THE SONS OF YMIR

THIEF OF MIDGARD – BOOK 3
ALARIC LONGWARD

THE SONS OF YMIR © 2018 Alaric Longward

Copyright notice: All rights reserved under the International and Pan-American Copyright Conventions. No part of this book may be reproduced or transmitted in any form or by any means, electronic or mechanical, including photocopying, recording, or by any information storage and retrieval system, without permission in writing from the publisher.

This is a work of fiction. Names, places, characters and incidents are either the product of the author's imagination or are used fictitiously, and any resemblance to any actual persons, living or dead, organizations, events or locales is entirely coincidental.

Warning: the unauthorized reproduction or distribution of this copyrighted work is illegal. Criminal copyright infringement, including infringement without monetary gain, is investigated by the FBI and is punishable by up to 5 years in prison and a fine of $250,000.

TABLE OF CONTENTS

MAP OF NORTHERN MIDGARD	7
PROLOGUE	9
BOOK 1: HILLHOLD	13
CHAPTER 1	15
CHAPTER 2	57
CHAPTER 3	70
CHAPTER 4	78
CHAPTER 5	95
CHAPTER 6	106
BOOK 2: THE ROBBER AND THE KING	123
CHAPTER 7	125
CHAPTER 8	139
CHAPTER 9	185
BOOK 3: THE UGLY BROTHER	233
CHAPTER 10	235
CHAPTER 11	256
CHAPTER 12	281
CHAPTER 13	308
BOOK 4: THE SERPENT SPIRE	319
CHAPTER 14	321
CHAPTER 15	347
BOOK 5: THE SERPENT SKULL	375
CHAPTER 16	377
CHAPTER 17	411
CHAPTER 18	431
CHAPTER 19	456
ABOUT THE AUTHOR	486

MAP OF NORTHERN MIDGARD

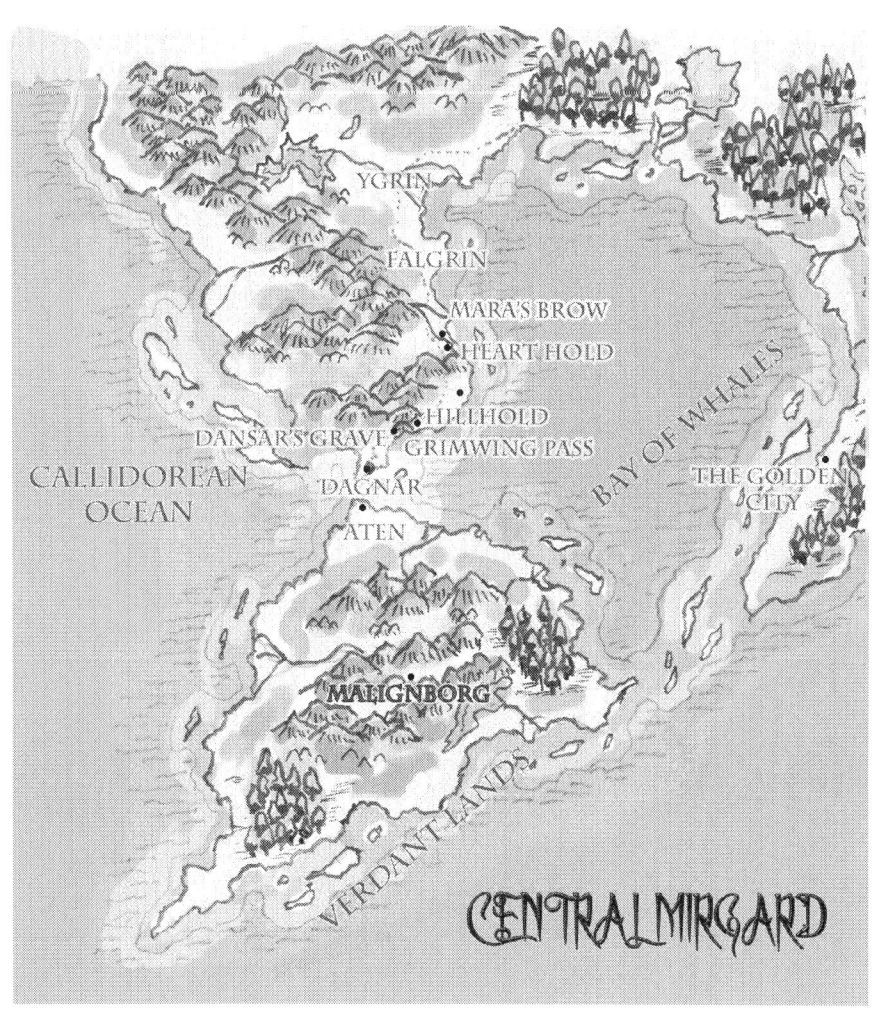

PROLOGUE

The realms of the north were shaking with the devious assault of Hel, and her draugr forces. The goddess of the dead, Hel, forever resentful for being a pawn in the game the Aesir and the Vanir gods played with Lok, the tricky god, the half-god, half-jotun father of monsters, and her father, had set her sights once more on the Nine Worlds. There was no reasoning with Hel. She was mad. Lok's crimes had led Odin to punish Lok's most beautiful child, and that punishment turned beauty in to half deformed horror, wisdom to resentment, kindness into cruelty. Lok couldn't help her. Lok's murder of Odin's son, Baldr, doomed Lok himself into imprisonment under the stone and root, until the time of Ragnarök.

But then, Hel was wronged again, and she sent legions of her minions to war.

The Nine Worlds were ill-prepared for Hel's War.

It had been fought many thousand years past over her stolen eye, and it had torn the Nine Worlds apart. The Gjallarhorn, the Horn of Heimdall, had been stolen by an elven lord, Cerunnos Timmerion, and he used it to close all the gates, in every world, thus dooming the worlds to fend for themselves, and the gods into losing their precious jewels, the Nine Worlds.

While Hel lost the war, and the gods, the gates, and godly quarrels were forgotten for long years, Hel's yearning for her vision of justice lived on. The ground grew fertile for new schemes. The elves grew greedy, the men proud, the jotuns still thought themselves gods, and the Aesir and the Vanir became legends many didn't believe in.

Then, in Aldheim, in the Jewel of the Nine, the evil gorgon Euryale had found a group of special humans, and amongst them, the one truly special human, and their adventure is a trail of bravery and suffering.

What took place in Aldheim, at the hands of Shannon, Dana, and Euryale would also touch Midgard, as some of these humans had found their ways to Midgard, using goddess Nött's thief wells. With them, they brought back the Gjallarhorn, the Horn, and hope for the gods to return, for they were seeking a lost Aesir, Baduhanna, the one who could blow the Horn and reopen the gates for Odin and his family.

With them, also came Hel.

A war and terror followed, and the humans allied with Morag, a jotun king hiding amongst humans with his clan. They saved Midgard, but only for a moment. Evil remained and worked its grip around Midgard's throat.

The enemy were numerous. The heroes, few.

The High King Balic, a seed of the great evil the King of the Draugr, reached out to bring down those who would threaten Hel's plans. He wanted Morag's gauntlet, the Black Grip, for it was a key to a secret Hel had tried to unlock since Hel's War, hidden deep in Mara's Hold, far in Falgrin.

Mir, the self-proclaimed Queen of the Draugr, had aided him, though she also aided herself, in the eternal struggle for power between the dead. It had been her mission to destroy Baduhanna, and the Aesir, almost the last hope for Midgard, was slain in the aftermath of a battle, a result of a long plan of the evil.

The Verdant Lands, the south, believed in the One Man, in Balic, and his long-battled armies invaded the Red Midgard.

Most of Red Midgard's legions were usurped by Crec Helstrom, a draugr, who took them away to Falgrin and left the land nearly undefended.

What stood against them was a motley crew of war-torn people of the north—a draugr raised jotun-king Maskan of Red Midgard, a renegade princess Quiss of Aten, the disgruntled nobility, thousands of refugees—and they had too many issues to solve.

With enemy armies crawling across the land, Maskan would have to find in himself the king who could save Red Midgard's people, who could lead the north to war, and victory, while dealing with the threat of Hel in the far north. He would have to find out what Hel seeks, and a way to stop it.

He would try. Standing in the ruins of battle, his people refugees, his soldiers mostly militia, the winter threatening all with starvation, it seemed unlikely he could succeed.

He would be a king of Red Midgard, a jotun-king of men, and the heir to his father's legacy.

Or, perhaps, he should be something else.

Listen.

BOOK 1: HILLHOLD

"You did something odd there. It was unexpected. I guess the jotun part of Maskan is finally taking over. It was there all the time, wasn't it?"

Sand to Maskan

CHAPTER 1

Hillhold held the end of Graywing Pass in its wintry grip, and the Hammer Legion on duty watched our miserable camp from its ramparts. The enemy was huddling over cauldrons, but archers and soldiers looked steadily on, prepared for anything.

They knew my tricks.

The enemy had plenty of its own.

Thrum stood with me, the short dverg lord apparently bored. He spat. "You have a bag of fancy rings, fit for a whore, or for a king. You think you might want to try them out and see if one gives the fort a good shake?"

I shook my head. I had indeed many of Balan Blacktower's odd creations, and one had saved us previously, but I had also seen the dverg Narag testing them, and dying as a result, and I had no wish to renew the experiment.

"We could have one of the damned prisoners play with them and see what happens?" he suggested.

"Yes, an excellent idea," I said, groaning. A jotun heals fast, but nobody heals fully from the punishment I had gone through. My face was in burned blisters, and I had wounds and nicks all over my body. My armor was a shamble, and I looked like a beggar knight. "Let's see if one of them makes the prisoner immortal, and all-powerful. He would likely give it back, eh?"

"He can be a she as well," he murmured. "There are some truly foul-mouthed ones in the ranks of the prisoners. But, I grant you, it might not be the best idea. Still, we have no real options. What about the Larkgrin, or Grinlark, or whatever it was your father called the filthy thing. We killed a lot of draugr with it."

My hand went to the brooch set under my armor. It was Blacktower insignia, and if you tapped it the certain way, the Grinlark would open a portal. It was limited in range, and in how many could travel, but it was a possibility.

"Let me see," I murmured. "A part of Aten's legion is in there. Six Spears, what is left. White Lions of Vittar and some of the Gold Guard, the Malingborg's draugr. Milas Illir, with the Griffon and the Hammer legion, squats in that hell-hole, Palan's Bears, what still breathes, and possibly some of Palan's Bulls. What else?"

Thrum squinted at the high walls. "Ontar's Ax and Minotaurs of Kellior Naur. The prisoners said Palan is split in three, and Vittar has one legion, her son leads the Bears, and the husband, Bulls. Palan's a split land."

"How many?" I asked him. "I don't care which way or form they are split into."

"They are skeletons of legions only, you nervous wreck of a jotun," he growled. "Some have perhaps three thousand men, and many, less than a thousand. We have as many men as they do."

"They have the keep," I said simply.

He opened his mouth, unhappy to be wrong, but shut it eventually. A man, one of the lords of the highest houses of Red Midgard, agreed with me. He was Cil Noor, an old man with a heavy chin and large brow. "They have a large siege train as well. I am surprised they are not shooting down on us, just to keep warm."

"They don't want us to keep warm. Running around, dodging their bolts would be keeping one warm enough," Thrum said.

I nodded, smiling and still horrified by the terrible situation.

I was a king. I had been ousted from the position by Baduhanna, when she had promised Hilan Helstrom the title of Regent; she had warned me to be patient and to earn the crown. I had eventually found her to be right, and had rejected the kingship.

Now, the army had made me one.

It should have made me happy. Instead, it felt … unimportant?

No, that was not it. It felt wrong. Father had ruled men. He had been happy, and had made his people happy.

Looking around, I didn't feel happy. I felt anxious. What would my house even be? Unlike it had been with Morag, I was a jotun even in the eyes of the people. There was no hiding. They would always challenge me, doubt me.

There was no Danegell House. My mother's House, the Tenginells, had been usurped by jotuns as well. I was an Ymirtoe and still, oddly, a Danegell, and I knew the men of Red Midgard, the women, all the citizens had made a huge sacrifice to accept me.

They would one day reject me again. Just because I was a jotun.

And what was a jotun? I didn't know. I had no idea what we were. I had seen glimpses of the great past when I had held the Black Grip. I had seen kingdoms in ice, chaos of war, spells invented by the mightiest of beings.

And now?

I looked back to the camps.

Shit, snow, and I a king of shit-digging, mud-shaping folk who would hate me, eventually.

And still, I went on.

I cast a critical eye on the camps.

There, the noble men-at-arms were digging a horrible fort. A muddy moat and root-plagued earthen walls were coming up around the noble camp, where the men of Dagnar and Fiirant were staring at the work, and not doing the same. There, too, was Hal Ranthor and Roger Kinter, the surviving lords of their Houses, and they had supported Hilan against me. I saw them watching me, and both were unhappy sots, likely dreaming of the crown themselves. They drank too much, feasted in their tents in the evenings with other nobles and decorated soldiers, and were slow to obey.

I saw Quiss speaking to those men of Aten who had joined her during the battle. She was speaking to them kindly, then, looking to some men of Dagnar, she gave them orders the men turned to obey.

Hal and Roger looked sour as they observed her.

They didn't like her, they hated the fact she was my ally, that everyone seemed to love Quiss, and so they found her presence disturbing.

They didn't think Quiss, or I, knew our business.

They could be right.

I took a ragged breath and turned and looked up to the walls. "We have some four to five thousand Dagnar and Fiirant militia. We have four thousand noble men-at-arms and five hundred of the bastards themselves, though only a thousand horses. We have a bit over two thousand dverg. There are nine hundred Aten legionnaires."

"The militia is unruly," Cil Noor said stiffly. "They cannot piss straight, and many will go home when the winter sets in. They say there might be a storm coming."

That was another issue. The winter.

If the winter brought a blizzard, or even a day or two of heavy snowfall, the army would die. I raised my hand and stopped Cil from going on.

I spoke harshly. "We lack food, bandages, tents, and experience, but still, we must get through Hillhold. We must get past the enemy and go north to stop Crec, who has Hawk's Talon, the Gray Brothers, and the Heart Breakers under his banner. They will go for Mara's Brow, and Falgrin, our ally, is going to be tricked. Balic has sent legions there as well. Three, four of them. They will release an ancient, trapped enemy, and we must stop it. They have my gauntlet, the key to unlocking a prison, and my blood…my father, mother. Both draugr. We cannot waste time."

Thrum Fellson sighed. It was an odd sound from the dour dverg, but he did. "Maskan. King. Maskan. Even if we take Hillhold, even if Fiirant has been saved from Balic for now, and even if the Stone Watchers finally march here from the east, we have no siege. None. If we take the fort anyway, perhaps if they forgot to lock the gate up, or we just stand on each other's shoulders and climb like ants, or gods fart and the walls break, Alantia is still mostly under Balic's thumb. We cannot march north, free like a young widow, because Balic will make sure we are stopped. We would need ships, but they control the coast. Do you see? Hillhold matters little. We cannot defeat it, and we cannot retake Alantia. Nött knows how many legions Balic is summoning to replace his losses."

I gave him a quick look. "You were in Mara's Brow long ago. Are you saying Balic should be allowed to release this Hand of Hel? There is a reason why they are trying."

He gave Cil a quick look, but the man had no interest

in the past, only on the walls of Hillhold. Thrum cursed. "I only know Hel's army fell apart back then. I know your father likely sealed the Hand in a chamber below. We didn't see. We saw your father, and Medusa, the gorgon general come up one day after we came to Mara's Brow, and she was thrilled. They found what she was looking for, and Hel. I saw Medusa leaving in rage. She had been insulted in some way. Then Baduhanna came with the human army. The battle was terrible, and she, the Hand of Hel was raising dead to aid us. She left suddenly, and your father followed her. He came back, alone, and we fled. I cannot tell you, if there is an undead elf, or something else they seek. I have no idea what happened. There was no real fort there, then, just a fortified hill, with a gate to Nifleheim. We held it. To be honest, Maskan, it might very well be just a disappointment to Balic. We should keep Alantia, and only when ready, we—"

"No."

"You mule-headed pig-eater," he rumbled.

"Let me think."

"Never saw a jotun who tried that before," he muttered. "Will get people killed, no doubt. Dverger too."

I gave him a furious glance, and he rolled his eyes.

They were quiet. I turned to look at my tent, a large, hide-built, muddy thing with a bedroll, a desk, and a chair, all looted from the enemy supply train. There was no Rose Throne, nor dignity. The chair I had in that filthy tent was the chair of a war-king, simple and with no glory.

Quiss had a tent next to mine, as bedraggled as mine.

That I was alive was a miracle. I healed fast, thanks to my heritage, but no jotun should survive what I had faced. How would I survive a war in Alantia? How would those who served me? They all looked up to me. They all trusted me. I had been lucky, I had skills to fascinate my allies and to kill my foes with, but we were far outnumbered and maneuvered. We were trying to catch up, and Thrum was right. We knew nothing. We didn't even know what father had hidden in the north. It could be nothing.

I looked back at my tent and hoped I would have time to read poor Illastria's book soon. *The Book of the Past* could answer some of the questions.

"Can you, lord, get inside and simply open the gate?" Cil asked, his voice cracking with hope.

I could.

I was a jotun, and gods themselves couldn't shapeshift as well as I could. I had sneaked into Dansar's Grave and many other places in my recent past, and I would in the future.

"They'll be ready for such mischief," Thrum said, crushing Cil's hopes.

Cil nodded and looked behind him. He wasn't looking at his compatriots in the noble camp, and he didn't get along with Hal, or Roger, at all, but was looking beyond them, to the pass.

Baduhanna had fallen there, and a cairn and a mound had been raised over her. An Aesir, a demi-goddess, it was easy to see why a jotun would not measure up with her.

All their hopes had been laid squarely on Baduhanna's shoulders.

She had been my wife, though I had had no say on it. She had married me, after she had tried to kill me, and she had proceeded to lead the men of Red Midgard against Hel with cool efficiency, a brutal blade, and still, thanks to the twisted, many-layered plans of Balic and the late Mir, she had perished at Hel's hands, but moments after I had led my army to save her.

She had abandoned Dagnar, Fiirant, and the people to Balic, just to buy her time to get to the north.

She had been cold as ice and inhuman in many ways.

Despite that, the people missed her.

Was a god better than a jotun? Or, were they just like us.

I had no idea. Did they expect me to be as brutal as she had been?

Perhaps. But I wasn't a natural hero.

An Aesir, a Valkyrie of the past, a heroine of the Hel's War, long trapped then released, was a natural heroine. The nobles feared her after she butchered Gath Bollion. The people loved her for it and her role in the butchering of the Bull Legion, and they loved her unearthly beauty. They had rallied behind her, had believed in her.

Now, they had a jotun, a scion of a clan that had killed the great families of the Tenginells and the Dagnells and had taken their place. They had a jotun, who had been raised by the draugr.

They had a jotun who was a thief, as well as a king.

Mir's plans had worked. Her plans inside plans, her filthy lies, and practiced treachery gave the One Man, Balic Barm Bellic, my gauntlet the Black Grip, the corpses of my family, and a dead goddess.

"Odin," I whispered. "Let me find the Black Grip again."

Thrum snorted. "The jotun who prays to Odin. Ymir's kin pray to *none*, if not to Lok, and the Ancient Ones. By the ball hair of Balic, you should know better."

"I have not had a teacher," I murmured.

"You need one," he said evenly. "You would be much happier being what you are. The people loved Baduhanna, because despite what she did, she represented law, and order. A jotun? The stories they still remember, speak of chaos. And they are right. Morag settled in, and chose to act like a god. He settled in, and made laws, and guarded people. It is not a jotun's way. Lead the people to victory, Maskan, and forget your fears. At all costs, Maskan, and come out with treasure, and glory. That is the way." He leaned closer, as Cil looked pale. "The boys would prefer that as well."

I shook my head and kept my silence. His words disturbed me. I pushed them away, but failed.

Teacher. I need one.

Not only did the ancient Black Grip have a power to seal stone and halls in a way even gods couldn't open, but it held the great history of my clan's past, the spells, the memories. It granted one power beyond one's abilities, and it was a great loss, due to my own stupidity.

The enemy held all the cards in the game. I was just a fool, and the game was played to the death.

Cil spoke. "What do we do?"

"First," I said, "we must deal with our issues in this camp. Then, I shall find some answers to a few questions. How do you think they like Hillhold?" I asked, squinting at the groups of guards on the walls.

"Maybe they are depressed as they have the warm barracks and supplies," Thrum rumbled, scratching his hairy chin. "What a damned mess. Well, it won't fix itself.

I grunted and didn't bother answering. "Cil," I said. "Go and tell Roger and Hal I will have words with them in a bit. With the prisoners. Tell them to come to me."

Cil hesitated and bowed. Then, he trudged away to the distant jeers of the Hammer Legionnaires above.

Thrum nudged me. "So. Here it is. No matter what

you decide, and how many people will die for it, they don't really need Baduhanna."

"Oh?" I laughed. "They will settle for jokes and lies?"

He booted my leg. "They will need ideas. You must provide them. If you don't have any, at least show leadership and lead them back to Dansar's Grave."

I pushed him off. "We *cannot* go back to Dansar's Grave," I said, and turned. I cursed as I watched the troops, settled in miserable camps under the darkening, cold sky. "What you said about our situation is probably true, but there must be another way. We simply must find a way to solve this issue."

"It probably means you will go," he spat, "and do something utterly stupid out there and then get your damned head chopped off. That's not a solution a king should consider. You send men to die for you."

"I have," I snarled. "But I need to do more than that. And first, I'll break some skulls in this here camp, if things don't improve."

Thrum nodded. "The bastards need to change their thinking."

He meant Roger, Hal, and all the other nobles, save for Cil and his banner men. I had led Dagnar to their aid, and still, the bastards acted aloof from the militia, from each other, even, when old grudges came in the way.

They had lost many of their mounts, but they still had trains of packhorses filled with food, tents, and weapons.

They seemed to assume they were an independent command, with flexibility to determine what orders they would obey, and what they could ignore.

They had not shared their supplies and tents with the militia, nor had they even assumed the walls and moats would cover the militia as well as them.

That would change momentarily.

"You think Lisar is in there?" I wondered as we hiked in the snow and mud, now also enduring the mockery of our enemy. I was worried of Lisar Vittar, the bitter foe I had beaten in Dansar's Grave. "Probably waiting for a new chance to rip my head off," I muttered. "That amulet of hers is a shit terrible thing to beat. Eats magic like mad."

"It won't guard her against a proper ax-blade, does it?" Thrum cursed. "Chop on the head, and any draugr will take an eternal nap."

"She is watching, scheming, and I'm sure she won't wait for us to get the first strike in," I rumbled.

"She is probably getting a good earful from Balic, eh? She's not there. She would be on the walls, hurling insults," Thrum said. "If she were a man, she'd piss on us. Well, she'd, or he'd have to be alive first. I mean—"

"I get the picture," I laughed, thankful for his levity.

"Seems like an unusually lively draugr, she does," he said with a grin.

"She is," I agreed. "She knows quite a few curses and

is cruder than a sailor." I looked at a train of horses drawing crutches away to the west. "The wounded are all gone now?"

"Not all," he said, and nodded for a large tent at the end of the huge encampment. It was guarded, and still, the red snow and the nervous looks the guards gave the tent spoke of the horrors inside. "So, you are determined to take Hillhold, eh? You will go in there, you will try to open the gates, and you think you can do it. If I were the poor bastard in command of the shithole, I'd keep the doors barred, locked, and I'd heap stones on the doors."

"They, too, must move men out to Alantia, and in," I said. "I'll find a way inside that doesn't involve trying to fly in. They will have learnt their lessons. You must figure out a way to siege it."

He winked as we circumvented the moat. "Oh, *I* must? Suppose we just do it the way I suggested. We can build a pyramid with the nobles. We can train them to make a human ladder?"

I sighed. "They are sending supplies to us. They are scrounging what they can in Fiirant, and they will send it here. They will send lumber, they will send hammers, nails, leather, rope—"

He cursed. "How about you let *me* build siege. Never go into details when you have no idea what you are talking about. Don't do it in public, at least. Quiss won't mind idiocy, but I do. Is she pregnant yet?"

I blushed and looked at him with horror. "We have kissed, and hugged, and I have no time to play such games. We haven't … I don't know what she wants."

"Oh, play the games, Maskan," he cursed. "I would, if I were young. And you have implied that you intend to marry her. At least a cook told me so. So did a stable boy."

"Aye," I said, horrified. "I have let her know she is welcome in Red Midgard. She is here. She has risked her neck. But I haven't …" I cursed and spoke on, looking at Quiss who was now grooming a horse. "So, we will get food in a day or two. Siege gear. People of Fiirant will send what they have over to Dansar's Grave, and you take over."

He nodded. "I have sent some of my boys along. It will take a week. Siege towers that high," he said, and eyed the twenty-foot-tall walls, "can be hard to move in this snow, and the ground must be cleared. There is sure to be holes and other nastiness beneath all the snow. They'll be firing all sorts of missiles down on us, they have their One-Eyed Priests, or draugr royals with their stupid horned hats, and it will be a place of tears. It will be impossible, but if it isn't, it will be costly." He winked. "They will get reinforcements, and we will, and winter will ultimately be the enemy that will beat us. Have you been thinking about the rest of the stupid traitor shits inside the fort?"

"Legion of Aten," I muttered. "I have. Quiss thinks

they might come over to our side, the rest of them."

"Aye," he said, knowing it could be our only hope. "But I guess they will be watched, and you'd have to talk to them. I'd not be surprised if they have not all been sent to hunt for rabbits and squirrels in the mountains. I'd not trust them in our midst. I don't, in fact."

His eyes went to the nine hundred or so of Aten's men, huddled in their separate camp, silent and uncertain. They had joined Quiss, but many would be rethinking their allegiances.

I hesitated and nodded.

I turned from my scrutiny of the legionnaires, and we entered the militia camp. Not far from my tent, Quiss was squatting over a fire and speaking to some of the men. I walked that way and nodded at Thrum, who walked for the prisoners, hundreds of them tied up under crude shelters at the edge of the militia camp. As I walked, thousands of people I had not sent back to Dansar's Grave began getting back to their feet. I walked forward and kept my eyes on them, despite the insistent voice in my head I should look down, lest I betray their trust.

A king must act differently.

A captain of his people must show he is confident.

To be honest, I wanted to ride the winds for the east, and there, work alone and try to find a way inside the Hillhold, one that promised me hope of opening the gates to the people and never getting one killed.

And yet, what Thrum had said, held some allure.

I would love to be less concerned, a thing of chaos, and never look back.

Let the men fend for themselves. And yet, I couldn't. I couldn't, for father, who had protected them

I eyed the people, despite myself, and gave them curt nods. Most grinned and saluted me. They wore the looted legionnaire weapons from Dagnar, from Dansar's Grave, and from the battle of the pass, and looked like battered hammer legionnaires themselves. Wide helmets, bloodied chain, and shields, they all carried uncertainly. There were shields of five different legions of Balic, and all the military gear from boots to brushes made them almost look martial.

Almost.

There was no going back.

Dagnar was gone. The capital was where they were.

I stopped before Quiss, who flashed me a surprised grin. "Did you spot a hole in their wall? Did they offer you mead? I hope you didn't have any, if they did. They'd piss on it first."

"No," I said, as I kneeled next to her. "No mead, no holes, no piss. We must figure out a way of getting in. You are sure Aten will speak with me, if I get in."

She shook her shoulders. "They will speak with you. I told you."

"And do you have a way in?" I asked with a smile.

She fidgeted. "What did Thrum tell you?"

"He told me to be a jotun, and start acting like a cruel, damned bastard," I said.

"What did you say?" she asked.

"I shall act like Morag did. You hesitated when I asked you a question."

She hesitated then. She looked deep in her thoughts, and then, finally, as if she were afraid, she nodded. "The men say there is a hall not four miles outside Hillhold, where the Legions have a small command post for scouts. They send mail and orders from Nallist into that place to be sent forward, and there is a captain from Aten in there. He has a brother with those who joined me and he says the entire legion has been unhappy over many things in the past. I hear they are regretting not joining us. That captain would be able to help us speak with Aten's men inside. He can get us in with him. He will find the right men to speak to. All we need to do is to ride in to Hillhold, carrying mail. I'm sure they want to join our glorious army, after all. They can get the gate open. It will cost them, but they can, if we help them. They are envious of our fine meals and accommodations, I am sure."

We looked at the muddy snow and the terrible camp. Both chuckled.

"I'll try him, then," I said. "They might be our only hope."

She leaned closer to me. "Tell them that I shall make

each one who joins up rich. A ship and hall for each man, and a title to the best. Some are fanatical, young, and stupid, but many saw the draugr as they are in the battle. Even if some agree, then we might succeed. The captains name is Antos." She winked. "We'll tell Antos he will be lord above lords in Aten." She frowned suddenly. "Wait, you said *'I'll try him, then.'* You mean to leave me behind?"

I pulled Quiss up and walked her to the side. "I have another job for you." She nearly slipped, but I caught her. I gave her a long look, and she smiled at me. I wondered at how well she had endured the entire debacle, and the adventures we had had together. Rescued from Aten, she was remarkably easy to work with. She had no objections to standing in the snowy mud, hungry, dirty, preparing for a desperate siege, with *no* siege engines, with few supplies, and with a quarrelsome army, half of which was an armored mob, at best.

I had saved her, and she had supported me all this time, and I needed someone I could trust.

"Can you take some people inside?" she asked, looking up at the fort. "In the night, you might be able to fly a party in. Or that Grinlark thing. That—"

"No, I dare not," I said. "Like it was in Dansar's, they have guards all over this place. Here, there are no mistakes made. They have them on the walls, around the courtyards, in any nook and ditch you could possibly imagine. It is lit like a bonfire inside, and every man is itchy. I cannot get anyone in," I told her. "I cannot be sure how many legions are inside, for they keep indoors when not guarding, but I am betting every doorway is closed and guarded."

She gave me a small, knowing smile. "But now, we have a plan. It is dangerous." She squeezed

"I know," I told her. "Let us go and speak with our dear friends, and perhaps with some of the prisoners." I tensed. "You will have to prepare."

"I cannot prepare for something I am not expecting. What did you have in mind?" she said, and lifted one exquisite eyebrow.

I smiled at her and nodded at the nobles, who were preparing their camp. The sergeants and soldiers were still digging a ditch around the camp, which the Dagnar's troops now tried to imitate. "We have to deal with Roger and Hal, and we must find someone who will take up the cause, should I fall. We must bring the troops together. We must change things."

She looked hard at me. "Wait. What do you mean?"

"You have to lead them," I said. "I need a Regent."

She stopped walking, and I tugged her along. She was hissing complaints. "They know I am *from* Aten. My father was Aten-Sur Atenguard. None of those northerner scum … nobles shall obey me. The people of Dagnar do, because I bled for and with them on the walls, but these nobles? Their men? Not a chance in a million, Maskan. They *barely* obey you. And some," she whispered conspiratorially, "think Crec is not with the draugr and should still be the king. Not many think like this, but some do. So, if you will tell them I lead, and please also note that I don't know how to lead an army in or out of battlefield, they *will* rebel."

"I need you, and they do as well," I said. "I will be back."

"You think you might not be back," she whispered. "That's why? Oh, Maskan. I—"

"I need you," I said. "Play along."

She beamed me a strained smile. "Well, of course I will, King Maskan! But—"

"I need you here," I said. "I *desperately* need you here. I need you to lead them and to give them hope. I need you to be the general of all of them, nobles and peasants alike. And I need you to back me up when we speak with Roger and Hal. Do say yes."

The nobles were gyrating from the military camp for the edge of the militia, where the prisoners were kept. Cil was following behind the two other men.

"What are you planning with the prisoners?" she wondered. "No, wait. Fine. I will do what you ask of me." She wiped the hair out of her eyes and looked hard into mine. "I am no soldier, but a sailor. All the men of Aten are, in their heart." Her eyes went to the men of Aten. "I will try. If there is a battle … then, damn you, Maskan."

We navigated the camp for the prisoners and came to a group Thrum's troops.

There, he had picked out two officers, both men, one old, evil-eyed, and one savagely scarred warrior. They eyed me, their faces unflinching, their jaws set, and dverger stood around them, holding weapons ready.

Roger and Hal arrived on their horses. Cil stood behind them.

"King, I would need a word," Roger Kinter said, his hugely bearded face gleaming with sweat. "The need to leave this place is urgent. I have already sent a third of my horses off, and men will march out this evening. Alas, we lost most of our horse."

"No."

He looked stunned. "King. We cannot *possibly* take the fort."

"We shall stay *here*," I said with finality, and eyed the prisoners. "We will not leave, and you will get *my* men *back* here."

Roger and Hal looked at each other, concerned. The latter got down from his saddle and gave the reins away to Roger. "My … king," he said, his voice trembling with emotion. "My king, the fact is, that we cannot take the fort. It was designed that way. It is a fort. Even with time, and siege, it would be very hard. It is filled with legions. There is a great chance … my king, that winter will hit us with its full force very soon. There are people here without food—"

"The dverger have a supply, and you had supplies," I interrupted him. "You will share the rations."

"They are ..." Roger began, but Hal lifted his hand, and kept speaking.

He bowed slowly. "Yes, *of course* we shall share. The supplies do belong to each individual House," he said with slight acid to his words, "but we shall share all of it. We must, after all. If we are nobles of the land and the king tells us to, we must obey, and, yes, we should have thought of it ourselves. It is our fault it didn't take place." He stepped closer. "But listen to me, King Maskan ... Danegell. To get past that fortress, and take our people after the traitor Crec, you must not only take the walls. You must ride through Alantia, which they say is crawling with the enemy. We are, I am afraid, too late." He hesitated as he grasped my arm. "Perhaps, if you would, you could, um ... shapeshift and scout the land, and see the truth of it. You might even go to Falgrin, and Ygrin, and warn them, though ..."

"The draugr will have poisoned them against me," I said icily, and removed his hand. "In fact, they have never heard of me up north. Not once. They think Crec is the king. We need you," I told him, "and the men to get there, and tell them what is happening here. It is very important. You know this. We all know this. I have explained why."

"Ah, yes," Hal said, bowing to hide his smile. "This creature of goddess Hel. Indeed. Lord. One day we must meet them in battle. We cannot take this fort. Let us plan for a battle, and not a suicide."

I nodded, subduing the urge to crack his face. "This is Red Midgard now. There is no Fiirant, no Alantia, no legions, no …

Roger spat. "Dagnar. No Dagnar, which you put on fire," Roger said stiffly. "Along with a great deal of our property, houses, and history."

Hal nodded and looked down. Cil looked away, frowning.

They all resented me for it.

The dverger all put their hands on their weapons. The prisoners shifted away and looked at me, expecting violence. They knew I was not a human, but a jotun, and had heard what I one might do when upset. I didn't act like expected, because I still had no idea how a jotun is really supposed to act.

I was upset, indeed, and cursed them in my head.

"Your houses are *gone*," I said loudly, for a crowd of noble soldiers had followed their lords and, with them, had come many of the people of Fiirant. There were hundreds of them. "They are part of history, mere mortar, stone, and now, rubble. They all burned down with hammer legionnaires huddling inside, screaming their way to Hel. They all turned to dust along with what you once owned. Balic's legions were made into ashes, and that is a part of our history, part of Dagnar. That is what new Dagnar shall be built on, after all of this is finished, no matter who rules there. Harrian, Malignborg, Xal Cot, Kellior Naur, and others bled away in our city. You, however, lost nothing."

Roger shook his head. "King. This is— "

They flinched as I stepped forward. "I know fully well not one of the noble Houses left your treasures in the city when you left. You buried them, hid them, sold what you could, and you will remain rich after everything is finished, should you live. Do not pretend otherwise. We *cannot* flee this place, we *must not* leave it, and we *must* get inside Hillhold, and I shall work on that. In the meantime, you are right."

Their eyes brightened.

"We must eventually fight the enemy," I said. "We will face them across a shieldwall, or in a fortress. We shall have to fight and beat them."

"With the militia—" Cil began desperately, sensing what was going to happen.

I pulled out the finger length piece of wood, the Grinlark, and growled the command word for it. They looked at the full-length staff my father had used and frowned.

I handed it to Quiss. "As the Regent of Red Midgard, you will obey her, as you do me. And you *will* obey me, or I'll rip your guts out." It sounded hollow. I tried lying more, and it wasn't easier. "I'm not Morag. I'll not negotiate or listen to you. I don't care about your rights, or what decision belongs to a king, and what to some obscure council. There is no Master of Coin, no Marshal, and no negotiations for your ancient rights. None."

The people around us, save for the hundred or so of the nobles, were murmuring approvingly.

Roger was wringing his hand. "She is not—"

"She is my choice," I snarled. "*Mine.*"

I pulled my two-handed sword, and gleaming in battered mail, my face scarred and hard, I stepped towards him. "Get down from your horse. Get down, or face what Gath faced, when he spoke to Baduhanna like you do. Do you remember what Baduhanna did to him?"

He hesitated. Hal went to his knee, a wiser and more dangerous of the two.

"Get down," I said softly, "from that horse. And then, kneel."

He blanched and leaped down, splashing in mud and snow. He went to a knee.

"The Ten Houses," I said icily, "are no more."

That was met with an astonished silence. The nobles around us were frowning, fidgeting with their weapons, and holding their breaths.

"What will be after the war, is what was after Hel's War. Nobles were made based on the merit of their actions. You shall merit your place not by what your ancestors achieved, but what you shall achieve for this nation," I said, speaking so loud, it echoed across the fields, and spread like wildfire in the whispers of the people. "Who survives, and has served the country, not their damned House, shall be rewarded by the king. What was, is now gone. Lords and ladies, your men and the common troops will fight as one, and not under House banners. You will lead wings of such men, as dictated by Quiss of Aten, who is advised by Thrum Fellson and if someone has an issue with any of this, you can take it up with Thrum." I pointed a finger at Thrum.

He spat and hefted his ax over his shoulder.

Nobody voiced complaints.

"Be gone," I snarled. "Prepare the men and heal the army. Your men are no longer yours. You are mine."

They bowed, shaking with fear, and anger. Then, they got up and were shocked as a raising scream of approval began from the men around us, and like a wave, it spread across the field. The men and women screamed their throats hoarse. I handed Grinlark to Quiss, and she smiled gently as she looked over the thousands of dirty, blood-spattered, mud-cursed bastards, who approved.

While the people screamed, I leaned down to look Roger in the eye. "I've had enough of trouble with the nobility. If someone breaks my peace, or disputes my orders, I shall break that man, no matter the rank or their self-perceived importance, and they'll serve the rest of their life farming pigs, if they are lucky. Is that understood?"

He nodded. Hal, as well, his face white as sheet.

"I need you," I said, "not your rank. You will serve the nation with Quiss of Red Midgard, as you will reform the army. I shall deal with Hillhold. Go."

They left, and I waited until the army went relatively quiet.

Thrum grinned. "See. Jotun-speech works miracles."

"I lied," I said.

Quiss shook her head, looking pale. "They will make trouble. You should be guarded, Maskan, at all times."

I turned to the two enemy captains and didn't answer Quiss. Thrum stepped next to me, as Quiss, looking harried, turned to her new duty. Dagnar's people were looking on, and I felt sorry for Quiss.

Then, I hardened my heart.

"Will they reform the army?" I asked Thrum, while considering the eyes of the scarred and then the eyes of the evil-eyed one.

Thrum was stroking his chin.

"The militia will do well, with veteran fighters," he said. "They'll have to learn fast, but by breaking them up, they will. The nobles will aid Quiss, and they'll make wings, and center, and a reserve. They might lose a battle or two, but if they keep their heads," he chuckled, "they will do well with what remains and turns professional. Now. How do you want the prisoners killed? Visibly, I take it?"

I nodded. I leaned down on a captain with the evil eyes. "One Man. One Man Balic, a shit-arse draugr, a filthy follower of Hel, an enemy of the living, and you lot march to his tune. Aye, we'll give this one the ax."

He said nothing. His eyes didn't flinch.

I placed my sword on his shoulder. "Twenty nations, twenty lands filled with fools, who listen to the lisping lies of a corpse. *Where* is the honor in that?"

The scar-face captain looked down.

The evil-eye one didn't. He looked back at me furiously. The silent prisoners stared at us intensely.

Thrum had chosen the two well.

I smiled at the man's fury, feeling the jotun's rage bubbling inside my chest, even if my father's laws tried to stifle it. "The dead took your damned kings and pretty queens, the rulers of your kin. I wonder how they died? How did Queen of Palan fall, and how did Aten-Sur get killed?" I murmured. "He told me he was murdered. His throat had been cut, but gods only know what happened. Do you ever wonder?"

He said nothing.

I went on. "Now, the One-Eyed Priests are walking about, dead as stones, evil to their eyeballs, when they have them, and you dishonor who they once were by marching to the tune of Balic, the False. Why do you serve them, and what do you get out of it? Coin? A pat on your head? Speak, man, or go to Hel."

"There are no gods," he said fervently. "No Hel, nothing. Only the One Man. I am," the man said thinly, "Dannac of Pelthos. I have served them since I was five.

There is nothing else for me. I shall tell you no more. The legions are not like that of Aten, craven and traitors, but will serve on. They will die for the One Man, for Balic, and his faithful One-Eyed Priests, his fine kings, and the enlightened queens. They shall be raised again. We shall all walk again, one day. It has been promised."

Fanatical fool, I thought.

"They won't walk anywhere, save the bridge over the Gjöll to Helheim," I told him harshly. "I'll show you, unless you answer some of my questions. Tell me about Hillhold. Tell me all you know about it."

He looked at me and lifted his chin.

I nodded and sawed the sword to his neck, watching his eyes enlarge. He fell on his face and twitched his life away, on a red snow. The prisoners were watching me carefully, and some with disapproval, though most also lifted their chins.

Brave, but fools.

I turned my eyes to the other captain. He frowned, waiting. I got up and walked to him. He eyed my size, the size of the bloody blade, and sighed as I squatted before him, the sword on his shoulder. I leaned closer to him, and he flinched.

"What in the blazes are you doing?" he demeaned. "Are you going to try to mate with me? Do jotuns honor the best fighter they take prisoner with love-making? No, thank you. I am not that kind of a man."

"Shut up," I said. "And wait. I shall tell you a story."

"Why?" he asked, frightened. "I don't need to hear one. Just put me back with the remains of my company."

"No," I told him, close to his ear. "Are you like your friend was? Brave."

"Of course I am!"

I smiled. "And yet, you look down to the mud whenever a dverg passes you. Most of the bastards are stiff-necked, fanatical shits, but some of you are not. The dverger know a sensible man when they see one. I need someone fresh to answer some questions. I've been talking to the draugr, and the men like that one, far too often of late."

"I'll not speak a word," he answered stubbornly.

I laughed aloud, placed a hand on his shoulder, and nodded. He flinched. The mass of prisoners frowned.

I leaned down and shook his hand, and then, I cut his bonds. "Thank you!" I said loudly.

He looked at the ends of the rope and then at me.

I pointed a finger at the man and looked at Thrum. "This man," I called out, "must be kept alive. We shall get everything we need from him."

Thrum nodded and grinned.

The man's jaw was hanging open. He looked over to the prisoners, and most everyone looked like they had just swallowed a rancid bit of gristle.

"Why, you bastard—" he muttered. "Oh, you shit. You damned ... king."

"Decide," I told him, smiling. "Will you go to them, or shall you speak? Later, you may go back to your service, because I doubt any of these men will return to the ranks again. They won't tell about you." I winked. "We don't have the supplies for them. We'll hang the lot."

"I have a pension and pay I need to feed my family, and ..." he cursed and rubbed his head. "Yes."

"So, you are not as fanatic as he was, are you?"

He shrugged. "I was recruited for my skills later than many." He smiled wistfully. "I also can put together simple thoughts. It makes no sense to fight a raging current. It takes your life, anyway." He watched the dead captain and the horde of simmering hammer legionnaires. "Shit."

"So," I grunted as I sat next to him. "Explain why most of them would sit on a stake for Balic."

"Well," he said tiredly. "We serve, either because we get paid for it, or because we were bred for it. The legions the Verdant lands once had are long gone. I mean, men who saw it as a profession. When the One Man—"

"*Balic*," I snarled. "Don't make him sound a god. He is a shuffling, curly-haired corpse."

"Balic," he echoed softly, as if terrified, "a man once, a draugr now, and no god, stepped up from the Eye Keep in Malignborg, resurrected, promising men eternal life once the world was rid of those who still believed in the old dreams. It had been, I recall, a day of treason in the city, where some of the royals killed his family. There had been his funeral, and a new king and High King were to be elected, and instead, Rhean and his family were murdered in battle. He raised many over the coming months, always a thing to see. He raised his valiant daughter, Filar, and also Silas, his son. They were dead, and then alive. Filar had died before Eye Keep to Lisar Vittar, and then, suddenly, she lived."

"You seem to have done your reading," I said. "Keep going."

He smiled. "I had rich parents, and I was grounded a lot, when not learning the sword," he said, and eyed mine. "Damned butcher's blade. No good for battle, only for a duel. But I digress."

"You do. As you said, it is a butcher's blade, so don't risk a butchery."

"I do not. I am talking, am I not? So. He publicly raised many of the dead. There was Lisar Vittar, the rebel. There were Rage Larran, the king of Harrian, Sarac, of Xal Cot. Dozen others, like Aten-Sur. Imagine, o King, how such … men, women, no longer dead, can raise a nation to fervor. Everyone wanted to bite that fruit. It was sweet as life. Balic promised the world harmony, peace."

"And he gave it war and blamed others, for Hel," I said.

He nodded. "I suppose so. He went about making

Midgard peaceful by launching a war on those who had rebelled. One by one, all of them were brought to the fold. Palan was broken in pieces. New kingdoms made. To do something like this, he began raising troops. From age of four, the sturdiest of boys were taken to his care, and trained. Only the very best, mind you. Those are the men that make up most of the legions. You cannot really reason with them, as you noticed." He looked at the corpse and shuddered. "They believe in him like they used to in Odin. The Eye Keep of Malignborg is not what it was, once. The Odin's Seat is gone. His One-Eyed Priests, some of them draugr, roam the lands, posing and praying, and causing havoc, and even in lands far away, some of the trouble is his." He grinned. "Some men who serve are like me. Latecomers. Most are poor as paupers, but very good with spear, and I am an excellent one with spear. When there are losses, men like me replace some of those who fell in wars. Now, after this war, there will be plenty of those coming to the ranks."

"Where is Balic sending his legions?" I asked.

He hesitated. "Now, King, why would I know that? Do I call him a friend? Does he hail me with wine when I come to his house? Nay."

"You know plenty," I said, and poked the man. "Let's not go back there, or I'll widen that scar."

"I do know a lot," he murmured. "But I have no idea what he is planning. I'm a captain. I know they are doing something up north, and I have no idea why, since the war in Alantia isn't won, and … well …" He looked around at the army besieging Hillhold. "They have the stockpiles … shit. This is hard."

"Dying is not easy," I told him "if I cut off your limbs first. Or if your men do it."

He glanced at the prisoners and forgot about his apprehensions. "There is a great city of Alantia, where the legions concentrate. That's the place where they drag all the gear and reinforcements, and one fortified village on the east coast, but mainly in Nallist."

"Nallist," I said. "On the south coast. I was near it, not too long ago. Had to sink one of your galleys."

He spat. "I hate ships. Sink all you want. As for Nallist?" He shrugged. "A pit of mud, misery, dysentery, and filthy soldiers. But the Ugly Brother, the fort, is nice and warm fort, large as a mountain, and that is where the reinforcements are going to come in from. The harbor's the best in the coast, and rather sizable for the north. Betus Coin, Aten, and many other navies are already ferrying in more troops, and perhaps picking up what you failed to kill in Dagnar. Half the legions are still over there in the Verdant Lands, of course, and many will stay to keep order, but—"

"Keep order against what?" I asked. "I wonder, since the High King has such a loyal following, all desiring life eternal. Odin is forgotten, and One Man rules all, and still, he needs people to keep order."

He hummed. "He has trouble with his own horned ones. They scheme constantly against each other."

"I know."

He smiled. "You would. My name is Mummion. Mummion of Lok's Bend."

"I didn't ask you for your name," I snarled. "I asked a question. If you think knowing your name will stop me from killing you, you do not know the jotuns. I tell you—"

"Lok's Bend," he said patiently, "is a county in Xal Cot. A nice place, really. Lakes, a bit of rural wonderland with small villages, and a large city filled with thieves. Lord Sarac rules it and consistently tries to purge it out of heresy. Or did, before he was killed in Dagnar." He chuckled. "It is not called Lok's Bend by design. It has another name. But it is, indeed, named after a god."

"Heresy," I wondered. "I thought my father was the only heretic."

"Your father," he said softly, "probably knew about the entire undead business beforehand. You lot … your kind live for a long time?"

I squinted at the man. He had opinions, ideas, and seemed not too afraid. "Are you sure you are not a draugr?" I asked him "We should probably just test it."

He looked at his thigh. It was slowly pumping blood from a shallow wound. I put my finger in it, and he flinched and tears filled his eyes. I picked one up and tasted it. It seemed genuine.

"Fine," I muttered. "What is Lok's Bend, then? Why is it important?"

"A city of caves," he explained. "A haven for the criminal types. It is said that out of all the gods, Lok still has an odd priesthood working the land. He is not one, you know, a god. They say he is a First Born, in love with mischief, tricks, and trickery. A half jotun, half god, a bastard if I ever heard of one. But these people do openly speak about the Aesir and Vanir gods and their past. Do remind the people there is another force in the land, other than the One Man." He stretched his neck, and looked at the horde of prisoners, not far. "You think I could find a place to sit in, King? I could use a drink."

"I'll put you in with the dverger," I said. "They know how to handle an ax, and you as well."

He looked at the milling army, where Quiss was leading a sullen force of nobles around their ranks and then giving orders.

"You do not like the lady?"

"I do like her."

"Are you in love, perhaps?" he mulled. "How does a jotun love a human? Do we not seem … inadequate? Short-lived and boring?"

"This jotun has loved a draugr," I said tiredly. "It was far too heart-breaking and exciting."

"Oh, that is … I mean…" He made a disgusted face. "I hope you forgive me."

"I try to forgive her, one day," I said sadly. "What do these heretics do?"

He winked. "They play nasty tricks on the Eye Priests, the draugr. They know well how quarrelsome and single-minded the draugr are—"

"So, you have noticed," I said.

"Yes, of course," he told me. "The Lok worshippers tend to get caught, but plenty of men and women join this cult. They raid the emissaries of Balic, and they steal what they can. They once managed to make two One Eyed Priests believe the other one had proclaimed Balic is as godly as a goat with a gout, and they caused a minor civil war. They never found the Mouth of Lok, as it is called."

"Have you seen him, or her?"

"Him," he answered and looked sheepish. "Him. So, yes, I have seen him. I was very young. He has a mask around his mouth but sports a blue and black mask on his forehead. He once gave a sermon to young people of the glory of Lok, the imprisoned one. He has reputedly been active for twenty years or more. I didn't join up. Many other did. All in all," he said as he stood up with a groan, avoiding the eyes of his former men, "he is a minor bother in comparison with you lot. Both shall fail, of course, but you are no alone in causing Balic trouble. Now, if you have ale or mead?"

I pointed the sword to Thrum's camp, and we settled there, sitting in my tent.

He had his eyes on Quiss. "She is young. Has she been in war? I heard you. It is a needed change, but she is ... not a warrior."

"She must make them listen," I said. "And the nobles must follow and help her. I have none else."

"She will be rebelled against," he murmured. "I have seen sots like your nobles before. They know their sword, but they have a black heart and douse it in wine every night to give it some life."

I nodded. "I'll raise better ones to the standards, if they do," I told him. "I shall slaughter each one of them, if they resist. They know this. I'll find them in their locked towers, and in their beds, underground, or hidden in clouds, if I must. They have heard the stories and know they are no lies. Midgard must change, anyway, if we are to survive this onslaught of Hel."

"Midgard ..." he wondered. "Oh, Lok's arse, this is a damned mess. You speak tough, king, but I think you are also trying to be a good ruler. Your people need the one who actually breaks bones of those he distrusts. Break those nobles in half, I say."

"Tell me about Hillhold," I told him.

He squinted at me. "Surely you don't think you can take it? The sots were right. They shall keep it. You don't have enough men, enough good men, no siege, no supplies or means to get them, nothing. Winter is soon here. They'll keep it."

I leaned forward. "Thrum told me something. I smell

something."

"What?" he wondered. "Did he compliment you on your nose?"

"I smelled something, indeed," I said. "Here." I handed him some bread and a mug of ale.

"Oh, gods," he breathed. "Oh, thank you. We haven't eaten in two days." He tore into the meat and, in mid-chew, stared at me. "Oh," he said. "Yes, you are right."

"You have no food," I said. "None?"

"We have horses?" he told me. "They can be roasted, like you will. I suppose they will supply us. I hear the ships came in, and they will find wagons coming in soon after."

I shook my head. "Well. That does give me ideas."

"Uhum," he said.

I got up. "You will be taken to Dansar's and held there until the war is over, or you are rescued."

***

Later that night, the camp in an uproar, as the nobles were restructuring the army. I sat and waited.

She didn't come.

I went out, looked around, and walked the camp, swathed in my bear-skin cloak. I walked and searched, and thought deep, afraid of the future, and then, finally, I saw her.

She was speaking with three nobles. They were handsome and tall, perhaps of the Kinter House. They were speaking, and Quiss was listening, and I was proud of her. The men were not happy, and she was unhappy and tired, as she leaned on Grinlark. Finally, the men bowed and left, and she placed her head on the staff, apparently exhausted.

I walked to her, and, startled, she looked up at me. She licked her lips, her eyes moist.

She was afraid and overburdened, and as terrified as I was of the responsibility. I lifted her up and carried her off.

While I did, she leaned her head on mine, and spoke. "Oaths are terrible things. The past, it haunts us."

"They are gone," I told her. "Your family is at rest."

She shook her head. "I am sorry."

The duty had sucked all the happiness from her.

I carried her across the camp, drawing some chuckles, and carried her into her tent. I was about to leave, when she hesitated and stopped me. "You are a widower."

"I am," I said, smiling. "Baduhanna is dead. I suppose I am."

"And jotuns marry many, anyway. As many as they wish, and think is wise."

I smiled. "I have no idea. Do you?"

"I think they do," she said. "In fact, I am sure of it. I think we both deserve a moment of happiness, before you leave for Anton, and I get to play a Regent, knowing absolutely nothing. Let's pretend we are married." She wiped a tear off her eye, and then, almost with desperation, pulled me to her.

I made love to her, and she was warm, full of matching love, and passion. She guided me patiently, and I followed her, and still, while our love was wonderful, I felt she was sad. I felt her, almost as if she was inside my heart, but I also felt she was heartbroken. I had not been sure of my feelings for her, but they were brilliantly clear then.

I loved her. I wanted her to be happy. I wanted her to survive.

I sat next to her and eyed her as she finally slept.

I touched her back and arranged her clothes around her. I hesitated to leave her and played with a large, red stone that had slipped out of her bag. I replaced it and dressed. I fetched my gear, the bag filled with the magical, odd rings, the Book of the Past, and the earrings Mir had used to trick us all in Dagnar, or rather, which she had forced Shaduril to use, and placed them in her hand. She looked up at me, saw I was leaving, and smiled sadly, afraid.

I kissed her, my heart full of love.

Then, I flew off.

CHAPTER 2

I flew over the Hillhold in the guise of an eagle, still happy for Quiss and the time we had just spent together. I let the thought of her flow from my mind, could see her face looking back at me, and I began scouting the fort.

I had done it a few times already.

The great keep held the pass in its snowy grip, and it was bathed in light. It was filled with legionnaires standing on cold guard, and not an inch of it was unguarded, or unlit. Standards of many legions were set up on the walls and the towers, and men stood in every nook and corner.

I had to find the command post. It was supposed to be along the way to Nallist, near the edge of the woods. It would have spare horses, a garrison of scouts, and captain Antos, and I wasn't sure I'd be able to find, or speak, to him. He could very well be a sullen mutineer or still loyal to Balic, even if our traitorous legionnaires of Aten thought differently.

A churned road ran for the south and Nallist, another equally churned road led deep into eastern Alantia, and one led for the north-east, the wide, bloody Iron Way.

The land beyond Hillhold was dark, save for specs of distant lights, which were likely enemy garrisons and burning villages and estates.

I flew around the fort one more time, found a

pleasant draft, felt the air joyously lifting me higher as I beat my wings. I glided south, along the slopes Blight, and looked at the churned road with alarm.

On it, I saw a marching column of nearly two thousand men.

They were swathed in their cloaks, their standard forlornly draped over the pole. They were miserable lot on a night march, and by the fish and ship symbol, it was clear they were men of Aten. They were the rest of the legion, perhaps marching for Nallist or to put down some local rebellion. I had no idea.

I was on a fool's errand.

Antos would, or wouldn't, help me, but it seems he *couldn't*. I'd not find men to speak to in Hillhold, for they were not there. Rebellious, disgraced scum had been ousted.

I flew around them, cursing. I circled lazily, and before I knew, they drew close to a great, dark forest. They passed an old inn nestled on the road's edge.

Some riders emerged from the forest and saluted the men. Few men exited the hall, holding bows. Out stepped another legionnaire, a captain in a gorgeous armor, and he spoke with the man leading the legion.

They embraced and shook arms, and the captain gave the officer a stack of orders before going back in.

Antos.

I waited until the legion marched off to the night forest and then, having made up my mind for seeing

Antos at least, aimed for the building's roof. I would talk with him, and perhaps the legion would come back, and all I had to do was to find out.

I flapped hard and then felt, and heard, something.

I looked up, and my heart nearly stopped.

A huge owl, snow white, was right there above me. Then, it crashed into me. I felt the peak coming down on my back, and I shrieked. We were plummeting through the air. Its claws tore at my feathers, the beak came at me again, the cabin, the woods were spinning closer, and then, the owl let go.

I crashed to the trees and among pine branches. I had to shapeshift and tried to grasp at the trunk but failed. The branches did slow me down, but then, I struck the ground hard. I lay there for a moment, trying to decide how many bones might be broken. I sat up, feeling lucky I might not have broken one, gathered myself, and inched up the trunk to stand. I tried to spot the bird that had attacked me and cursed the thing. I could shapeshift and fly, but I knew precious little about nature. An owl attacking an eagle seemed odd, but perhaps it happened all the time. I had no idea.

I was a thief, after all.

I saw the building not too far ahead.

My arrival had not escaped notice. The riders were looking at me from the trees, silent, not moving at all. I cursed, shapeshifted, and adopted the look of a legionnaire, and took Hal's face. I had no orders, no papers, and nothing more than lies, but perhaps they had not seen what happened and were trying to decide what and who I was.

I saw a group of men walking around the cabin, and one was likely Antos. His armor was gleaming in the light of the moon.

One was carrying something, a sack.

The riders were coming for me as well.

I stepped forward and raised my hand.

The sack-carrying man threw it at me. It opened and out rolled heads. They were men who looked like they had died in their sleep.

I had been expected.

I pulled my sword and held it high, feeling a wrenching fear in my gut. I watched them spreading around me, and my heart fell, for their eyes were glowing and faces shifting from those of the living into the decay of the draugr. They were shedding cloaks, and most all, save for the captain, wore black chainmail, decorated with bone-white symbol of serpent coiled around a skull.

There were draugr out to kill me.

One stood back, in the shadows, while the others pulled swords of night black.

The captain pulled off his helmet, looked at me, and smiled. His eyes were red, and skin white, and I felt fear coursing in my heart, stabbing ferociously. I considered those eyes, and the fear I felt. It was not natural. It was almost crippling.

That man was no draugr.

He grinned, and I saw his elongated incisors, like those of an animal.

I forced myself to step forward and to speak. "Balic's dogs run in the woods. Out to make a draugr out of me again?"

The man shook his head and spoke with a very smooth, cold voice. "Balic doesn't have a thing to do with this. It is time for others to take over. And, no, we do not want you. We just want you dead, finally, as you should have been a long time ago. Balic and Mir's squabbles, their pitiful rivalry, has put us all on risk. So, now, we deal with it. Put down the sword."

"What are you?" I asked, feeling compelled to obey.

"Not a draugr," he laughed softly. "King Maskan, put the sword down and get on your knees. No man can fight the command of a vampire."

I felt the need to obey. I felt the suggestion working its way to my head, and the fear aided it. I felt the sword trembling.

The draugr stepped forward.

I blinked, growled, and attacked. "I am no man."

I swung, and saw darkness. There was a cloud of shadows twisting away from where the vampire had stood, and then, it appeared behind me. It grasped my hair and pulled me back to the tree. Its arm was around my face, the hand tugging my head back, and I, a jotun, couldn't move. Perhaps it was the fear, the suggestive power, or simple, terrifying brawn, but no amount of struggle could rid me of it.

The team of draugr charged, swords high, except for the one in the shadows. They were all coming for the throat.

I stopped struggling, pushed the panic away momentarily, and changed. I grew to ten feet and thickened, my skin growing white, with thick hair and powerful muscle, and I adopted a bastard half bear, half jotun form. My face was that of a white bear, upper body as well, hands those of a jotun, and legs as well, and it felt terrible and unnatural and sickening, for it was, in a way, as unnatural as those things attacking me.

At least, the armor covered my body.

The dead were there, and their swords stabbed, the evil faces grinning, until they noticed the throat was no longer there to be slashed, and their blades sunk to the magical armor, and while many went through it, the thick skin and my armor saved me. I roared and swung the sword with terrible speed, decapitating one and splitting another. They stepped back and aimed for my guts. I threw myself at the tree, and the tree broke, so did the undead thing on my back, and as we rolled and rolled in the woods, the draugr loping after, the vampire tried to get away.

I grasped its leg, and it kicked at my face, stunning me, but the beast in the form recovered with rage, and I pulled it to me.

It pulled a dagger, but it was too late.

I sunk my teeth in its face and tore it apart.

I whirled and struck around with my sword, and a draugr's legs were cut out from under it. It howled, I stepped on it, and then, more came at me, rushing silently, so fast, aided by the darkness and the shadows. I was hit, stabbed, and pushed, and I fell and rolled in the snow-laden land, roaring. They were chittering and laughing amongst themselves as they hunted me.

I smelled them all around, and I was surrounded, confused, and then, a figure far in the woods braided together a spell.

Darkness rose around me—thick, suffocating, and familiar.

Sand?

I saw a glimpse of perhaps eight dead surrounding me, before the darkness enveloped me, and knew I'd fall.

I felt a tug. It was like someone was opening a door, a familiar relative, or a lover.

It was a weak voice in my head, and it suggested something Black Grip might have whispered into my ear. It was as if wind blew a thought my way, fleeting and loving, and it was speaking wisely.

Pray for your gods. Touch the snow, and pray aloud for aid. A life for a boon.

I acted without thinking.

I changed and kneeled, now a man-sized jotun.

I thrust my hand in the snow.

For a man, the snow and the winter was a thing of beauty and death, both. It stole lives and killed without mercy, and children still shrieked with joy as they saw the first flakes coming down. For a jotun, the ice and freezing winds of Nifleheim were a source of magic. We could braid and pull at the power of ice and fire, both, and create powerful magic, but icy spells came more naturally for my kin. That was the power I had used to kill hammer legionnaires and many draugr. I knew many such spells, and I embraced the power to do so. And still, such spells exhausted one, and sometimes, they would not suffice to save one.

Not alone.

The wind had spoken. I was to learn of the jotuns.

An ice giant, a jotun of Nifleheim, was more than spells and ability to shift. I was, the wind had told me, *a creature* of winter and magic. In the cold, my spells were more powerful. During winter, my power truly grew. I was one with the winter, I was an ally with snow, and I could beg it for aid? I did.

I thrust my hand in the snow, deep inside it, and even if the winter was only a blanket of snow on the ground and not very old, I felt it was suddenly … alive. Waiting.

A spirit of cold, something one does not see, sense, was intrigued.

It was cold as god, inhuman, and beyond human cares. And still, it felt familiar, a part of me.

It all happened so fast.

I begged it to aid me. The voice had told me how. Aloud.

"A life for a boon. A life for your aid," I whispered, as the dead raised their swords.

There was a power I had not expected. It came to my rescue. It clenched its icy hand around my heart and agreed.

Like a heartbeat, the snow around me jumped up. It blew high up into the spell of darkness, a thick, white blanket, and, not unlike a storm, it swirled in the air. And then, it grew in strength and power.

The darkness dissipated.

The draugr howled, swords high around me, holding their faces and eyes, filled with snow.

They were freezing, slowly, in pain, as the snow swirled around me, tearing at their flesh.

I struggled to break the connection with the spirit. It was reluctant to let go, happy for company, unyielding and harsh, and only reluctantly agreed. I felt a brief terror as the thing seemed to caress my soul before leaving, and then I went into attack.

My sword was humming in the air as I struck down a draugr.

It fell apart, and I danced to the next one. Its sword stabbed at me, resentful, dead eyes staring at me, rime-filled and freezing, and I hacked it down. They slowly regained their ability to move, but far too slowly, and harshly, with rage, and crude violence, I split their skulls, chopped through their chest and arms, and stamped them all to the snow. I spat and paced back and forth over them and then sensed eyes on me.

I looked to the depths of the woods.

There were two figures.

One spoke to the other, and it whirled and ran off.

The other one stared at me a while longer. It held two swords, curved and bitter black blades, and then, it stepped to the pale light of the moons.

It was Sand.

I laughed. "Just you and I, friend? Do you have more I must send to Hel before you dare to try?"

He lifted a rotten eyebrow. "You did something odd there. It was unexpected. I guess the jotun part of Maskan is finally taking over. It was there all the time, wasn't it?"

I kicked a skull of a draugr to a tree. The noise echoed in the frozen woods.

"Yes, it was," I hissed. "Balic's dog still, eh?"

He shook his head. "I serve someone else now. Just like the vampire said, Maskan, so it is. But you need not worry about it. I will be back. You cannot hide. For now, fare you well." He stepped back.

"Midgard won't let your lot rule them," I roared at him as I ran after him. "They'll hunt you down, Sand.

They'll find the strength to pull down Balic, and you, and all the Hel's things."

He disappeared into the shadows, and I stopped and whirled as his voice echoed in the woods. "Soon, there will be no army for you to command, Maskan. Soon, after they receive supplies, they'll make the Pass a graveyard of your dreams. Goodbye, for a while, friend!"

There was a silence.

I stood there, trying to concentrate.

It was hard. Our plans to enter Hillhold were dashed. There was a party of draugr and a new threat coming for us, for *me*.

And there was the power I had touched, the spirit of ice, the winter's very essence. I was a jotun, indeed, but was a jotun supposed to fear it or obey it, and what would it want of me, should I call on it again? I felt afraid, unfulfilled, and nervous, and then, I realized why.

I felt unease, and impatience, and I knew something ancient, and evil was waiting.

"Life for a boon," I whispered. I had promised it a life.

I had given it *nothing*, so far. The dead were dead. Their blood had no weight in our pact. I felt I was right, and also felt a demanding impatience of the thing I had discovered, a judgmental beast lurking deep inside the cold land.

The thing of winter might never aid me again. It might actually *harm* those whom I loved, or those who served me.

I turned to the cabin, its lights flickering far in the woods.

I heard a crash, and a muffled crash. I walked that way, and when I got to it, I heard noises inside. I walked to the doorway and looked inside.

The draugr had killed the soldiers in the cabin. They had been waiting for me. Quiss had been betrayed, and so had I.

A soldier was standing by an open trapdoor, having hidden himself below.

He was young, clever, and with him, there was a local girl, who clung on to his arm. She opened her mouth to scream and then closed it as she saw what was, likely, a living man.

The soldier, too, walked forth, hands out. "Thank Balic, it is over. I have no idea what they were. Rebels? I know not. Did anyone survive?"

I felt the thing watching. I knew it preferred the girl.

I grasped the man instead and struck him in the belly. I dragged him outside, and he struggled as I did.

The girl was there, beating on my back. "No! He is my brother! Do not!"

"He belongs," I said heavily, feeling sick, "to a jotun and, through him, to winter."

It was no battle. It was, in a way, an abomination.

What jotuns did in Nifleheim was not what men were supposed to do in Midgard. A dark rite, dark gods, and evil, depraved men might do what I was doing, and still, I had no choice. I had an ally, a jotun's ally, and the man in me had to step back. I could butcher a man in battle, I could kill them to save myself, or my friends, but the boy was weeping, and my heart broke.

I hacked down. The blood spread on the snow. I felt the wintry spirit, mollified, sated, and still, perhaps unsure I had given it my due.

Then, leaving the girl weeping, I changed back to an eagle and took off.

One day, that girl would do me great harm. Such a fate was also part of being a jotun. Chaos and blood on the snow follow you all through your life, until it is your blood on the snow.

Sand's words echoed in my mind.

The enemy would attack my army. All they needed were supplies.

And so, I headed for Nallist.

***

Later, at the edge of the woods, near the coast, I spotted a caravan of wagons headed south for Hillhold. I had no doubt Aten's legion had been sent to meet it.

I banked and circled it, and then, I dove down for the woods.

CHAPTER 3

I landed with a rustle of feathers. I stared at the supply caravan of a hundred tightly packed wagons that was stalled just inside the woods where a large hill ran down. There, just on top of the hill, a few wagons had slid off the icy road, and the men were trying to pull them back, save for one that had a broken wheel. A horse had broken its leg and was still on the side of the road, dead. In the dark, a swarm of Hammer Legionnaires were busily moving gear from that one wagon and loading them on others. There were guards on horseback and companies of soldiers staring at the woods, and men calming their bullocks and horses as the work went on. There were hundreds of men and almost as many animals.

Aid was finally on its way to Hillhold.

I'd make sure the men in Hillhold would not receive food, unless I was driving one of the wagons. Sand's words echoed in my mind, and while in a few days, the enemy would be chewing on leather straps, this load would give the enemy hope and strength, and perhaps they would indeed surge out and beat my army. Winter might do it anyway.

If possible, I could get inside, disguised, with papers to prove my identity. Aten's troops would escort me inside, and perhaps, after a successful adventure in Hillhold, I might find aid and indeed open the gates.

But first, I'd have to make sure there would only be a few wagons left.

I watched the enemy march, and when they had pulled the vehicles back on the road, made checks, and listened to the complaints of a fat officer, miserable on his horse, the hundreds of wagons began a slow decent down the hill. Far below, there was a small, dark pond and some snow-covered ruins. They would follow the road to the north and would, eventually, meet Aten's legions. I hopped on a tree branch to look at their progress. The hillside was icy, and the advance riders rode uneasily down, the bullocks and draft horses whinnied with fear.

I heard a noise.

I turned to gaze to the depths of the woods.

From there, a band of men and women sneaked forward. There were some fifty, perhaps more, and they were on foot, save for two. A clever looking, muscular woman, her thick, dark hair braided over her shoulder, was whispering to a bald man, who was dressed in barbaric splendor of furs and golden belt. They, too, seemed to have business with the legionnaires.

Hunters, rebels, or just robbers, the Alantians were out for blood and supplies.

They went to my right and disappeared deep into the woods.

I turned back to the wagons. I let twenty of them pass. A hundred men, perhaps sailors on escort duty judging by their lighter shields and armor, and archers a plenty stalked the woods around the road, and it seemed they were jumping at each creaking noise from the frozen pines.

Thirty wagons had passed down hill, the drivers screaming at each other.

One in the middle was in trouble. The horses slipped and took steps to the side, and there, the wagon toppled, spilling bread and grain in a wide arch. That stopped the progress for a moment as the soldiers pushed and pulled the wagon aside, cursing the winter. When they moved again, soon, half of them had passed me.

I took a deep breath.

I flew to the top of a tall, dark green fir tree, its evergreen boughs billowing in the wind peacefully. I landed and changed to my human form. I hung on, hoping the tree would not break. I maneuvered to look down at the road and found I saw much of it from that high. I tried to turn, but my sword was caught by a bough. I ripped myself free and was very still, as some archers below stopped to look at the woods. When they moved again, I ignored all discomfort and concentrated on what I'd need to do.

The slope would make a fine ally.

I called for magic. I felt the spirit of the winter wasn't far and fascinated, intrigued by what I was doing, but instead of it, I just called for a thick braid of magic, one I knew well. I braided it together in my mind, a perfect, fine mix of freezing wind, the vibrant, slippery ice of River Gjöll and her sisters, and made it thick and tough in my mind. The plate and chainmail around me jingled gently as I worked the magic.

The two archers from before strode back uphill, apparently not happy with their earlier efforts. Diligent soldiers, they came back and looked again at the woods.

Then, one looked up. He frowned and then spotted me, and he opened his mouth to scream.

I released the spell and threw it on the road.

Ice and mud cracked. Rushing, frigid water made crunching sounds that echoed across the woods. The hillside, from the top, rushing towards the bottom, iced over in thick, terrible grip of winter. Men were screaming, horrified to their core, their legs caught. Such a spell could envelop a man, suffocate, and turn one into a statue of ice, but I spread the spell, and the result was perfect.

The forest echoed with the animals and men calling out in panic.

Not all were panicked, though.

An arrow flew past me. Another struck the tree, and yet another clanged on my pauldrons and spun off to the night.

I ignored them and watched the road.

With even louder cracking sounds, accompanied by screams of horror, the heavy wagons broke off the grip of the ice and began to tumble down the hill.

The horses and the bullocks were dragged with them.

Even the archers below turned to look at the carnage.

I watched an avalanche of supplies, breaking wagons, desperate men, and draft animals sliding, tumbling, and pushing into each other go past. The forest echoed with the noise of the dying, a bloody slide of doom scaring most birds into a headlong flight. They flapped in the darkness around the hill, they croaked and screeched in an unholy concert with the dying caravan, and when it was over, on the bottom of the hill, there were a huge pile of scattered supplies, broken wagons, and thrashing draft animals lit by discarded torches. Men were rushing down, horses were running around in panic, bullocks were mooing in the woods, and officers, whipping their horses, were screaming for order.

On top of the hill, the fat officer sat in shock, his horse prancing, surrounded by twenty men.

Below from the ruins and the woods, the hunters surged forth to reap the rewards of the unexpected chaos of the caravan.

Fifty archers released arrows from the woods. Another fifty rushed out of hidden pits with spear and sword and began to butcher the soldiers that were pulling at their companions stuck under wagon and scattered supplies.

Arrows cut down men like a scythe. They put down

horsemen and killed troops that had been rushing down to help. Men fell on their faces, others ran to the woods to flee, and some few formed a wall of shields around the wreckage, killing a few of the robbers.

The officer on top screamed.

His men were being shot at, and he turned to flee.

I watched the carnage in dismay. What might be salvaged for my purpose to enter Hillhold was going to get looted and burned by the robbers. They were finishing below, their men stabbing down at the few enemy who still moved.

I jumped out of the tree and changed into my eagle shape. I fluttered after the dozens of the enemy that were fleeing, though few fell, struck by arrows. I spotted the fat man, a high lord on a black stallion, ploughing into the woods, his silver helmet over his eyes, a general of some sort. His heavy jowls were hanging on his chest over the armor, and he was yelling at his men, though not orders but curses, and who survived the archers didn't go after him.

The man was alone.

I flapped frantically to get ahead of him, and then, changing into a jotun, I landed before him.

I grasped the man from the saddle and lifted him face to face with me. I flicked his helmet up, and his eyes widened at the sight of an enemy, and not a human one. A pale blue, fierce face, inches from his, made him shit himself. I ignored the smell and his horror and spoke.

"Name?"

He blinked.

"Name!"

"Mine?" he asked.

"No, your horse's damned name," I growled. "I would speak with it about hay and mares. Of course, *your* name, you bastard."

"My name is Naris Malcan," he said. "Of Miklas. A … a supply general. Please—"

"Naris Malcan," I said with spite. "And your boys came from Nallist."

He nodded that way. "Yes, since the supplies are there and must go elsewhere, yes, we came from Nallist."

"Are there," I snarled, "any of the One-Eyed Priests in the city? Any of the filth?"

"Most died, they say," he stuttered with a shudder. "I don't know. They don't always wear the horns. Please, I've never done a thing to—"

"The fleet is there?" I asked him.

"Aten's, and Katar Kas Opan's, yes," he answered. "The merchant vessels will stay, but the other ones will go to Aten soon. I can help you, see?"

"You will help me, indeed," I laughed. "Is there a draugr High King there?"

He looked confused.

"Balic!"

He flinched. "The One Man. Aye, and no. Balic is

coming there, they say, his armies shattered in Dagnar. They will come here, and garrison the city. He sent some of his riders ahead, but he had not arrived yet when I left. He is, they say, visiting Aten first and then on his way to north. That's what they say."

"Since this caravan," I asked him carefully, "is history, will they send a new one?"

He frowned. "Yes, of course. Hillhold and the legions will need food. They will make sure—"

I nodded. "I thank you. And now, close your eyes."

He did. I snapped his neck.

I wiped sweat off my face and thought about Balic.

He would be in Nallist. I'd have to get to Hillhold, and I'd need to find a new supply wagon to infiltrate into in the city, but if Balic was on his merry way north, then perhaps, with luck, I could kill him and stop this entire business.

And then, there was the thing what Sand had said, and what that terrible undead had mentioned.

Balic wasn't in charge.

I should be a king. I should *think* like one.

Hillhold was the priority.

And still, I was also a thief, and a jotun, and jotuns were bitter, vengeful bastards.

I had business with Balic, for those who were dead.

I flew away and would be Naris Malcan, and my vengeance awaited.

CHAPTER 4

I dragged myself to the gates of Nallist. While the guards, already notified of the calamity by others who had fled, fetched help, I watched the twelve-foot tall, rough walls and small towers. The city was a large one, though nothing like Dagnar. Not even close. It was wealthy with trade, however, and the harbor far below was enclosed behind a sea-wall, guarded by sea-towers, and the true miracle of Nallist was the Ugly Brother, no doubt a rival to the Fat Father of Dagnar, which was a large tower. This one, however, was a huge, circular fort. It was a simple affair, with five levels and top bristling with siege machines, and it was part of the outer wall on the far edge of the city. It was far too large to house local troops, but it would suit well to shelter thousands of legionnaires.

The harbor I had glimpsed was filled with merchant vessels. They were being emptied of munitions, heaps of supplies to feed armies.

Finally, someone came to fetch me. The officer that met me at the gates was a handsome older man and furious at the guards.

He was pulling at me and hissing at the men. "A general! A general, and you let him stand outside like a beggar! I'll have you demoted. See if I do. I will find you, though I have no time now. For you, its best if a rebel puts a shaft in your skull. Indeed, far better. Come, sir, we go in!" Inside the city walls, the streets were empty, and people were staring towards the fort. There, far at the end of the streets, a great number of cavalry was mustering, and men were climbing on horseback.

I was pulled from my ruminations by my companion. "Come, Naris. I am the watch officer of the week, in case you wondered. All sorts of missions they give an idle admiral from Katar Kas Opan, eh? Our warriors aren't coming back? They told me there was an ambush."

I nodded. "We lost everything. I lost my horse, even. I loved that horse."

"All of it is gone?" he asked. "All? There were hundreds of men we could ill spare! Most were good sailors. Didn't you scout properly?"

I flinched, and my hands shook. "I did not send scouts," I said acidly. "I am no captain of war, you know it, but there were captains in charge of such activity. They reported nothing. Not one damned thing. The woods have occasional rebels and hunters, but we killed some, and they killed a few, and things were going well. Then, suddenly, hundreds of the enemy! There was no reason to expect a major attack from anyone in those woods."

"No reason!" the man huffed, his thin cheeks sucking in as he wrapped a red, woolen cloak around his tall frame. "There are a hundred thousand people in Alantia, and most have taken to the woods, unless they ran into a sword. No reason to expect them? There are twenty or more of these rebel groups, and this one is livelier than most. Some bandit called Saag leads them, a bald bastard with a fine-looking lass on his side." He rubbed his face, and nodded. "Aye, your captains should have been prepared. Let us blame them, and neither one of us should hang. I did, after all, pick the routes for you, eh?"

I nodded and watched the riders. Lances were being handed out.

There were at least a thousand such riders. Some few rode past, and I took a close look at them.

They were grimy, battle-hardened men, and the Headless Horse of Harrian was sown on their cloaks, prominently and proudly portrayed also on their shields. I had seen them in Dagnar. My host seemed to be in love with them. "Look at them. They have been arriving all day, and they all want blood. They barely ate, eh? Lovely men."

"They'll eat me, if they find I lost Hillhold's supplies. Look, I'd like to remedy my mistake. Surely, a new caravan must be sent. Can I be part of it? I'll not ask for the command, but I must, simply must make the trip and show I can—"

"Relax," he sighed and eyed the milling mass of Harrian's best.

I did as well, impatient.

Most horses looked like replacement mounts with

rudimentary gear. Still, they had them. We had a thousand horses, but only half were war-horses.

"Look—" I began, and he shook his head and guided me forth.

"How many survived Dagnar?" he asked, smiling. "They all ask me that. I know, since I am the watch officer of the week. I know what is coming in. Some. The legions are few thousand strong and will hold Nallist. Aten's ships will fetch them this coming night. They'll live in the fort. All save for Harrian. They have business elsewhere."

I nodded. That many had survived. A few thousand had managed to find a way out of the inferno, and perhaps they had hidden in the Temple of the Tower or used the Old City's tunnels, and that would mean death to many of wounded we had left hidden there. I heard the man speaking. No, he was chuckling. "Do not worry about anything, I told you already. But, no, you cannot join a caravan. We are out of wagons. See, there is already another one out there." He looked sheepish.

I gave him a confused look. "Sir? There is another caravan?"

He pulled me aside. "We were prepared. The road you and your poor boys took is the best one, but there is another, and you are late to join it, as I said." He fidgeted and sighed and pulled me aside as some riders left the gate. "I cannot abide to see good men so distraught, come."

He led me off, and I looked around the city, one of the largest ones in Alantia, and saw the population going about their business, no doubt much reduced, since the legions rarely believed in peaceful occupation, and on the other hand, the north didn't go down without a fight. At the end of the street, near the milling force of cavalry, there was a red-bricked house of four stories and, on its balcony, were hung the banners of ten legions.

The man saw my roving eye. "Yes, all the headquarters are there now. You noticed some new flags, eh? We hung them up hour ago. Some legions don't exist any longer, or basically only in name, and their scribes and officials sit there and wonder what they should be doing, save for sipping wine. We came here with near fifty thousand men, and now, two thirds are alive, mostly in the north, and out of those that are here, full third are wounded, and a part is starving. It's a sorry state of affairs, but must be remedied, eh? Unbelievable, indeed. The One Man will have to settle the score with the scum."

There was a pleased undercurrent in his voice.

"Is he here yet? Will he too, go north? We need more men."

"He will go up there," he said dryly. "There are two legions up north. He sent the fleet and legion of Betus Coin up north to follow the two legions that rowed that way in the early weeks of the war, and took all of

Malignborg legion out of here, and Dagnar as well. Left this morning. They are waiting for Balic near the Blight. Fifteen to sixteen thousand men. They have camped and are waiting for something. I know not what. Balic? Here, we shall have some fifteen thousand men as well, but half have been beaten once, and I think we should fetch the northern boys back. He, himself, is coming here today, before he follows the fleets, and I hope someone tells him to finish the south before some fancy northern adventure."

"I agree," I said.

That made him happy, and he was clapping my back. "Perhaps I exaggerate. He is bringing more legions. He went back to Aten to muster two more of the legions and will be here to sort out the strategy with the One-Eyed Priests who still walk about. All the supplies we have, all the men he can find, it shall all be here. We must forgive him the north." He looked at the wintry city and cursed softly. "Summer would be nice, eh? And still, warm or not, the One Man sent his orders, my friend, and those orders are clear. We won't give up Alantia while he goes north to deal with something bigger."

"Something bigger," I breathed, and wondered at what Thrum had said. Hand of Hel, or perhaps nothing awaited them. He had already sent my father and mother north with the fleet of Betus Coin. He, himself, perhaps, carried the Black Grip. "What's up there?

Goats, snow, and ugly people."

He clapped my back. "No, I told you. I know not. Come, wine! You sound depressed. I am happy you survived, for I need an excuse to sit down and eat. Let my men deal with the unfortunate affairs of the war, and you sit here with me for a while. You'll keep your head, I think, no matter your failure. They have bigger fish to fry, and no time for the little supply generals or displaced admirals. If we must, we blame someone else. You and I, eh?"

He wasn't worried for my head. He was for his.

He expected me to aid him.

"Of course," I said.

"I know a few captains I dislike," he said and winked. "Thank you."

"Very generous, lord," I answered. "Let them fry the other fish, and you and I pull the nets so they can catch them."

He chuckled. "A general and an admiral can be cordial amongst themselves, even if one is a lord." He laughed. "Especially if they fish together. Come, sit."

He pushed me on a table set in a fresh snow and kicked at a steaming clod of horse manure from his feet with a disgusted look. "It is best to be at sea, where such a sight is rare," he muttered.

"Indeed," I agreed, "though the sea robs me of my appetite."

"Appetite you must have," he laughed and slapped

my large belly, "after escaping with your head. I have just the thing. A dish from home. Smell that?"

Indeed, the smell of meat wafted to our noses from inside a guard tower. The man snapped his fingers at a soldier, who walked off and went to roar commands inside the doorway. Some answers echoed in the halls inside, and soon, servants were carrying plates of red stew and vegetables, and there was also and a bowl of syrupy, peppery sauce. It burned my nostrils even before it was set on table.

He smacked his lips. "Some comforts from home. Can't do without them, can we? What's your home again, General? What legion were you attached to?"

I made a noncommittal sound, while rubbing my face. I was served a bowl of the thick dish, which was then lathered generously with the sauce. While the servants left, I firmly grasped a tankard of ale, hoping to survive both the questions and the dish. "I have no idea which legion I belong to now. Six Spears of Miklas, I suppose, but I hardly know the men any longer."

"Indeed," the man said, losing interest in the banter as he dug into his dish. He heartily enjoyed it by the blissful look on his face, and I gingerly poked a fork into the mess and put some into my mouth. It took some time to manage a breath, but I did, feeling like a dragon might after scorching a village. I realized he had been talking. "But sure. They had their time. Now, it is time to put things into their right places."

"Why, I think I missed some of what you just said," I said, guzzling ale, which didn't seem to bring a shred of relief to the scorched cavity that had previously been my mouth.

"Ah, I just said that each new war has its difficulties. Ever since Balic," he mumbled, "the One Man, I beg your pardon, began raising the royals and turned the inbred shits into his loyal, ever-loving slaves, be the lot blessed, the armies he has led have rarely been beaten." He winked at me. "Of course, there never was a soldier that thought a war in the north would be easy. Never. Not once. And especially on the eve of winter! What was he thinking, eh? But winter had nothing to do with our recent humiliations. Nothing. That will come when the winter really hits us, and the rebels will make supply runs almost impossible. This blanket of snow is no more than a nuisance, though men act like they have been sent to Nifleheim for duty. They should try sailing the Bay or the Callidorean Ocean some time. That is cold as snowman's shit."

"They say the One Man lost a lot of men in Dagnar," I wondered, staring at the army of riders that was getting commanded into their proper places by captains.

The Headless Horse was a cavalry legion, and though they had done well on foot in Dagnar, it was clear their horses made them twice the men they had been. The pride, the confidence, was back, and I fidgeted as I watched them putting up their lances, tall as two men. I had slain their draugr king, a brave one to be sure, a devious one, and scattered their troops. They had bled over many walls, always first to conquer, always first to brave death, and there I was, sitting right next to them, drinking ale.

"They did," the admiral agreed. "They say they didn't, of course, but they did. A few thousand, as I said, are here. Perhaps some went back to Aten, I know not. It is their own fault. The enemy ran through the Under City. We know about the Under City. Balic should have anticipated it. He should have enforced a better order. The city burned down while the bastards had scattered to loot it. Not a single royal, save for Balic, got out alive. He has not raised them again. Punishment? I do not know. Perhaps you can only do that once, and I wonder where they go after? Is there Hel after all?" He shrugged, munching away, and I discreetly pushed the bowl aside. "But now," he went on, "all this bad luck will change. It is time for sweet victories again."

He saluted me and drank down his ale, smiling like a child.

"Oh?" I said. "I am under the impression that my former command had a role to play in that victory. No food for Hillhold means a loss. What if this other caravan is caught also?"

He shrugged. "Well, yes. It is possible. But victory will be ours. How could we not gain one? With Lisar

Vittar in charge and here in the city."

He went quiet, still smiling.

I had twitched so badly, the bowl scattered to the snow. Immediately, two dogs set upon it, though both ran away with their tails between their legs, yapping like someone had kicked them. One fell and then crawled away, farting loudly. I tore my face away from the dogs.

"You want another serving?" he asked dubiously.

"Ah, no," I said. "I'm afraid I shall die."

He laughed.

Lisar.

I had barely survived Lisar in Dansar's Grave. And now she was in Nallist?

Why?

"There, look," the man said. "Her symbol used to be a yellow flower on black as House symbol, but the Lion it is now, since Palan has been split in three. They mostly hate each other now."

I turned.

I saw her.

I spied her approaching the army of Harrian. With her, there were riders of her own legion, the White Lion on their shields. She was splendidly beautiful, a damned draugr, but a radiant lady, indeed, and I thought, though I couldn't be sure, she would still be holding the magical bone pendant that defied magic. Our battle had broken the tower of Dansar's Grave in half and nearly killed me.

"Redemption," the man said. "Balic's unhappy with her. She went and lost Dansar's to Maskan, and now, she has hijacked all the cavalry of the armies, and it will give back her favor of the One Man. It will be a splendid victory, indeed."

Victory against whom?

They meant to attack my people in the Pass?

I shook my head. Thrum's dverger alone would make it a butchery, and there were ditches and a new order.

"Surely they are prepared?" I asked him. "In the Pass?"

"They won't be," he said, belching. "A supply officer takes supplies from one place to another, eh?" he chuckled. "He doesn't draw strategies. But I think you must be drunk. More drunk than I am, that is."

"Why, yes, but—"

He shook his head at me. "I understand. Of course, it is a failure not to get the supplies forth. You knew it would be dangerous. You were upset you were stopped before you could get to where you were supposed to be going, and you barely survived. But you do know it matters little. They will survive a few more days."

"Hillhold. I was supposed to go to Hillhold," I said, sensing it wasn't so.

He confirmed it.

His eyes went large as plates. "No! No, that is not it.

You weren't taking the food to *Hillhold?* Surely not? Oh dear. Oh, dear me. We *left* Hillhold this night, not a few hours past."

"*What*?" I asked. "What do you mean? I just flew over …"

He laughed and poured me more ale. "I think it doesn't matter how much you drink now. You flew over it on your horse, no doubt! The troops are not in Hillhold," he said simply. "Oh, dear me, you would have been butchered, had you gone there. Our troops left the fort, quite noisily. I am sure it is in rebel hands now. That King Maskan is probably sitting in the great hall now, feeling smug as a king of frogs." He took a swig of his drink and looked at the walls around Nallist. "He won't stay in Hillhold. They'll go after the legions." He winked. "They cannot resist."

I fidgeted and frowned, anxiety building inside me.

The enemy was tired of being fooled, and I was sure what ever Lisar Vittar had planned would be deadly for our troops. My eyes drifted to the harbor. I saw the streets leading down to it, nodded at the admiral, and leaned back.

I would not have much time.

I had to get back to the troops, and Quiss.

"You said Balic's fetching more legions?" I asked.

He gave me a sly wink. "Well. The beaten troops of Dagnar are coming soon, new legions in a day or two with Balic, and people are moving. I am sorry I was so negative earlier. The victory must be near. His Black Ships arrived this morning, so there is that."

"Black Ships?" I asked.

He blinked. "Yes. He expects the battle to be over soon."

I stared at him.

He wrung his hands. "Gods, did you hit your head, my friend, when you fled? I am talking about the ships where the black robes store the fallen he wants to bring back to us. Black Wagons, Black Ships, they go where battle has been fought. Heroes, champions, worthiest of the fallen, and the dead enemy royals, of course, will all go sailing. They get taken to Aten and then down the Green Way back to Malignborg and what was once the Eye Keep, where he will one day raise them. We shall all, one day, walk, but the royals he raises first and these best of men and women next, and for now, they all sleep in Malignborg."

He shook his head. "His black robes will go and seek the battlefields, dig up graves, and they will find servants for One Man. It is always so. You have not been paying attention, have you, friend? They brought back plenty of corpses from the city. And some," he said with a wink, "they will pull from the fields in Hillhold soon, and then, the Pass. They have loaded the corpses we had here already. We'll get them all back, one day, but Princess Filar Barm Bellic will find the very best of corpse for the Black Ships."

I stared at him.

He eyed my mug. "I think this is enough, after all. Eh?"

"Perhaps," I said with a squint. "Filar?"

"Daughter of Balic. Balic's family deal with these matters. The beautiful Queen Rhean and his son Silas keep the dead. You know this, no?" he asked.

I rubbed my head. "I do not, alas. I am not one to follow the rituals of Malignborg, with all that is taking place back home and in the job. I merely try to float in a flood. My wife …" I shook my head. "She distracts me."

"Married, eh?" he laughed. "Good man. A distracting wife is a thing to cherish. You don't need a lover with such a creature in your bed."

"A *terrible* woman," I corrected him. "She distracts me with her constant demands of coin, and a lover would be too expensive to have, thanks to her. I have not noticed the Black Ships. Can one see them?"

He shook his head and nodded down the street. "You know the storehouses in the Opulent Yards as well as I do. They are down there, with Aten and Katar's merchant navy, all half-filled with supplies. As I said, Betus Coin's ships are out. The Black Ships are fat, and … well … black and don't go near them unless you want to end up in the hold as a passenger. You ask a lot of questions. I know nothing of Balic's comings and goings and the new legions. Not really. The grand admiral would know, down in the naval headquarters. If you dare, go ask him. Wait, they are leaving."

I looked towards the harbor and then realized he was talking about the cavalry.

Down the street, the massive number of horses were turning about. They were moving slowly under their banners, and captains and sergeants commanded the men with silent gestures. There were no horns, no emotion to the mass of grim men, only a thicket of lances and silent determination.

"Where are they going?" I muttered.

"To war," he said. "Obviously to war. What else?"

I saw a guard of men. Palan's White Lion flashed in shields and one of them, wearing chain and plate, with a long, barbed and hooked spear, was Lisar. Her face was free of worry, free of mars of death and time, and soldiers bowed before her as she passed them on a black horse.

Lisar smiled triumphantly, let her eyes go over the gathered nobles and troops, and, whooping, rode off to war, passing the city troops by with her hair streaming after.

I nodded and got up unsteadily. "I thank you for the fare."

"Oh, few like it. It is from home." He winked. "It is a boiled dog's arse and some of their guts." He laughed. "It the sauce that makes it bearable. It's not for weak-bellied men, is it? Keep hair growing on your balls, it does."

"Where are the naval headquarters? You said they are here. Are they in the same building you showed me?" I asked, feeling sick. "I would like a word with someone about a trip back home."

"That is a different place," he said magnanimously, eyeing the cavalry with critical eye. "They shall be seated in the harbor, of course. The wharf hosts a cherry red building, and a tavern called the Lamp of Lootan. There, we hold our headquarters. All the officers and Katar's admiral and other useless sods will be seated there, as well as the grand admiral. He is some fool of Aten's." He gave me a puzzled look. "Now, it is time for my nap. Good luck! And remember, if there is trouble, we find a fish for them to fry."

"Indeed! Thank you for the advice, and the dog's arse," I said, and left.

I had to hurry.

CHAPTER 5

The harbor of Nallist was a beautiful place. Nestled inside a sandy lagoon, the entire city built around it and with a beautiful red-bricked road on top of a wharf, it boasted taverns by dozen, and wealthy mansions. One could imagine peace and wealth of its occupants. Now, it was a den of warriors and military support personnel.

There were a dozen piers, and all were filled with fat merchantmen. There were fifty, and more. Most were disgorging supplies, but some also had troops. The legions from Dagnar, haunted looking men from Xal Cot and Harrian, and their officers were trying to find their quarters in the city.

The supplies were being taken into the storehouses and up to the fortress.

A long breakwater built from gigantic rocks guarded the lagoon. Walls that encircled the city ran over the breakwater, and a sea-gate was guarded by two towers.

The naval defense was Morag's design, and like it was in Dagnar, it was in Nallist and other major cities of the north.

I waited on the docks for a moment, staring at the galleys and other ships, and saw the Black Ships. They were at the end of a middle pier—fat-hulled, double-masted ships with a wide belly. They were merchantmen, obviously not in the business of hauling wheat around the bay, because they were armed with several ballistae. A dark flag of white throne and skull flew over them, as did the symbol with serpent and the skull, which I had seen on the chest of Sand's killers. Around them, the piers were quiet, and nobody went near them. Dark robed men stood guard, wearing black helmets, black robes, and black boots, holding black shields with spears. They were entirely dark and looked oddly statue-like as they stood on the decks and pier. They had already, and would again, collect the very best of the dead for Balic.

One day, he would resurrect them.

And once, all the dead of Midgard would follow them.

Hel would be happy to see no living humans walking in Midgard.

I watched the harbor entrance, where some galleys were being rowed in, and some were waiting for their turn to get out.

I whirled and marched off to the wharf, taking the path toward the east. I walked, looking for the headquarters, and spotted it soon.

A stream of naval officers was waiting before a cherry red building, which was lit by torches. There were at least fifty. All wore salty armor, and some were drinking to relieve their boredom, but most had their eyes fixed on the doorways, where whoever commanded the navy would be seated. They had reports to give, requests to make, and they would have to wait to meet scribes and officials, and they were all boiling for a fight. I walked over and saw one of the officers, a red-headed young man in a fine chainmail and holding a blue cloak over his arm, walking for the alley.

He was going to take a piss.

I hesitated and then walked after, looking down to my shoes as I did.

Trash, barrels, and cats filled narrow passageway, as usual, and it stank of piss, shit, and fish, but I did see the man ahead. He was leaning on the wall and looked up, apparently enjoying a long overdue relief.

I flexed my fingers and walked for him. I'd take his face, his documents, and his business, and then, I'd get inside. I'd find anyone who could tell me exactly when Balic would be there and what his plans were.

Hillhold abandoned? I must to hurry. And first, I will murder.

I took a long breath and stepped forward.

The man sensed me and turned his face to me, surprised. "Wait. I am nearly done—"

I reached out and snapped his neck so brutally, the head nearly came off.

I kept a hold of him and tried to see what he looked like, but I was distracted.

On her knees before him, was a whore. She looked up at me, and she still had the soldier's cock in her mouth.

Then, she fell back, horrified, and screamed. She screamed like a demon of the night and scrambled away. I dropped the corpse and ran down the alley.

I heard voices behind, the woman was still screaming, and then, there was the clink of armor and the distinct sound of swords being drawn.

I ran into a dead end.

I looked up. Old fishing nets hung on top, blocking the way. The walls were thick stone.

It seemed I'd be the fish that was going to get fried, after all.

I turned around.

There, a shadowy rank of naval officers stared at me. They saw a fat supply officer. I heard laughter and mocking whispering until a tall, bearded man stepped forward, his sword out. "What did you do, and why? A murder? In the middle of our own men, an army man stabs down a naval officer? Was that about a debt or over your wife?"

"Wife!" someone suggested, and they began to argue about it.

"It was an accident," I said softly. "I fell over him, when I was going to take a piss. Such a skinny boy, he hit his head on the wall. Look—"

"Fell over him," the man said as the party, some twenty strong, with more beyond, stopped arguing and walked forward, swords out. "The girl said you *snapped* his neck. You. Snapping a neck? Seems odd. Never mind. I'm sure we shall find a wound on Larken. Let the admirals deal with this, after we have cut you up a bit. They'll make the right choice. You'll hang, and then, you'll be drawn, and that is the way forward. Come. Give your sword to me."

I shook my head.

He and the others rushed forward.

I shapeshifted.

There would be nothing like I had tried before. There would be no bastard of a creature, confused and ugly. I'd be an animal, and the enemy would be corpses. I fell on my fours and grew terribly in size. Hair burst from my body, my snout grew and widened, and my mouth filled with fangs. My legs and arms were thick with muscle, and the claws were long enough to be considered daggers.

A gigantic ice bear faced the men.

They tried to stop, but it was too late. They crashed into me. I roared, over the brim with rage, and bit down on the first one of them, the bearded shit. My snout grabbed the man's skull in a grip of death. Blood, bone, brain filled my maw, and then, I rose to my hind feet and buried many of them in an avalanche of ripping claws and snapping fangs. An arm was ripped off, a chest crushed, and a leg severed as I embraced the battle-rage. The tight alley still full of foes, I rushed forward, and over them. Men shirked, a woman wept, crushed under my foot, and my claws and fangs gouged at the writhing bodies under me as I rushed on. Armor was rent, flesh torn, and the gigantic bear that I was, relished each bite, each kill with simple joy. I danced on bleeding bodies and hopped on the heaps of the fallen enemy and in the tight press, where half were pushing to escape, half holding on, even though their swords were of no use. Ten, then five left, I rolled up the street like a storm of anger. I saw the whore running out of the alley, her skirts flying, and then, I landed in a ball of rage on the few officers that were left, and we rolled out to the wharf. I heard the bones snapping, fingers groping for my fur with desperation, and I savaged them until they gave up.

Bloodied, panting, staring at the wharf around me, I found myself eye to eye with a troop of those black armored men and their leader.

Blond, in black clothing and black armor, a woman with a chain and ball dangling from her hand was staring at me with curiosity.

Her troops, spears aimed at me, shields out, were circling around me.

"Now that," she laughed, "isn't what I was looking for at all, when they told me I must find the grand admiral. An alley full of sailor bits and pieces!" She winked. "I think you are not really a bear, are you? No? I am Filar Barm Bellic, and you made a mistake, jotun."

I snarled, and then, the draugr let loose a spell.

She braided it together so very fast and skillfully, and

I felt earth itself tearing around me. Like a fist of rock, a force tore up from under, and rock, mud, and brick tossed me, a gigantic bear, up and through the air. It was painful, I felt my fur ripped, and flesh flailed by the power, and then, it was even more painful, as I struck the naval headquarters with full force and went through the doorway, rolled over few scribes and a servant, and end up in what used to be a set of sofas, now a heap of bear, wood chips, and screaming, crushed officers.

I jumped to my feet, sank my teeth into a man who had stabbed me from under, tore his head off, and saw shadows at the doorway.

I felt magic being braided together, and Filar was Kissing the Night there, swaying as she eyed me.

I changed again.

I felt air rushing and then came up as a large dog-sized wolverine. I jumped to the side, sunk my teeth into a meaty thigh of a fat officer trying to hide behind curtains and felt Filar's spell being released. It was a bolt of lightning.

It flashed and boomed, and I kicked off my victim and rolled on the floor, howling as the energy passed me.

She struck the fireplace, and the spell tore it to pieces. Debris was flying in an arc, burning wood scattering all over the room.

I got to my feet and ran at her.

I was so very fast. I pounded thought the floor, past

fallen chairs, and under a table and jumped to the air.

A black armored guard was before her, a shield out.

I changed shape and came down as myself. A jotun of twelve feet, buried in magical armor, hefting a bitter sword. Armed with an irate nature, I struck at them. My sword smashed into the shield and shattered it, and the guard behind. I stepped on the corpse, and Filar hissed with anger, her spiked ball smashing up at me, and I laughed as I grasped it out of the air and pulled her to the wall next to me.

She smashed into it face first, and I lifted my sword to slash her in two.

I saw a boy out of the corner of my eye. He was an evil looking shit with a weasel's face, wearing robes of black, and staring at me while Kissing the Night.

It would be Silas Barm Bellic, and I wondered why the youngest sons of the kings were always sadistically twisted shits.

I found myself standing in a field of black fire, and it sneaked up my feet and on my sword's blade. He was swaying and laughing, and the spell-fire crept on. I howled as my legs were burnt, I fell back inside, and a lizard, a long dark, armored sauk, took the place of a jotun, its claws drawing slivers of wood from the floor as I slithered for a stairway. The fire was still on my flesh, and I felt the tiny armor scales twisting with heat, my flesh burned beneath. I ran up the stairs and jumped, waited, and saw a shadow as Silas was following me. I thrust forward and landed on Silas, who was rounding the corner, giggling. I landed on him brutally, tore my claws into him, bit down on his shoulder.

Spears stabbed at me.

Dozen or more.

A fiery, burning ball and chain was coming down on me.

I jumped off Silas, who was nearly crushed by the ball, but not quite, and then, I fled. The horde of men rushed after, and I loped up and around a corner, and there, a door was closed. I changed, panting with exertion and pain, my joints on fire, kicked through the door, and dodged aside.

Arrows and javelins tore past me, impaling two of the black armored men in the stairs.

I cursed as an arrow transfixed itself on my thigh and came face to face with perhaps three admirals, one a kingly man with an oiled beard, and their scribes. Guards were backing off, pulling new arrows.

I rushed the admirals and wiped my sword savagely across them. Two fell, bloodied and screaming, and the oiled man tried to run, sheets of paper on his hand. I jumped after him, rammed my sword on his back, and struck his hand off. I leaned down, took the hand and the papers, felt arrow sink to my ass, and staggered for a window.

I threw myself out of it, fell through it, my back on

dark flames again, and changed into an eagle. I plummeted down, hurt, trailing feathers, and then, spread my wings, and flapping frantically, pulled myself up where I'd find favorable drafts. I was soon flapping over the dark ships. A stench of death wafted up to me, and when I looked out to the nightly sea, I saw four galleys being rowed.

On one, the emblem of skull over a throne was whipping in the wind.

Balic.

I fled the city, for the north.

I flew like a mad bat caught by daylight and worried myself sick over the terrible foes that gathered to call down our last armies.

I flew away, and in an hour, when the Lifegiver was sharing its first rays of light, I saw Hillhold.

On top of it, *my* banner flew. Higher than it, was that of Roger Kinter.

Before the Hillhold, there were corpses. They were scattered in line, dozens of them, and I saw they were the Aten's men.

I heard horns and drums and looked out to the plain before Hillhold.

I felt my blood turn to ice.

The legion of Aten was out there, much reduced. They were in a ring of shields, thousand and half strong, and rapidly being surrounded by our forces. Ten thousand men, elated by the unexpected capture of

Hillhold, it was the only army we had in the south, save for the Stone Watchers and the three legions Crec had stolen and led north.

It was also victorious.

It was arrogant.

Aten's legions had been surprised.

Our men, still in companies of militia and those of the nobles, were competing for the honor of capturing them. The nobles on their horses were riding around them, whooping like fools. I saw Roger and Hal's flags, the latter on the right, the former on the left. Their men-at-arms were rushing to encircle the enemy.

Only the militia, in the middle, was marching forward in a solid shieldwall. They had not yet mixed up the troops.

Not too far, an icy river ran lazily for the woods, and its steep banks were snow-laden.

I saw a glint of metal in that snow. Then more. I saw movement. I saw men getting up.

Horns blared.

The legions, the bitterly beaten legions from the Pass, suddenly filled the valley's end and began marching for the bewildered nobles.

And I was still far.

CHAPTER 6

It looked bad from the start. The historians would blame me, and Quiss.

They were right to do so.

I had threatened Roger and Hal and trusted Quiss and Cil, and that Thrum could coerce the new order on them. I had stripped the lot of their titles.

When Hillhold has suddenly capitulated, and Aten's lone legions had been surprised before the gates, historians wrote that Roger had quickly led his men-at-arms and other nobles out.

Quiss had followed with the militia and Aten's men.

Thrum had not followed. He and his dverger had started to prepare the place for defense.

I could see it all taking place as if I was right there.

A disaster.

The horde of Red Midgard's nobles and men-at-arms was still engulfing Aten's legion in a pincher-like movement, despite the wide shieldwall of southern veterans marching on them. The five hundred noble cavalry was still riding around wildly, many younger nobles, lances and spears high.

Most had not even noticed the enemy legions.

Only the horn blown by the order of Quiss, recalling them to the militia, stopped the charge.

Soon, they spotted why the recall had been given.

And then, half of the men out in the field, found

Roger calling for a shieldwall there and then, while was Hal retreating. Rogers men were pushing into each other, in utter confusion.

The thousands of Hammer Legionnaires were just a hundred yards out. They were a silent wall of professional killers, stepping in tune to their brothers, their shields up, a wall of steely death. Their eyes spoke of something else.

They finally, *finally* had their enemy where they had wanted it all this time. They would finally fight a battle on a level field, shield to shield, and they had much avenging to do.

The chaos in our ranks was complete. The militia was spreading into two lines, but slowly and chaotically. The men-at-arms were rushing to the right wing, but hundreds and hundreds were trying to form the wall on the left, and what was born out of that was corpses.

A milling mass noble cavalry was confused and not sure what they should be doing, so they were instead riding in all the directions

Aten began shooting arrows. So did the legions. Six Spears had many, and a cloud of missiles tore through the morning sky. Men were falling from their saddles, horse were crashing down, and the troops that obeyed Roger were falling in tens and dozens, often unprotected by shields.

Then the enemy shieldwall was blowing horns, the standards were dipping, and they rushed forward, their howls filling the valley.

I flew as fast as I could, but I was far, weary, and hurt.

Snow was flying as the enemy charged.

They rolled right to the nobles and the men-at-arms commanded by Roger. It was Milas Illir and Ontar who struck the chaotic lines with shields, and Aten rushed to cut most of the fools off. Spears first, stabbing at backs, shields, and faces, pushing men over, shields working in unison, the legionnaires pushed into, and through, hundreds of men, leaving pockets stranded in a sea of the enemy. Our militia, Aten's traitors, Hal's nobles, and the hundreds who had obeyed the recall on the left were forming ranks, staring in stupefied horror at the butchery before them.

One by one, standards high, shields pushing relentlessly, the enemy was victorious. Our men were butchered, and beaten to ground.

It seemed to take no time at all.

Roger led dozens of survivors to our shieldwall, while the enemy turned marched to join theirs.

The loyal Aten fell in with the bloodied Milas Illir and Palan's few Bull legionnaires, and when the killing was done, many heads were hoisted on spears, a field of thousand and more of our dead celebrated by the foe. The enemy stopped to dress ranks, to stand in attention, and to stare at our shieldwall with a promise of similar death clear in their sullen eyes. The silence—save for the screams of the wounded, many of whom were crawling away from the legionnaires—was chilling. Horses were running free, their riders slain.

Roger was again active.

He was howling orders, waving his sword amid the much reduced, thin left flank. It rippled and took steps back.

Hal was on the right flank, but they moved nowhere.

Cil and Quiss were sending riders to Roger.

The enemy marched forward. They stormed over the dead and the dying, silencing last of the wounded. In three ranks, spears falling to place, it marched to within fifty feet of our army.

The left flank retreated again, like a gate swinging open.

The legions stopped, and I saw arms pumping along the lines. Horned helmeted men and women were howling orders under their banners, and javelins and arrows shot up and at our men, especially the militia, and the traitor Atenites.

The missiles ripped through the ranks, which seemed to recoil, and then, people began dropping. Hundreds fell, then another hundred, and many others lost shields or took wounds. The line of Red Midgard looked like a wounded animal shuddering from pain.

They replied in kind, especially those trained for it. The militia had very few missiles. Javelins, stones, and arrows tore haphazardly into the mass of the legion, dropping men all along the lines, but it was a paltry price they paid in comparison to what the enemy had done. The numbers were still fairly even, but the left flank was still in turmoil and chaos as Roger was howling orders, clearly shocked and terrified beyond recall.

They stepped back again, and again.

Horn blasted a note to the air. It was a fast, high one and ended quickly.

The legions stepped forward together and then again forward, and then, they rushed forth, spears flashing, spears out.

They bashed into our ranks. They fell back, and back, and many fell under the enemy.

The spears stabbed over the first ranks and tore lives away, on both sides. The stabbing went on for a long moment, all along the shieldwalls, which were no longer straight, but looked like a snake slithering forward. It was a battle of attrition. The legionnaires had the skill, the routine, and the bravery, and so, while men fell on both sides, they killed two to everyone they lost.

Our men tried. They fought as hard as they could.

Hal's ranks held. They took the brunt and settled into brutal exchange of lives with no visible gain.

The center only held due to Aten and Cil's men-at-arms, former of whom fought against their own countrymen, and Ontar and Palan. They held in the middle, but the militia, ill used to battle and never really having endured the shieldwall, fell like dogs. More and more of them were eaten by the terrible veterans, whose shields pushed, pushed, and tied down men, and pole ax, spear, and sword stabbed them down in dead ranks.

The left, having moved back, had somewhat confused and delayed the enemy, but was now also fully engaged, and since they lacked so many men due to Roger's mistake, it was just a matter of time it would be enveloped and shredded.

There were no reserves.

I struggled against the winds that had so favored me when I flew south. I beat my wings, cursed my luck, and saw, how in the militia ranks, sudden holes appeared. Bashing down militia and tearing through a company of Aten, Milas Illar's men were abandoning the shieldwall to gain a breach, to hold it, to widen it. Enemy warriors were moved by keen captains from elsewhere in the ranks and moved behind such attempts in the hopes of gaining sudden, brutal breakthrough.

I saw Quiss, on her horse, guarded by some dverger near the center, yelling orders, which nobody heeded, and she had no men to convey the orders either.

A javelin went past her face. Another seemed to strike her, but she had apparently dodged it.

The broiling pits, where the enemy were trying to break through, suddenly gained great success. Near the center and left, where Roger's men suddenly retreated, an already desperate fight to plug a hole suddenly fell apart. The enemy butchered those who had tried to stop it and began stabbing men from the sides as hundreds poured in after.

A single hero was pushing from the left, stabbing and hacking with a sword, and few men joined him. For a moment, they stood there, falling men, and then, like swimmers in a tide, they disappeared.

Just to the right edge of the militia, a savage company of Six Spears Legion, led by near gigantic man with a hammer, smashed its way to a company of Dagnar and simply tore it to pieces. The man's men spread around him, and Hal, leading cavalry from the right that had somewhat regrouped, led a savage attacked to stop them.

Hal left his lance on the giant's gut and dismounted to hold the fragile line, but many an enemy turned right and began pulling the militia and Aten's men apart.

The enemy pushed, they pushed again, pushing back the entire line. There were cheers as the enemy took the standard of Roger from a torn nobleman. They took it away, holding it aloft.

They were all chanting now. It was a ferocious chant, a merciless one.

"Death! Death!" they howled.

They had won.

Nothing more was needed. All they had to do was to

push and kill, push and kill, and our men would run and many killed.

What came next broke the hearts and souls of Red Midgard for long years.

Lisar's cavalry appeared on our right flank. They came from the woods, and I cursed none had sent scouts to the flanks.

Thousand men were thundering in a thick column of glittering lances for Hal's men.

Our cavalry, most still trying to pluck the hole, nonetheless turned to counter it. There were no more than two hundred. They rode at the enemy bravely, like immortals.

A wall of fire burst from the ground under them. The spell's power was terrifying, explosive, fierce. A hundred of our men were caught in the inferno of fire, the horses hurtling in burning pieces on the snow, the men burning around them.

The spell died out, leaving just the smoldering corpses, and the noble cavalry that had not been caught in fire was milling in terrified chaos behind the corpses. Many had been thrown. All were stunned.

The thousand men of Harrian rode over them. They stabbed at the horsemen, they sent our men to Hel, and the enemy crashed forward. Stomping over the dead and the frozen ground, Harrian and Vittar's Lions rode behind the right flank, wheeled, and struck that flank from behind, the column spreading expertly into a line.

The hundreds and hundreds of lances dipped and tore to the backs of the panicked men, pushing them into ruin, into the spears and swords of the legions, and simply tore our men to pieces. One standard after another fell. The enemy cavalry dropped the lances, pulled swords, and began riding freely at our fleeing, desperate men. They lost a dozen men to a small counterattack by some of our nobles who had been late to abandoned late the breach in the line, but quickly overwhelmed the men. Soon, the right flank was in shreds, and Lisar's riders proceeded to ride for the center, and Quiss.

All the army ran.

They simply fell apart, no longer soldiers, and ran.

Most went for Hillhold, like billowing clouds of sparrows, herded be enemy right, left and front. Roger, looking around in panic, was gathering men around him and rode to the northern woods, being pursued by the enemy.

I saw Cil, holding the tide, and then, he was buried under shields, and spears.

Not all got away.

Many thousands were suddenly surrounded in the middle. There were perhaps four thousands of them. They were Aten's men, they were mostly militia, and many nobles with their men-at-arms. Hal was there, as was Quiss, who was saved from twenty riders of Harrian by her dverger, who bought her time to push to the milling mass of her men, before dying under hooves.

And it was then when I arrived.

I hurtled from the sky, heard the enemy chanting as they chased our people all over the field, and most ferocious were the legionnaires, who had pushed to the cut off men and women of Aten and Red Midgard. I saw them stabbing, stabbing, and then, I spotted Lisar amongst many of her riders, looking triumphal and proud as she gazed at the chaos, and the impending victory. She stared over the shoulders of her legionnaires at the surrounded thousands and lifted her spear high.

I shapeshifted as I came for them.

I turned into a gigantic wolf, bounded from the bloody ground, and leaped for Lisar.

She and I fell, my rear claws tearing chunks of flesh from her horse, and I buried her under me. My fangs ripped into her side. She placed her spear shaft into my mouth, and pushed me back. I tried to snap it in two.

I failed.

Men dismounted, swarmed me, and finally pulled me off, and I roared as I change into a twelve-foot jotun, straddling the falling men and Lisar. My sword cut the air and took down four men. I kicked aside few, stomped on a sergeant who rode at me with a lance, and looked for Lisar under me.

She was gone.

I roared and cursed. I heard her calling for her men, but I couldn't see her. Instead, I rushed forward to the enemy mass ringing our people and braided together a spell.

Icy blizzard grew around me, the braid wild, rushed, and powerful.

I had no time to perfect it, or aim it. I had no easy way to control it. Instead, I let loose a whipping storm of ice and wind amid thick ranks of enemy.

The spell tore flesh and bone from tens of the foe.

It tore the life from many of our people.

It moved along the line of both our men, and theirs, and ranks and ranks of men and women died, their flesh ripped, skin torn, eyes and mouths full with ice and snow. The Minotaur legion of Kellior Naur suffered worst, standard after standard disappearing into the blizzard, men falling and running away, two captains shredded and falling with their horses.

I screamed at Quiss and pointed my sword to the woods. "Quiss! Get them out!"

Her eyes enlarged as she saw me, her mouth moved in astonishment, and then in shame, and I had to call again.

"Hal! Quiss! Get to the damned woods! We must get there! Don't let them run!" I yelled, and cursed, as a spear entered my flesh in the calf.

I whirled and struck the man down with my sword and then another, and suddenly faced a draugr king who had pulled his helmet off to see better.

It had been a prince, judging by the young age.

He had been barely a man when he had died and been raised. His draugr father had likely fallen in the battles, and he ruled his legion now.

He had dropped his pretty face and looked white, skeletal, and his hair was hanging lank around his shoulders.

He Kissed the Night and aimed his finger on the ground before me. I rolled away just as our men began pushing out of the shattered legionnaire ring, commanded by Hal.

A large hand clawed its way out of the ground. Mud, snow, stone was mixed on it, and a face appeared next to it. I growled and stomped on the hand, hacking down on the head with my sword. The thing fell apart. The draugr cursed and braided another spell. Fire grew in the draugr's hand, and he produced a flaming whip, and he jumped forward and struck down at me. I dodged, but the whip rattled against my armor, scorched it, and judging by the look in his dead eyes, both full of surprise, he had not thought my armor might be dverg-made, near magical. I spat and grasped the whip, my gauntlet ripping apart, and yanked him to me.

I rammed my sword to his chest.

I threw him down and hacked him in two. For good measure, I stomped on his face with my heel until he resembled a fallen cake. I whirled, looked at the mass of battling people rushing for the woods, saw Quiss, and Hal, leading men and women over a line of legionnaires, and then, they were pulling down Harrian's horsemen, who had tried to cut them off.

Legions were turning to attack them, rushing after.

Harrian and Vittar's Lions were galloping wildly, a long stream of trouble, to cut them off.

I called for a spell again. I pulled at the great power of the ice, I twisted the coldest streams of icy water, the chilliest winds that blew across the nine rivers that tumbled into the Filling Void, and added more ice, in a braid I had only used a few times.

I pulled in all the power I could. I made the braid strong, thick and, my head throbbing, I threw it at the cavalry.

The spell struck the men. The horses tumbled down, thirty, forty, their legs kicking air. The men on them didn't object. They couldn't scream. Their mouths and noses were pushing out a stream of bloodied ice, as I had turned their blood into ice. The rest of the riders scattered, terrified. The spell had ripped out the heart of so many men, I could scarcely believe it. It was one of the most powerful spells I knew, and I couldn't use it repeatedly, but it had never been that powerful. I wondered if the spirit of winter had a thing to do with it, but it didn't. I was just growing in power, for it was winter, indeed.

An arrow struck my head, but the point had been cut off, and spun off.

I stumbled forward with a splitting headache.

I distantly heard my name being called.

I thought it was Quiss.

Then, I felt a spell being braided together. I knew it had been Lisar who had called me, instead.

I fell on my face and roared, as a lightning bolt kissed the air and ground, as well as corpses next to me, before hitting me with its waning force. I flew around and landed ten feet away. A pauldron had been ripped off, leaving part of my chest, back, and the entire shoulder exposed, save for chain and leather. The riders of Harrian were heeding Lisar's call and coming for me. I spat away the blood in my mouth, staggered up, and saw a horde of horses arriving, men leering down at me. One stabbed a lance at my back, other one at my leg, and one guided his mount before me and swung with a hammer, smashing it down for my head.

I caught the hand just in time.

Then, I saw Lisar looking at me ten feet away, standing on a corpse, her face twisted with unequaled rage.

She began braiding together another spell. I tossed my captive head over heels at her, and she fell with it into bloody snow and mud.

I raised my sword and rushed forward.

A lance tore to my bared back, and I saw bright lights

of pain. The man twisted the lance, and I twisted and hacked the man down, then another. Hundred enemy were milling around me, and many more were rushing for me, answering Lisar's calls. Hundreds tried to stop a few thousand of ours from escaping, pulling down straggles, cutting tired groups from the main body, isolating the slowest and the bravest, but a mass of our people were nearly in the woods.

I turned, sensing something behind me.

Lisar was there and charging yet again with her riders, all White Lion, this time. She wore her horned helmet now, and men saw her and followed her willingly, ashamed to show fear while a One-Eyed Priest led them.

I had a moment to prepare, and I lifted my sword high.

Her spear, hooked and deadly, was coming for me, as were the many lances from her riders.

I dodged left and right, and then hacked down. The sword whistled in the air and tore a horn off her helmet, killing a man next to her. I found her spear was tangled in my armor. Men rode to help her, all armed with hammers, and their mounts crashed into me. I fell on my knees, they pushed and pulled, and I fell on my back, struggling mightily. Lisar, holding on to her spear, jumped to my chest, her eyes burning with rage, and then, her foot on my face.

"I feel no anger for you, jotun. You have been a

decent opponent. I shall miss you, curiously enough," she muttered, ripped the spear out of my chain, and stabbed for my throat.

I exerted all my will and thickened my skin, calling forth the great bear.

Men were tossed off me, many losing their hammers. Not Lisar.

The spear tore to my neck. I shrieked, thrashed, and rolled over men and Lisar, clawing at her armor, at the men, and barreled out of their trap. Trailing blood, taking wounds from javelins and swords, men riding by me, I loped off after the mass of our men, passing many of the slowest who were being butchered. I ran as fast as I could, bit down on a champion of Six Spears, who had been just turning from a kill, and saw how twenty more men were converging on me, excited as any hunter would be when stalking the king of the woods. I saw Quiss amid the mass of people just inside the woods, and she was frowning as she saw me coming.

Men were rushing forward around her. All held brutally long bows.

They were not our people, but fresh arrivals from Alantia.

They lifted their bows and began losing arrows on the great mass of foes behind and around me. Men fell, horses tumbled, and suddenly, I was free. I slunk to the woods and shifted, felt a great wound on my throat, and went to a knee, trying to get up. The bald man I had seen leading the assault on the caravan was there. I saw Hal, and Quiss. They were all pushing and then pulling me up.

"It looks bad," the bald man said. "But he seems to have seen the like before. He heals faster than a man?"

"He is King Maskan," Quiss said. "He does. Jotuns heal from terrible wounds. He needs time."

"We'll find him some time, and then, we will speak," he murmured. "Follow the people and don't look back. We'll stop them in the woods."

I got up, bleeding heavily, and turned as we walked off. I watched many of our men dying before Hillhold.

Thousand, perhaps two, had gotten there. Another thousand had fled to the woods. With us, there were two and a half thousand.

On the battlefield, there were nearly six thousand dead.

The enemy cheered itself hoarse, and then, I saw no more.

BOOK 2: THE ROBBER AND THE KING

"And still, it is how you win. You risk all. You need to win your throne, Queen of Red Midgard. It takes more than extorting kings to sit in the Temple of the Tower."

Maskan to Nima

CHAPTER 7

The retreat was one of miserable chaos. It could have only been worse, had it been night. The enemy doggedly came after us and spread lightly armed men to the woods, while they marched hardy infantry after us. That infantry took horrible losses from the archers. Our guides, locals all, gave us the only good news of the day.

It seemed we would get away.

They led the stream of militia, a thousand and a half, thirty nobles led by Hal, and a thousand men-at-arms of Hal's and poor Cil's to the green and white depths of the woods, using trails meant for hunters and their prey.

The militia were shocked.

The men-at-arms were silent.

The nobles, serious.

Many of the militia wept. Some marched with no weapon or shield, and most of the weapons they had were spent and dull. Many were wounded, and the roots and icy trail were hampering their speed.

None could wait for them.

Many of them were left leaning on trees, too exhausted or hurt to go on. A boy, barely fourteen or fifteen, thin and handsome, walked to the woods, holding his bleeding belly.

It made me sick.

I held my throat and bled, not sure I wasn't dying. Quiss was walking just ahead of us and looking at me with a pale, shamed face. I gave her a look, and she opened her mouth and spoke softly. "It was foolish. We had no time to create the wings you asked for. The militia and the men-at-arms had to be kept separate. And Roger? He took his men out without order. We had just gained Hillhold and held it, and then, he went out like a fool. We had to follow. I sent him an order stay with the militia, but he rode off, and Hal followed him. But of course, the failure is mine."

The bald man leading the bowmen grunted. "Roger Kinter, eh? Powerful, rich, and stupid. Perhaps the lady should go to the front and see to our well-being with my lieutenant."

"I—" Quiss began.

"You lost a battle, girl," he said brutally. "And now, you must not look like you have been beaten, because some of these people will survive, and you must get your act together if you would not lose their trust for good. Don't admit to failure when they are listening. Go ahead."

She hesitated and handed me the Grinlark. I refused it.

"Where is the Book of the Past? And the rings and other things?" I asked her. "I gave them to you."

"With Thrum. He never left the keep," she said, and then walked her horse forward, dodging branches.

The man watched her go and looked behind. "Poor lass. Out of her depth, but who isn't?" He gave me a look that suggested he meant me. Before I could answer, he went on. "They'll hunt us like dogs, but they always do. That Harrian's cavalry force is a nasty one, and that Queen Vittar is giving Alantia a history we shall never forget. She has butchered up and down the land, before they all looked towards Dagnar, and she went to Hillhold." He smirked. "Now, she is back. Not good. Not good at all. It has been a hard fall here in Alantia, and winter seems to go to shit as well. You are Morag's boy?"

"I am," I said.

A boy?

I leaned closer to him, and spoke harshly. "I am the King of Red Midgard."

He chuckled. "*King,* eh?" He rolled his eyes. "King of a bloody mess, you mean. Dagnar is gone. They burned it. Morag is dead, usurper that he was, and no human king at all. And now, what you built in Dagnar and the pass with your sword, is shattered."

I bristled at his tone. "Yes. I am a king of ruin, and I'll not stop before I have pushed the enemy off. I am—"

"Bleeding to death, if that is not taken care of," he said as he eyed my wounds. "Those cavalry boys were expecting you. They were looking for you. I saw them waiting in the woods, like a pack of well-trained hounds. They watched the battle unfold and could have gone in sooner. They could have captured your pretty lass and shattered the entire line. Instead, they waited for as long as they could, and only went in after it seemed the battle had been decided."

I nodded. "They would like to see me dead, wouldn't they?"

"You called for magic," he said with a first hint of approval in his voice. "*Dangerous* magic. Deadly skill, worthy of a consideration. That is much more important in these days than a title of a king, eh? We would have done so much better here in Alantia, had we but not faced their magic. They are not alive, are they?"

"They are not," I answered. "It is a long story."

"Oh, we know much of the story," he said. "People travel in your kingdom, Morag."

"I am Maskan," I said. "King."

He chuckled and went serious, as he heard commotion, not far. A man screamed, a horse whinnied with pain, and after a while, he relaxed, as if he had seen the danger go away.

He spoke on. "One of their scouts found one of ours, and the usual thing happened. Those southern boys are no good in the northern woods. Like asking a noble to milk a cow." He eyed me with some interest. "Maskan, eh? Morag is what the king has always been called. All the Danegell kings were called *Morag*. They say the first Danegell after Hel's War took the name of a jotun king he had slain, and it had been the custom ever since. But, indeed, it was that first, stupid Danegell who had been raped with a jotun's ax, and it was really Morag all along. It has been the *same* damned Morag all the time? Aye. You can call yourself a brute, for all I care," he muttered. "There was a King Crec in the middle, wasn't there? A bastard of some Helstrom family? Greedy and stupid. Do not worry. You can call him a pig, and none shall so much as a flinch. We dislike him here in Alantia. He stripped us of our defenses. The Gray Brothers would have been much needed here."

I shrugged. "You call him *King* Crec, this Draugr, but you dislike the idea of calling me King Maskan. One must wonder why you bothered to intervene on our behalf, if you hold me in such a contempt."

He spat and thought about it for a moment. He looked like a man pondering if he should throw his dice, or if he should just walk away. Apparently, he tossed them. He spoke harshly. "All the nobility left us to our own devices. Granted, Crec took the armies, but Fiirant recalled the nobles. The left us to deal with twenty thousand hammer legionnaires. There were a hundred thousand people in Alantia. It is a spacious, mysterious, rich country with fine cities, peaceful towns, and harmonious villages, with gold and iron mines, and we have the very best hunting grounds in Midgard. Now, only the hunting ground remains, and we basically don't hunt for stags or deer these days. The rest, and the people along with it, has been burnt, looted, raped, and destroyed. And you wonder why we care little for kings? Where was *King* Maskan when our land was put to torch?"

"I've—"

"I know," he said reluctantly, and sighed. "You have raised the people in Fiirant to your cause."

"Our cause."

He smirked. "To a cause. You showed them the draugr deceptions, and you have pushed the people of Fiirant, those whom Crec and this goddess of yours betrayed. They stand together, and I agree your actions have been for … Fiirant. Alantia, however, still hasn't seen the good you have done. You are the first jotun king of the *west* Red Midgard, and you fight hard for your people. Everyone can see that, o king of scars. What I saw out there, that miracle of a shapeshifting, scares me as much as anything I've ever seen. I do not know if you are suited to be a king of the east. We might not want a king anymore. No, nothing scares us more than kings in Red Midgard."

He sighed.

"Save for the undead," I said. "Because with them, you cannot win."

"Save for them," he said softly. "I am called Saag, Saag of the Highwoods. But you err when you say the undead scare us more than kings of Dagnar. As part of your role, as a king, you have hanged many of my kind in the past." He flashed me a grin. "I am, sir, formerly a bandit."

I gave him a cold stare.

"One thousand gold for my head, before all this began," he chuckled. "Your father would have had me strung up on the Gate Gallows, and I'd pissed my thighs for all the crimes I've done."

I nodded. "I remember your name. I was a thief for years, see?"

He blinked and then spoke on, uncertain. "Now, I am the king of Highwood, *this* wood, and one of the dozens of bands of people who seek to survive this winter. Not all fight the enemy. There are people in Alantia who think by surviving, the High King Balic will one day give us peace back and will give us our freedom under a *new* king, and things shall be mended." He chuckled. "The people are turning to me, King Maskan. Even nobles live under my wing, and many local militia and men-at-arms, who used to hunt me. Alantia is divided and no longer a county, unless one for the robbers. The people brought us food, and I gave them shelter, and it is the same all over the country. There are five thousand people in the Saag's Hold, and that is where we shall hide your people as well."

I shook my head. "And *how* will you feed them?"

"They can go back to Hillhold, unless that bitch draugr takes it later, but for now, I am going to give you shelter and protection, and aye, it will cost us supplies we do not wish to spend on others," he said, and gave me a quick, worried look. "I'd not try to raise *my* people to your cause, king of Dagnar," he added. "They hate the nobles and kings as much as they do the southerners. You shall have shelter for now, until you heal. I am no beast, see?"

"You propose we sit on our hands," I asked him scathingly, "while they slowly kill us all off?"

"I suggest," he answered with equal fire, "that we let winter do its evil on their armies, and I shall summon other people during the winter, and together, we shall try to negotiate a peace. They want it as much as we do. They must. The draugr cannot possibly want more than the land. What good are the dead to them?"

I laughed, bled, coughed, and still couldn't stop laughing. "What good … they are Hel's things. *All* they want is to kill the living. That is their goal. They are seeking a powerful being of Hel up north," I answered. "Their victory won't stop with the death of a king."

He flinched.

"That's what you have been contemplating on, eh?" I said. "Kill me and offer the head as a gift? Lisar would go giddy over it, and she'd make a count of you. Draugr Saag the Count. This war will be the end of all of us. They don't want the living. They have no use for any of us. All of this is just a distraction."

He grinned, though he looked worried. "Truly?" he asked. "They want us all dead? It is hard to … fine.

Possibly. But you are saying there is a powerful being, and we are just a distraction?" He looked at me with pity. "No. They want power, and they will take Falgrin and Ygrin, and the Golden City, and then, they will rule what living people remains. It is no more than what they have done in the south, in the Verdant Lands. Those lands are *not* filled with the dead. They merely rule over the land, and the living do well enough, don't they? Saag's people will not budge from the holds unless to keep our people alive, to fight when it makes sense. That is all we do. We help retain what we have and shall have in the future." He smiled. "I must look after my people."

"And my head?" I asked.

He scratched his neck. "I played with the idea," he said. "I am not a man like that. You shall be aided, your wounds bound and stitched. Then, you get to leave, and you will take your nobles with you. The rest will stay. They will give me more strength for the spring's negotiations."

"As you bid on Balic making you a count?" I sneered. "You do know that the royals in the south, many generals, dukes, and counts, are all undead."

He shook his head. "I'll try to be something less than a count and a duke, and still important. I have my ways," he told me. "Do not make trouble. Like those riders, you will be kept an eye on."

In the shadows, archers looked on.

"The Princess of Aten shall stay," he said, and marched off. "I need an insurance, after all."

I walked on and found a clenched hand stuffed in my belt.

It was the grand admiral's, and there were papers in the fist. I pried them off, dropped the hand to the snow, and read the papers.

***

Later that evening, the pursuit had fallen off. We were being guided to a rocky path that led down a mighty river's bank and then up a steep, rocky hillside. We took trails through ravines that defended the land quite naturally and found another exhausting route up a steep side of hill, and there was a man-made barrier, for a gate barred the way, and a drawbridge over a steep ravine made it a near unassailable place.

We marched through and found a valley hanging over the river, nestled in an armpit of a near-mountain of a hill, and that hill was filled with robber-caves, and the valley was rich with several villages.

People poured out to see Saag's men leading a beaten army in their midst, and I found myself standing with forlorn noblemen and some of their men-at-arms. The remainder tottered to rest, to the caves, and all were kindly but sternly disarmed before they would be allowed to change sides.

Many would, I was sure.

We were closely watched. There were two thousand

archers around the valley, many staring at us while casually working on their duties. All had bows nearby, and bundles of arrows.

We waited until out people had been settled in.

Hal was shaking his head. "What a mess this is."

"What happened in the battle?" I asked, looking for Quiss. I couldn't see her.

Hal took a tentative step forward. "Hillhold was abandoned. We couldn't believe it. We thought they might have rebelled against Balic and gone to raid their supplies, and the dverger managed to climb on top. It took some time and skill. Then, the gates were opened, and we simply marched in." He shook his head. "The next thing I knew, Aten's legion was outside the gates and then on the run, after they took a few volleys of arrows. Then, suddenly, Roger is leading half of the nobles and men-at-arms outside and after them."

"Roger."

He nodded. "It was odd. He was totally composed. Then, we had to follow, to make sure they wouldn't get into trouble. Regent Quiss ordered it, though she kept sending riders to Roger."

"And you went right."

"Yes," Hal said, "I, too, led my men to the right of the legions, as ordered. You know the rest." He shook his head.

"You were ordered to the right," I said. "I see."

Hal took a ragged breath. "We lost most of the nobles

in the land. I guess you actually must remake the order after the war."

"Aye," I said darkly.

Roger. The dog.

Finally, we saw Saag in one of the villages, riding out and looking at us. He pointed a finger at a large, dirty white hall, and grudgingly, I walked that way with the nobles and many of their men-at-arms. Every man kept a hand on their dulled, busted swords and weapons. There was a throng of nine hundred, and little more. I still couldn't see Quiss.

It was as Saag expected.

Most of the nobles of Alantia had gone to Dagnar to seek help. Those who had stayed had been killed in battle. It was easy to blame them for the misery and the losses, for the hunger and hopelessness, and it was easy to listen to a robber lord, who only hoped to profit from the whole debacle.

He was using us to make his point. The hall was a center of attention and rude comments. People were mocking us outside, and the people who had aided us, refused to look us into the eyes.

We didn't belong.

I feared the people I had so recently been made a king by would forget as well.

"King," asked a young nobleman, watching my ragged wound. "What do you expect us to do?"

"I want you to keep your calm," I answered. "And

the rest of it, I shall have to figure out."

"What do you mean?" the man asked. "He means to turn us out."

Hal came to stand with the man. "He means to take your head. And ours."

I shook my head. "I was a thief before I was anything else. I told him. I know a thief when I see one, and I know he would not have let us up here if he meant to see us out. No. We are a risk. He told me that many times. He knows I can escape, so he isn't counting on taking my head. He knows a jotun." I smiled at them. "Your heads are a different matter."

"What, then?" the man said with a smile. "He hopes to deal with Balic. I heard it."

"The man is a robber baron," I said. "He knows fully well there is *no* negotiating with Balic. He knows it, though he pretends not to know anything. He is the sort of a man who plays cards, and he has told me they are strong cards, and it seems likely they are. He might hold all the best ones, doesn't he? Should he will it, he can kill many of us. He can give us shelter or take it away at a whim. He saved many of us, so he is kind. He is a killer, and he can act as a king as well. He has plans, and he makes them sound sensible. All the cards, see? And yet, none can truly claim the game will not end in his defeat, if Balic wins. He will, if I die. So, in the end, he wants to bargain. I shall listen, and we will see how it goes. I think he wants to rule Alantia and have my blessing." I looked up at the archers. "We need him on our side. And it will cost us a great deal."

CHAPTER 8

The night came, and the calls of the wounded echoed in the valley. Their miserable wounds and terrible pain were a constant distraction in Saag's Hold. Hel's song, the shrieks of the dying, reminded everyone of the cost of losing a battle. Bodies were being carried out of those caves, and men and women who tended for the warriors would come out, looking sick.

"King Maskan?" a man called out, as I leaned on a wall. He was an official looking little man, who seemed to watch me as if I had been born of the rocks themselves. "Your wounds need attending to."

I touched my throat. A jotun heals, and heals fast, from near fatal wounds, even, but the wound was still bleeding.

He went on. "Saag gives his word, you are safe. It is the truth, King. We do keep them, even in a land of a robber lord. How could we otherwise expect to survive?"

So, I waved Hal down and followed him.

He led me to the caves, through one filled with the wounded, and I passed them, looking at each and saluted who was awake. They mostly smiled back.

I was led to a separate, rough room with a bed, and a table with all kinds of supplies that one could use to heal a cow, or a man.

The small man nodded at the bed, and I sat down,

waiting to be administered to. Soon, I heard boots striking the floor. A girl appeared, a thick braid gleaming with blood. She had an apron, something a butcher might wear, and she looked weary. She nodded and approached me, looking at my half-destroyed armor, and the sword I wore on my hip, the terrible butcher's blade formerly of Bjornag, the Black Brother.

She lifted an eyebrow. "Off with it all."

I sighed and proceeded to stripping the armor. It was damaged, badly battered, but the dverger might help to fix it. I was certain Thrum was alive and would either be marching to Dansar's Grave or holding Hillhold still.

The armor came off easily, still magical and wonderful. My wounds made it a slow progress.

I finally managed to strip away the armor, and I sat on a chain skirt, and my thick leather pants, leaning onto my sword. The girl twitched to action and approached me.

"Carefully," the small man, who refused to name himself, whispered, and she nodded.

"She knows how," I said hollowly. "She's had plenty of practice this night."

"She has," the man agreed.

She inspected my throat and then my neck and shuddered.

"It was a close one," I said.

"Yes, King," she agreed. "It was just an inch away. I shall give you medicines to aid with infection, and I shall stich this one up."

"My back, and some other places have been hurt, and—"

"You are, King, bruised and battered all over," she said with a small, pretty smile. "Like a king should be. They seem to be on the mend? So fast?"

I smiled. "I am lucky, since I find myself in terrible situations all the time. Tell me, is Saag ever so battered and bruised?"

The official man wrung his fingers. "He is a lord of archers. They do not—"

I scowled at him, and he clamped his mouth shut.

The girl didn't answer.

"Where," I asked her, "is the Queen of Aten?"

She shook her head. "She is no prisoner. She is ... busy, and well enough. Is she the queen? Really? I thought she was a princess of some sort."

"If she is hurt, I shall remember what you and Saag promised, and betrayed," I told her.

She scowled, hesitated, and went on working, biting back a stinging comment. She made her way to my back and then began speaking. "Saag's not a man to break his words. You can trust him not to hurt her. And you shouldn't underestimate him."

"Indeed," I agreed. "I should not. I would like to trust him, but he doesn't seem like the sort of a man who has done any oath keeping in his life. His family is a spawn of criminals."

"You are a thief," she said simply. "A thief. Thieves have codes. They obey the rules, because to not do so means you have nothing to fall back to."

I nodded and flinched as her long, dark hair fell across my chest. She was half climbing on my back, to see my scalp. "A wound here, as well."

"I am nothing but wounds, girl," I grunted. "Do be careful."

"You can always fly away, if you do not like this. It needs stiches."

I rolled my eyes, and she smiled a bit.

"Tell me, King, what will you do next?" she asked.

"Apart from being thrown out of this haven? I will find a way to go forward," I told her. "I had an army, and now, I do not, and I need to beat my foes here in the south and then again in the north, and gods only know what will happen to Midgard if I fail. The enemy is complex and many layered and has been preparing for decades."

"Indeed."

"There is no negotiation with it, come next year, or the decade after."

"Oh, perhaps so," she agreed. "But how would you beat the enemy?"

"Not in an open battle," I laughed bitterly. "Not with what we have now."

"No, that was foolish," she said. "Your Queen of Aten claims a noble called Roger failed you all." She looked bothered and shrugged. "Perhaps it was so."

"I should have eaten his heart," I said with sudden rage, cursing Thrum for not forcing them to stop the foolish attack. "They must learn … *I* must learn faster."

"A rare, refreshing perspective."

"I will need to find out what your man wants," I told her. "I need to understand what he needs, because he does know there is no future in the land so beset with evil. None for the living, girl, no hope. And, yes, I am willing to deal with him, but not on an equal footing."

She smiled. "*My* man?"

"I never told anyone but him I was a thief. Besides, I am not sure, but I saw you seated next to him," I said. "Last night. You were raiding a caravan. I made it crash down a hill. You tell him what I told you. I'll deal with him but *not* on equal footing. I'll not listen to such suggestions."

"You crashed the caravan," she answered, a look of wonder in her eyes. "He is not my man, by the way. He is my brother. Here. I can do no more. Drink this. Dress up."

She gave me a wooden mug, and it contained a drink rich in herbs and medicine, and I gingerly smelled it. She rolled her eyes and took it from my hands. Then, she drank some, grimaced, and handed it to me, while audibly swallowing what she had in her throat.

"Thank you," I said.

"You might not feel welcome. It's made of … well.

As for Saag, you shall speak to him. He hoped you would be more desperate, but I shall let him negotiate with you. Yes, you are right. He is no fool, is he? He agrees, but he also won't risk his neck for nothing." She made a drinking motion.

I scowled, decided against demanding to know what is in it, and drank it down, and with her help, and that of the small, nervous man, began dressing in my ragged armor. When done, I turned to follow the girl, as she made her way to the deeper part of the caves. I followed, and after many confusing twists and turns in the well-lit maze, we climbed up a steep stairway, where water rushed down with gentle noise on both sides. She suddenly stopped, looked down at me, and gave me a hand. I took it, sure she was joking by offering me help, but she pulled me to the side, and instead of climbing up, she jumped to a dark hole and pulled me with her. She grinned, as we went through a hole, which suddenly widened into an almost palatial cave. It was filled with all kinds of loot and the best of gear and rich furniture.

Saag was sitting with his legs on a table, cutting his fingernails with a small knife. He eyed the girl with surprise. "What is it? You were supposed to speak to him and tell me what you think."

She smiled. "He is willing to negotiate. You should be reasonable," she said.

He grinned foolishly. "Nima is a fine one for making

people talk and to give me an edge on negotiation, but it seems you are no fool after all. Perhaps you are only surrounded by them and that, of course, might make you look like one."

I shook my head as I walked to him. The place was full of shadows, and I had no doubt the man was prepared.

I sat down on a stool before him, which was slightly lower than his. His eyes gleamed with small pleasure, and he gave an approving nod. "I think you and I might get along famously."

"What do you want?" I asked him. "We are still not equal, Saag. Listen to your sister and don't demand too much. I'm in no mood to haggle."

He leaned back, licking his lips, resisting just such an impulse. "I heard about your speech to the people in the Pass. You have already promised your people what I so desire. You promised to make men into nobles, should they earn it." He leaned forward. "I can get us four thousand men. That's nearly a legion of archers. That is more than a large city might provide. They are well stocked, and while they cannot go toe to toe in a war with the legions, they can make life terrible for our foes in any siege, or ambush."

"Us?" I asked. "You can get 'us' four thousand men."

"Yes." He smiled like a man selling a sick horse.

"You want to be more than a count or a duke. You want to be …" I laughed. "You want to be second to me."

"The second House in the land should be my House," he concluded, eyeing me with a nervous tick in his eye. "I will spend all the blood, of all the people who trust me in pursuit of that. Agree to that," he said, and pushed a paper towards me, "and you shall have your troops, this place, and my influence over Alantia's refugees. I can get you many, many men."

"I promised," I said bitterly, "that people who give their all for Red Midgard, shall be rewarded. A new nobility will be built out of those who shed blood for it. And now, you want an advance payment?" I nodded at the paper. "You want to hobble my rule with a secret you can use against me at *any* point. Can we not agree that I shall make sure your great sacrifice is noted and duly rewarded?"

"I also want Nallist," he said, pushing the paper towards me again. "The people are not as worthy as you might think. They are all greedy shits."

"Nallist," I snarled, "must be taken before it is given."

He nodded. "And I shall command the men I get for you," he said simply. "I will be their lord."

"Hah!"

He fidgeted and leaned back. "You have a point you wish to make."

I nodded and tapped my finger on the table so hard it nearly broke after each tap. "I need your *men*. I *don't* need a general. I don't want another Roger."

He blushed, and Nima shook her head, now holding a bow casually. He took ragged breaths and ripped a tangle out of his beard. He lifted a hand, as if to stave off an attack, and seemed to deflate. "I need to be *seen*. I have been seen already. They know I lead your men out to fight. If I do not show up in the battles to come, they will forget me. I must be present, at least."

I rubbed my face. "Where is Quiss?" I asked. "I would ask the opinion of my Regent."

A shadow moved. She walked out of the shadows. Two men were flanking her, swords in their hands.

"She is to be given back," Saag said stiffly. "I have no demands for her or for hostages in general. I only want the paper. On it, you promise to make me the second House in Red Midgard. You will give Nallist to us. I need a high title. I want to be seen, if I may not command my men. After that, you get your army."

I stared at him with smoldering eyes.

He pushed the paper for me a third time.

I pushed it back. "Is there a way to agree, without the paper?"

He smiled like a weasel might and nodded. I had walked into a trap.

He nodded towards Nima.

I was confused.

"This paper is needed, if you marry her now," he said.

"*What?*" I asked.

"Allies," he explained. "Marriage will make the paper needless. She is pretty. She is smart. She is a strong fighter and will give you powerful, tricky children." He frowned. "Wait. Can a jotun—"

"I know not!" I hissed. "How … you …"

"I can trust your word, *if* we are related," Saag said simply. "Say 'yes,' King, and we are done."

I sat up and glowered over him. "You think … I know not even your last names!"

Saag lifted an eyebrow. "Why, we are of the criminals, as you said it. We have no wealthy family, no past outside the gutters. We are, what we made ourselves, and what this war can make us. If you ask for our last name, then perhaps … Danegell?"

I rammed my fist through the table.

He got up and lifted it away, broken thing, brought another forth, and wiped it clean. He picked up the scroll and then laid out another, and another.

I pointed a finger at them. "You said no more papers are required!"

He smiled gently. He snapped his fingers. "I said that last one was not required. This one is. A formality for the records. Marriage is an official thing, is it not?"

Two men stepped forward from the shadows, both pale with worry.

"Law-speakers both, from local villages," he murmured. "They drafted it. In in, Nima is your wife.

She is also the queen."

He would try to rule through her, I thought and looked at Nima.

She looked at her brother with stone-hard eyes, and I had a hunch it would not be so easy.

Then, I watched Quiss, and her face was at least as hard as that of Nima. She was looking at me with fury.

Saag noticed. "I take it your Regent shares more than your power? Alas, but the north needs northern men and women, and the Regent only offers you few hundred men of Aten. That's what is left, I think."

Quiss kept her mouth shut.

"She also offers us alliance with Aten," I reminded Saag.

"So, marry both!" he laughed. "I hear Morag was not reluctant to share his bed, and the queen took it all in a stride! I guess that is a jotun's way, I know not. We do it too. No law against many wives."

"Or husbands," Quiss said stiffly. "None."

Nima smiled. She nodded.

Saag hesitated and spoke on hurriedly. "Yes, or nay."

The law-speakers looked supremely bothered.

I held my face and watched Quiss. She had a terrible, possessive look in her eyes, and her fists were clenched. The archers around her noticed it, too, and took steps back.

"I marry whom I wish," I said bitterly, "and how many I wish. There is no one queen. There can be many, no matter whom I have married first."

Quiss looked away and walked to the shadow. The archers hesitated, and one shook his head to the other. They stayed in the light.

Saag chuckled. "Well, of course. If you sire children with Nima, I care not who is the dearest after your heart," he said. "You *can* have them with humans, eh, jotun? Everything fine with the equipment, is it?"

I shook my head. "I told you, bandit. I know not. I have not had the time to …"

He laughed and held his belly. He poured himself a goblet of wine and rubbed his face.

I cursed him and leaned over the papers. "Two?"

"Two. One for you, one for the records, when we again have them in Nallist and Dagnar. See, we can do all of it! Pen!"

One of the law-speakers brought forth a pen and an inkwell.

I looked at Nima, who lifted her chin, and tried to smile. I wasn't sure she was keen on the deal at all. I signed both, and the law-speakers took them and began drying the ink, wrapping them in leather.

Nima and I avoided looking at each other. She massaged her powerful shoulders, and I fidgeted like an idiot groom.

Saag saved us, sighed, and massaged his neck. "Don't be awkward. We don't expect you to start producing offspring this very moment. It is a sad moment as well. My men are yours, and I am but a name, suddenly. Here. There's something odd you should see. Call it a gift to celebrate your marriage."

He pulled out a scroll from his jacket. He waved it around, like it was a magical artifact, before handing it to me. "A scroll from the south. As you know, bandits, robbers, pirates, and smugglers all have connections that run like veins in the shadows. Ever since Morag died, and your story came out, someone has been seeking you. It is hard to travel here now, and I hear this person, an important one in his own way, tried to see you in Aten when they dragged your arse under the Golden Chain and into the Lock of the Sea. He missed you then and has been frantic to find you. So, he sent a few of these to some of us, in case we stumble upon your highness."

I took it. It had been opened, the seal with a mask cracked.

"I dropped it."

I scowled.

He rolled his eyes. "I read it. It is for you. It has been sent from someone who claims he knows everything there is to know about this enemy. See, therefore, I don't think negotiations will work, even if I claimed they might. This man knows his business. It says he, the Mouth of Lok, has long worked against both the draugr and Morag, who was an equal enemy to Midgard. He has had plans, he has had allies, but he says he has failed. He asks you to go to Aten, and to seek a adopted horse. I bet it is a tavern. His allies, this man's have—"

"Those allies have turned on him," I finished for him, reading a part of it. I looked down at him with fury and rolled the scroll away. "My father was not evil," I snarled. "He was *not* enemy to Midgard. He turned his back on Hel, once."

Saag looked dubious. "Turned his back on Hel? The goddess? Did he also bend over? No, wait, don't answer. I know not what you speak of, but a man … a jotun might easily be an enemy to Hel and still also an enemy to Midgard."

"No, I—"

"Did you speak with him a lot?" Nima asked softly. "You know nothing of your kin. They say the draugr raised you."

"Wife," I said coldly, "he was a jotun, but also a good man."

Nima stepped forward, her hand raised in a calming manner. "What my brother is trying to say, is that we know little of the past. Morag brought the law, and rule of justice. But he might have benefitted from law and justice more than others."

"I have a book—"

"The famous Book of the Past, written by nobles," she said, "in noble city, full of rumors of the past, but the book doesn't know Morag, does it?"

I hesitated and refused to agree.

Nima stepped closer and put a hand on my arm. I looked to the darkness that hid Quiss and tried to chase away the fear I'd lose her. "Did you *ever* manage a word with your father?"

I looked down at her strong face and couldn't lie. "I spoke to him once. I know he served Hel in Hel's War, but also changed his heart about the service. He trapped Baduhanna ... and ruled well. He—"

"It is so," she whispered, "that he ruled well, though we disliked him. Bandits, pirates, and smugglers hated him, for a reason. For the rest, he was a good king." She touched the scroll. "But this scroll has been sent around the land to many others or our kind, so someone with a purpose is seeking you and is truly worried over what is taking place in Midgard. This Mouth of ... Lok sounds a rather ominous character. He is famous in the south, and you should seek him out, if we can. He has risked much. This scroll and the others might fall into enemy hands, after all. They have been seeking him for a long time down south." She gave a withering look at where Quiss would be hiding. "Ask her."

"I *know* the story," I said. "The enemy seeks to restore an undead Queen of the Draugr, a monster of the old times. To do that, they want Mara's Brow, and they have those who were there once and can open the prison. We must row after them, winter or no winter, and we must stop them up there in the north before they do to Falgrin and Ygrin what they did to us. They have my father's corpse, that of my mother, they have an artifact of power only my kin can use, and still, here I am, a king, trying to find a way to both save us and to thwart the evil that threatens us, and I am failing."

Nima squeezed my hand. "But that must change now. You need a plan to beat the enemy first. And I think, because I'm a rogue, that if you wish to be the thief of Midgard, the one who steals the land from Hel, you should heed what this Mouth of Lok says. You might not know all of the story."

The law-speakers moved, handed me one leather bound scroll, which I placed in my bag. They left.

Saag smiled. "I shall go and make ready the people. I assume you wish to speak to them? That is, of course, if you have a plan."

"I do," I told him. "I have a plan."

I sat down, and he left, singing. Nima sat near me, and servants brought forth food. Many archers, ten and more, emerged from the shadows, apparently overjoyed by the marriage, but I wasn't. Quiss was walking back and forth, just out of sight, and I knew she was furious.

I was too.

And still, I now had an army.

It was full of rogues and throat cutters, ill-suited for open battle, but I had a plan that would not require, with luck, such a battle before things were more equal. I thumbed the scroll of the Mouth of Lok and knew

Nima was right about reading it and considering finding the person who had sent it. It could be an elaborate trap, but it could also fill in some blanks.

Like the fact, Sand was serving someone who took no heed of Balic.

Nima leaned forward, and I looked at her. She opened her mouth to speak, but right then, a party of men came in and carried with them a small cauldron of stew. The archers proceeded to clearing a space for it, and soon, they were all chatting happily around it.

Nima smiled. "You want a serving? I suppose a king cannot get his own plate."

I smiled ruefully. "I've not had food in a day, but for some reason, I feel entirely full. I'm not sure I can afford to eat here."

She leaned on her hand and giggled softly. She was shaking her head. "It was a rude trick, I agree, Maskan. It was a very nasty bit of extortion."

I glowered at her. "A jotun might not have minded chopping off some heads before leaving you lot to your dreams. It is a risky business to make someone like me mad. A bull with bee-stung nut would not react differently than a cheated jotun."

"It was a deal," she said softly. "A deal you needed to make. You are a man rather than a jotun, are you not? You make deals, and do not think yourself above us. I guessed it was so. That's why we are all breathing and happy. I'll be helpful. You need someone who understands archers, after all. I'll fight hard for the crown, and for you."

I nodded, suspicious.

"I'll prove my worth," Nima insisted. "I know I might die. I don't expect anything else. I'm not my brother, am I? I'm brave, and I plan our raids, and I know the men. I have a mind of my own, but I can also serve you, and Midgard. What are you planning?"

I smiled. "We shall find a way to beat Lisar Vittar. Here is what I need. Listen." I leaned on her and whispered for a long while.

She listened, and then, she nodded. Her powerful muscles were twitching as she was thinking. Her eyes went to Quiss, who was still pacing the darkness.

"It is a terrible risk," she said finally.

I lifted my eyebrow. "Yes. And still, it is how you win. You risk all. You need to win your throne, Queen of Red Midgard. It takes more than extorting kings to sit in the Temple of the Tower."

She grinned. She was ferocious and practical, and still somewhat likable.

"I will find my scribes, and I will do it," she said. "My brother won't disagree. He will only be a nuisance, when I actually sit on that throne next to yours."

"Aye," I said. "I know."

She looked at Quiss briefly, then at the men lading food onto their plates, and she was silent as she was thinking. "We can make it work. Will the Regent," she wondered, "try to murder me?"

I gave Quiss a look. "She has been unhappy since I gave her the title. She was happy to fight for Dagnar, and she led men in the Pass, but something broke her when I elevated her to this role. I'm sorry I did. I need to speak with her, but now is not the time."

She nodded. "So. Will we stay the night?"

"We must move in the morning," I told her. "Can you prepare everything?"

"I can," she told me. "My brother … expects we will act like a pair."

I chuckled tiredly. "Your brother expects … and what do you expect?"

She shrugged. "I expect to earn that throne. I do not earn it in bed. And I am not in love with you, or any other man. I bed whom I want, as will you."

I leaned closer. "You cannot bed anyone you wish when you are the queen. It would smear the throne. It would be like taking a shit on someone's doorstep."

She lifted an eyebrow. "I will be very discreet and give you a full accounting of such activity, so the shit can be cleaned up quickly. You shall give me the same courtesy, of course."

"And if you get pregnant off some other … man. They will find out it is no jotun soon enough, eh?"

She slumped. "This requires some thought. I will have to be very careful, at least." She tugged her braid furiously. "I'll not easily settle for one cock, but I'll consider it."

We settled back on our seats, and both chuckled. She was ferocious as a ferret, and the jotun in me found her amusing.

"In the morning, then," she said, and got up. "I shall give the orders and may Lok dance in our favor."

"You pray to Lok?" I wondered.

"Nött and Lok," she said with a smile. "No rogue has forgotten the old gods. We all still ask for a boon from them. Do you not have one?"

"I used to pray to Odin," I told her. "Though, perhaps, I have recently found something else. I don't know. It might have been nothing more than a wood spirit. I can handle it."

I suddenly slipped away, and the odd, willow voice tried to invade my mind.

You fool.

A jotun. You are a jotun.

The voice had been gentle when it had guided me to pray on winter. Now, it was full of anger, and it made my head ache. I raised my head and heard Nima speaking. I nodded to a question I had not heard and held my head as the powerful, spiteful voice came back.

You think you prayed to the winter? To some fairy spirit of the woods? Something a jotun might be able to handle. Twice the fool. Think, Maskan. Would the spirits, unnamed and cold, need and heed prayers? Are they not truly uncaring and would they even hear a jotun? A life for them, means nothing. You understand not a single thing.

I shook my head, and tried to stand up, but the voice stayed in.

What are the gods, and what are the jotuns? They were carved of the same flesh, all part the very roots of Yggdrasill, ancient and powerful, and still ... two sides of the coin. They are the devourers, and the keepers.

"I am no—"

The voice pushed me back and spoke on.

Jotuns are the devourers. The gods, the keepers. One is irrational, terrifying, a power for chaos, and the other holds and creates the balance, the good, the laws, justice. Once, a great being called Ymir was born in the Filling Void, in the great Ginnungagap, and the race of jotuns was born of him when he fed on the milk of the cow, Auðhumbla.

They ruled, they invented magic, they built and prospered, and then, they warred. Tribes and tribes of lesser jotuns were born of them. They were, those ancient jotuns, the true gods. And yet, they lacked vision.

I got up and saw Nima next to me, holding my hand, and guiding me to the corner for a bed, worried. Some men were helping her, and Quiss was there as well, walking near me, her eyes on me.

So, it was that the great power, a lord none knew, a god of gods, the one who sits over Ginnungagap unseen and feeds Yggdrasill, gave birth to another race of gods. They were no lesser jotuns. They were born of the very strongest of the jotun kin, the sons and daughters of the kings of all the jotuns, of those who are the most ancient ones. Where the mothers and fathers of these jotuns were chaotic beings, these ones had a vision of a balance, of a need to limit, instead to devour. What that difference of a jotun and them was, I know not. It is there, nonetheless.

I was sitting on a bed and held my face.

Quiss was next to me, considering my eyes. Nima was giving orders to find men skilled in poisons.

Both were frantic with worry.

The voice went on.

Few of them, Odin, Vil, and Ve rebelled. They changed everything. They killed Ymir and doomed most of their fellow jotuns into destruction and pain. They isolated the jotuns to the primal worlds of Muspelheim and Nifleheim, and many they chased to Jotunheimr, and claimed many other worlds to rule with justice and law. They chose the best out of the uncountable worlds the death of Ymir had spawned, and they pushed away the dragons and other First Born, all spawned from Ymir's dead corpse, as they set to make their vision true.

I groaned and tried to get up but couldn't. I fought the voice, and it pushed back brutally.

They, jotuns, no matter if they called themselves the Aesir and the Vanir, squabbled, created, and struggled, and finally ruled. Their adventures were many, their justice swift, and the true jotuns and the chaos they represent was pushed away. While wars, plagues, famine, and these battles of Aesir and Vanir amongst themselves seem truly threatening, the great balance is still tilted for justice. One day, balance will swing back. *The prophesies speak of it. As Lok is released, and jotuns and their rebellious kin will battle and make things anew, perhaps it is jotun again, who rule. Perhaps none shall.*

The voice paused, and I was trying to win my thoughts back. I failed again.

Now, you, a jotun, would rule Red Midgard like a man? Fool, fool. You are the blood of the old jotuns, not of the gods. You are the son of Ymirtoes and kin to the most ancient of jotunkin. Be one! You need no allies save for your kin. Pray not to Odin. Do not heed the men. Forget Maskan. Pray to our god, the old one, the grandfather of Odin and his ilk. Guard our old ways and let the chaos reign, Maskan. Fight Hel but only to conquer. Guard your kin, o royal jotun, guard those the rebel Aesir and Vanir captured and defeat Hel, but do it for our kin, not for the humans, elves, or the gods. Let Lok slumber still and let Hel rot in Helheim.

But do not forget. You are also enemy to those who serve the Aesir and the Vanir. Humans are your meat.

When you pray, do not pray to winter.

She never answered your call.

Pray for the great Bolthorn. He did. Touch ice and snow, and pray for him aloud, and know you must pay a price. Do not ask for too much.

Stop living Morag's life.

It disappeared. Then I slumped, and went to sleep, my head aching.

***

It was late that night, when I awoke. I sat up on the bed,

my armor jingling. I held my face, and my neck, which was throbbing. I looked around and saw the ten men from a crack in a curtain that had been drawn to hide the bed. They were playing dice.

I shook my head, and I was terrified the voice would invade my head again. I rubbed my temples and thought deep. I tried my best to focus, but I felt sick. It was as if someone had held my face under water for too long, and I had nearly drowned. It had been terrible, terrifying, and still …

Bolthorn? An ancient jotun, near a god?

And I, his distant blood, above most jotun?

I smiled at the thought, and I was sure I was mad.

Then, a hand touched me, and I found Nima sitting on the bed. She held my face and looked into my eyes.

Humans, my meat.

The vicious thought fought with the human morals in my head, the cruel voice telling me to use them and never look back. The human in me, Maskan, put a hand in hers and another on her face. She looked shocked, trembled and tried to get up, but then stopped and settled back.

"Where is Quiss?" I asked her.

"She sleeps," she said. "She sat here for a long time and then went to sleep."

"My orders?" I asked.

"Wait," she said softly. "What happened? You looked possessed. You fell on your knees and held your head. I had to check you are not hurt and bleeding out in some other place."

She let her eyes go down briefly, and I smiled.

"No. It is … a jotun's issue. You cannot heal or aid me. It is gone."

She didn't look sure. "I was about to become the only royal in Midgard," she said. "The orders have been delivered. The men, all the army, is awake and waiting. Are you going to go down? We are all ready."

She was wearing an armor of chain, and leathers, and a cloak of fox fur.

"Yes, I shall."

Humans, my meat.

I pushed away the thought, hesitated, and pulled Nima to me. I kissed her lips gently and closed my eyes as I devoured her love, and not her meat. She hesitated only for a moment and pressed against me. She pushed me back and climbed over me, strong and greedy, and began pulling up my chain skirt, her hand trying to open the leather laces beneath.

I saw a vision of Quiss, and loved her, but Nima was there, and she was mine. I let her work, and then she managed to open the laces, and she, gasping, pulled and touched me with passion. She slid over me, and I felt her warmth as I entered her.

And then, the men in the room all got up.

We stopped, and she jumped up and rushed out. I saw her put a hand over her mouth, and then, I was there with her and saw what they all saw.

On the dark way out of the chambers, there stood a troop of men and women.

Formerly, that is.

They were draugr, and they had found me.

There were ten of them, they all wore the familiar midnight black chainmail and, on it, was emblazoned a white snake twisted around a skull. They all held the best of weapons, but their bedraggled skin, rotting flesh and wounds, and filthy hair made the men and Nima flinch from disgust and fear.

Quiss was up and staring at them as well, backing off.

I knew two of them.

With them, was Silas Barm Bellic, his face unusually smooth. There, too, was Sand.

He grinned, like he once had, missing half his flesh in his face. An unholy light burned in the eye socket, surrounded by blackened skull. "Maskan," he said. "I told you we'd meet again, soon."

I walked to stand before the men, and Nima, my sword out. They were spreading around, eyes round with fear. Quiss was pulling a sword and picking up a round shield behind us.

"Sand," I asked. "You found me again indeed. How?"

"I have my ways," he said softly. "I will find you again, should you get away. I have no other goal. You killed half my boys before, but this will be different."

Silas was giggling. He raised his hand and released a spell. A thick web of stone grew around the doorway. "There is no other door," he said.

"And how," I wondered, "would you know that? You don't look the sort that once travelled northern wilds and stumbled upon a bandit camp."

He shook his head.

I stepped forward, holding my weapon over my shoulder, trembling with anger.

Sand stepped forward. "As I said, I have my ways."

"Is Saag dead?" I asked.

He shook his head. "Best not to alarm them. They'll fall to the legions one day soon. We are here for you alone. Mir and Balic's rivalry is over, and everyone agrees you must go. Make it easy. You didn't last time, and it was very upsetting, friend. Very much so."

I would die there. It was unavoidable, unless we got very lucky.

I tried to play for time. "So, my father and mother are already on their way north? What if," I said, just coming up with a possible wrinkle in Balic's plans, "my father can no longer use the Black Grip? He is dead, after all."

Sand shrugged. "It is true. He cannot."

I blinked.

He smiled horribly. "What do you know of Mara's Brow, and the great ways and halls under it? Your father, Maskan, will show them the way. He is the only one who knows where to go. He has seen the door. He saw it before he sealed the Hand of Hel in. That is what I am told. So, he has his uses. As for the Black Grip?" He shrugged. "They have ways to open the door. Two ways. They will try, even if there is no key. It is her duty."

Her?

Silas walked down to Sand "Enough. My father doesn't approve this banter. He need not know anything. He is going to—"

"He was a friend," Sand snarled at Silas. "And I shall let him die with some answers."

The draugr around Silas stiffened and then spread to the shadows at Silas's nod. Their eyes gleamed, and I felt spells being braided together.

"Sand—"

He shook his head. "No. I cannot fight it, and you know it. One more question. Ask it." He looked like the one playing for time, not I. He didn't want to kill me.

"If you do not heed Balic," I asked him, "if Balic must heed someone else as well, then who is that? You mentioned a woman?"

"Balic was raised by Hel," Silas spat. "He was, and he raised us. Sand—"

"Whom do men like Balic heed?" he laughed softly. "Remember the first time you and I saw Shaduril? Do you? We both obeyed our hearts, and she held them in her palm. While it is not exactly the same with Balic these days, he, too once followed his heart …" He shook his head. "Never mind that. We need not give you more answers."

I stared at him. "I'll find them."

His eyes went to the scroll from the Mouth of Lok, peeking from my belt, and then to my eyes.

How could he know about that?

His draugr shifted on their feet and were moving around the archers. Sand shook his head. "You cannot escape. You cannot walk, run, or fight your way out. You cannot fly or slither. You are no fish, are you, my friend?" He trembled as he said that, apparently struggling with the words.

Silas pushed him aside, his chain jingling. "E-nough! That's it! Here, take it!" He grinned and threw me a kiss.

A familiar spell of thick black fog came forth from his lips and filled the chamber, robbing the living of their sight. The archers were calling out in dismay and fear.

I twirled and struck around with my sword and smiled grimly as the blade met flesh. A draugr's head and upper body fell next to me. I rolled down and heard blades striking stone where I had stood. I heard men shouting out warnings, then the sound of arrows hitting stone, and when I rushed to the edge of the room, breaking a table, I was, for a moment, out of the dark fog. I turned, sword up. I saw a shade of Silas in the far edge, with his sword on a throat of an archer, kissing the man's dying lips. His eyes went to Nima, who was nearby, and aiming an arrow bravely.

Silas smiled. "Oh, I've seen girls like you. Feisty. I'll make you mine, girl, when you die, and—"

She released the arrow, and Silas roared as it struck his chest, ripping the chain. He jumped over a bed and bore down on her, and then Quiss, pushing Nima aside, struck him with her shield. Nima grabbed a spear, and the two women faced off with the bastard.

I had my own trouble.

I turned to meet seven draugr, two rushing across the ceiling like spiders, other coming for me from all the directions, their eyes gleaming in the fog.

Sand was there, one of them, and I felt a braid of magic swirling around me.

I stepped away and found my armor stiffen with cold, and my eyes and face heavy with ice.

The draugr leaped forward, swords coming for me.

I feinted, forced my limbs to move and dodged, and feinted back and rolled under a blade, my armor struck by sword. My blade cut up and to the side, gutting one, beheading another, and then, one was stabbing for my face, another for my crotch, and two were ready to jump down at me.

Sand's spell lingered, his ice grew thicker in and out of my armor, it cracked as I moved, and then, I saw nothing, as it enveloped my eyes, my mouth, and my face, jingling and deadly.

I would be killed by ice?

No. Take it. It is ice. It is you! the voice called out.

It echoed in my skull, desperate, and I tried. I touched the ice.

I actually *saw* the spell.

I had not thought it possible.

I felt spell being collected, magic being called, but with ice and wintry killer, I could now actually almost see it.

I could, possibly, break it.

I could, possibly, do more.

I made a spell of my own first.

I braided it spell together. I added ice, wind, and freezing water, saw the spell and its braid was perfect, and then loosed it around me.

The spell thrust forward and grew on the stone, loot, and furniture, covering inches of ground in ice. It stopped the draugr in their tracks, and then I tugged at Sand's spell and ripped it off him. I could see his eyes enlarge in the fog. I took the spell and added it in mine, and what followed was a mayhem.

Spells twisted together. The ice grew in every direction in thick lumps of golden blue waves and threw me against the wall. A draugr was twisted into bits and pieces inside the grinding, moving, monstrous ice. One draugr, on top, scuttled to the shadows, but one was crushed against the ceiling. The spell looked like it might go on until it had filled the woods.

Then, a thick storm of dark fire struck the mass.

The two powers seemed to battle it out, and finally, fire burning fiercely, the flames thick and strong, the ice spell died out and fell apart in a wave of water.

The draugr, Sand, few others stood in the fog, and suddenly, the darkness filled even the space I had been standing. I saw fiery whips growing from their hands, their glowing eyes coming closer, and so, I shape changed and plunged into the darkness, rushing forward.

The draugr loved night.

So did this animal. There were some, even in Red Midgard, and I had seen one in the harbor, once. I was a gigantic black lion.

My thick paws and dark, short fur made me a prince of night hunters. I bounded from the stone, silent and fast, and jumped at a draugr. I swiped my claws on his face and neck and ripped him open. He fell under me, and I jumped forward, narrowly avoiding two whips.

"Ware!" Sand called. "Together!"

I slunk away and hid behind a pile of loot, just as the draugr stalked after me, sensing where I would be, without seeing me. They heard my breathing, saw traces of warmth, and perhaps smelled blood on me. I slunk off in the dark, went for shadow to shadow, passed one very close, and then saw they were again turning.

I saw them, and none of them was Sand.

Sand was hiding. He was waiting, one of the

shadows, cold as stone, and I couldn't spot him.

He would be there, waiting until I was found.

I stopped near a corner. They were around me, the fiery whips slapping around them, skillfully striking the floor, the air, and I knew I'd be hurt. My armor was in pieces already, and those spells could rip my arm off.

I might have to pray to Bolthorn. I was terrified to even think about it. I was also … thrilled.

And then, I was lucky.

I heard Silas screaming in anger and pain, beyond the fog, and the draugr turned that way, whips shivering still.

I charged and changed as I did and ripped through the fog with my sword high. I buried a draugr under my boots and hacked down on one, who dodged away. I charged forward, hoping to put a wall behind my back.

It was too late. A whip tore to my armored leg, and another burned around my gauntlet.

They pulled me over, and I fell on my face, the terrible weapons burning deep into the magical armor, heating it.

Sand stepped from a shadow.

He leaped over me.

His swords were up, and then, he dropped one and tried to tear away my plate. His sword was entering my shoulder, into a muscle, and then, likely my lung.

I howled and rolled. The whips rolled around my

legs, around my arms and chest, and the enemy rolled with me. I rolled over Sand, the whips burning his legs and my armor terribly, tearing off pieces. Together, like fishermen trying to harness a dying, raging whale, they crashed into a huge pile—eight feet or more—of loot, and I with them. We scattered coin, precious statues and destroyed fine paintings, and a pile of tables and chairs fell over us. I came out of the pile, again bleeding badly, and looked down at the two draugr and Sand, who were climbing up, pushing away burning furniture and coins.

I laughed and let go the same spell I had once. I did it fast, so very quickly, and the ice rushed from the floor and thickened around anything it touched. The two draugr were caught half inside a heap of coins, one with a statue frozen on his face.

Sand had disappeared.

I cursed, roared, and hacked down once, then twice.

The draugr didn't move again.

Then, I felt the fire again. Dark fire mixed with a billowing, evil cloud was spreading from the corner. Sand was standing there, swaying with great powers. The fires were spreading for me, and a filthy cloud of corruption was twisting wood, coin, and marble into blackened heaps of decay. He was pushing all he had on it, the fog was disappearing, and I would die, if I didn't move.

I retreated, and then, the fire was twisting around

me, my chain was smoking, my plate was melting with the corrosive power, and I rushed forward.

At the other edge of the chamber, I saw Nima, her spear in Silas's belly, and Quiss, her blade in his leg, tumbling and jumping around, until they fell together in an unfortunate heap next to an odd wall. As I rushed forward, feeling the fire dancing across my back, the corrosive cloud billowing behind, I saw the wall was flowing, and then I knew it was water, a thick, oddly silent waterfall of it, and realized what Sand had said.

I was no fish. I'd try to be, though.

"Stop him!" Sand roared.

Silas had finally pinned down both girls, his sword hovering over them. It was on Quiss's throat, and he cursed and turned it to Nima.

"Die, bitch. Remember what I promised!"

I got to them, my sword cut in the air and took his arm and half his skull. I tossed the sword into the waterfall, screamed as the mists and fire settled around my leg, tearing away chain and armored boot. Then, I grasped both girls and tumbled down to the water. We fell for a long while, though probably not that long, and splashed into a deep, brilliantly blue pond, graced by the morning's light. I kicked up, hampered by the armor, some more pieces of it falling away. I was soon dragging the two up with me, and came up to the surface. I saw my sword under the surface, and saved it.

Women doing laundry were staring at us in shock, almost as if they had seen an ugly merman. I realized my laces were still open, and my pants were sagging far too low.

They got up, and giggled as they left.

I held my face, and looked up to the waterfall. Sand wasn't coming.

Finally, men were rushing forward. I pushed Quiss on her belly. She was choking and coughing and vomiting water. I pushed Nima next to her and fell on my face, breathing hard.

The latter turned to me, while Quiss was breathing heavily, silent.

"My brother?" she wept.

I shook my head. "He wasn't there."

She wept. "Thank Lok."

I held a hand on her shoulder, and finally, she, too, vomited, though likely for the fear. She had fought like a mad thing, though I wondered if she regretted marrying the jotun of Red Midgard. Then, she got up, furious, and soon, was rushing through the camps. Alarm was sounded, and the men began searching for Sand. I watched them rushing about and sat there, tired to the bone.

Quiss finally sat up and held her face. "Gods, but that was close."

"They always have plans behind plans, and then more plans, and they are very good at executing such plans," I said tiredly, and looked at her. "Worry not. Nothing has changed. You helped me, I helped you, and nothing has truly changed, eh?"

"Everything's changed! And I must share your bed with a bandit?" she hissed. "Is that it?"

"Yes," I said. "You might grow to like it."

"A worm in comparison to us," she cursed. "You seem not too bothered by the idea!"

I shrugged and wiped water off my face. "They say Morag wasn't either. Perhaps I'm a shit of a man? She is brave. She is needed. I'll not … love …" I shook my head and went silent.

"A jotun and a man, and so damned confused," she hissed, and then breathed. "We need them. I know. Nothing … has changed."

I nodded, smiling at her. "I wonder how Sand keeps finding me."

"They have coin, and they buy traitors," she said, wiping some blood off her nose. She had a wound on her scalp. "What will you do with your new queen's army?"

"Well, Regent," I said. "We—"

"I won't obey her," she hissed.

I rolled my eyes. "Listen. Please. We shall get back to Hillhold. There, we shall muster the land, and wait for a moment. Her archers will start to harry the enemy supplies, and in the end, before the winter is over, we shall prevail."

She looked at me sadly. "And the north? What of that?"

"I shall have to go there alone," I told her. "I will first deal with the issues in Hillhold. And you shall still command the army. This time, you can. Thrum and Hal will help you, and Roger is likely dead, hung in a tree somewhere." I smiled. "Perhaps he is even in one of the Black Ships?"

She flinched. "You never mentioned those before. I didn't know you knew of them."

I shrugged. "No. They will get the dead to Malignborg. The very best, eh? So, perhaps Roger won't be there."

She frowned. "People don't usually speak about those ships."

"Do they speak of the Mouth of Lok?" I asked her.

She looked glum. "I heard Saag speaking about that. I did. We know about him. He is more like a bandit, than anything else. A common bandit, is all. And a mad one. An adopted horse? I know no such tavern in Aten. Seems like a waste of time."

I nodded. "I agree to all you said. I have no time for it. We must get back to Hillhold, today," I said. "We must march fast. You shall take the nobles and scouts of Nima, and you will lead the army off. You lead us to Hillhold and send her scouts back to report if there is any trouble. Make sure they are ready to march in two hours, and we shall follow you. Tell Nima as well."

She wasn't happy, but then nodded. I pulled her close and kissed her. She struggled and then sighed and looked at me with forgiveness and sadness. "Nothing has changed."

"Thank you," I whispered. "I trust you."

She got up and walked to Nima and Saag, and they were speaking. I watched them preparing the men briskly. The entire valley echoed with men calling out orders, and women packing gear and often, dressing in armor when they had it.

They all looked scared.

Some would desert.

Most would march with me.

I pulled out some items. I looked at the scroll from the Mouth of Lok. I pulled out the orders I had taken from the admiral in Nallist, and then the Grinlark, the mighty staff magically sealed into a stick-size. The last item I placed on my lap.

I eyed the orders again.

They were orders for putting up Balic and his family in the Ugly Brother's royal quarters for three days or until two more legions arrived in Nallist. They would be there late this very day. I looked at an alarming report of an incoming storm front, heavy with blizzard, cold, and snow, also set for this day, and likely early afternoon. Yet another was an order to seal the harbor, to keep the ships safe. A paper concerned some local ladies, whom they thought were spies.

Then, I gazed at a ruby red stone and finally threw it in the pool, watching it sinking.

Finally, I watched the scroll from the Mouth of Lok and opened it up again. I had merely eyed it, but now, I read it twice, trying to make sense of it.

"To the jotun-king of Red Midgard, from your humble servant, Caru.

The long years of waiting are past us. As the Trickster warned us, so it is seen. The Hel's curse endured and grew, and her servants have spread like a disease across the land.

You ask why Lok might care about this trouble?

You are right to do so.

Lok sees the chaos and finds amusement in the many tragedies he has witnessed, while suffering in his chains. Is it not Lok's pleasure to see such horror inflicted on those whom he often battles with, whom he hates?

It is.

And yet, there is a reason our lord Lok wants his Mouth to resist these dogs of Hel. To think it is Lok, who must save the Nine for the filth of Aesir and the Vanir, is beyond strange. And still, when a Mouth of Lok must work for the gods who imprisoned our lord Lok, he must ask himself: is this not the greatest trick of all? Is it not so that Lok the Hero will make the Aesir and the Vanir writhe in rage by his aid to their causes?

It is.

Here it is, lord of jotuns, a great trick to trick all the gods. Listen.
I was not there, thousands of years past, when Hel tried to take Midgard.
But I was here, twenty years past, when she failed again, though she did not fail completely. Morag failed. I was given a task. Others were given theirs.

They failed as well.

I endured, and I am still trying to complete my mission, though I am much hated by the filth of Hel and hunted by most everyone, even the living, but is that not the lot of Lok's Mouth?

It is.

We must endure shit and piss and do our duty.
It is ridiculous and tricky that I must trust the son of the one who has much of the blame in the current situation. Yet, I have no choice. The others failed. They betrayed us. I must see you. I must tell you everything. It is unfortunate, my lord jotun, that I cannot leave Aten, where I set up shop month past. I can send messages, for I have followers in the soldiery of the enemy, but I cannot risk a journey. I have sent these letters to those who are tricky, and perhaps evil, and yet, no

friends to the draugr.

If you see this, come and meet me in Aten. Find the Adopted Horse.
If you do not come, we will all have all failed.
I pray you are not like Morag. I have no other prayer left.

Caru, the Mouth of Lok, and one miserable bastard."

I rolled it up and waited until men told me they had had no sight of Sand. He might be hiding anywhere, but most likely, he would be afraid I would go after him, so he would be hiding, safe, regrouping, gathering allies again, and would be nowhere near. I got to my feet. I turned to see the columns forming in the valley. They were the men-at-arms. They were the militia. They were one, finally. Hal sat with the horsed nobles, fewer than forty, and Quiss was there as well. Saag and Nima were busy with the archers, and there were hundreds of local spearmen who joined the column from Fiirant. There were, too, many men of Aten, all looked upon with doubt. Many scouts were riding out already, and many others joined Quiss. A mass of them, three thousand, formed behind and before my people. I walked to them, in my full size and lifted my sword to the air.

There were nearly seven thousand of them.

Many were wounded.

Most had not followed me before.

Nima stepped forward, wearing a black chain, looted from the draugr. She lifted her spear, and the others followed suit.

"Behold the Queen of Red Midgard! Behold the Duchess of Alantia!" I called to the wonder of the people. Saag frowned, for I had not mentioned him. Nima beamed a smile.

Then, they cheered.

They screamed themselves hoarse. Where Quiss had been a foreigner, she was one of theirs, and not even the nobles seemed to mind they really didn't know her, or that she was a robber.

When the cheering ended, I spoke again. "Today, we are going to go back. We are going to surprise our foe, and we shall drive them to ruin. Mistakes were made."

Eyes turned to Quiss who didn't move.

She knew then I had not been honest she would rule over them still. She was a figurehead, a someone to blame, and I had just confirmed it.

"None more can we afford," I went on. "Not one loss. With our new allies, none more shall be suffered. Trust your queen, trust your king. Trust your generals and obey the commands. We shall ambush those shits of southerners, and then, we will hang the lot in Alantian trees. There are plenty of trees, and only some of them. But first, we shall march. To victory, and a new dawn for Red Midgard!"

A ragged shout echoed across the valleys and the

hillsides.

I nodded at Quiss, whose eyes were pools of anger and disappointment. Then, she turned her horse and rode out, leading the nobles and scouts.

We followed her.

The road was cumbersome, and the troops spread to navigate the trails. Quiss soon took her troops out of sight, and we struggled with the pack animals until she was at least an hour away from the main body. We marched for half an hour until we were all out of the valley, even the last mule.

I stopped the army and leaned down on Nima. "It is time, dear," I told her.

She nodded, and Saag rode to us, confused, looking at Nima speaking to scouts and officers, who began guiding the men around us, making sure none got past. We rode on, and Saag rode hard to catch us.

"Where in the name of Tyr's testicles are we going?" he called out.

I nodded to south. "Nallist. We shall take Nallist."

Nima shrugged. "We try."

Saag was trying to take in breaths, and finally managed some words. "But … that is madness. It is their capital. They have—"

"Only a few thousand men in the fort, and the city holds all their supplies," I said. "We shall take it, and the ships as well."

"They will retake it," he yelled. "Don't you see?"

"They will retake another Dagnar," I told him. "We shall hold the keep, and we shall burn the city down. Where fire claimed the previous legions in Dagnar, cold shall claim them there. A terrible storm will arrive this evening. It will be thick with snow, it will be freezing cold, and death will be bone white for the enemy. Let the bastards freeze and starve to death, while we watch. We'll sit on the supplies."

"They will come," he complained. "They will come, and they won't give us the pleasure of watching them die! They will come and take it. They have the best army in the land and even more on its way!"

"Yes," I said. "And we must hold it for a few days."

He went quiet and looked at Nima. "You sent orders and requests for me?"

"I did," she said. "I am the Queen of Red Midgard, and the Duchess of Alantia, am I not?"

He shook his finger. "About that. I should be the duke, and you …"

"You will have Nallist," I told him. "If Nima agrees."

"You will burn it!"

"You will rebuild it," I snarled. "You will use the bones of our foes, eh?"

"And the Regent?" he demanded. "She won't be there. You sent her to safety."

"I have my reasons," I said. "Safety is just one of them. We must have fewer generals, and no dissent.

Any spies will follow her. She will be fine. Don't worry. We will do well as well."

He looked pale as a sheet. "Lok's tears. Oh, this is not good."

Nima grinned. "Will you tell him?"

I leaned on Saag. "Balic and his family will be there. I'll take his damned heart, and I'll feed it to rats."

Nima laughed, and Saag shook in his boots.

CHAPTER 9

Nallist was strangely gray in the blizzard that afternoon. The snow was whipping across the ramparts of the city, and our troops shivered outside it, careful, nervous, and still, many of the bitter, angry men and women had determined looks on their faces.

They wanted to pay back for our suffering.

This was not an even battlefield. This was a place to surprise and butcher the enemy. They felt confident they could.

The blizzard had started before the Lifegiver sunk below horizon, and the harbor was closed. We had seen fifty ships and some galleys, and many others had been rowed inside. The Black Ships had left. Most were still half filled with supplies for the garrison of legions from Dagnar, for the troops in the field and for the new legions, and those troops would be arriving soon as well. Many wagons were busily disgorging those supplies from the ships to warehouses and the Ugly Brother.

The enemy had no scouts out.

They were tired, and lazy, and cold.

I watched the enemy sentinels on the walls, huddling in the graying evening, and all were miserable as shit. The guards that could be seen were so cold, they huddled under their cloaks and leaned on the walls to avoid snow piling up inside their tunics and armor.

They were men fresh from the inferno that had been Dagnar, and I had a hunch they missed even that calamity in comparison.

I felt empowered by the blizzard.

I closed my eyes and felt the power of the cold swirling around me. It was brilliant, beautiful, and chaotic, a power of awesome proportion. It was as raw as magic. It was part of me, and I was part of it, and for some reason, I wasn't cold at all.

A jotun, rather than a man, would think like that.

A man would think about Quiss, and how I had sent her away.

The jotun thought it was a brilliant ruse. A needed ruse. She was safe.

And thus, I had been safe in marching to Nallist.

There was a bell tolling. Soon, a change of guards came to the walls, and the relieved ones ran off. Who came, stood only for a moment, before sitting down in cover. I heard their curses that far. Xal Cot's men, they loved warmth, and the south.

The stretch of wall we were looking at was facing the east. It was not far from the Ugly Brother, which was part of the wall near the breakwater and sea-walls. The woods were quite near the walls and had not been cut for security.

I thanked whoever had ruled Nallist earlier, heartily.

Nima nudged me. "Well?"

"A bloodthirsty queen, eh?" I muttered. "I've seen

enough."

"You sure the two legions are not inside and only the survivors of Dagnar?" Saag asked.

"No," I said icily. "I am not. But the orders claim they shouldn't be. I think some few thousand men are in the fort, and hundreds in guardhouses and the walls, and some are moving supplies. Most will be huddling inside the buildings, hiding from this weather. You are prepared?" I asked Nima.

"We are," she said. "They know what to do."

I made sure. "Your archers will burn the city, and my men will march along the wall to the fortress," I said. "Later, your boys must get to the fort as fast as they can. They know the city?"

She rolled her eyes. "It might not look like much to you, but the locals know Nallist. They know every inn, tavern, and shop."

"Bring all you can to the fortress," I agreed, fearing the worst. The two legions might very well be there, for they would know about the storm and would have tried to beat it.

"We will, of course," she said acidly, spoiling for a fight. "I will lead them, and then, we hope for the best."

"Food, all the food," I reminded her. "Spare the ships but burn the warehouses. Carry what you can to the Ugly Brother and toss the rest to the harbor."

"We have three thousand men running around the city, and they know!" she hissed in my ear and slapped my shoulder. "Are we ready?"

I nodded.

"Get them," she said again. "We'll follow."

I watched the men. A long line of them looked back. Only the men of Aten looked unhappy, but they, too, were determined. A burly captain formerly of House Bollion, was now a general and saluted me. His name was Maggon. Sergeants had been made into captains. They all looked ready.

I nodded and changed.

A large owl, white and hoary, took to the air. I flapped my wings in the woods, dodging branches, and looked at the wall. The guards, three of them that I could see, two huddling together for warmth, didn't so much as twitch. One, a tall man, just got up to walk the rampart and was shivering like a dying old drunk. His beard was white with snowflakes and icicles.

I glided through the air, saw no movement in nearby, and much in the harbor, where ships were still being unloaded, and then flapped from the night for pair of men audibly cursing Red Midgard.

I landed and changed, and hacked down at them, once, and again.

The man who had been walking, turned.

His eyes went round as plates.

I picked up a spear from one of my bleeding victims and threw it with all my force.

It pierced armor, leather, and belly, tore his guts out

from the back, and left him a miserable heap on the snowy rampart.

I hesitated, felt a presence, and looked around.

A dog, what I had thought was a pile of snow, got up and looked at me. It shook its coat and wagged its tail.

I smiled at it.

Its legs went between its tail.

It ran off, barking furiously, snow flying.

"Hey, mutt, over here!" someone called out. "Where are you going!"

The man who called out knew the dog, and he was calling from the street, and I heard horses neighing.

I cursed, turned, and waved my hand at the woods. I grabbed another spear.

A dark mass of people moved out of the woods, snow flying. Ten or more sturdy ladders were with them, pillaged from barns and farms on the way. Their eyes were huge, as had been those of the guards, every soul stressed and terrified, but eagerly, they dashed forward, armor jingling gently, and prepared to top the parapet.

"Hey, up there?" I heard. "Why did Fierce bolt? Did you kick it? I swear, if you kicked the company mascot, I'll make a carpet of your arse-skin!"

I peeked over.

I saw a party of men, huddling in their military cloaks. All were from Xal Cot. They sat on their horses in the street below. I grasped a helmet from a man's head and pushed in on my head, as I returned to their sight, just barely.

"You!" the man leading them called. "Why did the dog bolt?"

I shook my head and tried to pretend I couldn't hear him.

"You, man!" he insisted, being the type of a man who felt slighted by everything.

"Sir?"

"What are you doing?" he called out. "Where is Sergeant Balt? He is the one who should address his captain, eh? The regulations must be followed. This is war, and no idle posting meant for tit-sucking toy-soldiers! Where is he? Did he leave his post? Name!"

"Mine?" I asked him, unable to follow which question I should answer first. "Monk."

He looked at me incredulously. "Bloody Monk what? You are not Monk. There is no Monk in the company. Stay there!" He got down from his horse. He jumped to the slushy snow and stomped for a stairway, not far. His eyes were bloody and enraged, and he likely envisioned gutting a private or two with his verbal skill, while serving the sergeant to his general as a supper. I stood up and stepped near the stairway.

He came up, his face a mask of rage.

Then, he slipped, his hands wind-milling, and fell down the stairs.

"*What* did you do?" yelled another man on a horse.

"You *pushed* him, you bastard!"

His men dismounted, looked at the captain with horror, and ran to help him.

The man who had called me out, looked up at me, then cursed, took a horn, and raised it to his lips, about to call more men to put me in chains.

I flipped the spear and tossed it.

It impaled the man, and he fell over his horse, spitting blood. His friends, alarmed, looked up.

I jumped down and landed in the middle of three soldiers, and their smitten captain.

They stared at me in horror. I slashed my sword down at one, then lopped off a leg of another and stepped on the captain, while I grasped the last one's skull inside my gauntlet and twisted.

I grinned, pleased with my handiwork.

Then, I heard a horse galloping.

I turned and saw my spear victim riding for the fortress, his guts flowing on the horse, face white with pain, fear, and the certain knowledge of impending death.

I growled and changed, and a huge white wolf loped after him.

I'd have to trust my people, the captain made into a general, the new officers. I had to stop the bastard from running to alert the city, and especially, the fort. I ran after the horse. The horse, terrified, whinnied and sped even faster. I gained on him. A dozen dogs began barking, a man stepping out of his house shouted in horror, and then, I saw the gateway to the fort. Men were coming and going, and guards conversing with soldiers driving wagons inside the gigantic, round fortress.

They paid little heed to the horse and the dying man on it, and I loped forth in the blizzard, three dogs on my tail, and prayed the guards would not turn.

Then, one did.

He was just guiding a wagon in a line of four to the courtyard, when he spotted the horse and the dogs, and then, squinting and taking a step forward, the man's guts flowing along the horse's side.

His eyes turned to the gigantic wolf running for him

"Guards!" he screamed, apparently forgetting he was one, and fell back. He began pushing the gates shut. Every eye stared at him with surprise, until the horse crashed past them for the relative safety of the fort.

Then, they all saw me, so very close already.

The wagon drivers whipped their draft horses and, yelling warnings, tried to push in. The first wagon and the horses crashed to the closing wooden and iron barriers, then past the guard and his friend who was helping him, and went through, wheel spokes drawing furrows out of the wood.

The others crashed together in a jumble of chaos, as the gates were again closing, and I jumped on the next wagon in line, bit down on the driver, and roared at the horse.

The guards were struggling, the door nearly shut.

It jumped and landed on the back of the horse, and the horse went berserk. It rammed the gate, we crashed at them hard, and they flew partly open again. The horse forced its head inside. Many guards threw their backs at the breach, pushing at the horse, and the gate.

I raked my claws along the neck of the horse, the horse fell, and when the men kneeled to push the head out, I swiped a claw on a man's neck and pulled him back to the breach, his head and body crushed between the gates, and over the horse.

The gate was stuck. Men were calling alarm, and up in the fortress, horn called out forlornly.

Behind me, the wagon drivers were grabbing spears, and then, the dogs sunk their teeth on my arse.

I shifted and turned into a jotun. I placed a foot between the gateway and turned to face the enemy. I saw their eyes go wide, and then, a captain snarled, and they lifted their spears and aimed. I fell on my arse, squashed two dogs I had forgotten about, the spears rattled on the wood above me. The enemy drew swords and hammers and charged.

I felt the enemy pushing the gate again, a spear stabbed at my foot.

I pushed myself up, braided together a spell, thrust my left hand into the hole, and released a blizzard inside. I pushed a terrific amount of power in it, and because of the winter and the storm, my magic was far stronger than usual.

A wind of ice was whipping inside the courtyard.

It grew in power, and it was a cruel death for those inside. I spotted men tumbling in the wind, flesh and armor torn. Snow piled up immediately at the great gate to the keep itself, and stables around it cracked, grew white, then pale blue with the power and fell apart. The ground was shaking, the wind was blowing so hard the noise hurt my ears, and a wintry wonderland of broken yard and torn corpses was forming inside the courtyard

And, apparently, the Ugly Brother was not in a great shape.

What should endure siege didn't endure the spell.

I didn't see what happened. The blizzard itself was thick, but the spell-storm was thick as porridge. I did hear men begging, wood snapping, and then, the ground tilted. There was a terrible, horrible rumbling noise as the keep's wall fell apart. Stones were falling, bits of wall were flying in air, and some crashed into the outer wall, and the inner courtyard wall, collapsing part of that. It seemed to go on, and on, and then, even the gate I had stuck my hand through, broke apart.

A side of the Ugly Brother had fallen. Up to the fifth floor, and the roof, you could see inside halls and rooms, and timber was jutting outside crudely. Men were looking down, shaking with fear, many in nothing but shirtsleeves. Calls to arms echoed.

I turned to look at the men behind me. A semicircle of legionnaires was staring at the fort, out of which fell furniture, bits of wood, some more stone, and official papers snapped by the wind. A horde of crows was flying around it, croaking furiously.

I thumbed towards it. "Well. We don't have to take the gate, I guess."

They roared and moved at me, their horses pulling the wagons away, running for their lives.

I smashed my sword on a man, whose sword snapped from blocking. I stabbed at him down, and then, a captain and another man crashed into me, and we fell against the remains of the gates and into the courtyard. I threw one off my chest, kicked at yet another, and smashed my sword down on the captain, who was getting up next to me, splitting him in half.

I panted, turned around, and came face to face with a scene of death.

I was fire and ice both, but a frost giant is a creature of wintry power, and while the blizzard had covered the land outside, the courtyard was a blue-white land of ice and destruction, filled with piles of wood and stone, and on the sides, swept there by wind, were icy statues of men's corpses, snow-covered wagons, twisted horses, and some dead, ice-white women, formerly locals working in the keep.

There was no gate. The courtyard was gone; its wall and part of the outer had collapsed.

It was a gutted fort, with a three men wide breach from bottom where the gate had stood, to the top.

I stared at it aghast.

It would be shit hard to keep.

But to keep it, we had to.

And before that, I had to take it. The orders had said Balic would take residence in the keep, and would arrive with the supplies, and so, he would be up there.

I walked towards the gaping hole in the keep and stared at the five levels on top, where you could still see people staring down at me.

"Balic!" I called out. "High King of the Dead! Come out and play, o great cadaver, you shit stuffed in a stinky corpse!"

There was only silence.

I looked up, way up to the top, and saw some ballistae peeking over the sides, but I also saw something else.

In the fourth level, there was a face, staring down at me. It had been a face of a golden-curly beauty, and it had looked shocked.

He was there.

Before I hopped over the pile of mortar, stone, and wood, I looked back to the town. I saw little from there. There were screams all over the city, and sounds of battle echoed. Out of the hole in the courtyard wall, I saw movement. Up on ramparts, I saw a mass of men running, weapons at a ready, screaming with anger, and even joy. They were rushing through the snow, almost looking like they were riding the blizzard itself. Guards and scattered Hammer Legionnaires were running away along the ramparts, some jumping over the walls, and many were getting cut down by the enraged mob, when they were too late to move from staring up at the Ugly Brother's gaping wound.

In the end, they would come to the tower, they would take it, and I had to hurry.

Balic and his family would do to them what Lisar had done the others.

I dodged inside the tower. There, the huge round main hall opened. I spotted quivering servants, and a company of Hammer Legionnaires holding spears at me, stepping back. Half of them were drunk, others half-dressed.

I looked at the servants. "You can stay."

I turned to the legionnaires, who were walking back to the depths of the gigantic hall. "You lot, decide where you will die."

They stepped back. They didn't want to die there.

At the end of the hall, near the soldiers, I saw a throne, red and gold, and a desk heaped full of papers, most tossed to the floor, and gilded trunk.

Balic's.

I looked left to see a stairway, and walked to it and began walking up, feeling the stone shaking slightly under my feet. Puddles of water were forming from the melting ice, as there were many fires still burning in the gutted tower, and it made the place look miserable ruin, instead of a haven.

The floor above was filled with corridors, hastily abandoned gear, and boxes and sacks filled with wood.

A captain of the Minotaur legion was there, in his shirtsleeves, staring at me with a bared sword.

I stared at him. "Live, or die? The boys below chose well."

He licked his lips and dropped the sword. "Live."

"Balic?" I asked. "The High King of a bastard? Is he up there? Or is he hiding in one of these rooms?"

He took steps away, and I stopped him with a raised sword. "There is a party of royals here. They arrived this morning. They are … about."

"Who? Where?"

He nodded upstairs. "Balic Barm Bellic. His wife. I saw them fleeing up to the roof, likely."

I stopped and hesitated. "You had better find your men."

He nodded behind him. "What didn't die down there," he said, and eyed the crumbled bit of wall, "is hiding here."

"Pray my people listen. They might, if you tell them you are not in love with the dead," I told him. I walked past him for the stairway, and he looked up at me.

"Don't go up there."

"Why?"

"He is not alone," he said. "His wife, as I told you, is there." He flinched. "They have guards. *New* guards. Don't fight them."

"What sort of guards?" I asked. "You make them sound like dangerous. *I* am dangerous, captain."

"Large guards," he said, and then ran off, calling for his men.

I walked up and passed empty, huge halls on four levels, and the final one with armory and storage of food. There were a dozen ballista, four catapults, and one gigantic ballista, with a box of terrifyingly large ammunition.

Up on top, the blizzard was whipping across an open trapdoor.

I walked up, and pushed to the open.

I turned and spotted four figures standing on the other edge. None seemed bothered by the whipping wind and the thick blizzard.

I walked forward, and they spread out.

There, swathed in a fur, and holding a staff, stood Balic. With him, a woman with a beautiful, cold face, not young, not old, but of course, dead. She had a red hair with golden ornaments, and a delicate, beautiful neck. Her hips were shapely, and she looked regal as a statue. There was something odd about her, and I locked eyes with her.

Fear, terrible fear coursed in my veins, and I knew she was no draugr.

She, too, was a vampire.

I looked away at the other two. With them, stood two men in silver chainmail and crude, black helmets, and large, double-bitted axes were over their shoulders.

I saw the hate in Balic's eyes. I also saw despair and fear. I had escaped him, and I had burned his people and killed his kings and queens, and there I was still, scarred and determined, and he was trapped.

He, the One Man, the golden savior of Midgard, the one who denied the gods, Hel's puppet, killer of thousands upon thousands of innocents, was afraid.

And yet, he wasn't in charge.

Like it had been with Shaduril, and Sand and I, so it was with Balic. Sand had said that.

My eyes went to Queen Rhean, who smiled gently, and leaned over to Balic. She spoke to his ear, and then, she took steps back.

Balic, in his turn, spoke to the guard on his right.

The two men watched me with surprising hate. It was a different sort of hate I had expected, and I, oddly enough, felt the same.

I turned my face to the queen, who lifted an eyebrow.

"So, it is you, then?" I asked. "The serpent and the skull. Your husband's emblem not good enough for you? He is just another plan, one on top of another plan, and you are the shit on top? You are the that, are you not?"

She smiled. "Well, Maskan. You have certainly made

a nuisance of yourself. A dreadful bother, with a foul mouth. Cannot abide boys with such foul language, no matter how bloody glorious and fine looking. How come you are here? Is Sand lost? And my Silas?"

I looked at my sword and then at her.

"I see. I see," she said, her voice cracking with some emotion. "Silas? Aye. I cannot bring him back."

"Shame that," I murmured. "He couldn't kill two girls. Weak-hearted bastard. His sort should lead all your troops."

"Well, Maskan," she said. "You have us trapped, you think? You have brought an army of the beaten to make yourself at home?"

I nodded. "There is no getting down from here, filth," I told her. "They are coming, the people whose happiness you have robbed, whose homes you have torched, and whose loved relatives rot in your Black Ships, and they will make an end of you, if not I. Or perhaps you have some fancy plan to get out of this one alive?"

The woman shook her head and pursed her lips. "You know, my handsome jotun, you are close to the end of the plans, even those that are hidden within plans. You are very close to the end, indeed. You are just one step to the top, near the serpent herself. But, alas, I can escape, fool boy. It is no spell. It is what I am. I am night, and I am darkness. Nay, not like Sand and many of the draugr who can walk the night. I am *the* night. It is a gift of Hel. When we were raised by the Mother, by the Hand of Hel, most became draugr."

Hand of Hel, I thought.

Hand of Hel had been lost thousands of years past. And Rhean was not two decades old. I was sure of that.

She spoke on. "Very few became something terrifying, beings of hunger, and those who feed on sorrow and blood. Even fewer became lich-kind, but we, Maskan, the sorrow, blood-drinking ones, we are vampires. I ride the night winds, boy, and Kiss the Night like the mightiest of elven nobles. My poor husband is naught but a cover. Oh, he and I were not like this always. We loved, once."

"What Hand of Hel are you talking about?" I asked her, and ignored her ramblings.

She shook her head. "I misspoke. Never you mind."

"Your boy, Silas?" I said, taking steps forward. "I took half his head. I bet I can take all of yours."

Her face tightened with rage, and she stepped back again. "You cannot stop what we are doing. Nothing can. We shall do the bidding of the Mother, of the Serpent, and she shall do the bidding of Hel, and only our few allies shall share in the success assured. One jotun and his bedraggled army cannot stop it."

She had grown fangs as she spoke, her eyes were ruby-red.

Balic turned to her and seemed to hesitate. "Rhean?"

She smiled at him. "I could stop him with only a

command. But I shall not. It is time for you to prove yourself. For all the times you have failed, dear husband, for all the mistakes you made with Mir, and this one," the queen said softly, "you will finally have a chance to pay me back. Kill the boy." She snapped her finger at the guards. "But I am merciful. You shall not go alone. You two," she said haughtily, "since my draugr have failed, Sand and my son, we have no more hunters to throw at Maskan. So, you shall step in, obey your king and, therefore, me. Go, and fulfill the pact your king finally made with me."

Balic pushed away his furs. Dressed in an ancient armor, that of the High Kings, and kings of Malignborg, the lords of what was once Odin's haven, the Eye Keep, the intricate mail clinked as he walked forward. Old when he had died, the draugr was a powerful creature. He had a familiar black orb in his hand, and the staff radiated power.

The two guards, casting Rhean unkind looks, flanked him and raised their axes.

I dropped something to the snow.

None saw it.

"Ymirtoe," one grumbled, thumbing his ax-blade. "A fool if I ever saw one. A lost little jotun, and barely of the royal blood. I've not killed one of the royals before."

"He is of the blood," the other one said. "But also of the blood of traitors, and cowards."

The first one shrugged. "Traitor, a coward, and still a king, no less. The last of his kin. They'll sing my praises in the halls, won't they, when we go back to our kin. Let it be soon. The Hel's bastards make me sick."

Balic waited as the two stepped before him. The other man pointed his ax at me. "Twenty years past, boy, your father robbed us of everything. He let the dead march on us, he sacked the Golden City, and left us homeless. It is no less than was expected from a Ymirtoe, but still, a coward's act. Now, we shall take your head to him, so he can try to weep. The dead do not, you know. He'll suffer without any."

I was confused.

Hand of Hel? These people made a deal with Rhean, or her mistress? And what was this war with the dead just two decades ago?

I'd have to find the Mouth of Lok.

Balic lifted his staff. "His head. It is not for you. Give it to me."

Rhean smiled and nodded. "Take it."

The two charged. Their axes came at me from high and the side, as they danced around me. They were as the wind, and those gleaming, almost living weapons seemed like feathers in their arms. I struck at one ax desperately and had to retreat from another, luckily avoiding it. The one I had blocked struck down with his weapon over-handed, the other one was already swinging again, and I crashed into the first one, grasped his mail, and tried to throw him to his friend.

He didn't budge. He pushed me off.

An ax was coming for my back.

It struck my armor hard, and I fell to my knees. The man was over me, pulling at the ax, wrenching it off the dverg-made armor, that had been split and broken, and I felt the chain beneath had saved my life.

The axes were dverg-made as well.

The one with a free ax chopped down, a savage, short, fast strike that would indeed have taken my head.

I kicked back, rolled away, threw my sword up, and blocked an ax, but not the boot that threw me back again.

I kept rolling, and rolling, and saw them running on both my sides. I stopped, got up, and rushed the one on the right, and was smashed down by an ax shaft.

I stepped back and fell down the stairs. I kicked off and came down hard, my sword high.

The two above me followed resolutely after, their chain jingling, axes ready, and Balic was coming after them, silent as a snake, a serpent of death, a meek servant to his queen. I got up and raised my blade. They smiled down at me, and one jumped from the stairway. He came up standing to my side, the other one crouched and came at me from the front. Behind me, was the gutted wall of the fort, wind and snow whirling furiously on the breach.

I heard the sounds of war.

In the courtyard, below in the tower, and across the city, battles were being fought. Men and women were screaming in triumph, or defeat. I glanced outside, and many streets were burning. The ships in port were being taken by archers and Nima.

I looked away just for a moment, and that was enough.

The two were there, so fast, so powerful, their axes cutting the air.

I braided together a spell of wind and ice and threw it at them. The fell back a step, their faces and armor hammered by rough ice and snow, the terrible power of the spell tearing at them. Balic stepped away, guarding his face, and looked at us from the stairs. He was moving his hands. The two savage warriors took another step back and another and grinned.

One spat out an icicle.

I let the spell go.

"Magic in battle, Ymirtoe?" one rumbled, spitting out the words. "No honor in that, Ymirtoe. You are Morag's boy, after all."

They should have died. Their flesh should have been ripped off their bones.

Then, I should have died.

Balic had braided together a spell. He had once, in Aten, sent a terrible, unseen force to kill me, and that force suddenly whipped in the air around me, tying itself around my arm, tightening. I stepped back and swung at the air, struck something, and then lost my sword.

The power came for my throat and slithered around me.

I shapeshifted.

The white bear, great and evil, ripped apart the power around it and charged the two guards. I sprung at them and stood up before the one on the left. I was thrice his size, a gigantic killer with a thick fur, and then, I buried him. I sunk my fangs into his shoulder.

Instead of dying in my clutches, he grew into similar beast, slightly darker and as powerful, and pushed me back to my rear legs as he wrestled with me. I tore at his fur, and he clamped his fangs in my leg. I bit down harder at him, raked my claws on his sides, and luckily bit him in his face.

He roared with pain, falling under me.

I went for his throat.

Something grabbed me, tore me off the bear, roaring with the effort, and tossed me down the next set of stairs. I fell heavily, rolled and crashed my way down the stairs, and landed in the middle of men of Dagnar's militia, some fifty strong, who were busy herding legionnaires down, men who had surrendered.

They backed off from me, prisoner and guard alike.

I shapeshifted and tried to stand, slipping in the snow and ice that had entered the tower from the gutted outer wall. I looked up, saw one of my enemies holding my sword, and then, he tossed it out.

The bastards were jotuns. One of them had knocked me down the night I had gone to meet with Antos. They worked with the draugr.

They shapeshifted together. I saw two figures hurtling through the air, white owls both, and land amid our men, tall, terrible, and fey.

The axes hacked around with lightning fast strikes. The axes killed men like sheep. They took heads and arms, split armor and skull, and they tossed and kicked men down the stairs, their eyes never leaving me. Men with pikes and spears were rushing up, many our allies from Aten. One jotun, having chased men away from the floor, straddled the stairway, hacking down, taking hits from long spears, and still laughing, while his friend turned to me.

"Jotuns," I sneered. "Hel's servants? How is that possible?"

"We are more than jotuns," the one approaching me snarled, his beard swinging. "We are kin," he added, white teeth flashing, "but also ancient enemies. It is the plan of our king, and none of your business. No time for the tale, boy. You are Morag's traitor ilk, and it pleases us to see you join them in their dark slumber."

"Come, then," I snarled.

His friend was wading down the stairs, his ax slaying men with every swing, like a butcher hacking at a cow carcass.

My opponent came at me with his ax flashing.

I lunged under the ax and picked him up. I turned him in the air and ran forward, crashing into the other jotun. We rolled down the stairs, cursing, breaking over twenty of our soldiers, beating, kneeing, and striking each other furiously. I saw a jotun's face just above me, felt his hands on my throat, and as we rolled down the stairs, I pushed his chin as hard as I could, and his skull cracked on a stone-step. His eyes rolled in his head, and we ended up below, and I saw he had died. The other jotun was getting up, cursing and howling, as our men were pushing pikes at him, and then, he remembered me.

I found my enemy's great ax and chopped it on his face, then on his neck, and he went to his knee, and toppled, pushed by our pikes.

The men around me were panting, frightened, as they looked up at me, unsure who was the enemy, and who not. I pointed the ax upstairs.

"Do not come up, and if anyone but me comes down, kill it," I told them. They backed off, nodding. "And if I don't come back," I said as I began climbing, "listen to your queen."

As I climbed, I called for magic, a braid of ice. I stepped over corpses, over battle scorched rocks, and found Balic was still standing on top of the stairs on the level I had left him. His eyes widened, he grimaced, and cursed softly, and he braided tougher a spell. He gleamed with a protective sphere, and then, he thrust his orb at me.

I threw the spell his way.

It was the simple, powerful braid of ice. The ice grew out of the walls and the stairs around Balic, and he was trapped. He fell on his arse, one arm stuck in the shifting ice, and the dark stone flashed as he released his spell. What had torn down Aten's palace, walls of Dagnar, and gods knew how many southern fort, released its power, not at me, but at the roof. The already gutted tower shook as stone and mortar, brick and siege gear flew in an arc as his terrible siege spell bit to the roof. I was battered by the debris, and as I dashed forward, guarding my face, the dust thick, I found the stairs. The ice was still spreading, but I stomped up the stairs, nearly slipping many times, pulling myself up with the terrible ax, and I was finally rewarded to see Balic struggling to get released of the ice.

He was still stuck, his ankles twisted, but his arms were free. He was covered in dust, and he didn't look golden and great, but frightened and surprised.

I roared and crashed my ax on him.

It bounced away from his sphere, and he held his hands over his face, clutching his stone and staff.

I hacked away, like a mad thing, limping around him, slipping, striking again and again at the sphere that kept him alive. It shimmered, shivered, and thinned.

Finally, he remembered to act, and his staff thrust up at me.

I acted fast and struck my ax down. The globe of protection was shattered, the ax went through it and split the staff.

Apparently, the artifact was one that summoned lightning.

That lightning exploded in our face. I was thrown back and fell down the stairs. My plate armor fell apart as I crashed to the floor, and I grimaced and felt my skin was on fire. I tossed and turned, found snow, and threw myself in it. I turned and got up and found I was dressed in my chain skirt alone, in one of my plate boots, and leather pants. My smoking skin was crudely burned across my chest. I rummaged in the ruins of the armor, and pulled out something, and stuck it in my pocket.

I got up, stepped forward and looked up. The ice had disappeared and was a powdery cloud, moving gently near the roof. It looked a brilliant, white rain, as thick as the dust had been.

"Balic!" I roared. "Baliiic! Did you run?"

Then, I saw him. He was stepping forward. His armor was mangled bits of gold and metal, and he held neither the black stone, nor the staff. His right hand was shredded, and his face and chest were black pits of mangled flesh and skull. "Look! Look what you did to me! I was the most beautiful of the draugr!"

I snarled. "So might a turd claim a kingship over vomit," I said. "Come, One Man. It is time to pay back for the lost lives of Midgard."

"It wasn't my fault! I was raised by the Hand of Hel and the Serpent!" he yelled, stepping back, and then, he stepped on the end of his blackened staff and roaring, hollering, rolled down. I picked up the double bitted ax and limped for him.

He twisted with surprising agility, and as I axed him, he managed to leap aside and come to his feet.

He braided together a whip of dark fire and struck down at me.

I moved under it and struck him across the face, taking his teeth.

He fell back, lost the spell, and eyeing me with desperation, rushed for the gutted wall, calling for some spell that might save him as he fell.

I was faster, and I jumped after.

I chopped down with the ax.

I smashed through his skull, chest—breaking some magical artifact that popped loudly— and lopped his corpse in half. Half fell out of the tower, and I stepped on the other half, before it followed in. I grasped the golden hair, hacked at the neck, and stared at the mess.

I shook my head and tossed it to the side.

I felt a presence.

I felt my heart beating faster, and fear was coursing its way down my limbs, making them shake.

I turned to look up at Rhean, who stared down at me from the top of the stairs with a look that was full of pleasure. Her eyes glanced at the mess that was Balic. She was excited by the entire thing.

"Will be hard," I forced myself to utter, while I leaned to the mess that had been my plate and chain and picked up something, "to make him lead your fanatics. Will look odd, won't it, when the One Man won't be around to resurrect his victims. Perhaps you can make some excuse?"

She shook her head. "I have a way around that. To be honest, he was growing tedious. The dead are terrible lovers, did you know? At least the males."

A way around that? The mess that was Balic? Who would raise their dead? Her mistress?

She opened her hands. In them, were items. There, the accursed earrings that Mir, Lith, and Shaduril had used and what had led to such terrible consequences.

The death of Baduhanna.

I forced a grin, and hid my dismay as well as I could. "Alas, Rhean, they only work when you take a female figure. Balic was, barely, a *male*."

Fury played on her face.

"You didn't know that, did you, vampire?" I mocked her.

She pocketed them and nodded. "No, I didn't. I have had no time to dwell on such details. Well, I am allied to jotuns, am I not? One must take his place, for a time.

I must make do."

"How are you allied to them? Who are they? How and why? What happened twenty years ago? And who is the Hand of Hel? Are there more than one, across different times?" I demanded, as I walked forward.

She looked at me with pity. She pulled out something else. I froze. "The Book of the Past. Almost holy to Red Midgard. It has an answer to your questions. Remember, a general of Hel, Medusa, led her army to the east. The jotun clan of Sons of Ymir went with her. Let us just say, that while not in love with us dead folk, they absolutely *loathe* your clan. There is a good reason."

"So," I said as I looked at the book. "You are as much a thief as I am. What reason?"

She had killed Thrum for them?

Or, perhaps, Thrum never had them.

"I am," she said proudly, "a queen, not a thief. I *was* the Queen of Malignborg, and I should have been the High Queen of Midgard. I was honest, I was good, I was kind, and I was fooled. I am now what I wasn't then. I am the death of Midgard, and its Queen, and I shall sit over its bones. The mistress promised me this."

"Bones won't feed you, will they?" I asked. "Will you not answer any of my questions?"

"We'll bring in new blood, boy, when the old one is spent. There are other worlds," she said.

I frowned. The gates were closed.

"These thoughts are too large for you," she said, and raised the book. It burst into a ball of blue fire, and she tossed it before her. I looked at it in horror, and she softened the look on her face. She was intrigued and not angered. She looked over my shoulder to the stairways. "Your men coming?"

I shook my head. "I will deal with you. You cannot turn them against me."

She laughed. "Ah, very clever. I could, you know. Men especially have no resistance to a vampire, and no mortal to me, save for the very mightiest ones. I suspect you will struggle, won't you? There is royal blood in you, but you are … raw."

She considered me for a while, and I took another step towards the stairway.

She laughed softly. "Few could deny me, when I was alive. I said I was good and honest, but I was also married to Balic. I was young, when I learned of love. I learned love is not something one is ashamed of. Alas, my last lover was pitiful. Poor Gal, Lisar's husband. I had him, though I didn't intend to make him my king, as it was claimed. He was just a pitiful relief. Oh, well. I am babbling. You know nothing of such past matters, champion." She tilted her head and looked dangerous, like a wolf about to devour a deer. She spoke softly, suggestively. "You fought well. I'll remember you. I could try to make you mine forever."

I snarled at the thought.

She nodded, having expected the response. "*Very* brutal, Maskan. A true warrior, you sound like. I could try, still. We, the few dead woven of this curse of night, can recall the spirit we have drained of blood, and sometimes, rarely, they heed the call and can become blessed like we were, but they are often lesser creatures. Very few can be like I am, or those who remain of the Ten from the Stone."

I had no idea what she was talking about. I stepped closer.

She noticed and shook her head. "You will not make it, boy. I can flee, or I will use my magic. I know my spells, and I'd not use ice on you. I see you have grown and find ice and cold your friend now. Still, I'd rob you of your skin, jotun, if you would challenge me to such a battle."

"I'll just ax you, vampire," I said. "No trouble with that, is there?"

She shook her head, her eyes twinkling with excitement. "I do like males who threaten me. I will not flee, nor will I call for spells. I need not do either. I will just *command* you. You will struggle, as I said, and it will be painful, confusing for you, since you are powerful enough to try, but you cannot defeat the night." She laughed softly. "Balic always wanted to raise you. I could try to make you like we are, but as I said, it is rare one heeds the call, and few are powerful. I'd not demean you like this. I'd not make you less than you are now. You'll simply die, and I'll have you buried under this fort. It will carry your name."

"Thank you," I said, stepping close to the stairs.

I wasn't sure what her weakness was. They all had one.

"You are welcome," she answered, and shook her head, her red eyes pools of madness. "If only I were alive. Such a man as you, or rather, a jotun, would have been a pleasing thing in the bed. Perhaps," she laughed, "I can make you an offer. I sometimes give my worst foes, those who are worthy, the bloody, terrible champions who shed blood to kill me, a pleasing end. All vampires have skills they are best in. Mine? I'll break your heart with love. I often break mine, as well, after …" She went quiet and smiled wistfully. "What say you?"

And that was her weakness. She was mad, dead, terrifyingly powerful, and still … partly a woman.

She wanted a man. She had collected them.

She still did.

"If die I must," I snarled, "then let it be a pleasing end. It would please me to see an ax in your skull."

She grinned. Her eyes flashed as she looked down at me, and I felt her power in my head. The voice that had guided, and chided me, had been a child in comparison. The power I felt was not born from magic, not a spell braided out of the Filling Void. The vampire could touch my mind, and it came naturally to her, like breathing to the living. It could simply force one to obey. It could make a king cry with fear, it could render a champion helpless, it could turn all mortals into her meek servants. She was a manipulator of the living, a perversion of life, a corruptor of lovers, and a slayer of the helpless ones, and most all were just that before her power.

That would have been me, once. A helpless mortal.

But I wasn't helpless, or alone.

With the aid of the spirit, the god, or an ancient jotun Bolthorn, I had a chance. I had an ally, an expensive, odd, and dangerous ally. It would cost me a bit of the human that was Maskan, for the voice would ask me for a price that any jotun in Nifleheim, Jotunheim, or Muspelheim would pay with no feeling of remorse, but not so a human I had grown up to, or the law-making Morag who made Red Midgard into a just land of honor.

And yet, the human had to die for a moment, as the jotun would have to fight.

I could call it then.

I opened my mouth to pray to it.

"Silence," she said. "No spells, jotun."

I tried. I struggled and fought and tried to speak. I thrust my foot to the snow, felt the cold ice on my skin, but I couldn't call for the creature.

I lunged.

"Kneel," she said simply. "Take your human form."

I stopped and nearly wept. I went to one knee. I shrunk to my man-sized shape. It was no trick I tried to play on her, for I had no choice. The vampire I had met before had been deadly. His commands had been hard to resist, but I had no chance to fight Rhean. She had been right.

She would kill me.

I pushed back at her power, but her eyes flashed, and she buried all resistance under her dark power, her mind stripping me of defenses, one by one, anticipating all my thoughts. It was as if her hand was grasping my soul, smoothing from it all thoughts of struggle, and I couldn't think of anything but pleasing her, of obeying her wishes. She was like a man wrestling with a young boy, toying with all my attempts to defeat her.

Trembling, I stayed on my knee.

"A mighty looking man-form, jotun," she whispered. "A mighty, if a raw mind you have, my boy. You do struggle, which is rare. I am tempted."

She walked down the stairs, came towards me, and dismissed her furs.

She was not young, nor very old, and the lines under her eyes made her oddly attractive. She was lithe, with a generous bosom and wide hips, and her shapely leg was revealed in a slit of an ancient silken dress, black as night, as she stepped down. She had a sword on her hip, gold hilted with a silver skull on the pommel. She released her hair, and the red wave covered her bosom and back. The red eyes never left me.

"I'll give you a kiss of death on your throat, Maskan, and you shall die," she whispered. "I'll take your blood, and it will hurt. Go on both your knees."

I trembled as she walked down to me. My other knee went down.

"Put the ax down, as well," she purred, and then, the demand no longer felt like a pleasant one. It was a disappointed one, like a lover to a failing husband, and I closed my eyes and put the ax down, not letting go of it.

She frowned a bit and stopped just at the bottom of the stairway, so close to me. She excreted her full will on me, and I felt my heart was bursting. I groaned with pain.

I managed to hold the ax.

It would do me no good. I couldn't even speak. I couldn't call for the creature or lift a finger.

"Love," she whispered. "You impress me. You do. Listen. Choose. I shall let you decide how you will die. I hold your mind, and you cannot break free. I shall kill you, and you will not be able save yourself, and you will die while struggling. I'll feast while I have a craving for warmth, jotun, and that craving will bother me while I feed, and when bothered so terribly, your death shall be a painful, cruel, and a long one. Stop struggling, jotun, and let me in fully. You will find my mind in the very depths of your soul, soon a part of your most inner self, and we shall be together, like wine mixing with water. Then, you shall love me, like I will you. You truly will. You will no longer fear, nor will there be pain. Give up and love me, even for a moment, and after, tell me you shall love me. Do this, and I shall give you an easy death, a gift from lover to another, a gentle kiss." She looked at me sadly. "Choose fast."

I fought the panic. I slumped in the snowy floor and knew I'd not break the hold she had on my head. I simply could not.

All I could do was to buy time.

She wanted to play, to take her time with me, and she would trade a terrible death for an easy one, if I just gave up struggling. She said she would get inside my head, into my mind, deeper than ever, and I would even learn to love her, if I did.

That was almost more terrifying than dying.

She was close, she was on guard, ready to rip me apart. She might do that *even* if I gave up.

Patience. I needed patience. I needed ... time.

Then I thought of what she had said, and felt a moment of hope.

I let go of the ax. I let go of the struggle and breathed deep, inhaling her power into me.

I felt I lost a grip on something much more important than the ax.

The terrible, oppressive power she had over me seemed to overwhelm me. Then, to my horror, it felt less terrible. It felt almost warm and welcome, and she was a lover in my head, caressing me, calming me. My mind was screaming warnings, but she was now deeply buried in my head, and soon, I looked up at her with admiration. She commanded me. She told me what I could do, and couldn't do, and I felt my heart quicken at the sight of her.

She smiled and came to stand before me.

I stared at her, as her cold hands touched my bare shoulders and chest, her finger playing in my wounds, drawing blood. She was trembling, anticipating the pleasure of my death, the taste of my flesh and blood, and she was whispering in a language I didn't know, soothing, almost gentle. She came to my side, her hands still touching my skin, her ice-cold touch exploring my body. She smiled, and I twitched as she moved my hair and kissed my neck, but there was no bite, no death yet.

I still smiled at her and tried to touch her.

I still couldn't move, nor speak.

She kissed my throat, slowly at first, and then with passion. She moved before me, her lips on my throat, her body pressing into mine. Her hands were impossibly strong, as she grasped me, and then, she ripped at the chain skirt, which came off with a jingle. She tossed it off, and her hands opened my belt, and she pushed her hand into my pants. She slipped her hand deep, and her fingers found my manhood. She caressed it, gently, patiently, and then, her cold hand pulled it out. Expertly, kissing my face now, she stroked it, until I, to my shame and still full of love for her, was fully aroused by the creature of Hel. She was moaning softly, and I gasped with pleasure, which made her smile, almost gratefully, with relief.

With mad, undead love.

I had seen it in Lith and Shaduril before.

The rebellious thought disappeared as I enjoyed her touch, breathing heavily.

She finally clutched my hair, while she stroked my belly, then my balls and ass, as she pulled me close. "Kiss me, Maskan," she said huskily, and turned my head down towards her. "Love me. Touch me, but better you have ever done to others. Let it be your last pleasure."

Her lips came for mine, dark fog issued from them. Sharp teeth flashed behind the lips, and her tongue, black as night flickered in her mouth.

Her lips crushed into mine, she tasted of wine, of herbs, of honey, and I struggled as much as I could, but couldn't stop, didn't want to end the freezing kiss, or her tongue from playing with mine. She pushed me on my back while devouring me and climbed over me with passion. My hands were pulling open her robe, caressing her breasts, her hips.

A tug in my mind disturbed me. It whispered of shame. Of loss.

I had let the vampire close, and I would never really

forget her.

She had also let herself close to me.

She pushed herself against me, pressed her body tight to me, full of cold love and passion. I raised my arms and put them around her hips, pushed my hands under the dress, and she trembled with pleasure. She grasped my hand and pushed it on her thigh, and then between her legs. She was cold, and still, due to her manipulative power, also desirable.

I touched her and stroked her, gently, then with desperate need to please her. She responded with pleasure.

She moved, wiggled and pushed herself on me, ripping her dress, and then, she enjoyed herself, as I did. She moved like a snake, rhythmic, and strong, demanding, and her lips were hungrily pressing into mine, as she panted and gasped, and had me.

Then, finally, the vampire moved with desperate need, close to climax, finding the perfect rhythm. Suddenly sitting up over me, she arched her back. Her eyes to the roof, she trembled as she ground herself on me, her hand grasped my balls, and she, almost like a living woman, had her pleasure with such power, she nearly broke my back. She held me down with terrible strength and moved on me.

She wanted to see my pleasure.

She aided me, moved and moved, her hands skillfully playing, and then, soon I had mine, and she, perhaps, again hers.

We lay there on top of each other, staring at each other, enemies, and what power she had forced on my mind, was weaker for a moment.

The love for her remained.

The control, her mind in mine, was … asleep, drowsy.

For just a moment, she was simply happy, like a living thing, and unable to do more than enjoy the warmth of my body, and what I had given her, and she to me. And perhaps, the vampire too, felt love, and not only lust, for she spoke. "Tell me," she whispered, "that you loved me."

"Yes," I whispered, allowed to speak.

I moved just slightly, and she tightened the hold on my hair, her face still full of joy.

Then, her face hardened.

She pulled my head to the side, savagely, and spoke huskily, the lust not quite spent. "Now, Maskan. Be still. It was wonderful, and I want to keep my promise. It will be fast and clean."

The deadly fangs came down, thirsty for jotun's blood.

My hand was buried in snow. Her command threatened to overwhelm me again, and the love I felt for her was confusing, nearly stopping me from struggling, but I forced myself to act. I had the moment and the ability to speak.

I also had her close.

"Aid, aid me against the terrors of Hel's minions. Lives for a boon. Bolthorn, heed me," I whispered.

And Bolthorn heard. This time, I heard him. The voice was old as mountains, grating and icy, inhuman, and cruel.

Ten lives. Ten faithful lives, the voice echoed. *Ten lives and you shall never fear or obey the dead again.*

And I, about to die, agreed.

Yes.

An ancient jotun, mighty as gods, a thing of chaos, a creature of bitter, ancient grudges, father and grandfather to jotuns, and rebel Aesir, and traitorous Vanir let his magic flow to me, through the great distance. Even when the gates were closed, his power touched me and aided me, his own distant blood.

A jotun is a natural, berserk fighter.

He fights like a wounded animal, like a father for his child, a mother for a babe, and fights to bring himself honor, and to his family. A berserk, mad creature can stomp over an army, can rip his ax at the enemy until the battle is over, and only then die.

That wasn't enough to stave off the vampire.

A rage a god might experience was needed.

Such anger filled my mind, and would, always when an undead tried to terrify me with their powers.

It burned away fear, it replaced compliance with bitter rage, and filled me with battle-power, making me tremble.

My fist smashed to her face just as she was descending on my throat, and the hand on her hip, took a hold of her dress and belt. I threw her to the wall, ripping her clothing. I rolled over, struck her again, and watched the red eyes filling with terror. I hammered at the vampire with burning rage, breaking bone, breaking skin, twisting her arm. The disgust at her touch, at what she had done, the fact she had forever made me love her, at least a bit, gave me such angry rage, I'd rip her apart.

She fought back.

Her dress in tatters around her, she struck hard and nearly broke my neck.

I spat blood and head-butted her, and then began to squeeze her throat, to twist it.

She thrashed desperately under me. She pulled at my hands, tore skin and muscle, but I kept at it. She let out a desperate gasp, and then, I felt terrible pain in my hip.

She kicked off, and I fell back.

There was a dagger on my leg, and I had to tear it off.

The rage wasn't gone. It was there, filling my soul to the brim, making me mad with anger. The creature was backing up the stairs, her arm and wounds already on the mend. She was shaking her head; a begging look on her face.

The spell of love, of seduction, still haunted me, still compelled me to obey her, but the rage overcame it, and

I managed to grasp the ax.

She fled, and I went after her.

She fled to the roof, and there, wind whipping around her bare, white skin, her hair whipping in the wind, the evil and the beauty seemed to blend with the shadows. She danced away from me, backing off.

I watched her go, and then, I pulled out and tapped the crescent of the Blacktowers which I had picked up from the ruins of my armor and saw Grinlark, which I had dropped to the snow, twisting, growing to full size, and Balan's portal opened before me, and behind her.

It had once doomed Morag to death, as I had unwittingly carried it to my father.

It had killed Lith, who had tried to take Dagnar for herself, before Mir and Balic.

And now, it gave me a chance to kill the snake of snakes.

I roared and jumped in, and before I even came up behind her, I swung the ax.

The blade struck her back, and she fell forward, as I straddled her. The ax sunk through her, it bit deep into her spine and ribs, and I placed a foot on her neck.

"Die, love," I roared, as I pressed her neck with my heel so hard, something broke.

Then, a spell struck me.

It was a spell of cold, bitter wind. It was strong, terrible, much stronger than most magic I had faced, and I fell on my face and rolled across the roof. I lost my

Blackthorn crescent, and my sense of direction, and the rage as well. The cold whipped at my skin, and while no jotun of frost should suffer so, the spell was powerful enough to hurt me.

I tried to grasp it, and found the braid, beautiful, powerful, and impossibly complex, but I couldn't rip it apart, or to capture it. It was made by someone like me, by someone of the old blood.

I saw, just a glimpse, of a figure kneeling next to Rhean, pulling the ax of her back. Then, just before the storm threw me over the edge, I saw the figure walking off and helping Rhean. I saw she held Grinlark.

Then, I fell and shapeshifted into the eagle, my eyes on the sky.

No owls.

Only snow.

I plummeted and twisted in the air, and saved myself just in time. I flew back, and circled the roof.

I saw my ax, I saw the roof and where the battle had been fought. I saw tracks, and then, I saw nothing.

She was gone. Whoever had helped her had seemingly disappeared.

I flew down and changed. I picked up the ax and looked dully at the partly collapsed roof. I was suddenly exhausted, tired beyond all, my leg was throbbing, my old wounds aching, and still, I knew I wasn't done, and had no time to rest.

Not, if I were wise, that is.

There was a throbbing feeling of a threat, of an expectation that was still unfulfilled.

I was due to make a payment.

I walked to the edge of the roof and looked down.

The city was mostly burning by now, Nallist's streets were dotted with embattled fighters, and judging by lumps, some already covered in snow, there were hundreds of dead, perhaps thousands. There were enemy and refugees fleeing in all the directions. The harbor street was a sea of fire, and thousand rebels were running for the shattered keep. Many were hauling supplies.

Below, I saw men.

I looked down at them, and they bowed. I took a long, ragged breath. "Any men of Aten alive?"

"Hundreds, lord," said a man from Dagnar. "They did well."

"Send ten up here," I said. "And tell them I need men who know the legions."

He hesitated and then went down.

I looked out to the sea, and in the blizzard, hugging the coast, desperate for safety, ships appeared. They held two new legions, and I smiled at the confusion, when they arrived at the sea-gates, and found the city locked against them. Nima had taken it as well. They finally began rowing past it.

It had been a long day of surprises and losses, and of a single, terrible failure.

But still, things were moving according to the plan. We had their most of their food.

"King Maskan," I heard, and saw ten men of Aten, looking dubiously up at their former enemy, a king of wounds, the jotun of the north, who stood in the blizzard half-bare, and smiled down at them.

"Come up," I said. "I have a need of you."

When they were dead, I, less Maskan than ever and the shame of my father, walked down to find armor and weapons, for a battle was coming.

BOOK 3: THE UGLY BROTHER

"Lisar Vittar? She is here, then."

Nima

CHAPTER 10

Men spoke about it later. None had seen it, but all knew, nonetheless.

They knew I had killed them.

Bolthorn had been sated. I felt my father watching. I felt I was losing the part of me that gave me the right to rule men. My kingship was defiled with rumors of my own making. Morag had been infamous for the harshness of his laws, not for the lack of them.

I had to wonder, if he too, could speak with Bolthorn. I had a feeling he had rejected the old creature's boons.

Everything what Rhean had hinted at, the morsels she had dropped on my plate, made me itchy to find out more. Medusa's clan, our kin, allied to draugr? A war with the dead, not too long past? And they had a way, no, *two* ways in, and Morag wasn't one of them?

What were they? A clan. Kin, they had claimed. And only twenty years past, they said, Hel had tried to take the land. The Mouth of Lok had claimed the same.

There was truth to it.

There was something about the northern quest of the dead, something about Mara's Brow I didn't understand.

I would have to find out. But before that, I had to win a war. I was stuck in a fort with all the supplies for an army, and that army would come for it.

I looked like a king again. I wore one set of the

gleaming silvery chainmail the jotuns had worn. The other one I had hidden in a trunk. I had taken their gear, their clothing, their steel-reinforced boots, and it was all dverg made. It was no plate, but it was more agile and mostly intact. I had a pair of long daggers, and I had their axes, one on my hand, the other one on my belt. One had had a large round shield on his back, strapped and ready to use. I held that now. I wore one of their helmets and wondered at the power of the figure that had saved Rhean. Surely, it, too, had been a jotun.

I feared keeping the fortress would be an impossible task if more jotuns joined the armies that would have to try to take it.

I was pulled from my thoughts.

The general of our men, Maggon, still alive, his face sweaty even in the gutted fort, was bowing before me. He had a look of fear in his eye and probably thought I'd invite him to the roof, should he have any bad news to share.

"Tell me."

"The men are tearing at the floor of the first level," he said. "It is hard going. The stones are heavy."

"Can you," I asked, "dig a moat inside the fort or not?"

He nodded. "We can dig it, but it won't be deep. They must break the floor, and it is sturdy as shit. There is an old floor under this top one. I have men who actually built this. They have looked at the beams below, and the pillars, and tell me the keep might fall apart, especially with the damage it suffered in … the battle. It was rotten to start with, the wall. Whoever designed this monstrosity had more ambition than skill. It was the old lord Wilred, no doubt. Thank Odin he is dead. They hanged him in the woods after he tried to hide from the Hammer Legionnaires."

"The courtyard of the keep itself and the wall around it?" I asked him.

He shook his head. "The courtyard is … not for us. The wall around it shattered in two places. The wall around the city is damaged as well, but the good news is that the keep itself is only breached right there, where the gate was. The breach runs all the way to the top. The roof, well …" He shrugged. "There is plenty of it left, but the supports are damaged, where not gone entirely. Something had a terrible effect on them. The doorways to the outer wall have been utterly blocked. They must come through down there. Unless …"

"Unless they have siege, but I doubt they will wait to set it up," I said, and was happy the dark stone Balic had used to knock down halls and wall likely had no twins. I had not found it. I had also lost the crescent of the Blacktowers.

"We man the keep, rotten or not," I said. I turned to look at Saag. "A thousand archers will go out. You will harass the bastards as well as you can. No sleep, no rest for them. Make sure what supplies from the ships will not easily be carried to the legions. When you find their ships, do not harm them."

Saag looked pleased by the order. He would be out in his own element. He had a role to play, after all. I had asked Nima, but she insisted she'd stay in the keep.

The fight in the keep would be one in a deadly trap.

He bowed stiffly. "Yes. And Nima?"

"Nima?" I asked him. "Nima will command the archers here. She wanted to rule Red Midgard, as did you, and it has to be taken back."

He bit back an answer and went to find his men.

"How many do we have?"

The general shrugged. "Two and a half thousand infantry in the keep and near two thousand archers, if a thousand leave. They'll be infantry when the arrows run out. We have the moat coming, and we are building a rough wall inside the hall, and getting everything set up on the stairways, as requested. I've added my own surprises. The catapults are ready, as are the ballista, and Aten's men shall use them. They know best how. It is their gear, is it not?"

I nodded. "Good. Now, we just have to wait."

I watched outside, wondered at the blizzard, and tried to forget Rhean. I would never fear her as I had, and I would have weapons against her power, but the seed she had sown in my soul would always be there, marring my love for Quiss.

The thought of the creature made me both curl my

fists with rage and to weep with loss.

And whoever had saved her would pay equally.

When the dawn broke, the blizzard thickened, and we heard the horns of the legions blaring across Nallist as the enemy had landed away from the city, unloaded in the terrible weather, and staunchly marched to eradicate the last king of Red Midgard.

They were hungry and cold.

They knew where warmth, and food could be found.

In the Ugly Brother.

***

I inspected the moat that had been dug inside the keep. It covered the breach and was not overly deep, as the captain had warned, but just deep and wide enough to give the enemy a pause. A rough wall of stone had been erected to stand before the moat and also on top of many of the stairways.

The tower was brimming with troops. The great hall housed most of them. All had spears, pikes, swords, shields, and even clubs. Heaps of smaller stones meant for tossing had been placed on top levels, where there were also archers, looking in every direction, ready to make life terrible for the attackers. On top, catapults and ballista had been readied, and in the great halls and on many levels.

The tower was a deathtrap.

Hopefully for the enemy.

We still waited. I looked to the upper floor and found

Nima looking down at me from between two broken piles. "Any sight of them?"

She nodded. "They spent the night in the woods. Their scouts are just riding the city and the walls."

"No shelter?" I asked.

She shrugged. "Most of the city is burned down. There are guard towers and some few buildings that survived. They might find it in the ships in the harbor. They will be cold as goat's arse, though. They'll be miserable."

I nodded.

The city of Nallist was a ruin, and the snowfall kept blanketing the ruins and the dead all over the city. It would be like a ghost town for the enemy.

"They'll come," I said.

Nima nodded. "There are eight thousand or fewer," she called down. "They have lost ships to the storm. A king and queen have been seen, their horns prominent. They'll know what happened from survivors. They might not know how many we are."

"They will come, nonetheless," I said.

"Hillhold!" yelled a man on top. "Hillhold! Come to us, for Hillhold!"

The battle of Hillhold had not been the doing of the two legions out there, one with a black skull on white in their standards, and another with a deep red flag with a grinning golden mask. I had no idea where they hailed from, but their troops stared at the smitten hold with fury and hurt pride.

Nima smirked. "They have a heap of corpses in the woods already. Saag's busy."

"Scouts!" yelled a man on top.

I twisted my neck to look up, saw Nima disappear, and heard her running up. There, soon, I saw archers moving and Nima giving orders. I climbed to the second level and saw a cavalry unit of a hundred from the Grinning Mask riding past the walls, huddled in cloaks.

Nima called out, and arrows fell among the cavalry. Men were pierced and thrown to the snow, and horses were whinnying with fear and pain. Some sixty enemy turned their horses around and madly rode for the woods.

There, I saw them speaking to the two draugr who turned to give orders.

I waited. Soon, I saw movement as men were crossing between the tents.

"King Maskan," called a man from the top. I leaned forward to squint up at him. "They are dismantling the camp."

"They will come inside the city," I said, "because they are hungry, their fame and honor demands it, and they think Balic will punish them if they don't. They'll test us this afternoon."

They did.

We watched the stream of men marching in with

caution from the main gates and setting up camp near the gate, and the other legion did so by the harbor. They pitched tents, took shelter in the ruins, some in the ships, and made a meager meal with what they had and found.

A stream of men were constantly riding and marching between the gate and their ships, which were out of sight. Those men began falling to the snow, and chaos took over as Saag made attacks on anyone who seemed ripe for killing. Bands of hunters rushed from the woods and back again, and the legions had to deploy their cavalry to deal with Saag's men.

They lost many men and soon gave up.

Before dark, the companies in each camp were taking their places as they shed their cloaks, took up shields, and formed companies around their standards. The Mask and the Skull were exhorted by their captains and the draugr, and soon, they marched forward, up the main street from the harbor, and the road from the gate.

They had no siege.

They would have to come in from the front.

Both legions would arrive in the same place.

We waited, silent, and the men were shaking, praying behind the wall.

I walked deeper to the hall, pushed past our companies, who were ready to take their places in the hall, and climbed a makeshift platform. There, I sat down on Balic's throne.

I would oversee the battle.

I would conserve my strength.

Echoing shouts and commands could be heard. From my seat, I could see the remains of the courtyard gate. The snow was falling heavily, but I could see the gleaming mass of shield and armor filling the streets beyond the courtyard. I poured myself wine as I heard the enemy on the walls, trying to enter the tower that way, but they were inaccessible.

The archers were looking at the enemy. They were well in the range now, milling all across the streets below. None had come to the courtyard yet.

Then, discovering there was no side entrance, a captain of the Grinning Mask climbed through one breach in the courtyard wall.

"Let them have it," I said. "For Hillhold."

"Let them have it!" called out a young man with a clear voice. "For Hillhold!"

On top, the archers began loosing arrows down on the foe. They sunk down to the masses behind the walls, but I saw the captain falling on his face, pierced by many. The ballista set on each level coughed up man-length spears, and the screams and oaths of the enemy echoed across the tower. There were a thousand archers working their craft on the enemy, while the others waited, guarded, and rested, and it was enough to turn the evening into a red one for our foe. We saw the air quivering as hundreds of arrows flashed down mercilessly.

I heard the catapults coughing high above us, and knew they would be throwing burning pots of fire on the legionnaire camps which were all in range.

A draugr, I was sure it was one, screamed, "Up! Up and through the wall. Take the keep! Do not stay here and die! Up for One Man. For Balic!"

The enemy charged.

They surged over the broken gates, passed the breaches on the wall for the courtyard in a chaotic mass of companies, men falling on their faces in the press, and their archers tried to take positions on the wall around the courtyard.

Ten fell as they tried and then twenty, dropping like dead flies.

Nima was calling out muffled curses and insults, and men kept firing from every floor. The enemy archers gave up, and then, our archers and ballista crews and even stone-throwers took the men pushing into the courtyard as their targets.

Deadly rain tore into legionnaire flesh.

A ballista bolt killed four.

More and more arrows tore into the groaning mass of the two legions.

And they kept coming, shields high, shields out, falling, crashing, and only some getting up. A few men looked like needle cushions as they walked forward, and some, in the terrible press of the enemy, were dead but upright. Twenty, a hundred, then more fell to the stone, ballista, and archers. Men screamed as they stepped into holes our men had dug, breaking legs. The ground was filling up with dead, dying, and those who were crawling to get back.

Still they came, proud as devils.

The enemy archers had given up on the courtyard wall, but were now shooting at the lower levels, and our men began falling. Some fell amongst us through the holes in floor.

The enemy finally surged up to where the gate had once stood, the breach, and, shields out, the first men were pushed through it and fell into the moat. Some fell on spikes and howled piteously.

A captain peeked at the moat and fell on his back.

Another, an officer with a gorgeous armor, peeked in and dodged away, an arrow taking a man next to him. We heard him calling, "Bridges, bring them forward! Bring the bridges and the ladders!"

They were prepared.

Such wooden ramparts were carried through the milling enemy. Ladders were pushed and pulled through the breaches, our archers falling as the enemy archers tried to stop them.

"Stop them!" Nima screamed, and our men braved the arrows, and tried.

The legionnaires fought with zeal.

Dozens fell, hundred and two, as our archers shot

their arrows at them, but doggedly, the bridges approached the breach, and many ladders were thrown to land against the walls, and some so that they leaned on the damaged floor of the second level. Men began climbing, falling, dying, and still climbing. One ladder crashed, and another took its places. Long pikes pushed at those who made it up, and then, the enemy archers began shooting concentrated volleys at the second and third levels. Tens of our men fell.

As if delighted by the horror, the blizzard grew in intensity and was burying the dead where they were undisturbed.

Two wooden bridges were finally carried to the breach, and laboriously hauled forth, so the mass of men huddling behind their shields in the breach, could act.

They began chanting.

"Balic! Balic!" and banging their shields. They got up, and moved for the moat, the bridge above their heads, and the first men with shields out. They filled the breach, their faces screwed with anger, their mouths panting, open, eager to get to grips with men they could fight.

I nodded and snapped my fingers. Around me, mostly hidden by shadows and on other hastily built parapets, archers and two ballistae prepared. The ballista shot first. They tore at the thick ranks, taking down ten and then more, throwing the shields into ruin and the men behind them as well. Then, the arrows began tearing men down, leaving them howling— some even jumped to the moat to escape the arrows—and still, the men were pushing in from behind.

Madly, bravely, the foe kept coming. They climbed the ladders, their archers tore down our men, those especially who braved fighting their men climbing up the ladders, and our men on top began firing on the archers, and it seemed like a game designed to kill everyone.

The bridges were picked up again.

Our ballista fired again.

The bridges fell yet again.

One was bashed to pieces by corpses falling on it and a bolt that tore at the planks, but the other one doggedly came up and over the carnage, carried up and forth by the madly brave men. A bald captain with huge moustaches was screaming at the men, who exerted all their strength. On top, some enemy had reached the second floor, and I heard spears finding flesh and armor as a furious battle was being fought. Men were falling out of the second floor in numbers.

"Fire already!" I screamed.

The ballista fired again. The captain was thrown back. The bridge, the men carrying it full of arrows, finally brought it inside, pulled it up, and it crashed down. The men, six, seven, fell one by one.

"Ready!" our captain yelled, and men lifted their

spears behind the makeshift stone wall.

Shields first, the enemy rushed to the bridge. The bridge was bounced up and down with their weight. Our end of it fell in to the moat and spilled the men forward.

New companies surged forward and saw the moat. Many fell to arrows and the final ballista bolts and still pushed through, pulling corpses out of the way. The stones were red with blood, and the walls heavy with snow. It all seemed almost unreal.

The enemy seemed as if it was made of stone.

They continued to advance, shields up, many falling to arrows, others falling into the moat.

One ballista had found one more spear, and it fired again, the spear impaling a young standard bearer and a female guard, breaking the bridge.

"Inside and fill it!" yelled a man in the breach. "Corpses will be our bridge! Get in and climb over them, you damned cowards!"

He died to arrows and a stone.

The soldiers heard him and surged over. They dragged stones and corpses and threw them down, rushed over, fell, and filled the moat. They wept, bled, and cursed, and soon, they began climbing out of it.

Our men pushed spears into their flesh, their weapons hefted overhanded. They stabbed down, back and forth, back and forth, and butchered the enemy. More came, more died and fell, and so it went on until the moat was full, the corpses filled the yard, and still, they came, crawling over their dead, pulling back their wounded and dying like it mattered little to them.

The standards of the Skull and of the Mask were moving near the courtyard gate. There, I saw a horned mask, the draugr screaming at her men. Another rode past her, whipping at someone who refused orders.

I got up and jumped down, pointing a finger at the breach. Behind, far in the hall, the great ballista, one that had been pre-sighted to the far gate, finally opened fire.

The great ballista, twice the size of the others, meant to sink ships, shuddered as the bolt was released.

The air itself seemed to groan as the bladed spear, the length of a small galley, flew past the breach. It tore through the thronging brave mass of the enemy, then ripped a man from a horse and disappeared into the horde of men, where the standards and the draugr were busy.

A standard fell. A man was rolling on the ground, armless. Two horses were kicking their hooves into the air. One general and many captains were still.

One corpse, half under a horse, was headless. A horned helmet was next to it, rolling around on a snowy, red stone.

The draugr king, screaming with anger, rode away.

The enemy, horns blowing, retreated. We let them go.

We proceeded to replace men, clear the moat,

recover the arrows, and then, we rested.

Nima came down to me and leaned her head on her arms. "We lost over three hundred on top. Fifty here below. Many are just wounded, but if they get in …" Her eyes looked over the terrible battle scene. She raised herself. "We will recover only half of the arrows and ballista shots. The catapults keep hammering their camps, and they cannot stay there. They'll sleep out in the cold."

"They'll be back this night," I said. "We sleep in shifts. I shall stay here."

She placed a hand over mine. "Will you tell me what happened here? You met Balic."

I nodded. "I met Balic."

"And they say there were jotuns here," she said. "Is that possible?"

I nodded. I showed her the ax. "They died. There are more."

She leaned back. "Is Balic dead?"

I pushed the thought of Rhean from my head, and she came back. I shook my head and felt cursed forever. "Balic," I said softly, "mattered little. We must win this battle, and then we shall deal with Balic's …" I went quiet.

"Wife," she said. "Queen Rhean," she said, and saw the sadness in my eyes. "She hurt you," she said.

I nodded. "She, and one other. It seems I must suffer for her, forever."

She punched me and got up. "Putting her under the ax will heal the wounds, eh? Now, I have arrows to find."

I could only hope she was right.

***

That night, they did come again. This time, they took the moat fast and pushed to the stone wall. They were bitter, angry, and desperate, and only after two hours of fighting and slaying them, archers firing volleys at them, they finally crawled away.

Resolutely, bloodily, we repulsed them to Helheim.

That morning, we slept, ate, and sat, waiting. I watched their miserable camps, enjoyed the terrible storm that kept brining in new snow to the land, and watched the enemy dead and wounded being heaped in the depths of the ruins so their live companions couldn't see them.

They had lost at least three thousand men. We, nearly eight hundred.

Soon, their horns were blaring, and slowly, the half-frozen legions got to their feet and moved up again. They came again—frozen, hungry, desperate. We threw them back, using stones and debris as our arrows were spent. They stayed out of arrow range, and no longer went back in. They burned wood, warmed themselves, and came again.

They came three times that day, and we repulsed them again and again.

We lost hundreds of men doing so. Our weapons were spent, and men tired.

The enemy was down to three thousand men, barely a single legion, and retired for the night, the men walking in the snow like a stream of skeletons.

They didn't come that night.

***

The next morning, they no longer came.

I watched the enemy camps from the top. Their remaining tents were heaped with snow that kept falling, and most of them were hiding in the ships. Fires were burning on the piers where men were warming themselves.

Maggon and Nima were there with me. I saw Saag far below, and men were hauling new arrows up to the keep. There weren't enough, but it helped. Maggon was shaking his head and scratching his chin. "I feel sorry for the pitiful bastards. They ate their horses last night. I could smell it in the wind. A soup of bone and gristle, and I bet they ate it mostly raw."

"I don't pity them," I said coldly. "Their last draugr, the king?"

"He keeps out of sight," Nima said. "We have done well."

"Any other draugr lord or lady the sentinels might have seen?" I asked.

"No," she said and gave me a quick look. "She's not there."

Maggon looked at the enemy and didn't ask what she had meant.

She wasn't there. I might have felt her, if she were. Nima was right.

"They have few thousand men able to fight," Nima went on. "Should we attack them?"

"The ships must not be harmed," I said. "But, alas, we have no time."

"Are we busy?" Maggon asked. "The men are actually bored now. They know they can keep the breach by now. We should harass them at least."

"No. Spare the arrows. Next time," I told them, cocking my head, "they will have catapults and other siege equipment. We will be tested to the limits."

Nima frowned at me. "Why?"

"Because I can hear them coming," I said. "And now, we shall finally face their full might. And hopefully, if things go well, they must face ours."

Through the blizzard, we heard deep drums. They echoed across the land, and Saag and his men below looked startled. Riders came from the blizzard and waved hands at him, and Saag turned up to me.

I nodded, and he turned and led his men away.

"Lisar Vittar?" Nima asked, massaging her neck. "She is here, then."

I nodded, and men on all the levels gathered to look at the enemy that was marching for us. Most had been told they might. Most knew what it would imply. The enemy wasn't marching to the city. They emerged from the snow and marched for the eastern edge of the city. There were heavy lines of infantry, men swathed in cloaks, their shields swinging. The great column looked like a snake or gigantic caterpillar. The White Lion's cavalry, those of Harrian, rode on the flanks. Aten's thousand came forth, and a depleted legion from the east, having marched from the coast to aid her, were there. Millar Illir and Ontar, Palan, and the others, victorious from their war near Hillhold, were there, company after company marching on, pushing resolutely through the snow. Low in supplies, their gear war-torn, they looked like a hungry beast preparing for a meal. Ten thousand strong, they were there to destroy us, to finally finish with us, and then, they would rule Red Midgard.

With them came a train of their remaining, stolen supplies and taken standards, prisoners, and slaves. With them, also a massive train of catapults, ballistae, and shot for the weapons.

They were led by the White Lion herself.

She was swathed in cloaks, held her barbed spear on her side as she looked up at me, her confidence unbroken. She wouldn't fail. Whether she knew I had killed Balic, I had no idea.

With her rode some ten to twenty draugr. Many were royals, or princes and princesses, easy to spot by the horned helmets. Many others had fallen, but what remained was prepared and gathered. Next to her, very close, she guided a king from Palan, the Bull proud in standard behind him. It was, perhaps, her former husband.

Gal?

Yes. Rhean had said …

I shook my head to clear her off my thoughts. Lisar was speaking to another, a short man, and pointing a finger at me. Her body-language looked like she was proud of him.

It was likely her son.

Lisar's army heaved past the walls and faced the Ugly Brother from the east, her troops setting up camps from the coast to the woods. They began setting up the siege. She rode back and forth the entire time, ignoring people demanding her attention, especially men from the two miserable legions in the city, and kept staring at the fortress.

Then, she finally stopped and called out.

Out of the masses of troops, a party of men walked out. They wore tunics alone, had no need for coats of cloaks, and held two handed axes. Their hair was blond, their beards as well, and all listened to Lisar, and then looked up at me.

I would have to fight soon.

She had jotuns on her side.

CHAPTER 11

That night, very few people slept. Instead, we prepared. The captains were building new defenses inside the main hall, ones that faced to the east. Wood, stone, and debris were being heaped into a wall. Men would face that way, as well as hold the breach that already had claimed so many of the enemy.

Maggon, muttering, was sure the whole thing would fall on our heads.

It was possible.

The siege would bombard us mercilessly. It seemed impossible the enemy could set them up in the snow, but magic helped, and we had watched the draugr casting fire fields to clear the snow and ice, and so, it would all start soon. Walls around the fort would go down, and the fort's side would crumble. In places, there would be more breaches, and so, the captains were trying to teach our companies how to disengage in an orderly fashion, so as not to get trapped by the enemy that would try to enter from the gates and the breaches at the same time. When the battle would move upstairs, we could make them pay.

Of course, the draugr and the jotuns would not let spears and pikes butcher their men like we had before.

They would be involved and, inside, calling for spells.

Oil, stones, and what arrows we had were ready. On

the roof, hundreds would make life terrible for Lisar's legions, and inside, others would try to hold the gate. The archers were now arming themselves with spears and swords looted from the dead, and the ballista, which had but few scavenges spears left, had been redeployed strategically.

Everyone prayed, save for me. I felt Bolthorn watching, and I knew it was alert, and waiting.

We would have to beat them. Surrender was not an option.

The prospect seemed dubious. My newly found mentor was silent. It had left me with Bolthorn, and I was terrified to ask it for anything.

This time, I'd not be below. I'd fight on top. The jotuns, I was sure, would come in that way.

I walked the roof. I watched the enemy preparing, and I watched the land beyond them.

We would have to last one day. At least that long.

I heard warning shouts.

"For Hillhold," echoed below, and then from every throat.

I saw why. There were enemy rushing around the ten catapults. Officers were yelling, and then, men pulled at levers. The weapons made an eerie sound as they tore through the air. The enemy began hammering the outer wall of the fortress, their crews working in the cruelling cold like ants, likely trying to keep warm.

First, they took down the city walls, to make it easy

to shift from one breach to the next.

We heard the outer walls falling apart and saw how the huge stone-shots arching through the snow-fall and rolling in the courtyard.

Then, they began breaking down the outer wall of the Ugly Brother.

It was thick. It took time.

Most hit the fort's eastern walls, near the second floor, and dust was falling with each strike, and the fortress was shaking like a man in fever. Eventually, stone and wood chips began dropping and rattling on the floor.

And then, suddenly, there was a crack.

And another.

I shook my head and looked around the keep. It might very well fall apart.

In an hour, a shot struck the wall where it was the weakest, and, like it had with my spell, the wall broke from third to second floor, and the debris spread around the bottom halls and created a slope of stone and wood out, and inside. I saw several shots coming down and rolling to the keep, and men were screaming in pain and horror.

Below, they took cover, and waited for the enemy to climb up the breach, and then inside.

The enemy kept firing, and our men suffered. Many, many died.

In the morning, the catapults went quiet.

Four thousand men of the Grim Mask and Skull legions marched yet again for our breach.

Ten thousand of Lisar's men marched for the breach.

***

I stood on top of the tower, looking down at Lisar's army. The Six Spears came first, bitter enemies of the men waiting below. With them, Aten. The snow was falling heavily, but we saw them yelling, mouths open, readying themselves for the butchery, for the terrible climb up the breach, and for the arrows and deadly stones that were sure to rain down on them. A new, small legion was jogging after them. It was likely one from the east, and had marched brutally hard to join Lisar. Their standard had a golden eye on black. The rest followed. Archers were running on their sides, unsure where they would be useful. A mass, ten thousand strong, was going to try to swarm Ugly Brother as ants might the carcass of a boar.

Lisar, her lords, and her kings and queens sat on their horses at the edge of the siege, and there, too, were five men in silvery chainmail.

I turned to the approaching enemy. Around me, hundreds of archers were looking down, shaking with fear and cold. Their skill would be measured, indeed, when shooting in the windy weather. Piles of dead from the night could be seen in the enemy camps. Saag's men had been busy again.

It wouldn't matter, if they took the keep.

The enemy stomped closer, ever closer, a thick column of spears. In the breach on the city side, there were men calling for warning as the miserable two legions were coming for the bloody breach we had defended. There, the battle began.

I waited and looked down as many companies of Lisar's troops reached the breach below, probing under the snow-topped stones, looking for a way to scale it. Many held their shields up.

I aimed to make it hard for them.

The enemy massed before the breach, like a tide trying to conquer a sand-castle. They began climbing it, hundreds of them scrambling up the terrible slope.

On the second and third floors, Nima yelled out an order. Hundreds of bows were lifted, and arrows loosed on both invading armies. The arrows sank down in the quivering mass below, and the butchery began.

The men around me joined in.

They stepped forward and began killing Lisar's exposed men.

I watched them, stood amongst them, and waited.

Men were dying and slumping down on the breach. Ten, and then twenty, fell on their faces. Captain and sergeants and their soldiers seemed to consider this a great opportunity for a good hand-grip as they pulled themselves up using their stricken comrades. They kept coming, at least half their army below.

The jotuns had not moved.

They stood and watched, and that might change at any time.

I stood there, feeling the power of the winter, relishing it, and let the snow caress my hands and face. The spells I'd call would be powerful, terrific things to kill men in great numbers.

I could call for magic to cover the breach in ice. I'd call wind and the terrible force of the blizzard, and it would rip apart a hundred men, more. Some might fall to their blood turning to ice. I felt that braid as well. There were others.

And still, that would not suffice.

It was not enough.

Not by far. A victory was needed, and a sacrifice had to be offered. It sickened me, it made me afraid, and it … thrilled me. I felt ashamed for that.

I looked at Lisar.

The draugr, they were waiting for me to act. I saw them all on their horses, seeing what move I'd make.

I'd have to make it something they couldn't counter.

I'd have to pray.

I had rested after killing Balic. My wounds were mending fast. I would be ready, as ready as I could be. I had let my soldiers do the killing, and the dying. I had planned, commanded, and acted like a king.

Now, I would trade lives for a spell to kill an army.

I told myself to be patient. I tried my best.

Below, thousands of the enemy were now climbing

up the breach. Thousands were concentrating on the slope, waiting for their turn. They were all there, the old enemies, and they were cheering, as they heard the two legions on the city pressing an attack furiously over the moat. Some of Lisar's archers were now shooting arrows to the floors on top, inside the yawning pit that would be filled by waiting soldiery. They were moving closer and closer. Harrian's riders and those of the White Lion were sitting still around the draugr and looking on. A company from Malignborg got up the breach first and jumped in and down the rubble, roaring with joy of battle, invading our hall. Many fell out, killed by arrows, and the sounds of battle intensified.

Our men, the archers below me, and on the roof with me were cursing and firing as fast as they could.

I looked down and closed my eyes. I kneeled, and put my hand in snow.

"Bolthorn, the father of jotuns. Twenty lives for aid," I whispered. "Smite the enemy for me."

There was silence. I felt a brief tug of irritation, of anger, of resentment.

I frowned. I felt unsure I had done it right. I looked to the jotuns, who stood in a row, staring at me, and suddenly thought they might be the reason for the lack of aid. One of them might hold the same blood as I did, in their veins, praying to Bolthorn as well. I might have sounded pitiful.

No.

The deal wasn't fair.

I took a shuddering breath.

"Bolthorn," I whispered, and felt the thing watching me. "A hundred lives of my own men for aid. A hundred men, and a sacrifice of jotuns."

I felt a moment of hesitation as the being considered me. Then, like a father to a stupid child, it spoke, the voice thick as ice.

Your kin, it whispered, *pray to me too. Your kin know better than to do so too often, or to ask for too much and to offer too little. And your kin, they will come for you anyway. I piss on your hundred men.*

I gritted my teeth. "Bolthorn, kill many of the foe below, do it, and I shall grant you much."

It was silent. Then, it whispered. *Much? You would grant the great frost giant, a god of all jotuns, much? You, barely a jotun?*

Yes. Much.

He laughed, and I felt his amusement. Then he spoke. *I have watched you. I have hated your weakness, and applauded your bravery. You think like a man, and then you kill like a jotun, and still you fight battles that are meaningless to me. No gold, no slaves, no honor flow to Bolthorn from your work. And yet, still … perhaps your road will re-make you. Perhaps at the end of it, you shall stand above all others. Aye. I shall give you your wish. You ask for much, too much, and promise me much in return. So here it is. Aid. I shall aid you now. I shall aid you now, and before I aid you again, or even listen to you, you must give me something.*

Yes, I thought.

You must walk a dark road, and you will give me a sacrifice of a great being, a living creature of ancient times. You will give it to me, as well the treasure it carries. If you do, your debt is paid. If you do, you will be what Morag never was, and you agree to serve me forever. We shall feast our great future together. If you survive, this is what shall be. Do not give me these things, and you are what Morag was. An outcast, a man, more than a jotun, and I shall aid those who hate you. Do you agree?

I shook my head and breathed deep. No more aid. Only a sacrifice of a great being, at the end of a dark road, and a gift. His thoughts about our great future, and my servitude to him were all terrifying.

And yet, I needed him. I needed him then.

I raised my ax at the army below. "Smite them for me," I yelled, my mind made up.

He did. He heard my call, he made his pact, and fearing what it would be, I felt him moving a great power around me.

The air seemed to twitch.

The blizzard seemed to twist in the air.

The winds and the twirling snow seemed to stop for a moment. The enemy soldiers, pouring into the keep, hesitated and stopped, and then, they looked up and around, confused, sensing trouble. Many of the archers were backing off, and I saw one of the jotuns, a man with exceptionally long hair, clean-shaven and angry, pointing his ax at me.

Lisar was shaking her head, apparently yelling back.

What followed was terrifying, and men would tell tales of it, and none who had not been there would believe them.

The storm was taken over by Bolthorn. A wind was howling so loudly, it hurt our ears. A mass of snow was rushing around the keep in a massive show of power, wide as roof, and as thick as the fort itself. It whirled on top of me, and the fortress groaned with its power. It snatched archers from the roof, it grabbed men from the other levels, and tossed papers, supplies, weapons, ballista, and broken furniture with it. A part of the breach widened, the stones falling silently as we held our ears. The powerful spell-storm rushed around, growing before our eyes, a swirling creature of ice and snow, and I watched the hordes of men below, cowering and praying, pissing themselves.

The price for this would be terrible. Bolthorn wanted something that would change everything. I was sure of it.

It would change what I was, and everything I had begged for, and prayed for, and hoped for, all my life. It would cost me my humanity.

Of course, I'd not have to walk that dark road.

I could be Morag, and settle to rule men. To rule well. The power suddenly stopped, and the snowy monstrosity seemed to stay still in the air. Then, it formed into a ball, and smashed down, looking like a fist made of ice and snow. It smote the breach, the stony slope, and the troops and archers around it. The power exploded in a brutal force of the god itself into the hapless men and threw them around for miles. Broken, beaten, torn, the legions suffered a terrible calamity. Stone, men, and armor fell in a wide arc, some raining to the bay, others around to the woods and the city, and white and bloody snow rained on who had survived.

Many thousands of the enemy had not.

Their corpses littered the ground, and their wounded were crawling amid snow, stone, blood, and discarded armor and flags.

The breach was gone, flattened. It almost seemed too good to be true, and it was.

The fortress seemed to lurch. A corner of the fortress, the one between the two breaches fell with groaning horror, and men were screaming inside as well. I watched as dozens of archers disappeared with half the roof.

The sound ended, and the wobbling half of the fortress remained standing.

I turned to look down to the gutted fortress. The wind and the blizzard returned to normal, and I had to shade my eyes to see what had taken place inside.

The breach where we had fought remained. The stairways as well. Half the levels were still there. Men were looking in shock at the fallen half of the fortress.

I saw Nima, sitting below on the third floor, and staring at the destruction below.

A thousand men and women had been crushed.

I looked over the enemy. They had lost multiple legions. Of the ten thousand, some six to seven were standing up, horrified, looking at the terrible destruction.

And yet, it would not be enough.

They would still keep coming.

Bolthorn, his immense power spent on my prayer, would exact a heavy price from me.

So many dead. So many.

A jotun wouldn't care. Father had spent his men ruthlessly, but felt sorry for it. But I still did. For a time, at least.

Men in the keep were gathering up their fallen arrows, bows, and rushing to create defenses around the stairways. In the lowest level, there were sounds of battle again.

Many of them looked up at me, as I stood there on the roof, and all thought it was my doing. Fear and anger were clear in their faces, and, also, looks of meek obedience.

I turned to look at the jotuns, and they were finally moving. They walked forward, pushing past the riders.

Lisar was yelling at her standard-bearer. He was riding forward and waving the standard furiously.

Horns were braying, and the bashed and battered remains of the legions answered. They gathered in companies. Their generals were pushing men together, companies to each other. Near decimated legions found their standards and took places with the others.

They marched forward, staring at the great, gutted keep with a mix of loathing and fear.

I lifted my ax, pulled out the shield, and watched the jotuns.

They shifted and took to wings. There were five, and then, there were seven huge, white eagles, as two joined them from the woods.

They took to the sky, beating their wings frantically, banking hard in the storm, and then, they suddenly dipped and flew to the storm, disappearing in it.

I rushed around, looking up to the sky, then down to the keep.

The Skull and the Mask legions were already pushing in, spreading around the once so deadly moat, and climbing over the heaps of rubble. The enemy were running across the fields in the east.

Maggon was yelling. "Move to the second floor! Fast, but orderly! Now!"

They began clearing the below, retreating to hold the stairway.

I had to find the jotuns.

There was no sign of them.

Archers around me were loosing arrows below,

desperately. Our men below were pushing spears at the legionnaires. Desperately, they fought to give the archers time to kill the teaming foe, and more of the militia were preparing with spears on each level, while others tossed down stones to the enemy.

The battle was born of a desperate chaos, and it would be lost.

I saw the thousands of Hammer Legionnaires, enraged, climbing through from the east. They came in ones, in pairs, in squads and companies, and with them were horned helmeted draugr. Arrows were falling around them, tearing to the heart of the enemy, and felling men by the dozens, but it wasn't enough. They swarmed through the debris to aid the Mask and the Skull legions, and far below, defending the stairway of the first level, our hundreds were determined to hold until an orderly retreat upstairs was finished. That stairway was full of men, all loping up.

What I thought was Lisar's husband stood forward, riddled with arrows, his horned helmet bobbing up and down.

He released a line of fire that cut our massed men around the stairway in half. It was a wall of fire, and it burned with terrible heat, and many died. The wall of fire spread to the stairs. Hundreds were cut off.

Arrows, stones rained down on the enemy, but finally tasting revenge, the legionnaires pushed in, hacking into the men isolated below, pulling them down, bashing them dead, and the draugr were laughing as they followed the men for the stairway that was filled with men, going up while fighting, streaming upstairs, where officers and Nima were pushing them further, so those below could get there.

The stairway was a butcher's block. The fire died away, and swords and spears took its place.

Slowly, agonizingly slowly, the men fled up, being pushed and butchered.

The draugr, calling spells to kill indiscriminately, loosed fire and more fire at the men holding on below, or up in the stairs. Dozens of men were jumping down, running up, flaming, dying horribly. Many were Hammer Legionnaires. Some of the enemy, dodging such fires, got to the second floor with the mass of our men, and spears began stabbing them down.

Gal Vittar was coming up the stairs, a fiery shield and whip in his hands.

He slashed the whip around, taking down men. He was nearly on the second level, where he bashed his shield on one of his own men, flattening him, and the whip slapped down and killed six of our defenders. He was trying to take that level on his own.

I prepared to call down a spell at him. I was robbed of the opportunity by Nima, who had all her remaining archers shoot down at the creature.

Dozens of arrows snapped into the draugr, shocking him. He roared and stepped up, tottering forward, and then, Nima hefted a rock and threw it. That rock tumbled true through the air and struck his helmet, crushing his skull. I watched as the enemy was rolling down below, where more legionnaires pushed up with few other draugr.

"Ready the third floor!" I yelled. "Retreat back up!" Hundreds of them were still on the second, and they were not prepared to defend against the draugr. They looked up and began running up the stairs. I'd have to stop the enemy undead at the stairway of the third level.

I turned to go there.

Then, I saw the white birds circling the tower, and they swooped in to the third level, and disaster struck.

I heard the calls of distress, the crunch of ax-born butchery, and wails of the fallen.

I shapeshifted into a white wolf and rushed across the roof for the stairway. I rushed down to the fourth level, where hundreds of Nima's men were preparing rocks and arrows. I rushed past them for the third level and found a mass of men looking down.

Below, six jotuns were in a terrifying shieldwall around the stairway—tall, dreadful, and deadly.

Their axes were heaving at the mass of men trying to get up from the second level and at the men trying to push them away on the third. Arrows were striking the jotuns, and they seemed not to care. Below, I could see the Hammer Legionnaires taking the second level, grimacing with rage as they tore at the men and women desperately trying to keep them down, while knowing there was no way up. The enemy were there to avenge themselves, pushing at the defenders with brutality. Our warriors were cut off in the second level, and it looked desperate.

"Come down, rebels, come down!" called out the enemy below, thousands strong and enraged. "We'll show you Hillhold again!"

Our men, bloodied to their chins, most wounded, fought in the stairways, in the second level, and sold their lives by taking lives.

I prepared to fight a desperate, last battle.

At least I'd not have to pay Bolthorn, I thought, and chuckled as I pushed past men on the stairs. I pressed forward and saw how the massive, gleaming axes claimed lives by the dozens. It truly looked like a monstrous butcher had set up shop in the middle of the stairways. Men tried to get past, and failed. A boy pushing up from below, managed to dodge under the legs of one, then another, but was stepped on by the third. He died fast, thankfully.

One jotun, the one with no beard and huge, flowing hair, hesitated and looked up at me as I walked down the stairs.

"Ah, cousin!" he laughed. "You fool. You'll pay bitterly for what you did. I wonder what he asked of you. Nothing cheap, I bet! No blood-kin of his should ask him for such favors. I would never, nor would my sister and father, but we are the lost ones, and you think you are not, eh? Fool. But perhaps I shall release you from such fear, eh?" He eyed his friends. "Hold them down. Give me room!"

They nodded and kicked and hacked down at our men, killing ten, twenty, so fast, so terribly that bits and pieces flew around the third level and over to the second.

The jotun shifted, and a white wolf, equal to my size, loped up for me. The jotuns tightened their wall of death around the stairs.

I snarled and jumped down as my foe came up, and we crashed together in the middle of the stairs, scattering men. His jaws snapped over the fur in my neck and ripped at it. I missed as I tried to bite his. He was shaking and tearing at me, his claws deep in my skin, and I rolled with him, a step down, then another, until I managed to clamp my maw around his throat. He yelped and changed, and I changed with him, two gigantic bears snarling down the stairs.

We landed amid the wall of jotuns.

They dodged forward, hesitating as their leader and I roared savagely and tore at each other in animal rage.

He surged forward, and I changed and jumped back. My ax snapped down fast.

It split into his arm, and he fell on his side, changing, screaming as he watched his missing arm, blood pumping out crazily. I kicked him, slashed the ax to his throat and spat on his face.

The jotuns around me stared at me with horror and then rage.

I charged forward and, pushing one, I fell down the stairs with him for the second level. We fell off the stairs and crashed amid battling men.

I was faster than he was.

I chopped down at the struggling jotun, who fell dead.

Bloodied Hammer Legionnaires and our people were staring at me, all over the level. I grinned, and looked up to see five jotuns staring at me.

I grasped the fallen jotun's head, and spat on his face. "Filth. Weak and cowardly. Come, and show me you are better!"

They roared, moved, and I rushed forward, my ax slaying legionnaires as I pushed into a company of them, hacking about.

The jotuns followed, heedless of who stood against them. They were emptying the stairs, axes chopping, their eyes on me. They tore to the legionnaires and our people, axing their victims down, eyes wide with anger, beards bloodied.

I turned, changed into a sauk, a white lizard of armor and claws, and pushed deeper into a surprised company of the Grinning Mask, who had been stabbing spears at me.

Still, the jotuns came.

"Kill the Ymirtoe!" one jotun roared. "Don't let him get away!"

The jotuns didn't let the Hammer Legionnaires stop them. Their axes went up and down, and they tore to my enemy and killed some of our fleeing archers. Blood, limbs, and bits of armor flew in the air as they pursued me. They stepped over and through the legionnaires, who died in scores to their savagery. A draugr had come up and hissed a command.

"They are all together. At them!"

And so, the enemy fought back, finally, pikes stabbing and stabbing again up at the giants, dozens of them, two taking the place of any that fell. Then, one lucky sergeant finally tore his spear into a jotun neck, stopping the giant in his tracks, and others pulled him down with hooked axes.

The other four hesitated, and stopped pursuing me, and hacked at the foe. I was now being surrounded by legionnaires armed with hammers, the blows coming with painful accuracy and strength, so I fled back towards the jotuns, changing into myself, and hacked into the backs of the men fighting the jotuns. I stepped into the middle of the jotuns, who spat, cursed, and hacked around, and I joined them.

The enemy came at us.

The pikes were thick as a forest, and our shields clanged with hits. Arrows rained down on us from below and above. Each ax-strike took down an enemy or two. The sweeping, terrible weapons cut down lines of them.

The draugr was pushing forward, and I felt him braiding a spell together.

I turned and did the same, and he and many of his men fell on their knees, spitting a near endless stream of ice.

The draugr soon understood the spell would not kill it, its blood old, cold anyway, and useless and, tearing its helmet off so it could see better, it stepped forward, calling for fire.

It met my ax, and I quickly retreated to the line of the jotuns.

It was utter, horrible chaos as the legionnaires tried to kill all the jotuns. It lasted for a while, until we began retracing our way to the stairs. We were all bleeding, all in a battle rage, and the enemy, despite their best efforts, couldn't stop us.

They tried, one more time.

They rushed to the stairs after us, many of their larger fighters holding hammers and axes.

There were a dozen of them.

The jotuns struck shields together and held the stairs easily. Tireless, cruel, brutal, they beat the enemy into a pulp, and it seemed our people, skulking in their dozens in the far ends of the second level and above us on the third, and the enemy simply stopped fighting so as not to attract attention.

There were thousands of the enemy below, but like the peace in the heart of a storm, the enemy stopped for a moment.

One jotun looked up at me. "This is no peace, you bastard-born thing of Morag. Know that."

I grinned and axed him in the face, kicking one other forward to the spears and fled back up, changing and rushing fast as a wolf.

I looked down and saw the jotuns changing, bleeding, and fleeing the tower, beating their wings furiously. There were only two left.

I leaned on the wall and looked at the mass of enemy slowly making its way up. Our men were running up the stairs, those who could, and our people began to prepare for defense.

Nima came to me. She looked exhausted, and she was bleeding from her shoulder.

"How many do they have?" I asked, holding my head. I was bleeding profusely all around my body.

"Six thousand," she said. "Perhaps five. We have less than two. Maggon is counting them. The archers are tossing stones now. We have no more arrows."

I nodded. We had to hold a bit longer.

The enemy tried to get up with pikemen. They swarmed the stairs and failed. Then, they came a second time. When they were resting, we listened with dread as they searched the floors below and hunted for our survivors in the gutted keep. The terrible calamity that had taken place, and what was taking place below, sapped our remaining strength. Others looked down, bitterly disappointed by what they had seen and endured. Some prayed, others wept.

Most all looked at Nima for strength. She was going from man to woman.

They looked at me with hope, for I was their strongest weapon, but many looked at me with distrust and fear.

They had a good reason.

Their suffering had been great, their losses greater, and still, they would have to suffer more.

And then, I heard something. It was far, but not too far, and I felt relief surging through me.

I got up. Men were watching me, shifting, thinking the enemy was coming again.

"The nobility of Red Midgard," I called out, and they all turned to look at me.

There was even silence below.

I pointed my ax down the stairs. "We have held the enemy, we have starved the enemy, we have put his best into bitter shame, his horned ones to graves. And we have not lost. We have endured against all the odds. You people will be rewarded for your glory. You shall all have your own castle, and as old men, and as ancient frail women, you shall tell the tale to your grandchildren and, no doubt, to theirs. Rich, affluent, and scarred with the enemy blade, people shall look up to you as gods for all time."

They smiled, too tired for more.

The enemy below, began banging heir shields, chanting. "Death! Death!"

"Listen to them," I called out. "Echoes of the dying. Listen to the woods instead."

And then, somewhere out in the snowy woods, men and women were cheering.

I heard the voices and smiled.

They would be refugees that Nima had called to answer the call of their king. They would be scattered, impoverished nobles and men of lost garrisons. They would be bastards and thieves, with good men. They would be men of Dagnar and Fiirant who had survived Hillhold's battle all the people Thurm had mustered in Hillhold. They were all out there and marching from the woods.

If lucky, there would be something more as well.

The effect of their arrival was immediate.

Below, in the keep, men were calling out orders. Harsh commands echoed, and the army turned to march out.

Nima was watching me.

I nodded at her. "A thousand men shall hold this. One thousand. And you shall command them," I told her.

"Will you go out to lead?" she asked, incredulous. "They are still boiling for a fight. You might die."

I nodded. "I must face Lisar in battle. I must pull her apart. I'll take half of the boys and girls here and join the army. Keep this place for me. Don't let them get past the breaches in the walls. Find arrows. Stones. Keep it."

"As long as I have a crown and Nallist," she said with a grin, "you shall have this fort."

CHAPTER 12

The enemy was deploying into a wide shieldwall. In it, were men of ten and more legions. They were all palest of ghosts of what they had once been. They had perhaps four to five thousand in the ranks, many wounded, all tired. Their standards were waving proudly, their men standing tall, ragged and hungry.

The remaining draugr royals were standing behind the men.

Most of the kings were gone. Few queens were left. There were princes that had been raised, cousins to power, lesser in power, commanding ranks of the living. Their horned helmets were visible behind the ragged ranks. Lisar was in the head of White Lion and Harrian cavalry, now only three hundred strong.

"They look ready for ax-business, don't they?" Thrum muttered, eyeing his ax and then mine with approval. "Suits you. I know that weapon, though."

"I cannot use it," I said. "I've barely learnt swords from—"

"Your Taram the Draugr," he agreed. "Keep your shield up and bash down with the ax. Usually that does—"

I saw Roger in the ranks. He avoided looking at me.

"He came back to Hillhold," Thrum said. "Tried to give orders. Had some support from some panic-filled fools. I put an ax to their necks, save for the high and mighty here. See, it is simple. You really only must make sure it is the blade part that touches the target. You have—"

"Did you know about the other clan of jotuns?" I asked him. "And why are they with … the enemy?"

He scratched his neck. "Well, now. There seems to me another terrified noble in the ranks today. Yes. I knew they had left with Medusa. She had an army and a clan of them. Some hundreds. I've not had time to wonder if any survived. They have chosen their side, and if you knew anything about jotuns, Maskan, you would know their king's oaths are their oaths. They are with the draugr. Not much you can do about that. Be glad you are alive. Balic's gone, then?"

"I killed him. His wife?" I shook my head. "Vampire. There are others."

He looked grim. "There are some in Svartalfheim. They hunt the tunnels."

I looked back to the woods. "Is she out there?"

He smiled. "Quiss is fine. She's pissed you sent her to safety. Came to Hillhold full of fury. She was anxious as shit. She is going to be here soon. She is bringing in five hundred men. They are late." He winked. "I made sure they would be late. I assumed you didn't want her in charge after the debacle, and since you sent her away … " He shrugged. "Your call."

"I would see her out of this one," I said. "Like I wanted to see her out of the way in Nallist. Thank you."

"A new queen," Thrum wondered. "A fast-moving bastard, you are. They say she is popular."

"She'll have to cut her teeth with the nobles," I told him. "She'll do well. She is quite ferocious. As is her brother."

He was silent. We watched the troops riding back and forth in the enemy ranks.

"There are two out there," he murmured. "Your kin. I sense them."

"My kind," I said softly. "Though, not of the most ancient blood."

He scratched his head. "If a jotun presents itself to me, I'll use the ax, ancient blood or not. It will flow just fine, no matter how high and fine the neck. I hear you did as well? One of them claimed to be more than just common, skin-changing shit? Men speak of it."

"One of them claimed to be of the high blood," I said. "Like I am. Like Morag was, and grandfather."

"Aye," he said tiredly. "That blood. Look, you have to take a grip—"

"Not a one word more about ax, and the art of axing," I snarled.

"Grip of your own destiny, Maskan," he said with asperity. "I told you this already. I hear …"

His eyes went to the fortress. It was a torn, tilted, bloody mess, and the ground outside it was littered with corpses.

I held my face. "I was going to die, Thrum."

"You were going to die," he agreed. "And yet, you survived. How?"

I shook my head. "It was that command post. They had set up an ambush."

He frowned and gave me a curious glance.

I spoke on. "I was surrounded. I was herded like a cow. Then, I heard someone telling me, so very gently, in my head, that I should beg for aid," I told him. "That I should touch snow with my hand and beg for help. It would feel stupid, except the voice was real. It was …"

"Magical," he said.

"I did, and I felt something," I said. "It was there, as if it had always …"

"Been," he confirmed. "We know. I've seen it before. There are just a few jotuns who are linked to the old gods."

"Ancient blood," I said softly. "It is terrifying."

"You are of the blood," he murmured, while watching our lines merging from the woods. "I know. Morag was. I know."

I gave him a quick glance. "Aye. Anyway, I received a boon at first. A small one, just enough to give me a chance with Sand. I survived. Then, later, that same voice that had instructed me, was almost enraged, and told me I am a jotun."

"I've been telling you that for ages," he said with a sigh. "Every day. You didn't know? Is the voice and this … being the same thing?"

I shook my head. "No. The voice I hear seems like someone desperate to guide me. A spell, perhaps. Something special. A link."

"Oh," he said softly. "A lover's mark."

"What?"

"Never mind. It is a little something I will speak with you after the battle. You called for it again?"

"I did," I said. "I called for it twice." I waved my hand at the fort. "No, thrice. It aided me, but …"

"It asks for lives," he said. "Or favors. Wicked favors. You must sacrifice lives to it, eventually, always lives. The more innocent, or unsuspecting, or unattached in your conflicts, the better. If you do not comply," he told me, "you will see misfortune when the winter arrives. Your kin, I know, once stood and fought each other. Both were of the blood, Bolth… this thing of yours, waited to see which one would give him a better boon. With such a contest, Maskan, you always lose. What did you give away?"

I gnashed my teeth together and stared ahead. "One life. Then, ten. Aten's men."

"That would have displeased him," Thrum said. "That is *cheating*. They are the least precious of your allies. And for that? How much?"

We watched the terribly carnage where the storm has smitten the ground.

"For that?" I whispered. "I must walk this road to the end. I must give it a great life, a great gift, and I shall receive a great favor. It will give me power, and demand servitude."

"Oh," Thrum said happily. "You had better pay this price, or he will take all that you love, have, or would have, and he will hunt you forever. You'll be a hermit, alone, and herded like a rabid wolf. Winter and cold will find you and your loved ones." He gave me a long, considering look. "It will change you. It might make you dangerous. Hel is one thing. Bolthorn, aye, I name him, is another. What will happen if he asks for my life in exchange for a victory?" He grinned.

"I remember you have been asking to die for a while," I said with a smile.

"You bastard," he murmured. "You are thinking about renegading on this pact?"

"I am. I would lose all I have fought for. Morag's realm would be gone to people like Nima and Saag, and Roger. I am torn. I see the humans who are so brave. They believe in what I believe. How can I just … leave them? And father didn't leave them. He loved them well enough to fight to the end for them. They feared, but loved him."

He smiled. "The people hate you. They loved him because they thought he was a man."

"They do fear me," I said. "But I just gave them victory. They do love me."

He hesitated. Then he shook his head, and I saw he had a large, thick scroll in his hand. I tried to take it, and he slapped my fingers. "Fine. I think we must fight this battle, and then you get this. I found it on Roger. We need to speak about some other things as well."

"If we survive, I must go to Aten," I told him. "But we shall discuss it after the battle."

He grunted.

He shook his head. "How did you survive a vampire?"

"In that," I said, "I was … lucky. It was … hateful, and wonderful. It still is. She made me love her. And I did, and I do. Then she let me speak, and Bolthorn saved me. I love her, and I had to kill her and I have never felt more confused. I doubt she can frighten me again, though."

He grunted again. Troops, mine from the fort and the new, were marching to the field. I saw Hal, who saluted me with his sword, and then led men forward to match the enemy line.

"Can you trust this Nima?" he asked.

"She is greedier than a rat in a larder," I muttered. "She'd swap me for a chunk of silver, I think, but she has kept her word, and she gave me victory. It cost them terribly."

We looked at the line of six thousand men and women.

Nima had summoned many to my flag, and they had gone to find Thrum in Hillhold. They had answered.

Alantia's warriors were there and took their places

on the left. Nallist's militia, a few hundred who had survived early battles in the city, a thousand men of the local nobles, their shields and gear filthy from hiding in the woods, walked grimly forward. The rest from Alantia were Saag's archers, one thousand and a half, including the men I had brought from the fort, and they spread before our ranks, and hundreds were bunching together on the far ends of the flanks, where they were pushing stakes to the snow and the icy ground below. They were low on arrows, but eager to finish the war.

Fiirant's people strode forward to the middle. There were men from the fort, and those who had survived Hillhold's butchery. They were all militia and men-at-arms. They were men that had marched from the broken fortress with me and looked grim as devils, and ready for revenge.

There were nobles, a hundred and more on horses, sitting in lines behind us.

Thrum's two thousand held the right flank, a solid block of terror. Some, mainly evil bastards with magic, were taking places along the entire line, to boost them and to fight the horned draugr.

Hal was on command on the left flank, nervous to the bone.

Magga was standing amid his men in the middle.

A pair of sturdy dverger stood around Roger, who was near middle position. He was not allowed to go and fight with the nobles. His hands were tied. His horse was slow and old.

He was dressed in a splendid armor, and looked bright as a morning.

Every enemy draugr were watching him, likely thinking on how to kill him.

Roger cast a begging look my way. I turned away, and watched the brave people, instead.

They were hunters, bandits, warriors, and fools.

The archers were placing more stakes on the flanks. Many seemed to be only for show, and simply stuck upright in the snow.

"They likely won't attack," Thrum said, bored. "But they cannot get away, either." Thrum smiled happily. "Vittar made a mistake. They should have marched to the city and taken the boats."

"They have no oars of sails," I said. "I made sure. The sea-gate is locked. They didn't bother opening it when they held the harbor for a day."

He smiled. "They are too proud, and make mistakes too. We might end this here. It was a good plan, King. Hal and I managed to make them all come here, and they obeyed. They know this is it. This will save the winter. They do have lots of men in south, though."

"Then, let's make sure they know in the south," I said cruelly, "that there are no survivors or mercy to be had, and the winter is sword-sharp up here."

He spat. "I am fine with that. Still must win this scrap, though. We will."

The enemy was not moving. They were chanting, perhaps singing. It sounded forlorn.

"No Black Ship for them," I murmured. "None shall pick up their heroes."

"Eh?"

"I'll explain later," I said. "What are the other jotuns called? Their name?"

"They are Sons of Ymir," he said darkly. "Ymirsons. Their king and your father were cousins. They, and you Ymirtoes, hated each other. Long grudges over women, lands, and treasure. They claim you stole Grinlark, and the Black Grip from them, once. Jotun-treasure means treasure that someone is seeking to regain. That's what they are, your grip and the stick. It seems that their general Medusa settled them somewhere when they left the battle in Mara's Brow, and before your father did something to that Hand of Hel."

"We need answers, and I have a hunch where one might find such," I said, tapping a scroll on my belt. "But first …"

"Yes," he agreed as he watched the singing enemy. "I think they are either waiting for us to make the first move or to send an invite, at least." He shifted. "Look. I hate to ask you, and I am not sure if you have thought of this, but—"

I turned in my saddle and interrupted him. "After the battle. As you said. When Roger came back, did you ask him why he attacked?"

He nodded. "I though you said you want to speak after the battle?"

"And what did he say?" I pressed.

"That it wasn't his fault. That he had been told to," Thrum said. "Roger's got faults, don't you think otherwise. But as said; after the battle."

"We'll make the first move," I told him, swallowing bile. "Are they ready yet? Are they there?"

"No," he said, sighing. He picked his nose and spat. "Soon."

"Sand is out here," I told him with a smile. "He and a party of killers have been trying to take my life for a while. If you see him, spare him. I doubt he'll fight here, though."

"He is not one for sparing, king. The boy has got wicked evil skill with shadows," he said sternly, eyeing the coast to the south and then the woods to the east. "Soon. They will fight well, the enemy. They have a chance. Our boys don't know sword and shieldwall like they do."

"They have twenty draugr," I said, looking at the undead nobles, silent on their horses. "They depend on them."

"We shall show them our arses," he muttered. "And then, we'll ax them."

"They will beat our militia in a shieldwall. We are short in arrows," I said. "Where are they?"

We both watched the eastern woods.

"They have been marching for a week and more," he answered. "They marched to Hillhold just when we got your orders. They should be in position. Don't you worry about that." He grasped my hand and smiled. "They are here."

On the right flank of the enemy, a forest of spears and flags appeared.

Enemy guards were running before the spears, guards from the ships of the Grinning Mask and Skull legions. There were dozens, and all screaming.

Men's heads turned that way.

Lisar turned to look.

Our men raised their weapons and screamed their approval to the winds.

Through the woods, Red Midgard's last legion, the Stone Watchers from the western coast, men who had been marching to aid Dagnar, had arrived in Alantia instead, and Thrum's people and chosen nobles had guided them well to the enemy flank. There were nearly four thousand of them. Some were holding Dansar's Grave, others guarding Hillhold, many had succumbed to illness during the march, but what was there, were coming forward with vengeance. Ranks of spears gleamed in the wintry light of Lifegiver, and though they were spreading out and not yet killing their enemy, the black and silver mass of the grimmest soldiers of the north promised the exhausted legionnaires doom.

Lisar stared at the enemy for a moment in shock and

then turned to look at the main battle line.

She leaned down on a man next to her, who turned to her standard-bearer.

The flag tipped. Horns brayed. The line twitched and moved. They strode forward. Then, they were screaming defiantly, surging across the snowy field.

Thrum spat. "They'll be coming for us, then. I guess the Watchers count as an invite."

Lisar's great drum beat a wild, steady rhythm and then a wild one, joining the horns, and the legionnaires charged forward in a wall of shields, in a rank of three lines, thousands of them still, the very best, the very luckiest, of our enemies. Chanting, begging for battle, hoping for loot, if victory was granted, their eyes shone with unholy happiness. Our men, obeying calls that echoed across the field, braced their shields. Militia, men-at-arms, and then, Thrum's evil dverger shifted and braced themselves. I rode back and forth, looking for the enemy draugr who all seemed to be riding behind their men.

Lisar's flag dipped, and the Harrian cavalry turned left and rode wildly behind their charging men, their eyes on me.

"Seems she thinks you are the key to the battle," Thrum chortled. "What a waste of good men. Come, King. Let us take cover. Fire when in range!"

Thrum's men lifted crossbows as we walked to the ranks. His dverger were in line, but five hundred at the right flank were deployed in a square.

The nobles on their horses were riding behind us, ready to support us, or any part of the field.

The dverger waited, aimed, and fired. Archers before our ranks and on the flanks lifted their bows, many guarded by stakes weakly struck on the frozen ground, also fired. The arrows sailed across the sky and sunk on the enemy force. Dozens fell, rolled on their faces and backs, and never got up. More arrows reached out, and enemy shields caught many, but men again fell, howling. A great officer, a general, perhaps, fell from his saddle behind the ranks, holding his throat.

The enemy kept coming and stopped for just a second, catching many of the arrows and bolts on their shields, and tossed their last javelins at us.

The javelins tore to our ranks, wounding and killing hundreds, and now, the enemy lifted their spears, their shields banging on each other, and they spurted through a murderous hail of rock, arrow, bolt, and now, spell.

Thrum's dverger, those who knew battle magic best, stepped to the front for just a moment. Their dark and white faces gleaming, white teeth shining like vicious pearls, they released twenty lines of wicked, dark fire. Those lines cut at the oncoming enemy. They burst through snow, shield and flesh and armor, melting iron and bone, leaving men heaps of skeletal, flaming remains to be trampled on by those, who, horrified one and all, filled their places.

It went badly for those legionnaires who were coming for us.

Thousand men had been charging our flank, had caught Thrum's crossbow bolts, and few lines of fire, and they were now cautiously coming forward, ignoring the screams of a draugr. Arrows and javelins fell at the dverger now, dropping one here and another there, leaving even some of the casters silent heaps on the snow, but all the cohesion was gone from the ranks of our enemy as their left flank stalled, while their center and right didn't.

We didn't have men to split them.

We'd have to wait for the Stone Watchers to start flanking them.

Knowing they had to be fast, the draugr and their men fought furiously. In the middle and left, the did. There, the draugr let loose with battle-spells just before the shields struck shields, answering fire with fire. When dverger cast spells, the horn helmets spotted them, and rippling storms of fire left our ranks shattered, and men burned into crisp. What had been a left flank was now a fierce battle of many shieldwalls, in the middle of which draugr rode wildly. Archers were running to the woods and turning to support our men. Hundreds of legionnaires were pushing to the holes, and hundreds of ours tried to stop them. Bitter battle, led by Hal, was brewing into utter chaos, and we were holding them, here and there.

Half the nobles rode that way.

"Rush, Stone Watchers!" I roared.

They were dashing out of the woods now, spreading into lines. Few draugr were calling for fire to stop them and, in places, pushed companies of the Watchers into chaos.

In the middle, the enemy thought Roger was in command. He sat on the horse, and the dverger, seeing the enemy draugr converging on him, dodged away.

Roger spurred his horse and tried to jump down, and failed.

A field of ice and spiky, deadly spears grew from under Roger and ripped him apart. It spread, killing men in the middle. A draugr was casting the spell, guiding it, sitting on his horse, another next to him, holding a fiery spear, and then, both fell from the saddle, one burning into crisp, another with arrow in his skull.

I grasped the ice spell.

I felt it fading as the draugr died, the braid dissolving like a cut rope, but I restored it skillfully. I took it for my own, the great power of the wintry death, I sent it back to the enemy ranks. Snapping, slaying, piercing, and splitting the enemy, I stopped many of the enemy from going forward.

The enemy still came, seeing the broken line.

Skidding, dodging corpses, dozens of them jumped

to the hole made by the icy death.

In the center, fifty nobles rode up, and jumped down, and rushed to block the hole. They banged shields together before the enemy, who thought of trampling them to the snow. They crashed to the skilled noble ranks, and lost so many men, men-at-arms had time to come to pluck the hole. The enemy pushed, tried, and stabbed; the line buckled and held.

In the left, the situation grew worse.

A draugr queen of exceptional beauty threw a spell in the middle of already pressed Alantian men-at-arms and militia of Nallist. It was not a visible spell, not by more than a gust of air, and still, the spell dropped twenty men and ten legionnaires. It robbed men of air, and many, holding their throat, were clawing out of the sphere. The queen, riddled by arrows, was laughing and calling for more spells, and I saw not what happened as the line of Dagnar militia near the dverger left-most ranks broke, and a company of Hammer Legionnaires surged inside, stabbing with swords, taking down a line of men, then hacking down dverger that came to help.

I rode through the ranks and called for magic.

Ice wall split into the enemy, cutting off many, and then, I let go of the difficult spell, the one that turned blood into ice. A captain, hacking down a female sergeant, and his company screamed and fell to the snow, crystal-white and red ice pouring from their bodies and mouths. Arrow struck my shield, another my helmet, and Thrum pulled me back.

The enemy left flank finally found their bravery, and charged the dverger. The shields of the foe banged to dverg ones, and axes hacked them down. Some brave ones jumped over the dverger, in berserker joy, or just eager to die, and soon the entire line was embroiled in horrible battle.

All along the lines, shieldwalls pushed into each other, furious men and women hacking over the shoulders of the first rankers. In many places, the shields made no walls, and terrible chaotic melee took place, embroiling like a cauldron of boiling vegetables. There, is such places, the draugr liked to hunt, killing men with spells of fiery whips, slashing all living equally cruelly. No matter what the battles were like, men fell in scores. I heard Hal screaming for their men to hold. I heard Maggon doing the same.

The discipline of the enemy was starting to tell.

I almost saw our people falling back, and back, and many falling dead as they tried to keep up. The enemy was chanting in many places through the lines. An enemy champion was dancing over a corpse of a captain, not far, before dying to dverg bolt, but the battle was turning.

I saw the Stone Watchers rolling over two draugr and loping very near the enemy right flank, their mouths open now. Some companies of the enemy were turning to hold them.

"Hold! Hold them! Hold them and take their honor! Take their fame! A bit longer!" I yelled, and rode back and forward, and for some reason, for some odd reason, they heard me.

A boy in an overgrown armor lifted his spear and pushed it over the shoulder of his father into a man's eye. "Hold the line! Take their fame!" he shirked. They pushed back. Men around them roared, wept, died, and pushed the enemy back.

"Hold the line! Steal their honor!" a female man-at-arms cried, hacking down with a mace in a wild melee where the Hammer Legionnaires were embroiled in a desperate battle to get though the lines and rip and roll over our men.

We held them. We pushed them back. We lost two to everyone we killed.

The enemy, howling, collected all their draugr. They rode like mad, gathering men to the middle, just when the Stone Watchers hit their right flank with vengeance.

The draugr stood forth. One died to a dverg caster, turning to ice.

The rest released spells.

Fire, a huge inferno, cut our center to ribbons. Snow melted, men turned to ashes, their armor melted, shield crashed, spears blazed, and steel and blood ran in rivulets. Black lines of dead marked the terrible attack.

The center fell. Hundreds died.

Maggon was rushing to us, his cloak on fire, yelling orders, and begging for more men.

The enemy surged forward to the space formerly occupied by our men, some thousand strong, and began to deploy in a circle of spears and shields, standing on the still blazing men.

The draugr were pushing to the shields and turning to make life horrid for the Stone Watchers, who were not butchering the right flank of Lisar's army and rushing for the center.

"Look out!" Thrum yelled.

I dodged instinctively. A spear passed my head.

I looked to the right and saw Lisar's men trampling our archers.

Hundreds were falling, the stakes useless, arrows spent. Many were running for the dverger ranks.

I cursed as I looked from one danger to the other.

The draugr in the middle were now releasing horrifying chaos on the Stone Watchers. I saw the standard falling in flames and companies turning to blackened corpses before the next line crashed to the enemy shield-ring. There, spears stabbed, swords hacked, and men fell, fiery draugr whips slashed, and then, I had no more time to gawk, for Lisar was coming for the dverger.

She turned her troop towards us, lances flashed, and she rode over hundred more of our archers fleeing before her. They did it brutally fast, in a thick line. They rolled over our men, stabbing little, letting their horses pound their enemy to the snow.

They eyed us and lowered the lances.

Thrum spat and called out his commands. "Brace! Walls! Shields overs shields, and Nött curse the bitch and her bully-boys! Let's show them what we are made of."

"Toadstools and boletus shrooms!" called someone, and they all laughed darkly.

The dverger right, the ring of steel, tightened into a thicker formation, with spears and halberds pushing out from holes in the shield fortress, and then, magic flashed at the riders.

Many fell, died in rain of ice, by bolts of lightning, as dverg casters called down magic on the riders.

They came on anyway.

They crashed into the fortress of shields and weapons.

Many fell over their horse's necks. Indeed, a horse was running *over* the shields, before falling and crushing dverger. The enemy stabbed, stabbed, and pulled swords, as ranks of them fell

I saw the queen.

Lisar had stopped and was looking for an opportunity. With her, was a horn-helmeted man, short and like a guard-dog. She saw halberds pulling down a man of White Lion, and then another, and she surged forward. Looking the dverger into the eye, she let loose a war spell. It was a forked lighting—terrible, powerful, and cast in the faces of our boys. It charred some of hers to crisp and then tore apart twenty of ours, their shields flying.

Into this place, the practiced enemy rode.

I pushed into the reeling formation to aid our dverger.

I hacked down a horseman, then another, the dverger pulling two more down. The enemy pushed in relentlessly, dismounting, and while the outer edges of the dverger were doing well, the center was suddenly a death trap where men and dverger were butchered like cows for a feast. There I stood, hacking down man and horse at a time. I was roaring, slaying, a king of bones.

Then, a fiery spell of fire struck my shield.

I fell back.

A fiery whip slammed to my shield again and then over my helmet, tearing metal. The horn-helmeted prince was there, his horse wide-eyed with horror, amid his men struggling in the terrible press. He had a White Lion painted on his shield, and his men suddenly knew I was their real target. They all tried to kill me, they all turned for me, pulling swords where the lance was useless, and fifty of them were trying to get to me, many dying as they abandoned their other foes.

Thrum's dverger pushed on the edges. Ten horses and men fell.

Thrum's wall closed the ranks, and trapped over

forty riders.

I saw Lisar just outside the wall. Her son, inside. "Fallior!" she screamed.

Then, I saw her falling from her horse, the horse a burning ruin braided by some spell by our boys. Outside, archers returning to battle were charging her and her men. Some nobles were there, stabbing at Harrian's riders.

I kept my eyes on the boy. He was glancing at his mother.

"Hey, worm-bait, here," I called out, and banged my ax on my shield. "Come! Let me give you a kiss of steel! Your mother's rotten tit can wait."

"Bastard," he cursed, and led many of his men at me.

The fiery whip came down again, and again, and I blocked it, though the end snapped to my chain, helmet, and boot. Thrum came and chopped down two horsemen, before a horse kicked him back. I kept blocking Fallior, for the boy seemed single-minded about taking my head, and kept hammering the weapon at me. The men following him were dying, one by one, until one managed to drive a horse at me, mad with rage, and I fell under the beast. The man jumped from the horse and crashed on my chest, and I saw the whip going up as Fallior was struggling with a spear in his gut, and ax on his leg. His whip went wide.

I pushed at the man before me. I snapped his neck and pushed at his horse.

"Maskan, look out!" I heard Thrum screaming, trying to get up

The horse changed into a man, a grinning man with a flowing hair, and the jotun kicked me back down and sat over me. He pulled my head to the side. The young man, fire whip high again, licked his lips as I struggled.

The jotun struck me hard across the face.

I cursed and braided a spell together. A brief, sharp, and deadly wind of ice ripped out from my hand, and the horse under Fallior fell into ruin. The draugr yelped, surprised, his whip killing two of his own men.

He was snarling his way up, but a dverg hacked a halberd down on him, and I heard Lisar screaming.

I turned my attention to the cursing jotun.

"I'll do it, then," he rumbled. "Here." He flipped his ax in the air and bashed it down on my chest. I tossed and struggled, and the ax missed my head. An owl swept down and turned into another of the Sons of Ymir. He came down fast, raised the ax-shaft, and tried to bring that down to my throat.

The first jotun also had his ax up.

Something grabbed me by my leg, and we all turned to see a white bear, lithe, sleek, blue-eyed, pulling me along. The jotun rolled off me, the other one crashed into him, and a pair of dverg died under us, and I was dragged over rank of dverger, then fully out of the battle, and for the woods with terrible speed.

I tried to see.

I saw a bear's ass. Then, I saw owls turning into jotuns and chaos as they struck at me. I rolled on the snow and shifted into a bear as well. I swatted at something in front of me, and it howled and rolled away. I had blood on my claws.

The bear that had dragged me out of the dverger ranks, was tumbling down a hill for the woods.

"Finally!" I heard a jotun saying.

I turned, and charged. An ax passed over my skull, the jotun that had swung it, fell over my head. He was screaming as I bit my teeth over his manhood, and then through them.

He fell under me.

I spat out flesh and a ball, and tore down at the face beneath me. I clamped down my claws at it and ripped into its face and clawed out his throat.

The other jotun, ax high, charged from the side.

I got up to my full length, and slammed into him, clawing at his face. His ax went flying, and I heard his knee cracking as I pushed him under me. He fell hard, hammering my sides, and I tore into his throat. He tried to shape-shift, but died in the middle of the effort.

Panting, I looked down the hill for the bear.

There was nothing there but bloody snow and woods swaying in the wind.

I turned to regard the battle.

I spotted Lisar.

She was standing in the middle of the battle. Her

standard was with her, some hundred riders were struggling to push the dverger back, but she was looking at the dead boy in their midst, silent, her hand on her chest.

I charged. Snow was flying as I pounced through the snow.

She turned and saw me coming.

She raised her head proudly, lifted her barbed spear, and called for fire. It roared its way out of her hand. It was a thick, pulsing, stream of power, and I fell as I jumped past it.

I shifted direction and dodged a man lunging for me and saw another spell coming for me, a rain of tiny fireballs. Few burned to my skin, and I rolled on the snow, growling. She kept calling for new spells and was gauging my movements carefully.

I changed direction again, and disappeared into a group of enemy riders, tore down one, ripped a man apart, and snarled my way through a pair of archers. Men were running everywhere before me, and then several flew around, some in pieces. The lightning bolt tore through a horse next to me, it ripped across my flesh, and my back was flaming.

I came out of the rout and saw Lisar very near. A line of riders obscured my sight, stalwart White Lion and Headless Horse yelling warnings, but I kept going.

I crashed into them, felt spear and sword cutting into my flesh, ripped down a man and his horse, and jumped at her.

I fell into Lisar's barbed spear.

I saw her eyes beneath me. I saw the yellow jewel in her bone-pendant flashing. I felt the barbs in my chest and then the spear breaking.

I sunk my teeth into her, thrashed her around, shaking and tearing at her, and then, I fell with her on a bank of snow.

I heard the yells of men, the cheers of so many soldiers, Thrum cursing, the weeping of the wounded, and smelled the piss and shit of battlefield.

The smells of victory.

CHAPTER 13

When I came to, I was in a chamber in the Ugly Brother. I was weak and felt terrible. I was shaking with fever, and I had apparently pissed myself several times. There was vomit in a bucket, and broth that had long gown cold. A pitcher of mead was empty, and I knew Thrum had been sitting there, helping himself to my fare. I was naked.

"Shit, damn," I cursed softly, as I tried to sit up. I managed it, though I also regretted it. It was pain here, pain there, and I was lucky to be alive.

Again.

The wind was whistling, and I heard the groaning of stone and flinched as I stepped on a dead mouse. I turned my head and stared. Nima was there, I found, sleeping in an angry heap next to me. She wore only a tunic, and she had a hand on my ax and leg over my shield, both close to the bed. She looked powerful, dirty, and vicious. I saw a dog looking at me and wagging its tail in the doorway, but he, or she, dared not enter as Nima shifted.

I lifted a blanket, and placed it over her bare ass.

I heard a chuckle. Thrum stepped thought the door and looked at her. "I think she is guarding her investment," he whispered. "She says she is the queen, but she wants a coronation and a proper wedding. She showed me a paper. Her brother has been demanding a title."

"I forgot to mention Saag," I said, and wondered at a missing end of a toe. "How—"

"You'll limp for good," he said. "You are much more scarred than Morag ever was. That's what you get when you don't have a proper father."

I nodded and looked at my chest. A bloody bandage was on it, and many others all across my body.

"In case you wondered," he said with a cruel smile, "we won. The line broke, but the Stone Watchers routed the enemy. They scattered to die in the woods. Some tried to flee to the city and past the tower, but none made it. Literally, none. We have two thousand prisoners who eat better than before. We have just three thousand men left ourselves, and the Stone Watchers. What now?"

I held my head, and shook it. "I must think how to secure the land. We need the ships to move between Fiirant and Alantia. We must find the best, and the fittest men to take north. It will take time. I will have a realm after this is over, won't I? I already have a queen." I smiled at Nima, who was snoring gently. "She undressed me?"

"Yes."

"Gods help me," I said. "I remember nothing."

He shook his head. "I wasn't here. She insisted we all leave. She was medicating you, and I don't know what she did. She's entitled to it all, isn't it? You made her your queen. Now. We must speak of two matters."

I smiled. "Yes. What was the scroll you had?"

He looked sheepish. "A manifesto of love."

"What?"

He tossed it to me. I opened it up, and a huge number of names had been written on it. There were hundreds, perhaps a thousand. They were noble names, and men of influence, and money. One name had been crossed over.

Hal's.

At the bottom, was a set of newer ones. One was Saag's.

I looked at Thrum. "What is this?"

He smiled sadly. "Hal gave it to me before the battle. He had retrieved it from one of Roger's men. While Roger was held prisoners, he was still gathering support."

"For what?" I asked him.

"That list," he said cruelly, "is a list of men who have sworn to challenge your crown after the war. If you win, they would drive you out. Seems your Saag's not happy how Nima holds all the power in the family. Hal retrieved it, and gave it to me. Seems he thinks he might benefit from your gratitude more than Roger's. There are others of Roger's family, that would be worth following, but he chose you."

"They gave me their oaths," I said. "They took my help."

He was nodding. I was thinking, and I felt cold rage settling into my soul. I wiped my face, and though for a long time, and then made up my mind.

"Tell Hal to keep his mouth shut," I said. "And spread word the men are going to settle in for the winter."

He nodded. "What of this other matter we were supposed to speak about? It is most important. Your life is at risk, and I have a hunch who—"

I shook my head. "I know the truth, and I have a plan. This is it. Listen. We shall need a map, men who know the coast, and few other things."

He listened, and nodded. He didn't look shocked, nor was he upset. He looked pleased. He bowed.

I got up, and rubbed my face. I felt empty, and angry, and I felt … different. I felt unfettered by duty.

"What else?" I asked him.

"I have placed the enemy draugr in a mound of stone and rock in the woods," he said darkly. "Their men are still lying about the field. No time to bury them, or to hide them from animals until spring."

"No," I said, thinking. "Who do we have left?" I asked, wondering at Nima.

"Hal, Magga, Tor Filon, who is the general of the Stone Watchers, some fifty nobles, a thousand men-at-arms. A bit over two thousand archers … and the Stone Watchers. We can raise new men, as we have the armor and weapons, but it will be months in the spring when they are good for something." He rubbed his head. "It was a terrible butchery. They held. They kept their fame and honor."

I nodded. "Send the prisoners out. Let them walk home."

He smiled viciously.

I watched the list of names.

I swallowed away the rage as best I could before I nodded and spoke. "Make a legion of our own of the surviving ones. The best gear possible. They can go home when the war is over, but for now, they are needed here. Tell them they can pick a name for the legion," I told him. "Let it be the same as one of the ones we have beaten. They have earned it. Let them take their gear, and flags."

"They will," Thrum said. "I have fewer than two thousand, by the way. Soon, I don't have to worry about my charges for much longer," he said almost happily. "The toad-eating lot will have died all."

"I am sorry," I told him. "Make the men ready. But not before this night. How long has it been?"

"Two days," he answered.

"Where is she?"

"She's riding the walls," he said. "Trying to keep away from Nima."

I smiled and nodded. I tossed away the scroll, and looked around for my clothes.

He rolled his eyes. "Your gear is here, mended,

washed, and ready. Go and have a stroll. She loves you, king. Quiss."

I nodded. "Make the preparations, Thrum. I'll leave for Aten this afternoon. Before that, find what I told you to. Nima will aid you."

"You should go to Quiss," he said.

I shooed him away, and turned to Nima. He shook his head, and went.

I wakened her up. She was startled, and sat up, her hair a thick wave around her shoulders. "What … you feel fine?"

I nodded.

She let her eyes run over my wounds, and then my nakedness, and she smiled. "I envy you your ability to heal."

I shrugged. "I am lucky."

She looked around. "Your Quiss is not here? She arrived yesterday, and I had to keep her out. You had a fever." She shook her head. "I feel like she wants to murder me."

"She does."

She chuckled and sat up. "And you love her. Truly?"

"I loved her, truly," I said. "At least for a moment."

"No more?"

I shook my head. "I was hurt by a vampire, Nima. And there is something else. But as for you, you need not worry. If things go well, you will have your title, and your nation."

She moved close to me, and I took a hold of her tunic. She smiled, lifted her arms, and I stripped her, and pulled her to me. She gasped.

"Tell me," I asked her, as I caressed her powerful back. "Can you arrange something for me. I need to find some help in Aten. You knew every lowlife here, and some there?"

She nodded. She caressed my face. "I can find someone. I tell you how to contact them. Just tell me what you need."

I kissed her neck, and she shivered. "I will also need a man, who knows a place in Aten. Someone who sails the waters. I need a map, and such a man. Right after this." I kissed her again, and she pushed me back.

She nodded. "I can … all of that. As for this," she said and touched my chest, and then put it on my cock. "I told you. I am no woman for one man. Don't grow too attached. If you want a child, I will do my best, of course. It is to my benefit as well. But I will not easily settle for one man, or one of these." She tugged at my cock.

I grinned. "I'm a shapeshifter. I can be as many men as you like, and I come in many shapes, though not at the same time."

Her eyes went round with shock and then I lifted her on my lap.

We were in no hurry, and everyone in the Ugly Brother knew the king and the queen were busy.

***

I wore a wolf-fur cape and looked over the battlefield. It had been mostly cleared of our dead, but snow covered thousands of enemy dead. There were broken spears, shattered shields, and blood all over a ragged line. Horses had been hauled to Nallist for food, but some remained, many of those horribly burned.

I rode for a speck of moving people, noble cavalry searching the woods around Nallist, and huts and houses that were just outside the wall. The enemy who had managed to escape would sneak in at night to warm up or even to attack guards. The nobles were hunting them with Quiss.

I enjoyed the sudden silence.

The storm had abated, and the weather was milder. While it was still cold, you could feel the warmer air blowing from the east. The Arrow Straits and the Bay of Whales were gray-blue masses of fog. Birds were singing. An icicle was dripping.

I rode until the riders saw me. They swirled around and pointed me out, and then, I waited.

She was coming. She rode for me, but was in no hurry. She was enraged, hurt, or something else. She was taking her time, and I chuckled and watched.

Then, when I could see her eyes, I knew she was not going to be happy. They were pinpoints of black and bright blue, and I placed a hand on my ax as she stopped her horse, waved the nobles away, and tossed a flask of water at me.

I dodged.

"You bastard," she hissed. "Do you know how embarrassing it is to lead an army to Hillhold, only to find there is no army. Do you know what embarrassments I had to endure when Hal handed Thrum a note explaining what *I* was going to do? They all knew Thrum was giving the orders!"

"I—"

"Then, when he led us out, he sent me to fetch a lost contingent. I came to a battlefield, Maskan, with a battle already fought! They all think you don't trust me. Your Regent!"

She guided her horse closer.

I lifted an eyebrow.

"That Nima," she hissed.

"She is the queen," I said.

"You bedded her?" she asked.

I looked away. "Yes. She deserved it. She must be accepted as the queen. So I did. Everyone will have heard, for she was full of passion, and I made sure she was happy. She had requests, and I fulfilled them all. Her throne is no longer just a piece of paper for Saag to show around. She might even be pregnant."

She shook with anger. "You bastard. Where are the men of Aten who followed me?" she asked. "Where are the men who chose to join you?"

I looked back to the fort and at her. "There are two

hundred of them alive. They fought well. Forget them."

"I," she snarled, "should have commanded them. You know this. You know it fully well. I should have been with you."

I shook my head. "No. I do not."

She stared at me and gauged my mood. "No?"

"No, regent," I said. "I sent you away to safety, Quiss. I sent you away because we needed another ruler to pick up the pieces if Nima and I died. I *was* disappointed how the battle took place. Roger and others disobeying you? Terrible thing. So, that is why I let Thrum lead the men here. We won. Now, we must build our force again, and make our plans here. We must solidify the land under our banners. We shall winter and take stock of the situation. This is what we will do. Nima will lead while I, however, go and seek out—"

She lifted her hand, and she stared at me. She didn't move for a long time, as if she was trying to read my mind. Finally, she shook her head, her eyes sad. "You have changed. Your heart changed. It is not Nima. She is a nothing, no matter how hard you make her scream."

"I'm changed," I answered coldly. "I have found many sides to being Maskan, lately. I need to find the rest of it."

"That scroll," she said tiredly. "From the Lok worshipping madman. You are going to Aten."

"I am going to Aten," I agreed. "The men will retake

Alantia and Fiirant, and I shall go and seek answers. It will be dangerous. None must know about me."

She looked upset, and then she held her face. "I will come with you. I've had enough of—"

"I thank you. And I agree," I said. "It is time you and I have an adventure again. We can, since we won the war in the north. Forget Nima, and aid me now. We might find our way together, again."

She hesitated and smiled.

I rode to her and grasped her hand. Later, I left her to prepare and went and prepared myself as well, armed with a map of Aten, and a man who knew the land. Nima gave me a name or two as well. I gave Thrum, Hal, Nima, and Magga orders, and left.

BOOK 4: THE SERPENT SPIRE

"The question Tris asked earlier is a good one. Where do they take all those corpses?"

Maskan to Hook-Nose

CHAPTER 14

"They are acting strange," Quiss said, her voice breaking. "Do you see them?"

I nodded.

Her hair was whipping in the wind as we stared at Aten's prison and main fortress, the dreaded Locks of the Sea, the golden chains over a wide road that ran from the harbor to the prison called the Golden Chains, through which I had been whipped as Aten-Sur's prisoner. The beating at Balic's hands, and that of Raven, Aten-Sur's mad wife, was heavy on my mind.

It was but for other reasons than the pain and the humiliation.

There, local guards were standing in long lines. There were a thousand of them, and parties of them left the lines after a captain was calling out orders.

"They lost their legions up north," she muttered. "They are nervous."

"They have five legions camped outside the city walls. They are raising new armies," I said. "They are nervous, but not too nervous. There are plenty of people asking questions, even with the city locked down. They don't like *our* questions."

"But—"

"They are seeking us," I said simply. "We have been walking about for two days and asking questions. They are trying to find us. They wish to meet with two odd merchants who ask about horses. They fear we work for … well, me. They fear spies and are afraid the terrifying jotun, bane to their legions, is coming for them. None else ask questions about horses. Adopted or not."

"*Adopted horse*," she murmured. "That is …"

"Aye," I said, frustrated. "That is like seeking a virgin in a brothel. None can understand us."

She giggled and shook her head. She had been much happier since we left Nallist, and Nima.

For a night, she had forgiven me, and shared my bed again, and unlike Nima, she had been gentle.

Now, it seemed we were running out of time. The guards were getting suspicious.

"I have to think about hiding soon," she said. "The mask is curious." I gave her a glance.

She wore a suit of chain under her thick coat and tunic. Her pants were of black leather, and her hair hidden in a hood. She wore a mask to cover her face. It was cold, after all, but it was a bit odd.

None had asked us for papers.

None had seen us entering.

I had flown us in, carefully, over the wall, when the guards were busy. But now? It was only a matter of time before they would accost us.

"Do you think my butler is alive?" she wondered, her eyes on the palace in the south wall. Its high walls were gleaming in the light of the Lightgiver. "He might be able to help. He is clever."

"We have some more stables to search," I said. "And we will have to go back to the Riddle and the Coin. The stables might be alerted, anyway."

We had been staying in the Riddle and the Coin for two days. It was a slow, silent tavern. It wasn't far, just a stone-throw away, and in an alley. We mostly spent our time seeking people who might know what an adopted horse was. It could be a joke, a nickname for a drunk, a tavern, a stable, or really a horse someone had adopted.

The people were in no mood for such questions.

Someone had obviously alerted the officials.

That night, at the last light, I had brought us to the roof of a very tall building to see the city from high, and there, we made our plans. The building was a hospital, and I had given away coins to the wounded when we came up. Most were from the battle of Hillhold. They would want more when we went down.

"Do you miss it?" I asked, looking at the rich city and the harbor.

There, a Black Ship had arrived past night. It would row down to the river and make its way to Malignborg.

Balic was dead.

They wouldn't be resurrected again. Unless … Rhean's mistress was cursed with that power.

The dead would be rowed to Malignborg, anyway, it seemed. I kept an eye on the activity.

Quiss noticed me watching the Black Ship. "Balic is

dead. Mir is dead. They are never rising again."

I nodded.

"That vampire?" she asked.

"She said," I told her, "that those she and her kind slay can sometimes be recalled. Sometimes."

She pulled at me. "See. Here is a general."

I turned and saw a high officer riding to the city from a gate. After him marched two thousand men and more, and they immediately spread out. Some stopped soon and stood around in the city's streets.

"They are seriously worried," she murmured. "We should find my butler. Not sure what you thought the people visiting this tavern could do for us, but it clearly is not the—"

"It has been empty," I said. "But Nima said she knows all the smugglers and criminals and told me that place is full of the smartest, best minds in the underbelly of Aten."

She chuckled. "I know my own city, I think, better than a robber-queen of Alantia. The place is empty. Balic has likely hanged all the criminals, smugglers, and thieves when he began this conquest of the north. Nay. We should seek out the scholars. There are some libraries, and houses of learning—"

"We will," I said, "if we fail to find anything this night. Libraries and houses of learning will be dangerous if they know we seek information and answers to riddles. In fact, moving about will be dangerous. They'll be looking for us, won't they? A man and a masked woman."

She touched my short hair, dark as night, and stroked my bearded cheek. I had taken the looks of a dead enemy captain and wore my armor under a heavy, dark-red cloak.

"It will be empty, as it has been, the Riddle," she sighed. "I am sorry we haven't found what this abandoned horse might be. It could be a joke. A trick. These people are in love with tricks. All kinds of tricks. There are plenty of stories about them, and Lok."

I nodded and watched the Black Ship. It had arrived that night. Another ship, a sailing ship with a low deck, was tied to a pier next to it. It was called the *Maggot's Nest*. It looked the part, with bedraggled rigging and dirty deck.

And if they were taken away, there was a reason for it. Where the corpses went, there, too, would be the one who resurrected them.

Rhean had said I had been near the end. Near the top, just one step away.

I was nudged by Quiss.

"We should get some rest," she said. "One should stay awake, though. They might search even the rat's nests, eh?"

I chuckled, and she pulled her mask down a bit. She had a sad, wondering look in her eyes, as she touched my lips. I looked back at her, saw Rhean's face, and then leaned down to kiss her.

It was a gentle, long kiss.

I broke it off, and she looked hurt and nodded. "Let us go?"

"Yes," I murmured, and turned to the hole in the roof. I went first and walked downstairs. Quiss walked after me, and her hands brushed the walls. I pushed through the curtain below, a filthy thing. The place stank of blood, piss, and corpses. We entered what was a highest level of a hospital, and a more miserable sight you couldn't find. Men were on beds and on stacks of hay, most waiting to die. Others were miserably seated by a wall, looking enviously at those who had even a bale of hay to lay on.

I pulled out a sack of looted coins, and kneeled next to some suffering warriors.

One gasped with gratitude as I put silver in his hand.

Another wept and held his belly. "Thank you, sir. Thank you," he said, and kissed my hand.

I went on. Quiss looked at me, unsure and sad.

I got up, eventually.

"A filthy rich city," I snarled to Quiss, "and they don't take care of the soldiers."

"Soldiers sign up to die," she said simply. "They do usually get taken care of, Maskan. There are too many wounded now. There's no king, nothing but harried rulers. Even Balic's missing."

"Sounds like a ripe time to take the war to

Malignborg," I said.

"Come now," she sighed. "Let's leave."

We went down many stairways and levels, and in the bottom level, where they were sorting out the wounded, I had no more silver. Hands went up, for they knew of me, and then, when I shook my head, they went down.

Save for one.

A man, bloody and face burned, his one remaining eye gleaming, climbed up to lean on the wall. He looked at me with curiosity. "You, a captain. Which company?"

I cursed. The risk of taking faces of people you didn't know, was great.

"Rest, soldier," I said. "I—"

"Sir," he said, frowning. "Why do you not wear your gear, sir? Have the legions been destroyed? Are there still men who—"

"We shall still fight," I told him. "Now, sit. I am moving on from the legions to something else."

He nodded, and then, suddenly, his eyes went round.

I turned to follow his gaze and found he was staring at Quiss.

She had forgotten her mask.

"The princess of Aten!" the man called out. It echoed in the barrack and across the levels above. Silence followed. Then, a soldier went to his knee. Another as well. A surgeon was staring at her, aghast.

Quiss smiled and stepped for the door.

"Greet them," I hissed.

"No, we must—"

The soldier who had noticed her grimaced. "They say she went to the side of the enemy! She was in Hillhold! Wait, she was in the Pass! She is a traitor!"

She ran out. I followed her, and together, we slammed against the door. It was being pushed from the inside. Men were calling out.

I placed a hand on the door and called for ice. It was a strong braid, thick and brilliant, made of wind, the freezing, gleaming ice of Gjöll and her sister rivers. I let it go on the doorway, saw the wood groaning, and then, ice running out of the cracks. There were dismayed yells inside.

I pulled her along and ran. We took to the alleys and walked when soldiers were in sight.

I dodged a pair of merchants, then we passed into an eatery, found a backdoor, and sneaked for the Riddle and the Coin.

We got in, and dodged through a silken curtain, stained by greasy hands.

"No mud!" called out the innkeeper.

We nodded and brushed our feet on a rug. I looked at the place, and it was empty. There was not a soul inside. Abandoned round tables were scattered around the main hall, and stairs led to rooms upstairs. The barkeep was singing forlornly and offered us nothing.

I chuckled and went to get us ale. He took his time,

gave me an unfriendly look, and then listened as I placed a coin on the bar. It was thick and heavy, and he gave me a smile like a draugr might, sour and evil. He went to the doorway and began preparing for dinner. I went back to our table.

"Rotten meat, ancient vegetables," Quiss said, and took the pitcher and a mug from me. "As usual. He'll not be in business for long. So, we must leave. I say we find my butler, and then, we will have a place to hide in the palace. He'll do it for me. Then, later, he will invite some of the better minds in the city to help you solve the riddle."

"I guess we have no other choice," I agreed, and watched the door.

The door opened.

A pair of dark-robed men came in, holding their full helms under their arms. They were men who served in the Black Ships. With them, there was an official, a man, and another, a young woman, both with Balic's symbol of throne and skull in their long, white coats. They looked around, saw us, and we tensed.

They ignored us.

Then, they walked over to the table next to a fireplace and sat down.

They appeared to be friends, whispering softly, and telling jokes, for three of them were laughing, and one, a heavy-set man, grunting. It might have been mirth, or anger.

Soon, the tavern keeper appeared, seemed delighted by the customers, and waved his hands at them, six fingers in the air. The men nodded. Six pitchers of ale were carried to them, and plates of bread, and a large pitcher of wine.

Obviously, they were well used to visiting the place.

They sat in silence, enjoying their ale, wisely not touching the food, and eyed the two pitchers with remorse.

They stood abandoned.

One, a hook-nosed man in the black robes, shook his head and sighed. "So many never coming back."

A white-coated official, the male, flicked back his long hair from his eyes and cursed as some foam from ale was on his chin. "Talic and Mun were good friends. One owed me money, and the other married my sister. Who would have thought the northerners fight so well, eh?"

The hook-nosed man winked. "They have been talking about it for decades, eh? How savage the enemy is? Yeah. They have. It was always coming, the war. Morag's arrogance and northern stiff-necks, and Morag's duplicity? No, it was always coming, even before this terrible business." He tapped the skull symbol. "Who would have thought? Now, we know. Next time, they will go in with all the legions *and* in the summer."

"They will have to be rebuilt," said the other official,

a woman with a copper-brown hair, braided around her skull. "All of the lost ones. Most all. Some companies got home. Only the fleets are intact, though I hear they lost the trader ships and many transports in Nallist. Forty ships and more. Not easy to move supplies without them. We will have to hire mercenaries."

She sighed and gave us a curious look. Then, she spoke on. "They will have to call new men to the colors, raise the youth guards into the companies, and I hear they will have to put new arses on many thrones." She leaned to the large black-robe. He was thick-necked, bearded man, and the beard jutted as she came close. He was either ready to fight or attracted to her. "Will they raise the royals again?"

The man grunted and wrung his hands.

The hook-nose smiled. "Gult is upset, Tris. Ask him nothing and don't pick a fight, eh? Alas, what is dead again is dead for good. Balic—"

"Some say *Balic's* dead," Tris insisted while staring at Gult, apparently relishing the risk of having a fight. "They say that jotun king killed him in Hillhold."

"Nallist," Gult rumbled. He waved a hand to indicate he had nothing else to say.

"Balic is the One Man," the hook-nose said reverently. "*The One Man.* He walked out of the darkness and brought hope to men. He cannot be dead. Gods curse those who robbed us of the gloriously raised kings and—"

"Gods?" Tris laughed. "I *knew* you believe in gods!"

Hook-Nose looked at her darkly, and the white-coated male, having won his battle with the foam from the ale, placed a hand on Tris's. "Shh. We are friends, remember? Relax. You are like an entertainer, poking a stick at snakes. We'll bite you back. Don't talk evil of Balic. And don't mention gods. We might all hang. They are really jumpy out there."

Their eyes roved over the tavern, visited us, but we were not looking at them, and then, the hook-nose went on. "We take their corpses back to Malignborg. That is where they will rest. They have all now been loaded up and dug from Dagnar's ruins, at least what can be found. One ship for them and another for those warrior Balic shall raise. He<< is alive, of course."

Tris bit her tongue. I could see it. She nodded. "I hear they look terrible, when they have been killed. I don't mean the wounds. I mean—"

Hook-Nose sighed and rapped his fingers on the table. "Shh. It is the unfortunate duty of a Serpent Guard. We collect everything. Do not worry about it."

"How do you decide," Tris asked carefully, "who has fought well enough to merit Balic's blessings, and who remains behind? I have no idea how you fit them all in Malignborg. Ships have been going that way for as long as I have been alive, from all the wars in the Verdant lands, from beyond the sea, even, and now, from the north. Where do they go?"

Gult spat on the floor. "The royals who die again go there. To the Eye Keep."

Hook-Nose shook his head, and Gult went quiet.

"But where do *all* the others go?" Tris asked. "There are always ships in Malignborg, and they push carts to the Eye Keep, and then, the ships leave, and come back with more—"

The white-coat pushed one of the abandoned tankards to Tris. She grasped it.

Hook-Nose sighed. "Look—"

Tris shook her shoulders, stubborn. "Look. Did you rescue our friends? That's what I'm interested in. Will they walk amongst us again?"

"The Black Ships sail," Gult rumbled. "They sail, and they come, and they go, and do not worry about it. Let it remain a puzzle. Let us toast our friends, instead. No, they will not come back. We didn't do that to them … I mean, we couldn't find them."

They toasted their friends, and then, the white-jacketed man pulled out a board and a sack of gaming pieces.

They proceeded to set it up.

They argued over dice, over ale, and then, we got into trouble.

Gult spoke up sourly. "It will be boring with but four. I know Tris and you," he growled and pointed a finger at the white-coat, "will make an alliance. Hook and I hate each other, and so one of you will win. At least usually we had one of the other who would play along with our schemes."

Tris snorted. "They played as Aten and Malignborg, or they didn't play at all, and you know they always allied with each other. Always. You lost then, and you'll lose now. So, just be happy they don't backstab you after suggesting you lead the attack on us."

The male official sighed, turned, and looked around.

We got up, hoping to get to our room. "You two," he said.

We looked at him.

"Do you have papers?" he asked.

Tris turned to me. "He seems rich. Merchant. I'd not—"

I frowned. "I have my papers." I clutched my ax under my cloak. "We came to the city last night for some ale, and—"

"A handsome one, nonetheless, no matter if he reads, or not," she purred. "Your girl has brains in her head?"

Quiss shrugged. "I do."

Tris nodded. "In that case, you'll retire later, you have an ale, two, and you fill in for our dead friends," she said simply. "This good for all?"

The other official opened his mouth to argue, but the others were nodding. The man deflated and waved his hand.

I cursed under my broth, and Quiss smiled, pushed back her hood brazenly, and walked over to the table.

She crashed next to Gult who looked at her gruffly. Reluctantly, I walked after her.

Tris winked at her over Gult's shoulders. "Girls play nicely with each other, eh? In fact, let us show them how to fool kings."

***

It was late night, and a third game, and Gult was frustrated beyond words.

The girls, in fact, were the only ones who were not.

Gult, however, was the worst off. He seemed to roar and shake with anger after each lost battle. When Tris and Quiss finally killed his last army, he held his face and shook again, this time so hard, the table shook with him. The other official had succumbed to the two devilish women earlier, and Hook-Nose had such a dreadful bad luck in dice, he had basically lost before he could start and had died of hunger and elements.

I was facing Tris and her armies now, and Quiss was actively helping her.

I threw the dice, and she did as well, and I removed two of my armies as she besieged Palan.

She whooped, Quiss grinned, and Gult downed more ale, making him, probably, the most drunk of all in the room, though that was hard to be sure of. Everyone else, including myself, was having a surprisingly good time.

I lost another army to Quiss.

"By the ball-hair of Odin!" he roared as he eyed my

slow demise. "By Balic's rotten nutsack! Beaten by girls," he wept. "You too. We should—"

Hook-Nose, half dozing, chuckled. "They'll beat us all anyway, if we try to play together. I bet they would. Look, we must hurry. They'll be searching this part of the town, house-by-house this night, so we cannot dilly-dally." He winked at me. "It is your turn."

I looked at Quiss and she looked back at me. "I pass. But I guess we should hurry, indeed."

Quiss smiled.

Tris frowned and shook her head. She tossed dice, and Tris took another part of my city. I decided I had not placed my armies in properly defended positions. She grinned, anticipating my demise.

Quiss was moving her troops to make ready for her and Tris's showdown.

She had no faith in me.

"So, they are looking for someone?" Quiss asked. "Who?"

She shrugged, as she watched Quiss moving on the board, calculating and worried. "They seek people who are looking for a horse. A man who serve the Black, the Serpent Skull," Tris said, as she eyed the two men in the table, "came seeking a horse. They turned out every stable in the city days ago. A true puzzle." She poked a finger on the table. "And now, they say people who are not serving the Serpent search for the same. They say there are spies in the city. They are jumpy as shit. The general blocked the city and the harbor at three days ago, save for the Black Ships, and we, of course, have to govern it. The guards are all young and stupid. Hopelessly so. Here."

She surrounded my keep, we threw dice, and she killed two of my armies and took the fortress.

She downed an ale, laughed, and winked her eye at me. "If you lose one more time, you'll have to be my plaything for the night."

Gult looked glum. "You never played like that with any of us."

"You are my friends," she laughed. Then, she went quiet and got up. "I need to piss. You wait here."

She got up and walked to a doorway near the bar. She entered, and we heard her cursing, for it was apparently dark.

The other official was looking bored. He was eyeing us, and then, he frowned. "Wait. Didn't you say you entered the city last night?"

I nodded.

"But the city was closed, wasn't it?" he wondered.

Gult nodded darkly. "It was."

The white-coat smiled at me thinly. "They have papers, though."

"I never saw them, did I?" Gult wondered.

The hook-nose looked troubled. "They are looking for *you*, no? You had best—"

I grasped Gult by the throat. I moved up and axed

him, smashing him to the wall. Quiss stabbed down the white-coat. I took hold of Hook-Nose, while Quiss turned on the barkeep. The man belched in fear and turned to run. I took a hold of a tankard and tossed it. It struck true, and the man fell on his face. She walked that way, eyeing the writhing mass legs and feet.

"Keep that Tris alive for a while," I told Quiss.

"Why?" she asked. "Will you be her plaything for the night?"

"She seems clever," I answered. "We won't stay the night."

I turned to stare at the hook-nose in the eye.

"You know," I spoke to him. "The question Tris asked earlier is a good one. Where *do* they take all those corpses? They say Balic raised the very best to the ranks, but the ships are packed with the dead, no?"

He shook his head and made a meowing noise.

"And still, most of the Hammer Legions are all living men and women," I said. "Balic grooms his armies, makes them up out of idiots and young fools, and then finds a war to find corpses. He seems to have had a war in his hand every year since he was reborn. I was going to follow the Black Ships to find someone, but you tell me something about them first. Speak."

"The cost," the man wept, "of changing Midgard is war. They must all believe, and if they do not, they must learn. He has a war, or two going, all the time."

"And still, you don't believe, and neither did your

friend. You don't, because you are not fools. Where do they go?" I asked him. "I shall make it fast for you, if you answer."

He struggled and gagged. "Wait," he said, his feet dangling furiously in the air. "Listen. The thing is, that those who die again, the royals and others that have been raised before, really do go to Malignborg."

"Many of late," I laughed. "Though not Balic. I killed him."

He looked at me, puzzled. Then, he gasped as I changed. I kept my size, but not my looks. I was pale blue, fiercely blue-eyed, and powerfully built jotun. "Speak."

"We bury the ones that do not fit the ships," he said in panic. "On average, if a battle takes some hundred lives, we take fifty, and those who still have a head, arms, and legs. Must have legs. That is crucial. We take those and bring them here, to Aten." He went quiet.

"And?" I asked, and watched Quiss stabbing down on the barkeep, then knocking on the door to the shitter.

"Come on out, love," she said. "We need to finish the game."

The door stayed closed.

"Speak on," I murmured.

He did. "Look. We change them on the pier. They take the pick of the corpses and put them on other ships," he said. "Usually, they pack all of them in another boat. There are many. Maggot's. The Vigilant

Wife. Many others."

"What?"

He took a desperate breath. "We take the royals and *empty* caskets to Malignborg. It is a show of empty caskets and wagons, and a parade of possibly dead royals. It is a silent, deadly solemn, holy procession, and people think all the dead go to Malignborg Necropolis, where Balic will raise his best followers, one day, and the rest, much later. What we have collected goes elsewhere. The other ships, not the Black Ships, take them away. I know not where the corpses go. North. I don't know."

I nodded. "Fine."

"Look. There is a Black Ship filled with royal dead. There are other corpses they will take off, but the royals will go south," he panted. "Some are rich as shit. They still have gold, silver. Let me go, and I shall let you loot them. Please. I—"

I laughed. "You think a jotun king is a grave robber? Now, I am going to steal kingdoms from Hel, and not trinkets from corpses." I snapped his neck and turned to see Tris looking at me, Quiss holding a sword on her throat.

"I asked her the question," Quiss said. "I asked her if she knows where the adopted horse might be found."

I walked over to them and stared down at Tris. "You know who I am?"

"The man whom they whipped before the keep," she

said with some acid. "You killed my friends."

"You get to down all six ale-tankards, Tris, if you know an answer to a puzzle," I said, as I showed my bloody ax to her. "I take no pleasure in this. None."

The jotun in me disagreed. She saw it.

"Your woman and a traitor to Aten, and aye, I know her now," she said softly, "tells me you need to figure out where an abandoned horse might be found. She said you seek a man called Caru." She smiled. "That Caru, I know of him. He is a man Balic and King Sarac have been hunting for long, long years."

"I know," I snarled.

She held her hands around her, afraid. "He worships the old gods and seems to have an uncanny luck on his side. Lok's Bend is where he has been brewing his trouble from. It is a land filled with ruins and misery, and woods and swamps ... a veritable hold of shit. Whoever tries to catch him finds his command in chaos, his supplies stolen, his officers at odds and even murdered. They have hanged thousands of this Caru's following. He claims to lead god Lok's depraved people, but only lately has there been a rumor this Caru is finally dead. Old age, you see, not sword. That's why they don't speak of it. But King Sarac's son has been holding a feast for his nobles in Xal Cot. King Sarac died in Dagnar?"

I nodded. "Where do we find Lok's Bend, then?" I asked her. "Let us forget this adopted horse. We could—"

She lifted a finger and shook her head. "Now, now. Let us not be hasty. Can you be a dear, girl...Princess, and lock the backdoor and the front one. I need time." She smiled. "As it happens, I was on one tour in Xal Cot, chasing rebels. I got to know the land and this filthy cult. They love tricks. They play deadly tricks, and they rarely speak their mind straight. They think they are mimicking their filthy god, but they truly cannot match him. Their tricks, jokes, and evil are paltry in comparison to the tales of Lok. You know of Lok?"

I shrugged.

Quiss rolled her eyes at me as she was barring the front door.

Tris looked up at me with disbelief and sighed. She leaned on the wall, holding her wrist. "The Aesir and the Vanir. Gods, they said, hated Lok. Tricky god, ever causing turmoil that threw the gods themselves into battle and despair. See why Caru might seem a pitiful thing. Calling himself the Mouth of Lok? Hah! The gods ... well, they don't say that anymore. No gods, eh?" She winked. "Is Balic truly dead?"

I nodded. "He won't go to Malignborg in a coffin. His bitch queen is the one running the family business. Always has been. They are dead, Tris. They want all of you dead, as well as us. Jotun, man, woman, man, old, young. Hel is real, the gods are, too, and Balic is the product of a cursed spell."

She looked at me with worry, then her friends.

I shrugged. "They got unlucky. You might be lucky."

"Yes, thank you," she muttered. "Tell you what. I told your lady I have an idea on the horse puzzle. I shall share that idea with you, for my life."

Quiss grinned as she came to sit on the bar and helped herself to ale. "At least she is cheap. The last one who negotiated with him managed to get Nallist and became a queen."

"Is that possible?" she whispered. "I mean, not becoming the queen, but—"

"She gave me an army," I snarled, and shook my head. "My bed is full, my heart is full, my body is full of wounds, my kingdom is much harmed, and I need answers, Tris. If you give them willingly, your status as a living, breathing woman will be continued."

She grinned, an impish, clever woman, and I felt she was already calculating how many cities she might rule. She was much like Nima. She leaned forward. "I told you. They are tricky. Their tricks are evil, like poison in your ale, or crude, like stealing the general's horse and replacing it with a goat. They are, simply said, secretive and childish. Lok, as I was saying, is a god. He is an evil god, kin to jotuns, and everyone says the prophecies tell us that when he is finally released—"

"Lok be damned," I snarled. "I—"

Quiss smacked my head. "He was imprisoned for tricking Hodur the Blind to kill Odin's son Baldr, who now sits in Hel's hall."

"When he is released," Tris said with some asperity, "it will be Ragnarök, and the end of all."

"Jotun kin?" I asked. "Lok?" I smiled. "All the gods are jotuns. So I have been told."

Quiss looked at me oddly. "Maskan?"

"Never mind," I said. "Get to the point, Tris."

"I?" Tris said with little patience. "Sure. Lok is a tricky god and cannot help himself. He meddles in the affairs of the Nine Worlds; he travels the lands causing chaos. He sometimes helps people, and sometimes harms them, but the price is always there."

"I hear all the gods charge for favors," I murmured.

I felt, perhaps I did, Bolthorn laughing in my head. It was distant and still real. It made me sweat with fear. His price would be terrible, and I feared it.

She looked at me like I was an idiot and nodded. "Fine. Whatever. Lok tricks are spawned by god's evil mind, and his followers?" She shrugged. "They are idiots. They are dangerous idiots, but idiots nonetheless. Caru is their Mouth and has been silent for months, but this business of you finding an adopted horse?" She rolled her eyes. "They have done this before. They simply scramble the letters in the words, so that if someone reads their text, it takes them forever to realize what is says. King Sarac found many such letters on his victims, and usually Caru simply had penned down scrambled words for a lamb roast or an ale recipe. This could be different. It is a damned anagram, or I am a fool. Here."

She leaned forward, hesitated, and dipped her finger in the tavern keeper's blood. Quiss grinned at her.

She drew the words in the dust.

Then, she mulled it over and we leaned over her. "Adopted horse," she said softly.

She was at it for a long while.

Finally, she drew again. "Adopted Shore?"

I looked at Quiss. She pushed me back and went to sit with Tris. Together, they were whispering, looking at each other like the best of friends, and then leaned over the words.

I sat back and let them work.

Then, Tris was nodding, and when they straightened their backs, I saw two words. "Deadtop Shore," Tris said. "It is a remote smuggler's bay and has a small fishers hut and nothing else. Ten miles out of Aten."

I nodded and smiled. "Tricky, and still, not too tricky."

"All right," Tris said and shrugged. "I know they have been rounding up scholars and people who are well versed in Lok. *They* are no fools." She gave Quiss an approving glance. "We are not, either." She turned to me. "And now? Will you let me live?"

"Aye," I told her. "You are coming with us. We need a guide."

"Wait," she said. "How? The city is locked down."

"Is there a roof to the building?" I asked. "I'll make one."

CHAPTER 15

We flew through the night. I beat my wings, and Tris, holding her eyes closed, and Quiss, eyeing the night, dangled from my claws. I held on tight on their arms, and we flew east along the coast. Soon, very soon, I heard Tris calling and saw her pointing. We saw the end of a small peninsula. It jutted out to the sea, and I saw the waves crashing majestically into high rocky walls. Then, when we were close, circling the peninsula, she pointed to a small bay on the eastern side, below the high sides of the peninsula and under a larger town.

I banked and glided down for the beach. I skimmed the waves and dropped both to the surf, landed, changed, and avoided trampling them.

Both were sitting waist deep in the water, drenched. A wave broke over them, and they struggled to stand.

I was looking around the beach. "Where?"

She nodded. "The cabin? Over there."

I turned to see where she was pointing at and found, indeed, a house hidden behind a set of bushes. It was twisted on its side, looked ready to collapse, and still, there was a bit of light shining on one of its windows. I pointed a finger at Tris and then at the shadows of the rocky wall. "Do not run, and I shall take you back home in the morning."

She frowned, got up, curtsied with mockery, her breeches dripping water, and gave Quiss a smile as she walked off.

"She is odd," she decided. "We killed her friends, and she thinks you are her best friend."

"She hopes I shall spare her," I said, "and hopes to profit. And perhaps she is bored and needs an adventure. Shall we? She won't be trouble."

We went forward, and the stones crunched under our feet. I went past two huge boulders and led Quiss forward for the door.

When we got close to the doorway, it opened.

A man had opened it, and he held an old shield and a thick spear. He smiled crookedly and was missing a few teeth. He had a dark-blue mask tattooed on his forehead, and his hair was white and black, long to his chest and back. He was in his fifties and had a limp and looked odd, dangerous. His eyes were on Quiss. "Come in, then. King Maskan?"

I nodded and stepped in after him. A large hall was lit with candles, and there were chairs, benches, and it smelled of fish.

"I am not sure if a jotun approves such rustic setting," the man muttered. "But then again, you have probably been sleeping in ditches during this horrible war."

I nodded again and looked at the place. The corners were dark, the walls hung with nets. Old barrels and a cold fire-pit were filled with straws and wood.

Caru turned around like a prince and crashed into a

seat. "This, here, a smuggler's paradise. They have a cave nearby, and its filled with fish rot and bones. Behind that, a cave to the city above. Smugglers and pirates, see, do—"

"We have such in Red Midgard," I agreed. "I have much to ask."

Caru nodded. "I have much to tell. I never thought I'd tell it to Morag's son, but I will. I am so happy you found me. It wasn't hard, was it? I hear someone else has been seeking that horse as well." He looked down, bothered, and brushed a speck of dust from his leg. "It is unfortunate," he murmured. "But we shall see. Do sit, King."

I sat next to him and leaned on my head. The ax dangled in my hand, and then, I took out the shield from under my cloak and put it on my lap.

Quiss stepped fully into the hall. She looked at Caru in silence.

"So, ask away, King," he said. "It is high time we find some common ground."

"What were you doing in Aten?" I asked.

Caru was looking at his fingers. His eyes went to Quiss. She looked uncomprehending.

Caru spat and spoke. "That's for you."

Quiss Atenguard turned to look at me, puzzled.

I snarled and spoke. "Yes, that was for you. What were you doing in Aten? When I was escaping from Balic's clutches and found you in the dungeon, what were you doing? Why did you stay, after Balic decided to make you into draugr? You could have left anytime. And what happened to the real Quiss?"

Caru lifted a blue book from his side. "The older sister Quiss died in Malignborg, during the siege and rebellion that killed many of the loftiest royals in the land. It was twenty years ago. Back then, Balic had died during the Cataclysm, and Hel's servant had come back to Midgard, as had few very special humans seeking to restore the gods to the Nine, but it all ended terribly." He shook his head, deep in his thoughts. "Quiss. She died with her father, Aten-Sur, in the Necropolis of the Eye Keep. She wasn't raised. Sometimes, they just cannot be called back, not even by Balic, Mir, or …" He licked his lips. "Her younger sister took the mantle and name of Quiss and was deemed too young by the draugr-mother Raven and draugr-father Aten-Sur to be turned into one of them. So, the young Quiss lived on until this one took her place."

Quiss looked at him and the book with trepidation.

"Where she is?" Caru muttered. "I don't know."

"Did you kill the girl?" I asked. "What did you do with her?"

Caru cleared his throat, but I watched Quiss. She said nothing, and her eyes were dark with fury. I knew that fury well.

"Why?" I asked her.

She lifted her eyes and looked outside. I heard a

noise. Then another.

Caru shifted in his seat. "She has lost her voice," he said. "Emotions. They do that to one."

"Tell us a story," I told Caru. "Make it a good one."

We both looked at Quiss, but Caru spoke. "Hel's War. It was fought over the Eye of Hel, stolen by two gorgons, First Born. Hel blamed it on an elf lord, instead. It all resulted in that elf stealing away the Gjallarhorn, the Horn that closes and opens all the gates in all the Nine Worlds, that the gods and mortals used to travel. The gates were closed, the elf kept the Horn, he kept the eye, and the gods and Hel, both, lost the war and were abandoned. The elf turned into a lich. The gorgons, who had hoped to conquer worlds while Hel destroyed others, waited."

Quiss was walking back and forth, her hand on her sword's hilt. "You know much," she said.

Caru nodded. "I was told much. I have learned much. I have had two decades, you bitch. I have learnt it all from one of your kind."

"Go on," I said.

He cleared his throat. "And then, humans, *very* special humans," he whispered, almost reverently, "came to Aldheim, the elven world, summoned by one of the gorgons. They could see the great power, and she, that gorgon, employed them to regain the Horn and the Eye. Many died. Aldheim was in war, and in the end, Shannon, the greatest of the humans, died in battle with the lich. The gorgon took the Horn, but Shannon, holding the Eye of Hel, died. She found herself with Hel, in Helheim, after crossing the bridges, carrying her Eye."

He rubbed his face.

"Hel rewarded her with a title and power. She was the new Hand of Hel. She was given Hel's dagger, Famine, a terrible weapon, and sent back for Hel's and Shannon's revenge. The gorgon, meanwhile, had made war on Aldheim, had opened a gate to Svartalfheim, and it looked dire for the elves. Shannon changed all that. She defeated the gorgon, and the gorgon's newly arrived sister. She defeated the armies. All of them. Both elven and svartalf. She did it with Hel's magic. She created draugr by tens of thousands of the fallen. Others. Not all are draugr. The spell resonated across the Nine Worlds. The Cataclysm in Midgard was part of that."

"Twenty years ago?" I asked.

He nodded.

He went on. "Hel had a purpose for Shannon. Hel wanted the Horn, she wanted the worlds to feel her pain, and Shannon led Hel's draugr after the Horn, which …" He took a deep breath. "Her fine sister, Dana, who had conspired against her earlier, causing her death, took to Svartalfheim. There, Shannon conquered Scardark, and only goddess Nött, the lady of the night, could stop her. Dana, and one Anja, and their guard, a dragon, used Nött's secret magic to come to Midgard. You see, only a god of a First Born, like all the three gorgons are, may blow the Horn and open a gate. Here, there was another, one—"

"Baduhanna, trapped," I said.

"Baduhanna," he agreed. "Trapped by your filthy father."

I swallowed the rage. Quiss was pacing back and forth, shaking her head.

Caru sighed, and went on, his eyes on the doorway. Shadows moved there. "They tried to find Baduhanna. Hel's minion followed them and brought forth the dagger Famine and deviously turned the kings and queens against each other. A great calamity, rebellion, and battle in Malignborg followed. Vittar, Aten-Guard, Harrian, Bellic … So many deaths occurred, so many high ones fell; a great magic was granted to Hel's minion by those deaths. From Famine was recalled ten terrible beings, who had died on it before."

Quiss held her face and leaned on the wall. She spoke. "Ten from the Stone, so they called themselves. Seven were vampires. You have not met them. Rhean is not one of these. They are elsewhere, doing their own evil, those that survived."

"Hel's plans on plans," I muttered as I looked at her.

Caru smiled. "Indeed! Seven vampires. Some fell. Few remain. I killed one, once. The three beings that were not vampires, were the most terrible curse on

Midgard. See, Hel wants many things. She wants to punish the gods and their worlds for her deformed existence. She wanted her Eye back. And then, she wanted one more thing, and that thing can be found in Midgard, in Mara's Brow."

"What is this thing?" I asked.

He leaned forward. "Wait. See— "

Quiss looked at him venomously. "This is not your business to share, Urac. Aye, it is Urac, and not Caru, because the imbecilic fool really thinks he is Mouth of Lok, instead of that Dana."

Caru, Urac, shook his head. "You keep your mouth shut, traitor. Hel seeks vengeance. That is why she attacked Midgard ages ago. Her Hand of Hel fought for her vengeance. These Ten from The Stone, twenty years ago, as well. The vampires I mentioned. Two others were Stheno, and Euryale, the gorgons Shannon killed with Famine, and the latter one is your current bane, jotun. She is the one evil that remains in Midgard, and is causing all of this. She is trying to get in to Mara's Brow, into a room sealed by your father, because Shannon, who came out of the stone last, set Euryale the Lich, the Serpent Skull in charge of a long-term plan. She was to take Midgard, and Euryale invented the One Man. Shannon set out north, for a short-term plan. If she were to fail to finish what Lok's first Hand of Hel failed to do, Euryale was to come and release her."

I stared at him. "Euryale set to do so? This is all about

that? And how would she have gotten in there? The Black Grip only works with one of our kin holding it."

He laughed. "Euryale would chew down the mountain, for Shannon's order is powerful. However, Euryale knew one of the special humans had a skill. She could open anything by touch. Anja, her name is. Shannon had captured her, she went after Dana, and the Horn, raised the northern dead with Stheno, the other undead gorgon, and found Medusa, who knew Mara's Brow and the location of the sealed room where their goal was. Dana and a warrior named Gutty aided Morag to fight them. What followed," he said sadly, "was terrible. Morag and her kin," he said, nodding at Quiss, "made a pact to fight the enemy, but in the end, Morag put down both the dead army, and their kin, and I hear sealed Medusa, Dana, Shannon, the brute in a chamber before Lok's prison. He took this Anja away and hid her."

I was nodding. Quiss looked down.

"Morag was never a good king," he said. "He made laws to protect his greed, his gold, his power. He abandoned old jotun gods, and sent them no treasure. A jotun of old blood, I know, is powerful when he serves his kings, or if he is of a royal blood, he serves his true gods. Morag hated men, he hated laws, but used both to cover himself in gold. He looted their Golden City," he said and looked at Quiss, "and sealed the Horn, Famine, and the heroes in, and took Anja, so they couldn't escape." He shook his head. "The dead have Anja now. Morag told them, the poor draugr. He will guide them to the door. Euryale will want to get in. She is plagued by Shannon's command."

Quiss spoke. "Maskan. I am sorry."

"Sorry," Urac laughed. "Your father was saved from Morag by Dana. He gave an oath to kill Morag, to get Black Grip back, and to save them. He was too weak. Where Morag is greedy, yours is weak. Opar agreed to help Euryale. He agreed to kill you. He betrayed us all."

Quiss shook her head. "Wait— "

I lifted a finger. "What did Hel want in Mara's Brow."

"That is a secret!" Quiss insisted.

"Don't play tricks with me," I told Urac, tired with the games. I was looking at the shadows outside. There were many, and they were looking inside. "You said vengeance."

Quiss stepped forward. "That is not for you to share!"

Urac went on, not taking heed of Quiss. "Like Shannon had set Euryale to save her, so Dana set these Sons of Ymir, freshly betrayed by Ymirtoes, to recover the Black Grip and to kill Euryale. Dana set me to spy here in the south and to aid the jotuns against the dead and Morag both. Now, Dana is dead. She was a human. She will have starved. Shannon, if she survived Dana, and Medusa are out there … poor Dana. I tried to take her place, but Lok doesn't speak to me. He doesn't ask me for protection. I—"

I leaned forward. "Wait. Lok *spoke* to this Dana?"

He wiped some tears off his eyes. "He did. He chooses vessels ... from birth. He seeks those with power, and he grants them more. That power, it comes with a cost. Dana survived all five times she asked for his help. That should have sealed her fate. She would have been Lok's slave. See, Lok is imprisoned, and he walks the land through these few, very powerful vessels. While writhing in chains made of his son's guts, tortured by snakes, he has ways to get his will out. With Dana, he sought a vessel to protect him in his prison. Dana bargained with him, and he had to make the bargain. He had no true hold over her, if she only fought for him. She tried. She is lost, thanks to Morag. But *Lok* is still in danger."

"Lok," said. "Hel was seeking her father."

"She is seeking *revenge* against her father," he said softly.

"That means ..." I began, astonished.

He grinned. "Because Lok's tricks made Odin wrathful, and Hel ended up punished for Lok's crimes, she wants revenge. She wants her Hand of Hel to conquer the Nine Worlds, to punish the Aesir and the Vanir, but she, most of all, wants to see Famine pushed to the heart of Lok, even more than she desires Odin's head. She wants him dead, seated next to Baldr in

Helheim."

Quiss shook her head. "But if you release Lok, by death, or otherwise, the world will end. Ragnarök might begin, the end of the Nine ..."

"Lok is in Mara's Brow?" I asked, holding my face. "Truly?"

"The jotun friend Lok, god of tricks," Urac said softly, "is imprisoned deep below Mara's Brow, where Yggdrasill's root touches Midgard, and now, perhaps after they release Shannon, who might still be the Hand of Hel and might still have Famine, they are trying to get back in there to finish the job. With their help." He looked at Quiss scathingly. "Her father, Opar, agreed to use Black Grip for the dead ones. They fought hard to stop Hel from killing jotun-friend Lok, and now, he just ... capitulated. That is why I had no choice but to trust son of Morag, who, perhaps, sees the light."

Quiss spoke, her eyes clouded with tears. "My kin, like yours, Maskan, left Hel's army when they tried to kill Lok the first time. No jotun took part. And my father, Opar, tried to do as Dana, the Mouth of Lok, asked him to. He took Urac's aid and information, he sent our people to war. He set me and others to spy on the enemy. I was a spy, Maskan. I spied on Aten and took the place of the girl. She is alive, by the way. She lives in the Golden City, a modest life." She stepped forward. "Opar tried to kill Morag many times. Many. So did the dead. We fought both the dead and Morag, they fought all of us, and Morag did the same as well. In the end, he lost half our people. Morag lost half his. There are now just fifty of us. And only one Ymirtoe."

"You failed," Urac said mercilessly. "Miserably. Euryale's dead killed Morag before you."

Euryale. The undead lich gorgon. Rhean's mistress. I know how to find her, I thought.

She held her face. "Yes. When he died, it was sudden. Then … Baduhanna," she said. "Baduhanna was released. She should have been able to stop Euryale. My father told me to help Maskan, and that way, we could have …"

Urac spat again. "Your father should have taken his jotuns to her then. He should have bowed to her, and aided her, guarded her, and this would not have come to this. And now? When Baduhanna died? He has agreed to *help* those dead shits." He held his head. "Help *them*! Morag cannot use the Black Grip, not when he is dead. Your betrayal," he said acidly, "is worse than failure and inaction. It is a complete reversal in everything he promised! The enemy has both Anja, and your father's oaths. He is betraying us all."

"He has made his mind," she said. "I know not what he— "

"He wants the Grip," Urac sneered. "He wants to go home. He abandons the worlds to evil. I bet that is it. Shit-pants of a jotun."

"Why," I asked her, "did you aid me? Only for

Baduhanna? You saw a way to Baduhanna through me?"

"I aided you, because of Baduhanna," she agreed. "Morag died, Hel was thriving, and we thought Baduhanna might do our work for us. Opar, my father, told me to aid you. He dared not bring our people to her. She might have killed the lot. She might fear us, she might hate us, and we'd die. Opar put all our hope on her. But I ..." She went quiet.

Urac smiled. "It was more than about Baduhanna. I see it. She liked you. Her bitter enemy, she fell in love with you. She aided you, and then, she liked you. She did."

She said nothing.

"And then, after Baduhanna died, and we both failed," I said. "Things changed. The deal was made."

She nodded.

"Opar, your father, devised a new plan," I said. "He went to Hel's spawn and made a deal. He commanded you to help slay me, because that is the price you will gladly pay to get into this Euryale's good side. Do you have another rock? The red one?"

She nodded. She pulled it from her belt. "I thought I lost the last one in the pool. The dead can follow me."

She looked outside, and I smiled. "Let them wait a bit."

She shook her head. "You cannot beat them."

"I picked your pockets," I said, ignoring her words.

"I picked them when we fell in the waterfall, threw it away, and gained time. I sent you away after. I knew when I found the stone. I suspected earlier. None else knew I was going to see this Antos but you. You were there, with Sand. You set your clansmen on me. You guided Sand, vampires, and killers on my tail. You gave Rhean my rings, the book, the earrings. You saved Rhean." I leaned forward. "You betrayed our army in Hillhold. It was not Roger who sallied forth from Hillhold. You told him to go and followed. You commanded him to surround the bait so the enemy could beat us easily. You gave him an order to form a shieldwall out there. You did all that for your traitor father. Euryale commanded him, and he commanded you, and you claimed you love me?"

"I never," she said miserably, "lifted my hand against *you*. I just … had to obey. I had to … the cause of my father …" She held her face.

"Is a coward's one," Urac said.

"You are an excellent actress," I said. "You are. You played Quiss very well. Too well. I … liked you well."

She shook her head. "You can only act so much, Maskan. I like you too. I … do. As for my father? He doesn't want to go home," she whispered. "He is no coward. I don't think he is. This is his last act of defiance. He told me. He failed, and he is trying to atone for it. He tells the enemy he wants to go back to Nifleheim. He tells them he wants Black Grip, and then, he shall open the ways in Mara's Brow to the enemy, if Anja doesn't, and they will open a way for him in return, the gate with the Horn, in Mara's Hold. Let Lok care for himself. So he told them. But he truly is going to try to surprise them, after the way is opened."

"I see," I said. "And love is nothing. You loved me, and betrayed me."

"I am a jotun," she said harshly. "We obey the king, or the queen, or our … gods. I am a chaotic thing." Her face shifted, and her body changed. Silvery chainmail gleamed, and a sword glittered on her side. She didn't grow, but her blue-green, bright eyes shone and a huge, white hair billowed out, behind her. Her face was cold as snow and sculpted as if of ice. "I, too, am of the old blood. My father, my brothers, one of whom you killed in Nallist, and my grandfather, and a line as long as yours are of the ancient breed. Oath to our family. That is what matters. No human, no elf, no dverg, nothing, goes above. Not even love."

I nodded. "So basically, they all must go in. Hand of Hel might be dead, but Famine and the Horn will be there. As will the First-Born. Medusa. She will not die?"

Urac shook his head. "She can heal herself. The gorgon kin, the lives ones, anyway, can drink the blood from their right side, and it can heal anything. It can bring the dead back to life. She will be there. Shannon … perhaps. The others are dead. In any case, Euryale has all the guides, all the keys, and if Shannon is gone, she will be the Hand. She will rule Midgard, she will take the worlds one by one for Hel, and there might not be any, if she also opens Lok's prison." He looked at Quiss. "You say he is playing a game, and you imply, he will not let Lok's prison be opened, and let's pray it is so. He plays a dangerous game, for he must kill Anja."

"Is Anja on Hel's side?" I asked.

He shook his head. "She is not. But Euryale is a lich, and she commands vampires, and while draugr jotun loses his ability to shapeshift at death, a vampire Anja might not. Besides, perhaps Rhean will just force her with her power. It is a terrible power."

Quiss spoke. "How do you know this much about these matters?"

"I had an adventure," Urac said with shivers. "I spied them once, before I was caught. I heard Euryale teaching her draugr. It is a story meant for another time."

I rubbed my forehead. "You led the lot after me, Quiss. I can never forget."

She lifted her head. "My father, no matter what he is planning, has given us *orders*. I cannot disobey him. I have aided you as well. I have begged you survive, but I cannot deny his command."

I snarled and pointed my ax at her. The shadows outside moved to the doorway. I saw gleaming pair of eyes.

"You bedded me," I yelled. "You loved me. But you

cannot break your oath to him."

"Only death can! You are a Ymirtoe … I …" she began and looked down.

"The lass loves you," he laughed. "Ymirtoe or not. Oaths or not."

"But you do not love me back," she said sadly. "You *did*. You did for a while. You cannot lie to me."

"Aye. Thrum spoke of a Jotun's Kiss," I said. "You felt me. You, despite your father's orders—"

She stepped towards me. "Jotuns who love each other are linked. Yes. It is a rare thing, but it happens. A female can hear her male. She can feel him near. Males, stupid brutes, feel nothing like it, but we do. I felt your thoughts. I felt them since the battle of Dagnar. I have loved you since then. I couldn't help it. You loved me as well. Our love was real. I know it was, because I could feel you. I could …" She looked sad enough to break my heart.

"You broke your oath to your father," I said brutally, "by teaching me about our god, our ability to call for it."

"I—"

"Yes. You did. You betrayed, and saved me. Again, and again. You saw me and Nima marry, and you tried to make a jotun out of me, ashamed of such a marriage, ashamed of my plans to follow my father, and of my hope to serve my human kingdom. You tried to make me into one of you. You were so jealous, you nearly broke my head with your furious thoughts."

She took a shuddering breath. "I am sorry. I was. Nima …"

"Humans are my meat," I laughed. Urac shifted in his seat, uncomfortable. "I have recently seen, they shall never love me."

"They shall not," she whispered. "You are a jotun. No matter what father ordered me to do."

"You can no longer hear me," I said. "Or feel me."

She shook her head. "No. I felt the bond grow weak after Saag's Hold. I guess you knew then, or guessed. Then, after Nallist? You … I guess you simply and slowly fell out of love with me after the battle. I missed you being so close to me. I miss it now. You cannot love a traitor. You shut your heart to me. Nima took my place."

I smiled. "No. Nima's a human. She is my meat, no? It was my anger for Sand's attack in Saag's Hold, and what happened in the legionnaire outpost. But what really broke it was Rhean," I told her sadly. "She charmed me. I fought her, but I had to … let her close to me. I cannot stop thinking about her. I am sorry."

She looked furious and closed her eyes. "That bitch. The first one raised by Shannon, the Hand of Hel, she was special. Balic came only after her. She has done this for decades."

"Where is Grinlark? You took it."

"With father," she said. "That, too, as was Black Grip, belonged to us once."

"Where can I find your father?" I asked her.

She opened her mouth and shut it. "It is too late for that." She stepped aside. "That far I won't betray my oaths. And they are here."

I shook my head. "I loved you. I shall not forget this."

Sand entered. So did a man, who was clearly an undead. He was a vampire, a cold-faced man in a large coat. There were four hulking shadows that shrunk as they stepped behind him. Axes out, they stood still.

I got up. So did Urac.

"Welcome," I snarled.

"Why?" Quiss asked. "Why did you take me along, if you knew I was …" She went quiet and squinted. She hid a smile. "You want peace for your own plans. You …"

"Sand," I said softly.

"You made a mistake, Maskan," he told me, the half-skull gleaming and eyes bright spots of madness.

"I know. Tell them, Sand," I said. "Your Euryale is going to betray Opar and the Sons of Ymir. Isn't she?"

He smiled. "Enough, Maskan. Enough. I heard you. Opar's the one who is doing all the betraying, not mistress Euryale. Now. It is time for this to end, finally. Your paltry victories shall be buried on this beach. Then, soon, the men of Red Midgard shall follow. We have a bigger issue to deal with in the north, first."

"No," I said, and held my shield before me. "The two are the same. My armies are moving north. They have ships. They are tired, hurt, bloodied, and in no condition to sail anywhere. They are still going to Mara's Brow. Well, not all. Some of the dverger are not in the ships. They had to go elsewhere."

"Eh?" he asked.

The vampire stepped forward. "Enough. He has made too many clever guesses. He must be silenced, and the mistress warned of Opar's treason." He walked for me and cast a baleful look at Urac. Urac fell back, held his face, and went to his knees. The red eyes turned back to me, and the fear he cast over me, made my heart beat fast.

With rage.

"Kneel, jotun," he said. "Kneel, and I shall—"

I slashed my ax down at him. He fell apart, and I kicked the remains, my blood boiling with anger. "No undead shall ever again scare me. Never. I will pay a price for that, won't I? Quiss, what is your real name?"

"Asra," she whispered, and smiled softly. "I see. Bolthorn. And you are prepared here."

I pointed the ax at her as Urac got up, holding his chest. "I did. I did indeed ask help. And do you really think I cannot read anagrams or figure one out?" I asked her with a sneer. "Do you think I cannot set a trap for you, like you did for me? Tris and Nima, time, and a ship, and maps are all I needed. I kept you and I busy for days, while they came here. And you," I said, and turned to Sand. "I have always been the brains in our outfit, Sand. You were the brawn, I was the smarts, even back in the streets when we were still thieves. It is time, Sand, to make my move. My own."

"No, that's not true," Sand called out, and let out a spell of darkest fire. It burned from his hands so fast, I couldn't blink. It was scorching hot, a touch of death, and it struck my shields and rolled over me.

And died.

I pulled out Lisar's pendant, bone with a yellow gleam in the middle.

Urac took a sharp breath. "That … I lost it to Lisar ten years ago! It was hers, once. You …"

"It is mine now," I said, and bowed to Sand. "Goodbye." I stepped aside.

From outside, ballista bolts shot inside. Heavy, deadly, they tore into jotun backs. Two fell on their faces, howling, their guts torn out. I saw the illusions of stones falling apart as the dverger picked up crossbows. From the corners of the hall, twenty dverger stepped out of a spell of concealment. They lifted crossbows and fired.

The two remaining jotuns howled, their shields and faces, throats, and bodies filled with bolts.

Sand hissed, pulled his sword, and called for darkness.

I lifted my shield and found myself standing in a sea of light, surrounded by mists, Lisar's pendant protecting me. Sand appeared next to me, bewildered by the light, and dodged my ax. He stepped past me, under my shields, and whirled.

There was a spear moving out of the darkness, and it flashed to his neck. Urac, moving like a viper, was pushing him down. "I've done a fair bit of fighting in the dark in my time," he said. "Say goodbye to him."

The spell of darkness died.

Sand looked up, trying to get up, his sword up.

I stepped on his sword and hacked down. He twitched, and his skull was cloven. He was still.

I turned to look at Asra.

She was taking steps back.

"You will take me to your father," I snarled.

"No, he will meet her soon, in a day or two," she said. "I don't want you two to meet. It won't end well. Happily, you do not know where Euryale is."

She shook her head, stepped back again, and then, she changed into an owl, great, white, and fast. She flapped for the doorway.

She flew into a heavy net, and that net entangled her.

I watched the dverger surround her, to pull the net together. I watched her changing into a raging bear, into a wolf, a small wolverine, and finally into herself, eleven feet tall and fierce, beautiful, and she remained stuck. In the end, Thrum stepped next to her and bashed her in the knee with a hammer and then in the temple. She was down, moaning.

Urac walked for her.

I stopped him. "I will aid Lok," I told him. "But you will have to obey me."

He licked his lips nervously and then bowed. "Lok thanks you, surely," he said, face full of mad relief. "My Dana will be dead, but Lok shall survive."

I nodded. "Do you know where the Serpent Skull is. This Euryale."

"This I know not," he said sadly. "I have no idea."

"If you follow me to the end," I told her, "and I succeed, you shall have a great task. You will get your heart's desire. It will be a great trick, worthy of your god."

He bowed. "I agree. I have none else. What, pray tell me, are you fighting for now?"

I grinned. "For me and a promise. Thrum?"

"King?" he said, as Urac stepped back.

"Take the ships you came here with," I told him, "and join the legions. Take Urac here, and Sand. Row north, and I shall meet you on the coast. If not? Then, you find a way to die in a manner you find pleasing."

"Aye, King, of course," he murmured. "I'll start planning for just that."

I walked out, my eyes on Asra. I found Tris leaning on the doorway. She lifted her eyebrow. "Well. My dear Nima warned me this would be interesting."

"You brought your friends along to the Riddle," I said. "Why? You must have known it would end badly for them. You were supposed to come alone, and we were supposed to ask you about the anagram. You were simply supposed to—"

"Oh, hush. Friends. We knew each other from years past, all serving the legion of Aten. Why?" she said. "I owed the hook-nose money. Lots of it. Gult was insufferable dolt. You saw him. Barely coherent. And my captain, the man you killed, bedded me every chance he had. He knew I helped smugglers and took a cut, but it wasn't enough. He wanted and took more. It was an opportunity, see? And still, you learnt something from the Black Ship scrubbing turds?"

"I did," I told her. "You did well, even if it wasn't intentional. In fact, it might have saved Midgard. We needed the time to get Thrum here. You made it all perfect. None is hunting me now. I have a chance. You will be well rewarded."

She nodded, pleased. "I cannot stay. They know I was there in the Riddle. So, I am coming with you. How will you find this Opar?" She shrugged at my look. "I listened. I did. So what?"

"Where I go, you cannot go," I said, "but as agreed, you and Nima can figure out how to reward you. She'll give you a piece of Red Midgard. Any piece. I care not. Excuse me."

I went to crouch before Asra. Her eyes were open, and she held her temple. "Where … can I find your father?"

"I cannot," she said. "I cannot tell you. My oaths are

to him, and our clan. You could be wrong."

I nodded and smiled. "I too miss that bond."

She smiled. "When I first saw you, I despised you. You were without your jotun's powers, a human more than one of us. And still, that human, he was brave. You went against Raven, Balic, and tried to save Baduhanna. You fought armies with rabble and challenged the south and prevailed. No human could do that. Jotun might. I saw you in Dagnar, planning devious traps for our foes. You were madly brave and strong. No oaths. No old ways. Just Red Midgard. I envied you. No burdens of your kin to weigh you down. But you must know the humans hate all of us. They will never—"

I stroked her cheek. "I know now. I also know my father, and your kin were greedy, selfish, and forgot to share it with our gods. I shall not do the same mistake now. I spit on all my dreams."

She shook her head. "Don't find Father. He hates you. All Ymirtoe. He won't listen. Don't stop him from his quest. He might save us all."

I rubbed my face. "Aye."

I got up and turned away, my heart pumping.

"Don't try to find them," she called out. "I will hate the jotun who kills my father. It would release me from my oaths, but I will hate you!"

I looked back at her. "He makes his own decisions. And I care not if you hate me, if you and I will lead our kin to victory, riches, and power. You and I shall marry, and rule well, in love, or out of it. Alas, that I love Rhean."

I left, and spoke with Urac, Tris, and Thrum. Then, I took to wing.

I had a way to find the enemy.

I had to follow the corpses.

BOOK 5: THE SERPENT SKULL

"Alas, it matters little if you betrayed us or not. I still must kill you."

Maskan to Opar

CHAPTER 16

I slid across the sky and then beat my wings furiously as I lost altitude. It was dark, overcast, and the wind promised more snow for the north. While adopting an animal shape, a jotun instinctively knows how to take advantage of its unique powers and learns how to enjoy the wonderful sensations of flight, the enhanced sense of sight.

It took experience to fully understand how and when best to utilize those skills.

Where a sensible eagle would be asleep in its nest, I was struggling with hail, wind, and general misery. I flapped my way through it all and passed over the Arrow Straits. I hugged the coast and searched the snowy, relatively calm sea until I finally spotted our naval force. There were the food transports and the transport galleys of the Grinning Mask and the Skull legions. I spotted the standards the new legion had taken. They had chosen the Six Spears. There were others, picked up from the battlefield. There were over sixty such ships, and I begged the enemy would not send the galleys south. They would sink our fleet. Some were sinking, nonetheless. The sea had not iced over yet and wouldn't for week or two, but I spotted two ships that had floundered and several that leaked.

I left them. I'd meet them in the north, if I survived and if they did.

I flew north and cut out to the sea, cursing the darkness, the unpredictable weather, and circling the Bay of Whales for hours. I saw a few ships. I saw the crews working hard on the decks, and they were mostly sailing for the east, for the Golden City.

Then, I spotted something.

There was a ship sailing for the *north*. It was silent and had not a soul on the deck. The name was *The Vigilant Wife*. The hook-nose had mentioned it.

I banked and flew around it.

It would be filled with corpses. I smelled them immediately, the stench of carrion.

It was a fat, lonely ship in the middle of the gray and black sea, and a single lantern shone in its cabins. I flew down for the ship, and around it, seeking a sign of life, but found none. The helm was housed in a sheltered aft part of the ship, and no pilot, officer, or captain stood on the decks. The crow's nest was also empty. If it was crewed by men, there would be a watch on the deck.

The crew would be draugr.

It looked like a ghost ship. It was the one.

I approached the ship again and made a relatively graceful landing on the aft deck. I hopped around the slippery railing, then the deck, and considered the aft part of the ship, which had been covered by leather canvases. There, I saw a man holding the black-wooded helm. He was staring ahead, over the horizon, and was long-dead. Not bothering to hide his condition, he was a rotten-faced man with filed teeth and lank hair in a ponytail. The draugr needed no guidance as to where to go. They stood no watch. They wouldn't be asleep. They would adjust the sail and go back down. They knew the route very well.

I hopped on the deck and flapped my wings to keep my balance and then saw an open hole.

I didn't hesitate and shapeshifted.

I, a huge rat, slithered down to the stairs. Assaulted by smells and sounds, I was careful. I descended, hopping softly from one step to the other. A galley, used a decade ago last time, was to my right. Bones littered the floor, and old kettles held the aroma of beef stew, long rotten. In front, behind a ragged screen, I saw glimpses of a lower deck.

I sneaked forward and found dozen draugr sitting around a table that had been nailed down. A hundred long-forgotten hammocks swayed with the movement of the ship, forlorn. Some had a skeleton in them. The crew was playing cards and cursing.

"Again and again," said one, a nearly skeletal draugr. "You have been cheating even before we died."

"I cannot help it," said a draugr in a rich, red coat and a flamboyant, wide hat. "I never could, and even less now." His voice was soft and unapologetic.

Another one touched an old bottle filled with liquor, stared at it, took a swig and smacked his lips. It didn't please him, and still, he tried again.

The skeletal draugr was shaking his head. "Not long now. I'll be happy to see this duty end. They'll put us on shore soon. Stop using the cards in your belt! I see you!"

The flamboyant draugr spat dryly. "I'm the captain, and I cheat all I want. I'll be careful ashore, I will, if we play with the living. With you lot? I need no subtlety."

"Is it true?" asked the one who had taken a drink. "They are nearly ready?"

"They are," said the captain, pulling out a high card from his hat. The skeletal one was grinding his teeth together in rage. "The Serpent Skull is nearly ready with the lot. All geared up, put into companies and armies. She has her generals and captains and plans. I doubt we shall be on the land for long, eh? The victory will be swift, and we own Midgard. Soon, we'll go where we please, eh, loved ones?"

They all looked glum.

"No," said the skeletal one. "We'll be left to rot in some scummy port until they put us to work again. They'll not let us go. They'll find new wars, new continents, new damned worlds, and we'll be hauling the stiff ones again in some god-cursed river of piss in Muspelheim."

The captain pulled all the coin on the table to him, his eyes gleaming. "I doubt they need to haul them anymore, boys. You have seen what her highness has built. We are past those times, my lovelies. They shall enjoy Midgard and start planting carrots, maybe. As for now, a few days to Ygrin and then to work, my sweet boys. Then, we'll see." She caressed the skeletal one's face, cracking his skin with a ring.

I realized the captain was a female.

"I hate the Dome," one of them remarked. "Filthy hive of villains. Too many candles. Seems like a waste."

"It is a waste," the captain agreed. "But they are rich, and waste what they like, eh? And it is our filthy hive, isn't it? Better than what's on top. No place less liked in the north. Filled with the sick, the dying. I don't mind the dead, but the dying? They are all so noisy and whine like children. Never could abide children."

Ygrin.

They were going to Ygrin, our ally north of Falgrin. Dome was their city. I had never heard of it.

"Damned nasty island," the skeletal one muttered. "I hear they'll take Mara's Brow in a day or two. They say it shall be glorious."

"Aye, they will. And the army will march as well. Mara's Brow is but a personal business to the ladies in charge. Nothing but a silly scheme they are running, though a good base … wait," the captain said, looking at her belt, seeking a card that would give her the victory. Then, there was a call, and most all got up, cursing.

They were going to trim the sails.

I slipped out and found a stairway to the hold.

There, I found the corpses.

A hundred or two lay in piles covered with sheets, blankets, or leather hides. Their feet stuck out towards the middle, in four rows, heaped high over the ballast stones. They were mostly officers and sergeants of the legions, most fallen in Alantia and in various battles, and had likely left Nallist just before I took it. I stalked through them and alarmed some fellow rats, who soon went back to their snacks of flesh and eyeballs. The heroes had been hacked to death, many killed by arrows, and few even strangled. They all had legs and arms, and were, I supposed, prime corpses to be raised.

The draugr had been doing it for twenty years. They had been collecting them in a city of Dome, some sort of filthy island filled with sick and dying.

Opar, he would be there.

I blocked the anxiety out of my mind and settled in a corner to wait. I waited and watched my fellow rats feasting.

Two days later, half starved, I found I had arrived in Dome. I heard scrambling legs on top, the call of gulls, and soon, they were opening the deck above. Light shone down all the way to the hold.

A draugr looked down and grinned, his eyes gleaming. "Rise and shine, pretties. Join the brotherhood, aye, even you, sisters! Welcome to the Serpent's Spire and the Dome under!"

***

The island, located off the coast of Ygrin, was a dismal place. A terrible one.

Slinking along the deck, my whiskers assaulted by the smell of dead things of the sea, I could see the barren coasts of Ygrin far to the north. Even further, where the Bay's northern independent counties and duchies began, beyond them, I could see the great steppes blended with the Blight, the mountains far, far away.

The western coast held cities and valleys, which would, come spring, be bountiful and rich, but only for a while. The capital of Ygrin was located far in the hills, but their harbor and trade city of Illon was visible to the west. There, spires and walls gleamed in the pale morning light.

Then, we glided past the southern peninsula of the island, and I only saw the villages and woods.

There were dozens of miserable communities.

People had gathered to watch the ship arrive. They were madmen, hermits, filthy and dangerous. I saw them walking on the shores, fingers clutching sticks and stones. Others were sick. They were missing parts of their body. Hand, fingers. Leg, nose, ears. Many were old, poor, and destitute. This was the place the north sent her unwanted, those it wanted to forget, and no solider or noble came to it gladly.

There was a small harbor ahead with a stone pier and a tiny fort that jutted above a miserable village. The fort was made of wood, and some sort of soldiers stood on the walls, likely made up of the worst scum the north had to offer.

The island itself was long and barren, and beyond the village, the center of it was filled with forests and high crags.

"The count's waiting," said the draugr captain. "He sits on his horse like a sack of turds. Looks sullen, doesn't he. I don't like them sullen. One would think he knows better than to irritate us. I took the head of his brother-in-law a year ago for sneezing. Can't let go, can he?"

"Aye, he cannot," said the skull-face. "He might follow his brother-in-law soon."

"Cover up, boys," the captain said. "They'll all join us soon enough."

I felt them braiding spells together and saw the dead taking living appearances. They were sailors, pirates, smugglers, and bastards the lot, but now looked alive. The captain's face smoothed into red-painted cheeks and highbrow and her men into salt-bitter sailors.

The count, I saw, and his men were all silent and waiting.

The village was empty, the doors closed. Wagons by the dozens, muddy and old with bedraggled mules and horses, were waiting.

One of the count's men was coughing.

They were likely all alive, but not on the side of the living. They took coin and kept their mouths shut. The count watched the ship mooring in his miserable little harbor, where fishing boats and small dinghies clanged against each other in their moldy misery, and he said not a word as the draugr commandeered wagons and horses, silently dropped a bag of coins on his lap, and proceeded to unloading their grisly cargo.

He stood there, waiting, sweating, terrified, and knew very well what was happening.

Soon, the first wagons were pulling out of the village.

I slithered out of the ship, ran down the gangplank, and rushed under a wagon. Then, I slipped inside, squatting under a former captain of Aten, a young man once.

I bided my time, and the wagons lurched forward. The sounds of the harbor filled with the sounds of the birds. After some more waiting, I poked my nose out from under the cover.

I was grabbed by the neck. I squealed with surprise and prepared to shapeshift.

"Well," said a white-bearded, rotten draugr driver, whose friend had seen me. "Fat and juicy, eh? I mean them corpses, aren't they, my rat friend? Haven't seen this one before. Must sail the other ships usually. I'd remember one that large. Looks like a dog."

"I like rats," the draugr holding me murmured. His eyes were gone, and fires burned behind the dead flesh in his skull. His lips were dry and black. "I remember I used to like cats and had a dozen. But now, rats. Rats are smart and survive anything. Well … except being squeezed."

He didn't squeeze, to his luck.

The driver scowled. "Cats. Cats ate my shoe, once. Give him a morsel, eh?"

The draugr looked behind and considered ripping a bit of flesh of a body, but then shrugged and kept stroking me.

I relaxed somewhat and looked over the dozens of wagons rattling on a rustic road, over a land of snowy landscape, for the craggy hillsides still free of snow. There were glimpses of green grass, bright as morning, and even some late flowers. The hills were rugged, and huge tower-like ravines ran between them.

"Will they be ready," my draugr muttered. "I doubt they are ready."

"They'll be ready," the driver grunted. "They are all on their toes with the high and mighties here. The four vampires and her darkness make things work smoothly." He poked me viciously, and I bit at the finger. He clutched it away and chuckled. "Beware, Ilk," the driver said. "I once saw a rat pet. It belonged to that lady of Olin in our barracks, and she used it to torment those who didn't give her love and appreciation. If she had held a shroud on that face of hers, she would not need a rat to punish anyone with!" he laughed. "Ugly for a draugr, she is. That rat ate some brothers who denied her fun, didn't it? Make sure to lock the rat up, if you *sleep*."

They chuckled. They didn't sleep. They missed it.

"I like her, the lady," the draugr holding me muttered. "She has a personality, rather unlike others in the Spire and Dome. She has no agenda but love making. She spreads it."

The driver hooted. "She spreads what? Her legs? Her rotten thighs? She does! You have *had* her? You fool. No dead one should love. You cannot forget her, ever! She must treat you terribly to lift the spell! Or you must have another, better than she is. That just feeds the affliction, of course. You are completely lost."

"It is my misery and not yours. I'll give the rat to her as a present," he murmured, his dead, intense eyes glowing with single-minded purpose. "I'll tell her you don't think she is pretty."

He looked glum. "She would prefer your jugular, I bet," the driver laughed. "You won't find her. They will be moving. You might just want to snap the rat's neck."

The driver eyed me, and I could see it grew attached to its own idea.

The draugr that had me, on the other hand, took the opposite view. "No, no. I'll keep her."

"*Him*," the other one crumbled. "Got balls you could play dice with. Fat and juicy. Maybe just fat. It looks dirty, after all."

"Whichever, but I'll keep it. Just should find it some flesh to nibble on," my friend muttered. "I'm sure our people left some bits and pieces behind, if they left."

They laughed hollowly.

The remainder of the journey I spent sitting in the lap of the rat-loving draugr. I watched the hills as we came closer and closer to them. They grew out of the dark gray fog like forgotten behemoths, and soon, we saw there were old ruins on the hillsides.

"I wonder," the driver murmured. "What happened to the poor bastards in the hill, long ago."

"What happens to poor bastards all over," the rat-lover answered. "They get cooked in their own guts, that's what happens. Annoyed a wrong king or just caught a nasty disease of snot and shit. They all suffer, love. They will, again, soon."

"I hope we make some treasure, if they let us go," the driver said.

"We'll rob the corpses, as usual," my friend lamented. "The boat-scum hope the same. They want a break from this labor. The generals? They'll not take us. Besides, they'll need us to collect the corpses soon enough."

The words were ominous, and the silence oppressing until we reached the edge of a craggy hills, and a captain commanding the wagons raised his haggard arm to the air.

On the closest low hillside, doors were opening. The hill was suddenly a beehive of undead activity. A streams of walking corpses rushed down the hill, and I saw a larger cave opening halfway up the hill, inside which lights flickered. We rode forward again as horn blared in the evening air, briefly and lazily, and without any apparent urgency.

On the very top of the hill, on the crest, a cavalcade appeared.

There, wearing a brilliant red, rode the queen of Malignborg, and the mind behind many of the undead plots looked down. Rhean was speaking to four others. They were pale, dangerous looking men. They were her spawn, her former lovers, and all watched her with adoration and servitude. Her eyes went over me, and even from afar, I felt compelled by those orbs. I felt the love for her.

The dread she instilled in a mortal heart made me also angry.

I bit down on my draugr, who didn't notice.

Her bastard ilk wore gold and black, all looking splendid, as if the dead were having a party. Their horses stood silent as the nasty creature took her time to oversee the activity below, and then, she whipped her horse and rode from the hill.

She didn't go to the hill above us, but she rode to the crags. Then, I saw some light.

Deep in the hilly lands, amid crags, was a tower of stone. Lights flickered from small windows. It was thick as the Ugly Brother, a fortress with a natural wall, part of the mountainside, but still likely hollow. It overlooked a great deal of the land around it. As I watched, it seemed to change, to be covered by magic, and appeared exactly like any part of the mountain.

The Serpent Spire.

The enemy was well-hidden in plain sight.

The wagons rumbled the last moments for the hillside, and I, looking up appreciatively at my new friend, let go of his finger and slipped from his hands.

"Hey!" he called out. "Get back here! I'll find you something later. I promise!"

"See, I told you—" I heard the other one complain, but I rushed into a snow-filled ditch and around the hill and eventually to the crags.

Nothing was moving out there. Not a thing.

It was late when I looked up the stone tower. I circled it and scurried about in confusion.

There was no apparent way in.

I ran around it again, sniffling, pushing my snout in every hole, and scraping the rough stones on the base. I smelled nothing but decay and rock, snow and grass, and horse manure. Nothing gave away an entrance. I looked up. There were no lights. No windows.

Had I imagined it?

Still, Rhean and her ilk *had* ridden this way.

I looked around the crags around the Spire. Rough ways wound up and down the craggy hillsides. There were horse tracks going past the great stone spire. They disappeared into the depths of the hills. Some ran left, others right.

No horses had trampled the snow and mud around the great spire. None had entered it.

There was no entrance.

Then, I heard cows mooing to the west. I turned and hastened for a well-churned route past two hillsides. I scampered up and down, cursing the slippery mud.

I came to an edge of valley, not far from the stone spire, and looked below.

A herd of cows and many horses were running along a rough stony side of the hills. They were driven for a village below me and had left the northern edge of the valley, where pastures were still rich with grass. The trail they took by the edge of the hillsides had been churned into a huge, muddy rut. Men or draugr were herding them.

There were small villages in that valley, with pastures, and the sea and the far-away coast gleamed on the west edge of it. It looked like a hidden paradise amid the terrible island.

I rushed down to the closest village, and it was dark when I got there.

There were dogs prowling the streets, and I hesitated. Men were riding the streets as well and looked well-armored and alert.

And still, the houses were rustic and seemed to be all involved in making dinner. The smell of lentils and cabbage wafted from each doorway. A rat was never wrong.

Rhean would not be there.

I turned to the north and looked at the stony hillsides. They were spattered by mud, and I wasn't sure if there was another track in the north end of the valley. I ran along the track anyway, suffered indignities from muddy horse shit, and sneaked forward along the wall. I ran along it, until I saw something odd.

In one place, the tracks were *right* next to the wall.

In that place, it seemed like horses and cows had galloped against the rock. I sniffled the tracks and then nearly died.

A troop of draugr burst from the wall. Their horses neighed wildly, and their riders grinned as they thundered away, rotten and terrible, in armor both of the Hammer Legions and archaic. Some were merely skin and skeleton. There were more and more, and I shivered in a rut as hooves splashed seemingly all around me.

It seemed to last forever.

Then, suddenly, the cavalcade was gone.

I found I was still in one piece. I heard the creak of a gate and sprung for the wall that was hidden by magic.

I passed through an illusion and crashed into a gate, bounced back, and charged forward again through a tiny crack in a massive gate set on a side of mountain and dodged between the legs of two draugr who noticed nothing.

I sprinted to the side, found a barrel, and hid behind it. I looked around.

The hall was meant as a muster-hall. Beyond it were dark doorways that led both up, likely for the distant Serpent Spire, and down. They were heavily guarded and closed, though now another troop of draugr was going to move out, for a doorway down below was shuddering. Then, it was pushed open and in rode a troop of riders out of the depths, their eyes cold and their voices harsh. Halberds, spears, and poled hooks were swinging over their shoulders.

I noticed two creatures emerging from a hall to the side. There, the guards would spend their miserable time. These two were captains.

"Hurry up," yelled a draugr with a golden bracelet, rotting white face, and lustrous, blonde hair. She was standing in the middle of the hall. "Must not linger. Hurry up and get out and do your duties. We march, we march, and you must guard the land when we do. Hurry your bones, you dog-faced bastards."

And they did hurry. Gear jingled, blades clanged, and they all were rushing.

With the commander of the gate, there stood another figure. It was a woman dressed in embroidered gown, her face white as snow, and lips blue. She wore enough gold to feed a fair-sized town for years, jingling and blinking in the torchlight. Her eyes were not on the army preparing to ride out.

They were on the shadows. She was casting something, and then, her eyes went white.

She had sensed something? She had smelled the manure on my coat?

It mattered little. She was seeking something, and she was sensitive and dangerous.

She was a draugr with special skills. I stayed still, very still.

She hesitated and frowned.

Then, she whistled.

It was a long, high whistle, and it was answered.

Out of the guard loped four hounds.

They were not your usual guard dogs.

They looked large like ponies, and they were not barking. They were, in fact, dead. Their ribs showed under their shaggy furs, and one had a skeletal snout, filled with sharp bones.

They looked up at their mistress, listened to her hissed instructions, and then began sniffling and walking about.

Like any rat would, I shivered with fear. The hounds, with their snouts on the stone, would make me very uncomfortable in a moment.

I looked at the shadows and knew my time would soon be up. The dogs were meticulously seeking every spot.

One dog raised its snout, his eyes on the barrel that

hid me. Its shaggy ears twitched. It walked forward, snarling softly.

I cursed, waited, and sprinted forward.

I did it so fast, the hound simply stared at me dully as I slipped between its legs, bit at a dangling, rotten nut, and tore away as fast as I could.

The hounds turned and sprinted after me, in mute silence.

Their draugr mistress saw me and frowned.

I jumped on a horse of a splendidly armored draugr captain, waited for a moment, and then sprung on another.

The dogs bowled to the horse.

What followed was utter chaos.

I jumped for a horse to another and bit down on each. The draugr were thrown, the horse bolted, and in a moment, the entire herd of horses were whinnying and rushing around the hall, back down the passageway. Draugr, with their spears clattering together, were howling with anger, some with fear, and when I last saw the hound-master draugr and the captain of the guard, they were about to be trampled on by tens of horses. Two of the dogs were but broken bones and bits of meat on the stone.

I laughed, it came out as a squeak, and the horse beneath me whinnied and kicked.

I flew and landed on a draugr, whose mount was galloping onto the bowels of the cave. I fell off him to the rear of the horse and bit down. We, the draugr and the rat, both hung on. The horse and twenty others were riding like mad down the occasionally lit tunnel, which seemed to go on forever. I hung on for dear life.

One horse fell and took down another. Then, a draugr was crushed to the wall, and the horse fell on the path of most others.

Ours jumped over it, skidded on the wet floor, and we went on.

"Stop! Stop it!" the draugr screamed, losing his spear to a low hanging ceiling. "Why won't you stop?" he begged and kept begging until we came to a land under the mountains, a seemingly eternal land of darkness, and it felt like we were riding across the night sky.

Still the horse went on, panting, its legs bloodied.

Then, I realized I was biting down on it.

I let go, fell off, and landed on my feet on a rock.

The draugr and the horse went on, riding to the darkness beyond.

I stood on the rock, sniffling the air.

I heard noises, the groan of rock, the shuffle of feet, the song of an underworld. I realized it was mainly under the sea.

That the miserably island had such a secret, was breathtaking.

The darkness beyond, I noticed, was dotted with lights, far and wide. I heard the dripping of the water and then the clink of armor. I heard whisperings, I smelled blood and old death, and felt familiar terror.

There, somewhere in the vast darkness, Rhean, and perhaps her mistress, would be hidden.

I saw a cluster of lights to my right. There were many such blinking spots. They were weak, but still, my best bet to finding something useful.

I charged forward. I rushed for the lights and then, after scuttling a long while in the dark, stopped.

I had found, no doubt, Dome.

There, below the ground, were the ruins of an ancient city, a settlement of buildings that rose higher and higher in layers and did indeed resemble a rough dome.

It looked like a *rough* dome because many were broken buildings.

Who had built it, when and why, was a mystery. It had obviously been there for ages.

Candles and torches burned in the depths of the buildings. The walls were finely crafted, with intricate details, and only the roofs were missing.

I was lucky they were.

I changed into an owl and took to my wings. My sight was immediately much improved. I flapped around the area and nearly plummeted from the sky in shock. I noticed that all around the great city, there were statues. They stood in ranks around the place. They were black and gray and looked like a gallery of some mad god sculptor. There were tens of thousands of them, perhaps more, and some were kneeling, others looking up. They were eerie and looked old.

I glided around the structures of the dome and found a great market-place. I saw more massive statues surrounding the huge area and remains of old booths. There, I saw a terrifying throne.

It was a throne of snake-headed woman. There were a hundred growing from her skull. The female was kneeling, and you could sit on her lap. She was looking up to the sky, her four arms wide, palms up as if she was praying. The seat was dark as night and surrounded by fire. Before that seat moved a figure.

Nay, I saw *many* figures.

It was Rhean and many others.

I watched from high as a vampire was being dressed. She stood in the middle of the great city, in her own domain, in her finest dress, and her four vampires were next to her in battle armor. They wore white chain, and all held swords. Two women, likely draugr, were removing Rhean's dress, and two were waiting with white armor and a fine sword and shield, one with the skull and serpent symbol.

I fluttered around the market and then landed high up on a ruined wall. I watched the party of evil below. I watched Rhean.

And loved her.

I loathed, hated, and loved her. I should have feared her, but Bolthorn's boon gave me a way to fight them. That rage was churning deep in my chest, mixing with the love, and I felt sick for it.

Rhean was listening to a draugr, an old king of some sort with an ancient iron crown on his head. With him stood a lady of golden hair, golden skin, still as the throne and silent.

On Rhean's belt was the Black Grip.

The gauntlet, made of simple steel with pale jewels, didn't look exactly like it once had. It seemed of different color, it had undergone subtle changes, and I knew its magic gave it odd powers of change over times.

And yet, I knew it immediately.

An artifact of vast powers made by the eldest of the dverg, the same who made the weapons of the gods, it was linked with the most ancient of royal jotun blood. It was a sentient thing, a magical storehouse of memories, capable of giving you great power, of teaching you mysterious spells of the past kings and queens who had used it. It could speak you of the past, if you only listened. One of those spells, a mighty spell of binding, could seal entire rooms, caverns, making them impregnable to efforts of opening them.

I had released Baduhanna from one.

Opar hoped, I was sure, to restore what my father had locked inside Mara's Brow.

Below, Rhean was enraged. "You will fix it this issue very instant! There is no time for such failures!"

The king nodded and kneeled, speaking softly.

I hesitated and flew down towards the party of foes. I dove around statues and stalls, and then, deepening my feathers into black, I settled on one of the statue's snakes. I watched Rhean preparing.

She was speaking to the king.

"Pray tell me, King Marc Tenginell, is everything well otherwise? I will not hear of trouble in the ranks," she asked, her dress off, and servants bringing forth silken undergarments, leather battle gear.

Tenginell.

The Tenginell House had been destroyed by my father, as had the Danegell one. My mother had taken the House as her own.

Was he one of the very ancient kings of Dagnar?

He rasped his answer. He was dry as parchment, and his eyes were milky white. Long, silken hair hung around his shoulders. "All is ready. The gates are going to be opened, and the quarrelsome captains have been beheaded. The enemy in Ygrin is moving nothing on the board, and we will surprise them. The draugr inside Mara's Brow will be ready, and the cavalry is near the keep, also waiting for you. Morag and his wife are there—guarded, hidden, and ready. He will guide you. Red Midgard's army and Crec Helstrom are facing our legions, which wait for you as well. Falgrin will join the battle on Crec's side. We shall take the keep fast."

"Good," Rhean said. "And her?"

They all looked at a woman in robes. She was

kneeling, and her eyes were absent of emotion.

The king looked sad. "Morag, your highness, told me he had put a spell in her to cloud her mind. Perhaps you should make her one of ours?"

She shook her head. "Draugr? Nay. She will lose her special power. A vampire might not, but it is a risk. She could very well refuse to come back to us from death." She shook her head. "It matters little. Opar told me he cannot heal her, not likely even with the Grip. We have our deal with him, and hostages. We shall soon speak with Opar, and seal it. All the arrangements are made. Proceed with our plans, King Marc."

I smiled bitterly. Opar was there.

"It will be done, as you say," Marc said, and kneeled. "We shall begin this very night."

"Very well, as ordered," she said, and eyed the golden-haired woman. She was an odd one, with glowing golden skin and a beautiful face. She could have been a vampire, but for some reason, I thought she wasn't. "Will you fetch Sarman of Illon, good Morginthax. After that, I shall speak with the jotuns."

"Of course, Mistress Rhean," she answered, and didn't bow. Instead, she turned, and I felt the vampires were all tense and insulted. The golden lady disappeared to the maze of streets, and I watched Rhean as she allowed her servants to pull leather pants on her before they would armor her. She was perfectly healed, I noticed.

"She must be respected," Rhean said. "And you and I shall endure her insolence, no matter how hard it is."

The vampires bowed, and Rhean waited.

I hopped forward, dipped down low, and took to my wings.

I stared down at them, a dark blot in the night. I saw Morginthax disappearing, a golden halo in the dreadful darkness, and dove after her. Out in the city, a horn blared—hard, long, sonorous—and the voice echoed across the great cavern. When the horn stopped braying, and I heard draugr cheering, I knew they were marching to war. I flew and dodged above ancient mazes, keeping my eye on the golden one.

I saw the army.

Filling the streets not far from the marketplace, finely armored draugr, a guard dressed in red armor, their spears swinging, was following the crowned Tenginell, who was riding a skeletal mount. He looked supremely pleased, saluted Morginthax, who ignore him, and then, he waved hand forward. A thousand or two marched after him, the horn braying again, held by a dead elf. It must have been one, for the eyes, even in death, were bright as rubies, and the hair still lustrous and thick.

Morginthax was turning right and abandoned the army. I followed her. She headed straight for a doorway on a wall of red murals and didn't knock.

The door opened.

Inside, a surprised man got up with his followers. He

was blond, young, and had three men like him on his side. He walked to the doorway and leaned on it. His face was pulsing with anger, and fear was in his eye. "Tell me," he said huskily. "Why do we have to come to this terrible place? We could have met in the light, above ground."

Morginthax shook her head. "Because," she said simply, "*she* wished it. They want you to know where your sister must live or die, or walk again, all eternity, if you do not agree to our terms."

He blanched and looked down. "And if I do, I must live with the fate of Ygrin's dead on my conscience."

"Yes, can you?" Morginthax said. "It is a simple choice. Mara's Brow has a captain who had to make the same choice. He helped us. He let our scum inside and will be responsible for countless of lives. Save your sister or buy your people some time. You will open the gates to the Serpent Skull in Illon, and you shall bow before her. You will be amongst those humans who will survive our conquest, and you will suffer for your crimes in silence." She stepped forward. "I thought you had gone past such remorse?"

I wasn't listening.

I felt something.

I looked across the street and saw a blond, thick-jawed, silver chainmailed man staring at the confrontation. There was a look of shame and disgust on that face, and I knew it was the jotun I was seeking.

He turned and went inside an ancient house. Sitting in shadows, he soaked in misery.

It was the jotun who had ordered my death.

Opar Ymirson, king of the clan.

I landed on top of the ruin and looked back to the street. There, the men of Ygrin followed Morginthax, ready to betray their kin.

I turned to look at Opar.

Opar had his ax and his shield and stared at Grinlark, the simple staff, intently. It was a powerful weapon, a surprising weapon, and with Balan's manipulation, a portal, but he simply stared at it with wonder. Aras had sent it to him.

"I do think," he said sadly, "that if you killed my daughter, as you did one of my sons, and many of our kin, Maskan Ymirtoe, I shall not even listen to what you have to say."

His deep, blue eyes turned to me.

I flew down before him, shapeshifted, and waited. I stared at him, and he at me. He shook his head and sneered. "You didn't answer my question."

"I hold her," I told him harshly. "She is alive. I didn't bring her here, to the den of evil and traitors."

He lifted his hand and shook his head. "You are the last Ymirtoe. No other remain. I hunted for your kin. I filled many a tomb in that Tenginell crypt. But Morag, he was a crafty one. A traitor, as well."

I walked closer and stood face to face with him. "He

had fewer jotuns than you did."

He smirked. "Envious shits, they were. We held the Golden City. That's where Medusa led us, and she gave us great wealth. Baduhanna, she chased your father, and killed so many of you, that you never fully recovered. Red Midgard." He snorted. "A land of fighters. The Golden City? A city of riches." He laughed bitterly "Imagine, what could have been done, together. But my father and your father and our old ways ..." He shrugged. "Morag offered us help when the dead tried to take Golden City."

I shook my head. "I do not understand. If the dead tried to take the city, surely someone would remember. It seems to me that the living consider the dead a myth."

He nodded. "This Urac told you a tale?"

"He told me," I said bitterly, "that my father betrayed you."

He shook his head. "Had he stayed faithful to his own word to the end, had he just aided Dana and not led the draugr to the Golden City, had he not stabbed us in the back, *while* we fought for the city and fought the dead, things would be different now. You wonder why no-one knows of the dead? Why your father hid all he could of the battle?"

"I do wonder," I said.

"Because he was a gold-loving monster," Opar spat. "Traitor to his oaths and words. He looted the riches of the Golden City. He hunted us. He had his army hunt ours. Dana, the Mouth of Lok, told me to hide. She did. Even after I tried to kill her. She made me take an oath. I did."

"You were to recover the gauntlet and to kill Euryale," I said. "And you didn't succeed."

He nodded. "Yes. So many died. I tried." He gnashed his teeth together and shook his head. "I hated him enough to try for two decades. He betrayed us all for riches. He coveted gold, he would have eaten gold, if he could have. Trust me. He hid it well. After the war? His own legion, the Hawk's Talon? He sent them away, one by one, on fool's missions, to hide not the truth of the dead, but the truth of the stolen gold. He raised men to rule the Golden City, and those men wiped all evidence of the dead and were paid well. They paid tribute to Morag."

He wiped his face from sweat. "Yes, he tried to find Euryale on his own. He grew rich, nearly got rid of us finally, he faced Balic and others and failed because of his greed for gold, power in Midgard, for his love of his paltry nation. Aye, we had been the same. Gold and trade and power, and we forgot who we were. We all killed each other brutally, but only the draugr grew with the deaths." He reached forward and pulled me close. "We cannot beat their armies."

"I have beaten—"

"We *cannot* beat them," he whispered. "You do not understand. What did Aras tell you about my plans?"

"That you hoped Baduhanna would lead all to battle against the foe," I said.

"She did, once," he said. "And did she tell you I would try to fight Euryale, when the gate opens?"

"Yes," I said.

"And you? What do you think."

"I think, Opar, that you hope to find Medusa," I said sadly. "And you hope she might be your Baduhanna. I doubt she cares. She has virtues. She is honorable, she is mighty, she is First Born, and she is clever. Her blood is precious. But she likely doesn't care."

"Euryale is the last of the foe who can raise the dead," he said. "At least Medusa could hunt down her sister. Undead sister. The cause of Hel's War, Euryale. That bitch …"

"And if this Hand of Hel defeated her?" I asked.

"Shannon was dying at the time," Opar answered. "I will release Medusa. I will bury Dana and her friend Gutty." He fidgeted.

I pointed my finger out. "There, they are guarding a woman. Not just any woman, but a living one. They think she had special skills."

"Anja of the Ten Tears," he agreed. "Morag took her. We heard he hid her. And we could never find her. Dana told me to try, if things went badly in the Mara's Brow. She told me to see if Anja was alive, and Morag's prisoner. She didn't trust him. Dana told me many things." He stood close. "Why did you come here?"

"You know why," I said. "Liar."

He looked like he had been physically hit. Then, he looked away.

"Coward."

He twitched.

I pushed him. "You had no plans to release *anyone*. You clung to lies and would-have-beens. I offer you a sliver of honor, and you grasp it. Medusa, Medusa. Nay, Opar. That Anja is broken. Magic-struck by Morag. They know she cannot easily be made to open a thing. They trust you. They trust you well." I spat, and he took a step back. "After Baduhanna fell, you really betrayed your kin. Only some agreed with you, no? The rest didn't. You lied to Asra. Go home like beggars. It was the plan, though you lied about a great risk and a battle after you betray the dead. You were going to do what they told you to do," I said sadly. "There was no hero, Opar. You simply gave up. Why did you intend to aid the dead?"

"I was … I cannot say," he answered, and looked frightened. "You will see, perhaps." He held his face. "You do not understand. I know I…I regret it. But how could I undo this now?"

I smiled. "I might forgive you. I can still accept you, and your kin. Asra would be proud. Where are your Sons now?"

"Forty of us," he said, with relief. "They are camped in a village, north of Mara's Brow. The village is called

Warthill. Could you really consider … we could still try to--"

His eyes shone with hope.

I nodded. "Good. You know, I told your daughter I believe you were a hero. That you were out to do a great, desperate deed. She had doubts, but she believes it now as well."

"Thank you."

I shook my head. "I did that for a reason."

He frowned. "What was it?"

I placed a hand on his shoulder. "I did it so she would be proud of you after you die. I shall tell her you fell in the hands of the dead who betrayed your brave attempt before it got fully on the way. And that's the way it will be for her. She'll serve me, and I'll marry her. She'll be the queen of a new clan. We'll remake our world. There won't be Ymirsons. Nor Toes. We'll find a new name. Alas, it matters little if you betrayed us or not. I still must kill you. I cannot have a coward, who hunted for my father and my people, betray me as well. And, alas, I need your warriors."

He stepped back.

I grasped him by the throat and rammed my ax-blade to it, and again, and took the head. He fell and died.

I pulled Opar up and considered his eyes.

I smiled. "But your treason can be useful in one final way."

My face flowed, and I looked like Opar. I took the head and stuck in in a leather bag. I stepped outside to wait.

Soon, Morginthax arrived.

She gazed out at me. "You ready to make you oaths?" she asked. I walked to her and waved my hand for her to lead us out.

CHAPTER 17

I walked to the courtyard and saw the enemy waiting. Tense, eyeing me with distrust, the vampires stood around Rhean. She was wearing her white armor now, splendid with gold and silver links in the chainmail, and her shield was on her side.

I struggled with the love I had for her. I struggled, pushed, and fought it.

I looked away with difficulty.

She smiled as she sat down on a chair before the huge throne of a serpent-woman. "Opar Ymirson," she said. She pulled out the Black Grip and hung it around her knee. "The time is nigh. The legions my poor Balic sent to push Falgrin into turmoil are all deployed. They shall fight tomorrow morning. I have draugr even inside the fortress, and we shall take the gate when their troops are outside. I have my guide," she said, and looked disappointed, "and I have a mad woman."

All their eyes went to a figure kneeling next to her.

The blonde woman was Anja. She was forty, pale, her hair grown, and an absent look in her eyes.

Rhean shook her head and put a finger on her lip. "You cannot heal her?"

I shook my head.

She sighed. "I *can* take her life. I *might* be able to recall her. She *could* be brought back as one of my brood. I prefer males, but I could make an exception." She shook her head. "But that special skill of hers might also be gone. Morag cannot, as a draugr, take animal shape. He has spells, but they are draugr spells. Darkness, fire. He used to be ice. Vampires regain skills, I think, I believe. And yet, not all bitten, killed, and prayed to return, do so. One out of dozen, if you dared recall that many. Unruly lot."

I watched her and closed my eyes.

I struggled with a need to reassure her, to make her happy.

She was speaking. "What did Morag do to her? She was being held in a cell with the Gray Brothers, that fortress in northern Alantia. Locked up like many criminals. Morag had spared her. He had not spared her mind. I ask again. What did he do to her?"

I shook my head again. My eyes went to the Black Grip.

She looked at it too. "Ah, yes. Entirely useless to the rest of us. You think he used a spell from it? Can *you* heal her?"

"After," I said. "I can try. But I told you; it is not likely."

She frowned briefly. "Such a strong voice, Opar. Like a true jotun. After, you think? After you and I open that doorway and see what lies inside. It might disappoint you and me. There might be no way home. There might be no Hand of Hel, and Famine? Or even the Horn? Medusa might have died, even. We could only find bones."

I shrugged.

She smiled and shook her head. "And yet, there the mistress must go, as ordered. After, indeed. After you let us in, you and I shall do each other services. After such, you shall be released from this world and free to walk through that gateway you so dream of." She was nodding. "You have delivered your three sons to me. The fourth died to Maskan, didn't he? Your daughter has not come back with the head of Maskan?"

"Matter of time," I answered, and admired her cool confidence. I closed my eyes and fought the rage and love, both. The rage was steadily growing inside me, for the vampires were getting restless and couldn't help themselves. They were trying to intimidate me with their power. I spoke hurriedly and walked back and forth. "Your killer and ours will not fail again."

She nodded. "We are running out of killers with this Maskan. He is a vexing one. He fooled the lot of us and came to Nallist with mere bandits. He challenged the army, my husband, your kin, and me. And now, the Red Midgard yet stands." She shook her head, enraged. "At least I gave him a gift he shall never forget." She smiled fondly at the memory and leaned forward, grabbing the gauntlet. "I am grateful to your daughter for saving me, but I am most grateful when we have finished with the duty the Serpent has given us. You and I shall leave for Mara's Brow this very night. They are ready for us. We shall act fast." She looked at me with suspicion. "If you fail, your sons shall all die. I'll hunt your kin to the ends of Midgard."

I looked around. "And where," I asked her, "is your mistress? Will she not join us?"

She looked at me coldly, and I felt the fear, the rage that followed and took a step forward. I forced that step to change into a kneeling position.

"I am her mouth," she said, surprised. "She is not going to share her plan. Why would you—"

"And if the Hand of Hel survives inside the hole," I said, "and if she disagrees with our oaths and deals? If she decides there are *no* oaths? She is, after all, the Hand of Hel."

She shrugged. "*That* is a chance you must take. With luck, we shall befriend Medusa, we will free Hand of Hel, we shall wield Famine, and hold Horn, and you will be free to go home, if we can persuade either Medusa, or the Hand of Hel to grant you passage. Hel is no enemy to you. Never was. You chose it yourselves. You once served her, and now, you serve her again. Hel will approve." She leaned forward, and her will touched mine. "Betray us. And you will join Morag in servitude."

I shook my head.

"Good." She gave Anja a glance. "She will be useful later. You will try to heal her, if you can. I don't want to risk her unique skill, unless I must." She looked at me.

"Now. Before you will get the gauntlet," she said, and lifted it, "you shall have a thing to do, Opar Ymirson. It wasn't part of our deal, and I ask for no oaths. I merely want you to drink this."

Morginthax stepped forward. She held out a goblet for me. It was filled with red liquid.

I took it and looked at it. I looked up at Rhean.

She tapped her fingers on the shield where the Serpent Skull was prominent. "Euryale's poison. One from her many snakes. It will kill you in two days. It will eat out of your gut, Opar. It won't be painful, not too badly, but one moment, you will see your belly falling out. If you fail, you will not escape." She leaned forward. "Your sons drank it already."

The treacherous Hel-spawned bitch.

She lifted the gauntlet. Morginthax stepped near, and the vampires had hands on their swords.

Rhean smiled. "I can make it pleasant for you, Opar. I have appetites for your kind, the kind who have hunted ours for long decades, and lost. It is exciting. I can make it pleasing, if you like, though, I was just dressed."

I was enraged, jealous, and still intrigued.

To hide my confusion, I lifted the goblet. "And how will my sons and I survive this vile thing?"

"You will be given an antidote," she answered. "Euryale has a long history of poisoning elves. She knows how." She lifted a clear bottle of pale blue liquid.

"In this, you must trust us, as we trust you. She will keep hers." She eyed me as she put away the bottle. The vampires surrounded her and drew their swords, looking at me with morbid fascination.

I drank down the goblet's contents.

It was bitter, raw, and poisonous. I could feel it surging inside my veins. Then, it settled as a cold ache in my guts.

Rhean smiled and got up. Sensuously, she pushed through her vampires, all four of whom stepped aside, bowing. She lifted the gauntlet. "My offer stands, Opar. Let us seal out sweet deal with love."

I took the gauntlet and eyed it.

I hesitated and looked back at her. She placed a hand on my hand and slid closer. The darkness in her was suffocating, intoxicating, and my heart beat hard as she came close to me. Her fingers brushed my face.

I fought it.

I fought the temptation.

I fought it with all my power. I could just ... leave. I could simply go. I could do it so easily. I just refuse her. I just tell her no. And fly away, with the gauntlet.

I leaned forward instead.

She tiptoed up to me, and her lips combined with mine. I pulled her to me.

Her eyes shot open in shock and then terror. She tore herself from me. The vampires and Morginthax looked on, confused.

I grinned at her.

I pulled on the gauntlet.

The power coursed in my veins. It was nothing, if not divine. The memories of the past, of old ages, when the Nine Worlds were young, flashed past my eyes. I saw, for a moment, a vision of an underground room, one that was scarred by battle. There, a red-haired corpse lay, corrupted, dead. Over her, stood a woman of dark-haired beauty, a mark of a grinning mask on her forehead. A beastly warrior, ax and shield high, was eying a short woman with snakes for hair, wielding two swords. Her eyes were bitter pools of pain.

Spells to kill her and her kind slowly, I thought. *Teach me.*

Many spells went past my mind. They were a jumble of memories. They were flashes of terrible battles. I saw Morag, Father, fighting a terrible creature of the night, a being dark as coal with four swords. I saw him forcing the thing down to the corner of a library after a terrible battle, and I saw him pushing his hand through the being's chest.

I saw what he did. I saw the braid, thick with winds of Gjöll, the sharpest flows of the young ice, and the thickest currents of the oldest rivers.

He released it in the black heart of the foe. I saw the heart freezing and spewing sharp tears of ice, steadily, ripping into the flesh, filling the insides of the thing. I saw Morag, screaming at the creature, and I knew it was the one that had once killed Mellina, my mother. I saw the thing crawling away, ice falling, tingling, clinking, ever ripping new wounds to his skin, until it would die, slowly ripped apart.

Heart of Ice. A slow death, demon, Morag yelled after it. Slow was fine with me.

Rhean was stepping back and back from me. Her eyes commanded me. They commanded me to flee, to run, to go to my knees.

I felt red rage and snarled away her commands.

I reached for her so very fast and grasped her hair. I rammed my gauntlet into her chest, through it and grasped the old, cold heart. "All mine, and I won't share," I laughed. I braided together the spell and released it. I felt her shuddering with horrible pain. Then, I slapped her across the room.

"Maskan!" she screamed, as she got up, holding her chest, bright tears of ice trickling from it.

"Die slowly, bitch," I laughed, enraged and full of vicious cruelty. I let my face change to my own.

"It is Maskan!" she howled and spat ice. "Kill him! Fast!"

I laughed and turned to her vampires. I lifted my shield and banged my ax on it. I grinned at them. "Come. Scare me."

They tried. They reached out and forced their will on me.

I roared, suddenly brimming with rage, and grew to

my full size, stepping on one so hard, he fell apart. I lifted my shield against the other three. They called for darkness. They called for fire and ran through the darkness to attack me from behind.

Their spells struck me and died. The darkness dissipated around me. Lisar's guard made me invulnerable to magic.

I lifted my gauntlet, and laughing merrily, I braided together a blizzard. It was thick, powerful, and whirled around me, turning the market into wintry scene in but moments. I saw a vampire fall on his face, dragged by the wind. I stepped to him and hacked him in half.

I saw another, spewing snow, trying to get his bearings, and I kicked him so hard, he was twisted in two.

The last one was backing off, and off, calling for fire, trying to see in the snow.

I thickened the spell around him, and he froze. I walked to him, watching Rhean who was scuttling back, her eyes huge with horror, ice in the corners of the eyes, her mouth, and chest spewing crystal clear bits of it. It was painful and deadly spell, and she knew it.

I put the ax on the vampire's forehead.

I grinned at Rhean. "You will wish it was so simple as this." I pushed the ax down and grunted. The skull was split. The vampire died. "Like killing sheep."

She shuddered and fled, turning into a cloud of crows.

"Run, Rhean! I shall find your corpse, love!" I called out after him, my heart suddenly broken, as I held my face. The curse would haunt me forever. I could marry a million women, or jotuns, and bed each one of them, but Rhean had cursed me profoundly. I'd kill her. I'd likely visit her grave after and weep.

"Maskan," I heard a voice calling.

I turned. I didn't see Anja anymore. She had been taken away.

But I saw Morginthax.

She stood behind me, and she was swaying.

"Go away, dog of Rhean," I snarled.

She chuckled and shook her head. "There was a day in Malignborg, jotun, when I played a silly game with a stupid girl and fell victim to her tricks. Dana, may she have died badly. I shall not play such games with you, jotun, and no, I am not Rhean's dog."

She ran at me.

I laughed at her face and lifted my ax and shield.

She shifted. First, her beautiful, golden skin twisted, and I saw a rotten, burned skin filled with battle wounds. I saw hideously punctured eye and then two pale lamps of cruelty in her skull-like face as she leaped.

She grew. She changed.

She twisted in the air, and a skeletal, rotten, serpentine, thirty-foot-long creature of death came for my life. It missed a few claws, but what it had were sharp and long as swords. Its skull, elongated and large as a horse, was filled with deadly fangs, and the tail was thrashing the air behind it. It had one wing, and still, it could fly.

It had been a dragon.

Now, it was something like a lich, and a terrible guard of Euryale.

She crashed over me, and its fang came for my face, its claws sunk to my armor and flesh, and I screamed as I hacked the ax at the skull.

It hit the snout squarely and pushed the skull aside, and molted fire scorched rock and snowy, rotten wood around me. It was no magical fire, but dragon fire.

It could kill me.

We rolled around and around, and I held on with all my life. I pushed the shield into its mouth, and it nearly tore my arm off. The claws were deep in my shoulder and leg as it tried to tear the limbs off.

I wept, cried, and then raged as I pushed the ax to the skeletal chest and summoned a spell. A storm of ice shattered against it and tore out skin, organs, and scales. The bones withheld the assault.

It laughed. The front claw pushed my shield aside, and the tail whipped around to grasp my ax. "Let's have that gauntlet, jotun. I'll take the arm too."

It was pulling me apart, and then, cursing, and bleeding, I considered Bolthorn.

It would grant me no wishes. It expected a great boon, but not this one. This one was a dead one.

I tried to listen to the Black Grip.

I couldn't. The pain was too much.

Instead, I shifted. I shrunk, and a ferocious wolverine thrashed under the dracolich, which roared in surprise. I jumped on the foreleg and scrambled for the back.

The tail whipped up and down, and I howled as it struck my back, tearing off skin and fur. The skull was turning about and looking at me, golden, dirty, rotten scales crackling. It opened the maw as I jumped for the skull.

I shapeshifted and turned into white bear.

Without Black Grip, the beast I changed into had already been huge, fifteen feet tall and deadly with claws the size of a dagger, strong enough to break a company of spearmen.

With Black Grip, the power was much more powerful.

I grew into a twenty-foot-tall, terribly heavy ball of claws, fangs, and anger.

I crashed into the head, the neck, and tore into the rotten face.

Morginthax screamed with anger, and together, we fell to the floor, breaking Rhean's seat. I pummeled, ripped, and tore at her. A great gout of flame tore from her mouth, and she tried to push me away, but her claws were drawing sparks off the stone, her forelegs were crushed under her and me, and I clamped my jaws around her neck and bit down so hard, the scales flew in all the directions. I felt, heard, the bone cracking and ripping. I roared, tore with savagery, and trashed the great beast.

There was a cracking sound, a snap of bone, and I came up, holding a huge head, devoid of life.

I dropped it and shapeshifted into myself.

I was looking around. The market was empty. It was quiet.

I laughed. I held my ax high and screamed, full of primal joy. "Maskan Ymirtoe! Maskan Ymirtoe is the master of the dead! The head breaker, the undead breaker! Who rules the Dome? Here, Rhean, look!" I lifted something to the darkness, where Rhean would be watching while she slowly died.

It was her bottle on antidote.

"See this! A thief, and a king!" I yelled, and poured it to my mouth, and felt the poison dying inside my guts. "And let sons of Opar die with you! I piss on them!"

And then, something happened.

Horns were braying all over the cavern. I heard them echoing across the undersea. I heard chanting, and terrible, harsh laughter. It suddenly seemed the entire land was filled with sound.

I hesitated and took steps away.

And I noticed movement.

I turned to the great throne of a woman with snakes for hair.

I noticed one of the snakes was moving. It was

swaying and twisting as it turned to look at me. Then another, and slowly, a hundred more. A sea of snakes was moving, slithering over each other. An arm turned, so the palm was no longer up. It was an exquisite arm, as was the other one, this one holding a long sabre. Two other pair of hands curled from the sides, and the throne, that was an undead gorgon, stood up.

A black as night creature, it looked down and not at me. It was dressed in nothing. It had black wounds, black bones showing here and there, and some of the snakes were cut.

I took a step back.

"Well done, jotun," it whispered. "For decades, I have hidden and let others do what I loved to do, once. Killing, jotun. I love slaying. I love scheming well, but killing is the crown on any good scheme. I am the one who stole the Eye of Hel, I am the one who defied Hel and the gods themselves, and the one, who caused Hel's War. It was I, my sister Stheno, and Cerunnos Timmerion, but I thought it up. Hel's thing I am now, friend jotun, but you shall not cheat me at the last leg of this journey. I shall obey the Hand's order, and gods willing, I shall have a unlife of my own, after. You will not stop me from ruling Midgard and then, one day, Aldheim."

She lifted her head, and those eyes glared at me.

Like staring down to bitter brightness of the Lifebringer itself, the pain was terrible. It tore through my eyes, it stabbed at my thoughts. It purged me of bravery, and I felt my skin itching, stone rolling down my brow. I stumbled away and hacked back with my ax.

She was laughing, mocking, bitter, horrible slayer of hope. I missed and missed again.

"No spells on you, I know," she was whispering. "We do it the old way."

I felt her moving, and moving around me, but I dared not open my eyes. I felt a sabre stabbing my side, then cutting my leg, and I fell away from the cut and found a leg which I tripped over. I felt her powerful foot on my chest, and her fingers on my throat.

"Open them!" she roared. "Open the eye, one is enough!"

I slashed my ax at her, but she blocked it and threw me across the room.

I got up, panting.

I was struck in the back, and I fell. I felt snakes slithering around me, slithering around my limbs, around my throat. "You cheated jotun, did you? You cheated. A thief, are you? My venom's not good enough for you, is it? Here."

I felt fangs in my arm. They tore through my skin, and I felt the burning pain as I was infected with death. I pushed at her, desperately, with all my strength, and then pulled suddenly. She fell over me, and I tore myself off the snake's grasp. I felt the cold lump of pain in my guts again, this time, much more painful.

I rolled, shapeshifted into the owl, and flew away in panic. I flapped my way up to the darkness, dripping blood, and finally, dared to look around.

I didn't see her.

I saw Dome. I saw the lights. I heard horns.

Then, I saw the hundred thousand statues turning. They were not really statues. They were draugr, all the dead that had been collected by Rhean and Balic's wars. They were turning, moving, answering the call to war. Black on black, their skin painted in black, their armor painted in black as well, led by old, terrible kings, young, dead, once great champions, the legions and companies of the dead were forming for war. This was what Opar had meant when he had told me I didn't understand. This was an army to end Midgard. They began marching for the west, a tromp of their feet echoing, old and new standards swaying.

They were singing.

> *"Sword to the man, ax to the boy, a whip for the lass, and spears for the mass.*
> *Together, we shall see, oh, we shall see, all their lives pass.*
>
> *Ho, here is old Corinol the King, and there, the rotten Sur, who stole the queen's ring.*
> *There marches Tarn the Slasher, and Ular the*

Wedding Crasher ..."

They marched to the drums, horns, and flute, a black mass of death, no longer silent. With them, rode red riders of the old Tenginell king and, in that army, marched dead wolves, bears, and even rotten jotuns. Savage draugr in dark furs were leading a train of siege, drawn by huge, skeletal mammoths. They marched under the sea for the west, and I knew, somewhere near Illon, they would begin their war on the living.

I shook my head and felt the poison in my veins. I flew away, far away, and found a way out, one where water was dripping.

"Come, Maskan!" I heard a voice calling. Euryale was screaming, from the top of her voice, enraged by my escape. "Come to Mara's Brow! Bring yourself there, Maskan, and beg on your knees, boy! Perhaps I'll give you your life back! Perhaps I don't need to! I will take the fort, Black Grip or not, Anja's power or not! I will take it, and I will get inside!"

I had the Black Grip.

They still had Anja. Euryale would rip what remained of her mind out to make her theirs. Rhean would make her one of hers, if she survived that long.

And I?

I had to summon help. We would all risk whatever was inside that stony hole in Mara's Keep.

***

I flew all that night and found a certain village. It was Warthill. I had to stop to ask directions, and it was hard, since so many people in Falgrin were fleeing what they heard was a war coming. Many were going to Mara's Brow, others to the mountains, and then, finally, I located a small village in the edge of the Blight, not far from Mara's Brow.

I flew around it. It was a simple affair of drab halls. Hunters and few farmers would call it home.

I saw movement, and then, many blond men emerged from the halls to watch me. They saw me, even through the night, and held hands beneath their cloaks, clutching axes. I landed and shapeshifted.

There were many.

Some were female, just slightly shorter than the males. They were no men, but the Sons of Ymir, Ymirsons, the commoners Opar had set to save, and yet, who would not have understood the shameful decision.

They watched me, their foe, nearly forty of them.

I swayed, felt the poison in my gut, and exerted my will, pushed the pain away, and stood up straight. I pulled out a sack.

"The clans have been feuding forever," I yelled out. "We have hunted and killed each other. It is time we fight for something truly worth dying for."

One of them, a man, a jotun, really, with a scar across his face, took a step forward, holding his ax. "Our king is out there, finding the enemy. He is—"

"Your king," I said simply, "betrayed you. Your kin, his closest family and few others of your clan, worked with Hel's minions, and he gave up his sons as their prisoners. Only Asra survives. She and I, we shall marry."

They looked incredulous at the words.

"Never," said the scar-faced jotun. "Never in a million years. How could she?"

I lifted small bit of wood. I whispered words and struck it on the ground. Grinlark was there, proud and tall, and I showed the Black Grip. "The enemy is moving. Your kin betrayed you, like mine did. It is time we build something worthy, together. Grinlark is yours. And the Black Grip is mine." I pulled Opar's head from the bag and dropped it before them. "I am your king, Asra is your queen. And, together, we shall find a cause worth following."

"What cause is that," a female asked, her red hair swaying as she shook it. "We came here as mercenaries. We came here to serve Hel, and perhaps our gods. We took the north and lost it. Should we fight to save it? Should we truly save the humans? Should we fight for riches?"

"We shall fight," I said simply, "for jotuns. We shall fight like jotuns fight, and we shall be unnecessarily cruel. I have a plan. It will likely kill all of us."

They stood still, silent. Then, the scar-face took a step forward. "If Asra agrees, we agree. But she had better agree, then, we say yea. They have been whispering of Opar, and his dark thoughts. If the plan is one that will get us killed?" He spat. "That's the kind we like."

I smiled. "Listen."

***

Later, I flew along the coast, then over the sea, and finally, seeing the Blight, the mountains cutting deep into the sea, I found a beach where I landed.

I fell in the shallows, and then, dragging myself up, I finally found some peace, holding my belly, which was … moving.

I sat on the sand and admired the Black Grip. I searched it for an answer to my pain, the poison coursing in my veins, and laughed bitterly at the thought of my victorious dance after I killed the dragon. I had failed, and I had succeeded, and I would still die, unless something saved me.

I touched my throat and winced at the pain.

I sought for another answer in the Black Grip.

There were still none. If my plan worked, and things were as I had seen, I might have a chance. It would call for good timing, bravery, jotuns, dverger, and betrayal. I would be a jotun, and for a moment, the thought made me happy, free of doubt, and fears.

I fell asleep, and in the morning, I saw our fleet rowing past for north.

It was the day the enemy would take Mara's Brow.

It was the day I'd live, or die.

CHAPTER 18

The fleet was soggy and weather-beaten. There were armored throngs of men and women huddling on the decks, everyone miserable with cold and hunger. There were people of shattered villages, sacked towns, captured cities. There were seven thousand of them, and my nearly two thousand dverger. Some of the people had been left in the villages along the way, too sick, or the boats too leaky to go on.

Not one of them should be there. They had suffered too much.

But humans were my meat, and I cared not.

We were lucky no enemy fleet of fighting ships had seen them.

Galleys would have stopped the transports and would have driven them to the rocks, but Rhean and Balic's plans had not considered a rabble of rag-tag soldiers beating their legions in the south.

We had a chance.

Thrum and Nima were on deck of a blue galley and pointed a finger my way. I hid the bite-marks on my arm and got up, feeling pain in my gut. I lifted my gauntlet to the sky, and they greeted their king, banging on the shields. I waded out to the water and got pulled on deck.

Nima looked at me and shook her head. "You never look rested, Maskan."

"I'll rest in my grave, unless I get raised. Asra?" I asked. They blinked. "Quiss?"

"Below," said Thrum. "She's still in the net. Gets irascible when you try to feed her. No trouble otherwise."

I chuckled and made my way below.

"What is the situation?" Nima called out, joined by Hal and the generals of the army.

I stopped, midway down. "We must get there fast. There is …" I began and didn't know what to tell them of the great terrible army of draugr marching to Ygrin. Instead, I spoke of the immediate battle. "There are over fifteen thousand enemy making a diversion on Falgrin. Crec is going to see Falgrin's army betrayed and humiliated, and ours as well. In the meantime, the enemy … a terrible enemy is going to take Mara's Brow with infiltrated draugr and cavalry. We shall have to hurry. We shall have to save Falgrin's army. We must kill Crec. After that?" I shrugged. "We shall see. We must hurry. Now. Let me speak to her."

"You need bandages and stiches, Maskan," Nima called after me, and I heard her speaking to Tris, calling me a fool.

I found Asra in a hold, and she sat up as she looked at me. Her eyes were round with surprise, and her eyes went over my disheveled condition.

They settled on my gauntlet.

I went to her and cut and pulled the net off her. It

took time, a long time, and I finally managed it.

She didn't move. She simply stared at me.

"Your father," I said, "and brothers," I added, "died heroes."

I handed Grinlark to her. She stared at it in shock. "You killed him?"

"He died a hero," I said. "I was too late. I will probably die as well." I showed her the wounds on my arm.

"He died a hero?" she asked, holding the staff, her eyes on my wounds. "Was he going to betray us? And why did you give me this?"

"Because you are right," I told her. "We need a new cause. A new king and a new queen."

"And Rhean," she said darkly.

"With time, I might forget her," I told her. "I gave her a present. She will die slowly."

She stepped up and kneeled before me. "What do you wish to do? You have been poisoned."

"Listen," I said, and turned my back on my father's love for Midgard and the people I had once called mine.

He had failed. So had the Sons.

I found Thrum and spoke to him at great length. He bowed. Then, I found Urac, who was seasick and then solemn as he listened to me. He kneeled.

***

We rowed on, and not far, just beyond the Blight, the mountains that ended abruptly in the sea, we saw the north through snow whipping across the slopes. We came in sight of a high plateau and a ravine with steep sides, where River Aluniel marked the border. A fortress lay on Red Midgard's side of the river and was called the Hearthold, and Mara's Brow was impressive and high on the other. It consisted of three round keeps around a large one and was made entirely of white and light gray rocks. Flags of Falgrin's many lords flew on top of it, a duke ruled it, and the Queen Mara, for Falgrin always had a queen called that, was absent, as the central keep had a blank, black flag. Falgrin's troops patrolled the land on their side, riding the ravine's edges, looking down to the river and the beaches.

They had a good reason to.

What they thought was Balic's army, was moving up the steep hillside for our fortress.

There were around four legions of the enemy. Three were ones we had not fought, and one was a mix of many, including Malingborg's own. There were fifteen thousand of them. The ships had been their camps, and many had been dismantled for firewood. They had been there for a long while. You could see corpses on the hillside where skirmishes had taken place.

The rowers, thousands of them, were now hauling gear and supplies out of the ships into a makeshift fortress in the middle of the beach. That camp, too, had been built of dismantled ships. They were abandoning the defensive tactic, would distract Falgrin, and were not going anywhere.

The distraction was working.

On top of the plateau, we saw Crec's great, filthy flag and a milling mass of our own troops who thought he was the king, and a just, brave one at that. There were Hawk's Talon, the Gray Brothers, and the Heartbreakers lined up. On the bridge milled Falgrin's local legion, marching to the battle. They had feared Crec's army for a while, confused by the legions marching north, but with the arrival of the Hammer Legions, they had no reason to doubt our alliance.

We watched them for a moment. I turned to Nima and the generals. They looked up at the mass of the enemy struggling up the hillside and our people waiting on top.

Hal was shaking his head. "A massive battle. Hopefully, the last one. I am really tired with this war."

The generals, soldiers, both, didn't say a thing, but I sensed they hesitated and agreed.

Nima looked dubiously at the troops, and the hundreds of ships along the beach. Ours would fill it. "What if they turn about and rush us?"

"We'll die," Hal said.

"What if," Tris, not part of the military, but still loud, "Red Midgard on top actually beats the enemy and thinks the Six Spears are still an enemy legion?"

"We'll die," Hal repeated with little emotion.

I pointed my ax at the massive wooden fort on the

beach. "We shall drive the sailors away. Then, we hold the fortress. We shall rally on it, if we must. You will march the men up that hill, and archers go first. You will make life miserable for the foe. Crec, no doubt, will order our men off the field and will abandon Falgrin, but that is not the only battle. We must make sure the keep doesn't fall. The enemy is inside already, ready to open the gates."

They didn't look happy with the prospect of the battle they would bleed in not really being the only battle. "Inside?" Nima asked.

"They will come for Mara's Brow. The battle is important. We must kill Crec and defeat the legions. But we also cannot lose the fort. The main battle will take place up there," I murmured. "Out there in the gate to Mara's Brow. So, I shall deal with that. I will try to get there and so will the dverger."

They looked at me like I had lost my mind.

Hal looked at Thrum. "They are coming with you? Where…how will you get there? We need you and them in the battle."

"You need swords, bow, and courage, not me," I answered dryly. "Didn't you hear me. The fort must not fall. We'll march over the river, on the beach, and up the hillside there."

"It's impossible," Hal said, eying the steep incline.

"If I die, follow Queen Nima," I told them. "Keep steady. March at the enemy back and link with Falgrin.

Send men to tell the generals Queen Nima rules, and they should obey them. I will guide our troops up the hillside. The Duke of Mara's Brow doesn't know the dverger, they might not listen to reason and might think we are against them. I shall find a moment to take down Crec. Nima shall wear the crown he stole from my father."

She nodded, a fierce smile on her face. "We shall do well."

I smiled. "Yes, love. You shall."

She stepped closer to me and hesitated. "I have something to tell you. It is about Nallist and—"

"No time, love," I told her. "Later. Take us on the beach."

The ships turned, one by one, and aimed for the beach. There, in a chaos, they disgorged the men, and the entire beach was so full of ships, the enemy and ours, that on the right edge, our ships and men were intermingled and fighting. Most of the enemy were trying to rush to the fortress, but some loved their ships more. In places, we had to abandon ships in the surfs to get to the beach.

By the time, we had unloaded our troops, the enemy was already halfway up on their long climb up the slope. In lines of shields, the four legions, Malingborg's included, were going up with single-minded drive, ignoring us and their sailors below.

The sailors, a few thousand strong, kept the fortress.

It was built of makeshift wood and broken hulls of the ships, and I saw fear on the many faces looking over the parapets. Their spears glittered bravely in the morning light as they looked up at their men, hoping for salvation, and then at the mass of our men, and they knew there was no hope for them.

We marched forward, and Hal led the assault, leaving the Stone Watchers marching behind them. The men of Fiirant and Alantia were staring at their enemy, moving forward in a mass of shields. They marched straight for the fortress. The enemy, without any ceremony, released arrows, and light ballista fired deadly stone balls which tore to our ranks. Ten fell, then lines of men. Our men screamed, and the battle, surprising both our people and the enemy on the hillside, began below them.

The men I had led to victory in Nallist were hungry, lean, wounded in body and mind.

They were also soldiers now. They knew the war would end after blood had been spilled.

They suddenly broke ranks and rushed through a hail of arrows. They rushed forward like mad dogs and began surrounding the fortress. The enemy threw javelins now and, as our men climbed the ten-foot-tall wall of wood, soon began hacking down with axes.

I watched stoically as men fell. They struggled, died, and soon littered the edged of the fortress.

"They'll break," Nima said coldly. "Soon."

Indeed, our men were swarming up the sides, furious at the resistance. They climbed like ants, and soon, in many places, they took the fortress walls.

Soon, the gate facing the slopes was pushed open, and a stream of men surged out, only to be cut down by archers. On and on they came and scattered, threw away their weapons, and our men began killing them as they tried to get past our ranks. Hundreds got past anyway and rushed up the hillside.

I turned Nima around and smiled at her. "Take them up and fight well. They will be fully encaged. Find Crec's crown after he is dead, and our generals. Fare well, brave Nima the robber."

She looked serious and smiled. "I shall. I shall do my best, Thief of Midgard. For Red Midgard, we shall both rule."

"Aye, for it," I told her, and kept marching. The army killed off the wounded in the fort, and the slope and the beach, and then was being called to colors. Slowly, Hal and the others managed to start pulling the people into their ranks, and Nima was running back and forth, yelling at them to hurry. Some companies of archers began jogging up the hillside.

We marched in a block of steel, Thrum and me. We looked at the calm river ahead and the waters from the western hills as they rushed for the sea over the rocks and the beach. There, sailors were wading through the sandy creek and climbing out. Aluniel wasn't a terribly large river. It would be in the spring, but now, it was lazy and partly iced over. The depth of the water was the least of our worries. The slope for Mara's Hold, which was a terrible climb, was also in range of the Falgrin's archers.

"Looks like a place to die in," Thrum muttered. "Finally. I'm almost done nursing you, my king. They won't take us as friends, will they?"

I shook my head.

"And when we get up, if we do, you are saying there's a place to go?" he asked.

"You have a job to do."

He nodded, unhappy. "I don't like hope, King. It is easier to seek death until you die. But we obey. It will cost us dearly. The ballista shall be in place."

"We need luck as well as ballista," I said miserably, and nearly threw up as I felt the cold pain in my belly shifting. It was almost as if it was moving.

"Speaking of ballista," Thrum muttered. "They are looking at us. They don't like what they see."

I looked up. The ballista in Mara's Brow, on one of the three forts around the central one, had lots of activity on the walls. Some of the ballista, far above us were firing. They were testing the range, and the bolts struck the river not too far away. It was clear they were jumpy with Hammer Legions out to kill them and could make no heads of tails what was going on in the plains and the beach.

"You said they'd be busy," he said. "You said they'd not have too much time to worry about our lads."

"They will be," I told him. I was looking up and saw Asra flying far above. She was banking in the winds, and then, she seemed to plummet.

It was time. I knew what she had seen.

She would see a horse-army of draugr, riding from the north, where they had been hiding. With them, would be Euryale, my father, my mother, perhaps, and possibly Rhean, should she still be alive.

I felt the burning pain in my belly and grimaced at the fear. I'd have to survive a bit longer.

We splashed into the river. We stomped through the mud and the sand, waist deep for me, and neck high for the dverger.

Ballista bolts began landing amongst us. One smashed down a wide dverg so fast, it seemed he was never there. He simply disappeared under the water. A scream and a splash turned our heads, and we found a headless dverg floating on the river for the sea, his armor dragging him down. The first dverger were climbing out of the river and already were going for the rocky hillside. I frowned as I watched it. The terrible climb led up to the Mara's Brow, and it seemed like a man would die of exhaustion climbing it. Not the dverg, of course, or a jotun in his prime, but I wasn't. Arrows were now falling on us. There were archers on the bridge, where their legion had passed over to stand near

Hearthold.

There were horns braying on Red Midgard's side. There were more calling out on Mara's Brow.

I knew what that meant.

They, too, had seen the draugr army. Ten or more ballistae were now being split between us and them. On the other parts of Mara's Brow, the garrison would be frantic, looking out at the mass of their foe that was coming from nowhere. Some ballista were hauled about in the parapets and then pulled away to face a new threat. Asra was now flying over something far away, beyond the fortress.

The troop began stomping up the hillside in one solid mass. Some were falling and saying nothing as they did.

I turned to watch behind. There, the legions were soon at the top. Falgrin had nearly deployed near the bridge and on the left flank of our legions, which stood proudly.

Arrows were flying back and forth, and soon, javelins would tear the heart out of both formations. The draugr would kill many. Our men would hold and butcher the tired legionnaires below.

That is, if they were led by a true king.

Something took place near Crec's flag, and I saw many other standards dipping.

Companies were stepping away from the edge of the hillside. Then, legions.

Crec was betraying his people and allies.

I turned my head back just in time to see two ballista bolts tear eight dverger to pieces.

Thrum shrugged. "Weapons. That's what the boys are. You have been learning it well. Don't worry. We'll get some two out of three of them up there. Just damned well plan this well."

"Aye," I whispered, and nodded, spitting blood. "I hope I will do well enough and fast enough. Go and march. I shall deal with Crec."

He laughed. "Poor fools, the lot of them. I'd rather march this hill."

I nodded and shapeshifted. The eagle was huge, graceful, but not entirely out of place in the north, and I begged the men in the plateau would not take note of it. I flapped my wings hard, made my way up to Asra, and saw what was happening.

A mass of two thousand draugr riders in red armor was charging past Mara's Brow, leaving fallen behind. It was led by draugr calling for spells, and on the walls, many ballistae burned with their crew. One had a horned helmet and looked familiar.

Filar. Rhean's daughter.

Arrows and bolts rained down on the enemy. The enemy took it stoically.

Amid the army rode a group of riders, robed and armored. One was tall and mysterious and rode a black lizard.

Euryale.

Another was Rhean, her white battle armor gleaming brazenly. There, too, would be Morag and my mother.

I banked after Asra, and we watched Crec's treason.

Red Midgard's army was stepping back from the edge of the hillside and was retreating for Hearthold. It was split from that of Falgrin's, who was sending men to ask what was going on.

And then, javelins from Falgrin's legions tearing into them, thousands of legionnaires were rushing haphazardly over the hillside and over the land where our men had just stood. They were rushing like a thick stream of steel, their flags over them, between our and Falgrin's army, and running for the bridge. They were trying to cut off Falgrin.

Falgrin was making a shieldwall and tried to keep the bridge. A ferocious battle took place for it. The legions, ignoring the danger of the massive army of Red Midgard, tightened around the Falgrin's legion, and they were pushing thousands of shields and spears at the hapless men. They were stabbing at them from all directions, and though brave, Falgrin was shuddering under each blow, leaving men behind as they tried to keep the bridge.

Most would die anyway, if they managed it.

The fury in our ranks was clear. The Hawk's Talon, the Heartbreakers, and the Gray Brothers were sending dozens of riders for Crec's standards, only to be dismissed.

Some companies stopped marching, and few, braver ones were running at the Hammer Legionnaires, only to be savaged by spells from the draugr kings. They were riding amongst their ranks and calling for fire. They were tearing down files and files of our countrymen, and Crec was doing his best to make the chaos even more terrible by refusing to see the riders that came for him, demanding to know what was going on. I could see him smiling, even from such distance, and he kept touching his crown.

My father's crown.

Falgrin's men were losing hundreds, falling to blade and spell, trying to force their way back to the congested bridge.

Crec was simply…watching.

A glimmer of hope made Falgrin's men cheer.

Behind the legions, our people arrived, out of breath, exhausted. The archers began taking down files of the enemy. Then, soon, companies, sweaty, shivering with exhaustion, thousands of them, pushed to the backs of the legions, pushing deep to their ranks, hacking and fighting desperately, trying to open a way to Falgrin.

It wasn't enough.

Spells split our men, and a gigantic inferno, called by a horn-helmeted queen, roasted hundreds of ours and theirs. The flames were spreading down, and our people had to rush away, then back up, the Stone Watchers leading them past the flames.

It took time.

A solid rank of spears had turned against them, and even if our men marched steadily to those spears and shields, they were too few to save anything, or anyone.

The enemy held our men and kept pushing at Falgrin, some of their spells and arrows tearing at the braver, most mutinous of the companies in our legions, and soon, I saw many companies of Malingborg's push to the bridge, hacking and fighting furiously.

I flapped my wings and flew higher, ever higher, and turned.

I soared down for the battle. The Hearthold fell away under me, and aiming for the great standard of the Helstrom's, I saw Crec ordering some of his men to go back inside Hearthold.

More companies rebelled. Many more were marching back to battle, to aid Falgrin, to aid our people, while others stood still, and only a few companies were marching back inside.

I saw Crec's hateful, pale, and proud face flash a grin as he rode back and forth. His aides were half staying, half deserting him. The standard bearer was whipping his horse like mad to get back the battle, so was the general of the Hawk's Talon, screaming insults, drawing his sword. He spat at the king.

Crec turned in this saddle, eyes full of rage.

He braided together a spell of lightning.

I felt the air electrify as a stab of lightning tore at the

general. The man fell from his saddle, as did two of Crec's adjutants who had left him. The standard-bearer's horse was torn to bits, the man's leg flying in the air. The standard was burning. Two more aides were screaming, their eyesight gone, and Crec was laughing as he aimed his hands at a general of the Heartbreakers, who was calling for his captains, not far. He had not seen what had taken place and was staunchly commanding his men to attack. A fiery spell was whirling around Crec's wrists, and that's when I arrived.

I changed as I did.

I fell on my enemy with my ax held high.

His eyes came up, saw my scarred, grinning face, my hair billowing behind, as all twelve feet of anger landed on him. The horse rolled, back broken. Crec was rolling under me, arm torn, leg twisted on the side, as he let out terrified curses. We rolled in the mud, and I came on top, my hand on his face.

I squeezed my hand closed. I hacked the ax on his corpse.

He was gone.

I got up and looked at the general of the Heartbreakers. He was trying to control his wounded horse and was eyeing me with horror. I walked over to him as men stared up at me aghast.

"General," I said.

He hissed. "Traitor! Danegell and a jotun, I—"

"Silence and listen," I snarled. I remembered the man was a Kinter, Roger's Kin, one of the few left. "There is precious little time to tell you what has happened in the south. Dagnar is gone, Balic's troops were ravaging Alantia and Fiirant, and most all our troops are here and will get slaughtered. Most of the nobles are dead."

He stammered. "My people? My family? Roger?"

I shook my head. "Most are dead. Roger as well. Listen. You are of the highest Houses in the land. One of the old blood. There is no king. Crec was one of the dead. A draugr. Aye, they are real. They are making a bid for power. I will stop them. Fight the legions and lead our people. Do it as a king. You are the King of Red Midgard now." I pushed a crown to him. "You. Red Midgard needs a warrior, and a noble House must lead it to victory. I want no part of it. It was a stolen throne to start with."

"It was…Crec." He shook his head, and greed played on his face as he held the crown. "I accept, since Crec lost his head!" the general said, eyeing the shocking mass of death not too far and then the crown. "I need to win a war. What about you? I—"

"He did lose his head, and you keep yours. Don't let anyone try to steal it," I said, and wiped the smashed bits of skull off my armor. I grimaced with pain as the poison inside me seemed like liquid fire now. I spat some blood and smiled at his incredulous face. "Defeat the enemy, King. Make sure none usurp the throne. It is your duty."

He nodded and placed the crown on his head.

I shapeshifted and took to my wings. I found Asra, and together, we watched what was taking place.

The chaos in the plateau was complete. Our legions were now marching to fight the Hammer legions.

Over the River Aluniel, the dverger were climbing, taking terrible losses, and still going forward.

At the gates of Mara's Hold, a calamity had met Falgrin.

The horde of riders had entered the fortress. The massive iron gates had been opened. Men had been slain, and the towers were congested above it. I saw parties of draugr pushing out of the gatehouse to the walls, like dark maggots, shoving the defenders relentlessly. They were over a thousand strong and rapidly disappearing inside. Many companies of Falgrin's guards and the duke's nobles were trying to push them out, and a furious melee was taking place in the courtyards. Civilians were fleeing for the central keep.

The enemy was holding the gates, and there seemed to be no stopping them.

I watched the draugr milling around the gate and saw the group of ominous riders passing in. Soon, I saw Rhean and Filar leading a phalanx of draugr for the central keep. I saw the men of Falgrin blocking the doors to the main keep behind a shieldwall, and then,

Filar led her dead against them.

A furious battle took place, Filar's fiery ball and chain hacking down a brave champion, and the enemy fled. Inside the main keep, I heard a man exhorting his troop. The duke was preparing for a last stand.

The draugr began hacking the gateway with axes. They did it brutally, while the last of the riders, releasing fiery spells at men on the bridge and at the ones on the walls, were entering the keep.

I saw a draugr captain, and he was screaming up to the gatehouse, hoping to close the keep.

I beat my wings and flew down. I went fast, plummeting, and Asra was with me.

Then, suddenly, many others joined us. Forty huge birds of all kinds and colors, joined us.

We flew down like a hail of steel. We shapeshifted as we landed, stomped down dead and the wounded before the gates, and promptly shifted to fit inside the gateway. The draugr turned to watch us. They saw a bitter, angry party of forty jotuns, shields out, axes flashing, filling their sight. The draugr before us were stuffed in a corridor with many horse. It was ten draugr wide, just enough for a pair of wagons, and there were a hundred or more of them milling in the confined space. Some were going up to the gatehouse but most had been ordered to hold it.

Their grins of victory turned into screams of death.

We locked shields and stomped over them, crouched

low, our helmets scraping the ceiling. We hacked and kicked into the mass of horse, draugr, and tore them to pieces or simply crushed them. It took no time at all. We soon held the gateway, and Asra was nodding at some of them. Jotuns were rushing upstairs. We soon saw pieces of draugr falling down the stairs.

Asra turned me around and nodded at me. "We will hold the gate, and we shall wait until Thrum gets here," she said with glee. She was free of pretense and her father.

"Let no man or draugr take it back," I said. "Tell Thrum to hurry. He knows what to do." She nodded, and I walked forward. She laughed brightly as she set about killing draugr who were still alive, and ten jotuns joined me as we entered the courtyard.

Before us, there was an utter chaos. It was a battle of pairs, of singles; a butchery of desperate men and evil dead that one couldn't make any sense of.

We cared not to try. We walked for the doorway for the keep, which had been breached. We walked with shields high, and we slaughtered anyone on our way. We marched into a party of men who were trying to get to the keep and hacked through them. A champion of Falgrin, his spear gored, standing on four draugr, was fighting four horsed draugr just before the gate.

I swiped my ax to the draugr and the horse, then stepped over it, caught the spear of the man, and kicked him inside the keep. The other jotuns hacked at the foe, and we stepped inside the keep.

It was a round hall hung with expensive tapestries and decorated with rich statues and busts. Tables and round chairs littered the place, and the duke's throne commanded the center of the floor. The upper floors were many, and their people would be holed up, begging for their duke to protect them.

The draugr mass was still engaged with the garrison. Many hundreds of them had surrounded the throne and a hundred of the duke's guards. Shield pressed on shields, and the draugr, deviously clever and fast, were braiding together spells of fire walls, cutting though the lines. There, when men burned, they jumped through, often died, as the duke's own family, handsome knights all, led men to pluck the holes.

"Take them, take them now!" I heard a female calling out. There, Filar was riding around on a skeletal horse, exhorting her men. She had arrows in her body, slashed shoulder armor, and a horn was missing, but she was laughing, in love with war. She had probably been in life as well.

One of the duke's knights was on the first rank now. He pointed his sword at Filar and then used it to slay two draugr. He danced before her, and she laughed.

She suddenly rode forward, and her mount crashed into the ranks, her flailing, fierce ball smashing down.

The knight threw his shield up, the ball crashed through it, and took an arm.

The knight stabbed at the mount, and Filar fell amongst her draugr.

"Kill her, fast!" the duke called out, and many men converged on her. "Then, cut a way out of here!"

I led the jotuns forward.

A draugr turned, holding a standard of Serpent and Skull. He wore a gorgeous red crested helmet, and he was missing half his face. What remained gave an impression of terrible surprise. He looked at my belt, then up at my eyes.

I axed him.

I nodded, and the jotuns spread out. We called for spells of ice, and winter made them more potent.

The Black Grip made mine terrifyingly powerful.

I let go my spell first.

I tapped my ax on the stones before me.

A blossom of ice grew behind the duke's legs. It opened its leaves, and a field of whitest, coldest ice spread from it.

The throne groaned and broke.

The Duke screamed and held his legs, his sword buried in ice. Men were turning to see what was taking place, and then, they were engulfed with the bitter cold, freezing ice. It was so cold, it burned the skin and tore at armor and boot. Men, dozens of them, were falling heavily, some against each other and the draugr. The draugr, too, were falling, confused, trying to extract themselves. A hundred and fifty more were caught, while others retreated.

I saw Filar, who was on her hands and knees, cursing.

Her eyes turned to me.

I smiled.

"Kill them," I whispered. The other jotuns released the braids they had created. Terrible spells of icy brilliance tore into the hapless fools. Icy hands grew from under the draugr and tore down ranks of them. There, on the icy floor, they were torn to pieces. Icy spikes tore into men, and I saw the duke butchered by two, his corpse lifted high as he bled. Snow was blowing around the hall, whirling and herding the enemy, and soon, I let go of my icy spell.

What remained was a shivering mass of dying men and ice-trapped draugr.

Some were fleeing past us, throwing away their weapons. There were not many.

"Clear the hall and then guard it," I said.

They nodded, and half turned to hold the gate, heaping table, stone, and corpses across it.

Others walked forward and hacked about in that room, stomped on the dying, and chased the men and the draugr who had been hiding until nothing remained alive.

I was waiting and saw a shadow, just barely catching it in the corners. I smiled.

Then, I turned to see another shadow coming for me.

A huge, fat rat jumped before me and changed into the scar-faced jotun. He grinned and spoke. "I will show you where, King."

"None spotted you?" I asked.

"Nay, lord. I have been hidden since last night and ate well in their larder," he laughed. "Will you survive?" he asked.

I held my belly and found a stain of blood. "Only, and perhaps if we hurry."

He nodded and led us off. He walked to the edge of the great hall, dodging corpses. There, we passed a shady part of the hall, where ruins seemed to have been built to house a pleasant corner with couches and tables. I raised my hand to touch the ancient stone, and hesitated. Then, I turned and walked after the scar-face. He pushed through a curtain and led me along a corridor that had recently been busy with maids, cooks, and servants, but which was not empty of life.

He led me to the kitchens.

He winked. "The ancient world below has been hidden in the one place no lord willingly enters. A broom closet. Come. Morag knew exactly where it was."

CHAPTER 19

We rushed through the kitchens, found a small doorway, and took a set of stairs below, and there, we entered a large room that was a mess hall. Breakfasts had been abandoned.

We sneaked past tables, and then, he pulled me for a corner and pushed open a gray door.

There, a wooden wall had been torn down. Brooms, hooks, barrels lay scattered and destroyed around the room, and rags were in heaps on the floor.

Behind the destroyed wall, was a dark, ragged hole.

"In there," he said. "They went that way. There were two you will not want to meet. There were two vampires, though, I couldn't see one properly. I smelled the disease, though."

Morag and Mellina. Anja, perhaps, and Rhean. They had managed to raise Anja.

I nodded. I looked back to the mess hall and listened. I heard nothing.

I felt something, however.

I stepped forward, man-sized, and looked down a long stone stairway. The air smelled of decay and mold, and a cold air was ruffling my hair. The walls were rough, and the stairs ancient, dark, and huge, not made for men, or perhaps not even for jotuns.

Far, far down, there were lights. The lights flickered as a party of creatures were making their way down.

"What are you called?" I asked the jotun.

"Heimdr," he answered.

I saw movement below, far below. I shook my head. "Go back, Heimdr. And be ready for anything. Hel and I are both about to wager our lives away. Aid Asra, if I do not come back."

He nodded and grinned. Then, he left.

I changed into a huge panther and made my way silently down the tunnel.

It took a long time to travel. Beneath the ground, the air turned thin, and breathing was hard. It could have been the poison coursing in my veins, or just the fact we were deep, and perhaps the land was close to the root of Yggdrasill, and odd.

To think Lok was close, was thrilling.

And still, he wasn't my god. I had another.

The steps went on and on. A musky odor invaded my nostrils.

Beneath, somewhere fairly close, I heard Rhean's hissing voice. "Hurry. Here?"

"Yes," I heard my father saying.

I hesitated, closed my eyes, and concentrated.

He had failed. He had failed to please Bolthorn, he had failed Hel, he had failed even the paltry kingdom he had built.

And still, he was my father.

I slunk forward softly, never alerting my foe to my whereabouts, and then, finally arrived at the bottom. I came to a huge room with a dark pool of water, and more water was dripping down from the ceiling.

The room was so huge, I couldn't see its edges. I could see thousands of doorways and tunnels leading off.

It was bewildering.

Thousands. Gods only knew how far they took one. There were so many, in so many levels, you could spend years and years there, trying to get anywhere.

Across from me, beyond the pool, I saw my father, dead, rotting, kneeling before an open white stone doorway.

"There?" asked a voice I knew and loved. I saw Rhean, stumbling from behind my father's kneeling body, and looking down. Her chest was open, and ice was pouring out of it. She looked terribly weak, hopelessly cold, and it was an irony the dead could die of ice. The ice was dripping from her lips, and I saw her throat had a wound, where diamond like icicle was forcing its way through.

Next to Rhean, stood the cloaked figure.

Rhean hesitated and turned. Her eyes pierced the dark.

She looked at me.

Morag, my father, did as well.

Then, I realized I didn't see Mother.

Eyes glowed next to me.

I was grabbed by my neck, something struck me

hard, and I rolled in the floor as the rotten Mellina Tenginell, Queen of Red Midgard, dead two decades before and nearly a skeleton, walked for me. In her hand, there was a battle ax, which her skeletal hands, skin hanging amidst fatty remains, raised as she walked for me.

Rhean eyed me, almost with disdain, and spoke to Morag. "Help her kill your son."

"You promised me not to resurrect him," Morag said with almost despairing voice.

"You are a soft draugr, Morag," she said, and tossed him a huge sword. "I suppose jotuns do not make good slaves. Here. Use it. I found this in the snow when I fled Nallist. It belonged to—"

"Bjornag, and then him," Morag said, getting up. "Wait. Mellina."

The skeleton, long hair filthy and lank, hesitated. She turned her eye sockets to Morag.

Morag took a step forward. Then, he stopped.

They both hesitated.

Rhean looked at them with disdain and pulled the robed figure to her as she addressed Morag. "Morag. Your son there will one day find your gold. All of it. You have hidden it well, but he looks like he might indeed find it."

Morag's eyes flashed with suspicion and resentment.

"And he married," she said with pained smile. "A Ymirson."

"You didn't?" Morag said. "You didn't marry one of the dog-spawned bitches? Not Asra?"

"I have not, *yet*," I answered. "But I will, Father. It is not I who failed in life. It was you, and the Sons. I will—"

"You *will* marry one?" he said, fanatical madness burning in his rotten face. "You *traitor*."

Morag approached me fast, the sword high. Mellina did as well.

I braided together a spell and threw it at Morag. Stone-dotted, icy hands grasped Morag's legs. He roared and kept struggling, breaking one. The other one held him.

I turned away from him and parried Mother's ax. I pushed her back.

Morag was roaring as the spell hand kept clawing at his skin and flesh, and he fell heavily on his face.

Mother hacked at me again, fast, then again, but I parried hard and tore the ax off her hand. She growled and burrowed into me, and we fell in a heap, rolling to the water. Her breath stank of rot, her claws raked my sides, her fangs sought my throat, and I fought her, weak with the poison. I spat blood, and she grinned. She placed her claws on my throat, snarling above me.

"Mother," I gasped.

She stopped. She shook her head and was breathing hard.

Morag pushed her aside, limping. "My gold? You

shall shame our family! Filthy Ymirsons. You shall not marry one of them. You'll marry Hel."

"The night they took you from me. I remember it," Mellina was saying. "My boy."

Morag didn't hear her. I kicked at him, got up, parried the sword, and pushed up. Morag kept coming, his sword humming.

I parried again.

I hesitated, and he kicked my shield so hard, I went to my knee and spat blood as my belly bled. The cursed poison was about to kill me.

I tried to get up. I was too late.

Expertly, the sword was coming for my throat.

An ax was coming down as well, flashing in a huge arc, and it sunk into Morag's head. The king fell like a stone.

I got up and saw Mellina looking down at Morag. She looked at me, her eyes burning with resentment. "I couldn't ... They want you dead. Please, son. I must…"

She began pulling the ax off the skull, and I hardened my heart and struck down.

The mass of my weapon cut into her thin neck, severing it from her shoulders

I turned and saw Rhean and the cloaked figure were gone.

I walked forward, spitting blood. I looked down and saw my belly was bleeding badly. The poison was moving fast.

***

Below, rushing forward and down, I saw Rhean. Then, I lost them and hurried forward. Soon, I saw them again. Rhean was leaning on simple stone doorway.

I felt the magic of the Black Grip on the wall. Morag had sealed not only Lok's chamber beyond, but this one.

I saw a discarded robe, and Anja.

She was leaning on a stone doorway. She was smiling and then shaking, frowning. "It is a long ago. I remember."

"Anja," I said. She turned to look at me. Her throat had a ragged wound, and her eyes were red. She was confused, and afraid.

"Dana. Shannon," she said. "They are inside."

"Fast," Rhean said. "We have no time." She was holding her chest, looking up as I came down.

Anja was shaking her head. "I obey, but I hate you as well. I shall not weep when you are gone."

"Open it up, fool. Vampires do not weep," Rhean gasped. "Let us see if the gamble is worth it."

I didn't stop her. She still had the skill. She touched the stone, and it opened with a shudder. Dust billowed into my face, and I saw Rhean pushing Anja inside.

I leaned on the doorway and looked around.

Inside, there were stalactites and pools of green water. There was a simple closed doorway at the end, one with scratches, and marks of struggle. I felt Black Grip's power on it as well. Old, scorched rock walls marked a magical battle and damaged floor spoke of spells of power. On the side, was a slender, yellow skull.

There were three stone statues in the room.

There were no horns, no daggers, and no Medusa. Certainly, there was no Hand of Hel.

I laughed, and Rhean looked at me with fury. Then, she stumbled around the statues, examining them.

One, was of a warrior.

It was a greatly detailed statue of a huge, seven-foot man, kneeling and holding his ax. His face was a mask of pain, his arm was up, and his mouth open. Rhean was walking around him, her fingers running through the surface. I looked at the pair to the side. One wore ragged armor and torn skirts and was half naked. Her hair had been hugely long and her face beautiful as it looked up as if welcoming death. One, the last one, held the hand of the other girl. She had a look of relief on her face.

"Dana and Shannon, I assume," I said. "Mouth of Lok, and Hand of Hel. And no Famine and no Horn."

Anja was shaking her head. "She is Dana," she said, and pointed at the one with a look of relief. "I hated her. I hated her for so long and then trusted her. The other one was the Hand of Hel."

We watched the half-naked statue. I smiled. "Well. I suppose she was alive when that was done to her by Medusa. What now, Rhean?"

She shook her head and held it. "Hand of Hel told her, and she told us to open it up. It was her duty, our duty, and there is nothing? Nothing!"

Her eyes went to a part of the wall, not far. There, a very weak outline of white on gray door.

"We shall see Lok, at least," she hissed. "Hel wanted him dead. I'll roast him in his chains and spit on his face, if he cannot be slain. Anja, open it up."

Anja looked at me, with a brief, begging expression on her face. She stepped forward and walked that way. She lifted her hand to touch it.

I stepped after her and axed her down. She fell, her skull cloven, and a smile was on her face.

Rhean leaned on the wall, exhausted, tired, and disappointed. "There is nothing here."

I shrugged. My eyes went to the pool of water.

Then, I felt something moving behind me, and I closed my eyes. "Euryale," I said. "Are you not disappointed?"

I heard her hissing and laughing. "Nay. I am not. Lok's murder was Shannon's duty. Hel be damned. My duty was to release her. That duty is over," said a relieved, melodic, hypnotic voice of a First Born monster. I looked back briefly. Behind me, on the ceiling, slithered the gorgon Euryale, her eyes hurtful, dreadful, even in the darkness of a hooded cloak. She was naked under it, the horrible, black wounds visible on her otherwise perfect, black body. She jumped down and walked around the chamber, her face still masked by a hooded cloak, her black body moving with grace.

She put a hand on Shannon's cheek. She was chuckling. "I would have spent the eternity trying to open the doorway. I would have killed all of Midgard and made slaves of the corpses, and I would have had them dig out the mountain and the root. I would have, because that was Shannon's order. I could not ignore it. I worked hard to get here. I fought the Sons, Morag, and raised more and more draugr, and hid my plans under so many layers. Dome was a wonderful discovery. Balic, a suitable fool. We would have tried until ages passed, Maskan, to get here. And now? Nothing. There is nothing. There is only my Shannon, a creation of my poor sister Stheno, and mine." She kissed the lips and smiled. "Medusa brought her back to life. Her eyes would not have turned this one to stone otherwise. She must have liked her. I wish I knew how she escaped here. It seems impossible."

Rhean spat ice, and Euryale was shaken from her nostalgia.

She put a hand on Dana's head and looked around the room. "No Horn. No Famine. The dagger is back with Hel. The Horn? Perhaps never here, perhaps in Dana's pocket. I cannot undo stone-death. Medusa could, with her sweet blood. Her blood was always the most potent to heal, while mine, to kill." She glanced my way. I looked away from those eyes. "You will join them, jotun. You will not be as monumental, but you will join them. I am free to rule my own destiny." She shook her head at the sight of Rhean, who sat down, ice pouring from her ears and mouth. "I shall take Midgard and make it my plaything. Hel be damned." She spoke to me as she leaned down on Rhean. "Poor thing. I shall have to find a new captain." She took her by the neck and concentrated on a spell.

Rhean's mouth fell open, ice and darkness rolling out of it.

I felt terrible sorrow, anger, and a need to avenge her, and stepped forward.

I hacked my ax down at her.

She danced under the ax, a dark saber appearing in her hand. A fiery whip of many tails rolled out of one of her hands, and a shield of fire came to being.

She pulled down her hood, and the dark, terrible creature turned to face me.

I shut my eyes and hacked down again.

The shield took my ax. The whip tore to my ankle, and she pulled me down.

I howled, for the foot was torn off. I tried to hack at her, and my shield was torn from my hands, and my left hand with it. I felt her pulling me up. Her hand was on my face, and she was trying to open my eye.

I struggled, and she hissed.

Her saber was in her hand and then pushing to my belly, very slowly.

I hacked my ax on her with a final effort, and she roared as it split her side, drawing some black blood.

She called for a spell, and I felt vines slithering up from the ground and tethering me in a place.

They fell away. Lisar's pendant saved me.

She stood over me and stepped on the ax.

She pressed the saber under my chin.

At that moment, something climbed up from the pool of water.

I opened my eyes and looked between Euryale's legs.

It was Medusa, dressed in a shredded and old cloak, her hood low over her face, and a threadbare skirt barely covered her. She looked like a powerful fighter, a bit like Nima, and had only a pair of arms. Her snakes, red and angry, were slithering around her head. Dripping wet, her muscles gleaming, she pulled out two long swords, both sharp and ancient. She looked at the abomination of Euryale, snarled, her eyes gleamed painfully in the shadows, and then, she attacked, her swords swinging. Euryale turned, yelling with surprise. She dodged under the blades that were moving fast, so very fast. Euryale's fiery shield moved rapidly to block the next attack, and her whip slapped at Medusa, who hacked through the spell, severing the spell. Euryale was swarmed by swords, but she pushed Medusa back, and stabbed her dark saber at Medusa, who again parried skillfully.

They took a stock of each other.

"Sister," Euryale laughed. "Oh, to see you here! I so hoped to see you here! I prayed for the Horn and you, but not for the Hand of Hel or her dagger. It feels I have been granted my wishes!"

Medusa circled her. "Your greed, your evil, caused all this. Hel's War, our break-up."

"You chose not to follow our lead," Euryale said sadly. "You joined Hel out of spite. Little sister, what good did abandoning us do you?"

Medusa laughed bitterly. "Coming from a thing of death, a slave and a miserable miscreant, that is rich, indeed. There is nothing more to say."

I bled, the pain in my belly made me see dark spots, my hand and leg were on fire, and still, I admired the battle.

Medusa was so very fast. She moved like a lightning and herded Euryale around.

And still, the undead loved the battle. She parried with the fiery shield, and her saber stabbed forward a few times and always nearly wounded Medusa.

Then, dodging the saber, Medusa dropped a sword and reached out to grasp a snake.

The snake hissed and bit down at her hand, but she yanked Euryale forward and for her sword that was coming up to meet her.

Euryale roared and bashed the fiery shield at the sword, and sparks flew as they crashed together. Euryale pushed hard Medusa, threw her back, and roared as she rolled with her against the wall, their blades striking stone. The shield was gone. Euryale placed a hand on Medusa's chest and braided together a spell. A spell of black fire tore down, and Medusa slapped Euryale away, her skin burning fiercely. She hissed, and both got up. She rushed the undead monster, her clothing on fire.

Euryale tripped.

Medusa's blade stabbed down for Euryale, but the off-balance monster grasped the blade, losing her fingers. Howling, she pushed the sword away and threw Medusa back, the saber stabbing at her. It pierced Medusa's side, and Euryale's snakes entwined themselves around hers, and the snakes were furiously biting at each other. The saber was pushing, pulling, ripping at Medusa's flesh. Medusa screamed with rage, pushed back, fought, and hacked down, only to have her sword blocked. Euryale was too strong, and she too weak, perhaps due to her long imprisonment. Euryale threw her to the floor and crashed over her. Struggling like wrestlers, Euryale kept her pinned with the saber and her arms and smiled down at her sister. She braided together a spell of darkness and pressed it on Medusa's mouth.

She writhed with pain, dark fog pouring out of her mouth, nostrils, and eyes.

Euryale laughed, kept her down, smiled, and sunk her teeth on her right side. Medusa screamed and visibly weakened.

I got up to my knees and dragged myself forward.

The undead thing, still biting down, was laughing softly, her mouth full of flesh.

I got up to my knees and hacked my ax on Euryale's skull.

She fell away, surprised, but I grasped a snake and pulled her over me. I rolled, and I fell over her, hacking again. The ax tore to her face, deep to the skull, just when the eyes burned into mine. She stiffened under me, and fell still.

I fell over her, weeping.

I felt little and saw nothing. I touched my eyes and found stone. I felt my belly opening from her poisons, my guts flowing, and felt death close.

Then, I felt someone turning me. I felt the taste of sweet mead and then of blood on my lips. I fell into a fitful slumber that was full of dreams and nightmares. I felt pain all over my body, I felt bone and flesh knitting, I felt even hunger cured.

I sat up and looked up at the hooded face of Medusa.

She was looking at me, a sword in her hand, a hand on my face. She had no wounds, and she had covered her eyes. "How do you feel?" she asked.

I grasped her hand gently and shook my head. "Alive. Better."

"You are Morag's son," she whispered. "Kin to those I commanded, though ever at odds with each other. You came here an enemy of those abominations?"

"I did," I said, and shook my head, holding my face.

I could see. I had a foot. Hand. I looked to the side where my shield and hand were. The hand with missing digits was mine.

I flexed the one I had now. It was perfect.

I watched Rhean.

I groaned. I still felt terrible sorrow.

She looked at the dead vampire and smiled. "That, I cannot heal. It is not a disease." She poked Euryale with one of her swords. She was covered with a cloak, her snakes still. "Great evil, she was. There are many kinds of evil in the Nine Worlds, and the Filling Void. Hers was the honorless kind. She and my sister, both deserved to die, a million times over. For fighting her, you deserved my blood. It is a cure to those who deserve a second chance. I don't willingly share it."

She showed me the right side of her beautiful body and smiled. "One side heals, the other side kills. You have been blessed."

I nodded. I looked at Dana, Shannon, and the last warrior. "You spared them?"

She sighed. "I raised Shannon after Dana killed her. She came back, healed of Hel. And still, Morag's magic is strong. They had no way to survive. They hoped for a long while Anja, whom Morag stole out of here," she said and looked at the dead Anja, "would come and open it up. They hoped Morag would have a change of heart. It was not going to happen. So, yes, I helped them. It was a loathsome thing to do, for I loved them well.

One sister tried to save another. Shannon had tried to recover the Nine, Dana followed her. The warrior, a loyal brute. I liked talking with them before I spared them a sad, hungry death. I waited after, slept, and fought boredom. I resisted the urge to put a drop of my blood on their mouths and to bring them back, even for a while."

"And now?" I asked, picking up my ax, and shield.

She smiled. "And now, I must decide if I shall bring them back at all." She shook her head, her deadly eyes gleaming inside the hood. She touched Shannon's face. "She, a sad creature, who found peace, finally. She is a powerful human, able to heal. Frigg's blessing is strong on her." She smiled as she held Dana's hand. "And this one? Afraid, for so long. Lok as a companion, Lok's curse chasing her across time and space, and then, she finally found her bravery. They do deserve to be brought back. Even Anja there. Perhaps, one day." She lifted something to my eyes. "The fate of this must first be decided."

It was the Gjallarhorn.

Silvery chain hung from it and spread across the floor, gleaming. Silvery and golden, the dragon on top of the mighty artifact looked like it was alive.

"What say you, jotun," she wondered. "Are there anyone else, other than I, who might blow it?"

I shook my head. "Baduhanna is dead. Your sisters and Hand of Hel are gone. Unless someone received a boon from a god, none."

She nodded. "And how is Midgard?"

I shrugged. "War. It is torn by your sister's abominations."

"And if I restore the gods?" she wondered. "If I bring them back? It seems my oath to return the Eye of Hel is finished. I owe Hel nothing. But do I owe the gods anything?"

"There are a hundred thousand draugr—" I began.

"I care not," she said simply. "Draugr are draugr. They take what they can, and they can be mastered by brave men and women. Let them fight for Midgard. I care about this."

She lifted a stone dagger.

Famine.

It was a dark, long, and deadly looking stone dagger that had a disquieting aura.

"When," I said softly, "the Hand of Hel fell here, the first one, it was recalled to Hel."

"Aye," she said. "So, Hel seems to think something might still pick up the mantle of being her Hand. A new Hand of Hel? I doubt there is anyone, but still, it is here. It was here for twenty years. Morag's spell might have hampered Hel's ability to recall it, but certainly she could, now. I do worry about it. Perhaps I shall hunt here for a bit. I shall think deep, if I will let the Aesir and the Vanir back to their precious worlds. I must seek their good deeds and weigh them against the evil they do, as they pretend to balance chaos with law. I will ponder their fate, and the fate of these friends of mine as well. I must not be hasty."

She touched Shannon's mouth and hesitated. "A drop of blood, few more. It would do it. But for now? Show me the keep."

I nodded. "Your people and Morag's are all gathered by the gate to Nifleheim. Up in the great hall."

"A hall? They built a fort here?" she said, smiling. "I have been there before, on that gate," she said softly. "Wait. We travel. It is exhausting, but I want to see the world again! I wish to taste mead and feast."

"A feast is set up, lady," I said. "A fine feast."

Her hands glowed, and she smiled with unchecked happiness, free at last. A gate glowed and opened before her. It was white, silvery, and beautiful, and she pulled me along as she stepped in it. I turned and grasped a body, pulling it with me, as I followed her. I was disoriented for a moment, and then, I could focus.

I dropped the corpse.

We were in the bloody hall, where ice was melting fast, and bodies filled the room. She looked back at me, smiling. "A feast? Looks like the feast is over, though it seemed to be a lively one. And you brought your own dinner?" she asked, and eyed the corpse. "Will you make the introductions?"

I bowed. "I thought you knew most of them."

She turned and observed the group around her. "I

do. Most of them."

There, standing around the hall and the ruins of the ancient gate, stood Thrum and hundreds of his dverger, and my jotuns, only thirty now. The draugr had tried to get in, sending hundreds of against the main hall. A steaming mess of horrible battle-dead littered the doorway.

Urac was by those doors, looking on with worry.

Medusa smiled and looked at the creatures she had once known. She smiled brightly like a star in the sky and lifted her hands high. "I salute you, companions in arms. Free, finally! I am free, and you are as well. I know not what trouble you have faced, but it is time for us to stand together. We are free of oaths, free of prison, and free to have an adventure."

I nodded.

Thrum whistled.

Four ballistae fired. Steel javelins shot out at her, pierced her, and threw her on her back. The javelins had chain secured in them, and the chains were tied to pillars, and she looked in horror at her wounds as she thrashed her way up.

"What is this?" she roared.

Many jotuns lifted axes and charged.

She whirled in surprise, saw the axes high above her, and ripped off her cowl. The terrible, fierce eyes smote down two of ours, then four more, creating a macabre gallery of statues. Her swords whipped around and butchered two more.

Dverger pulled at the chains, and she fell, cursing.

The dverger lifted their crossbows and fired.

She howled and fell on her back as dozens of bolts struck her. A jotun leaped forward. Ax smote her, then another, and the sharp weapons drew blood.

A heaving mass of jotuns descended on her, axes coming down brutally hard.

One turned to stone, another howled and fell as swords stabbed, and one stumbled away, his face snake bitten. I walked past the jotuns with Asra. The jotuns struggled to keep her down, and then, three fell into a stony curse, howling briefly with their eyes gone, then their bodies were statues that showed all the signs of terrible agony in death.

She moved, got stopped by the chains, and cast a spell. She was terribly hurt, wounded all over her body, but she released a spell at Thrum's dverger, a forked lightning which carved a way through a group holding one chain. They were torn to pieces, and she ripped the chain free. She gazed at a party of dverger holding the other chain and killed half, the fools who had watched her. She tore that chain free as well. Jotuns pressed her, and she hacked up and down.

I saw the desperation in her eyes.

She moved fast and summoned a gate, snarling, her snakes snapping, swords swirling at the enemy that was close, their axes and blood raining down around her.

She turned to jump to the gate.

I moved fast and bashed the powerful Grinlark down. It struck her skull.

She went down heavily, her skull crushed.

The remaining jotuns took steps back, led by Heimdr. Asra stepped forward from the side, and Thrum, holding his ax circled her.

Medusa looked up at me as I kicked her swords away. Her eyes were losing their potency, and I managed to look at her.

"Why?" she asked. "Jotuns, chaos, betrayal, but you seemed—"

"Because I am tired of being a man," I said tiredly. "I am tired of being a victim of old, evil bastards, and greedy nobles. I am no longer a lost jotun in Midgard, fighting for men, for scraps, and against my own kin. I am tired of dreaming of the return of the gods, and instead, I found my own. I made a pact with my own god. For victory in battle, I'd give a grand sacrifice. Alas, lady, you are the only sacrifice worth giving. I shall give Bolthorn you, and I shall be granted a place in his table, a jotun more powerful than most First Born. My kin failed in Midgard, and forgot to pay our own god their due. They forgot to serve him, and to be what we were born to be. Conquerors, not rulers. I will not fail. I am … free. Like you were, just now." I lifted the Grinlark and bashed it down.

She died.

I held my head. If a god can laugh, Bolthorn was laughing. I felt his mirth, the sullen beast amused, hopeful, and happy. He was full of cruel happiness, and at that moment, on the moment of my deceitful victory, his spirit reached out to me. I felt Black Grip changing. I felt it twisting around my hand and fusing to my flesh. I smelled the burning meat, the terrible hot iron becoming part of my bones. It didn't hurt.

It felt glorious.

And for once, and for all time, until Bolthorn would raise another to take my place, long after my death, I became one with the ancient ones, a Son of Ymir, a true son of the great god, his blood, his chosen champion. I was full of power, I saw the magical flows of the Filling Void like never and knew all the spells of our kin, all the past of our old family.

I got up, crashing to the roof, twenty-foot-tall, and I grasped the Horn from Medusa's belt. It grew to accommodate me.

I lifted it to my lips. And I blew it.

A sound rang out. It was an odd one, seemingly coming from a thousand such horns. It rang out with clear notes, it rang out bravely, it rang like a horn of conquest, and it was just that, indeed.

The air before us shimmered.

Snow and wind blew in the room, scattering letters, goblets, and clothing.

I hesitated and closed my eyes.

Bolthorn. I have delivered, I thought. "Thank you."

And he answered. *And you have, Morag of Ymir, Son of Ymir, Champion of Jotuns. You shall carry your father's name, which he kept even after pretending to be a human. You shall return home. You shall bring me the Horn, and you shall lead the armies of Nifleheim against the Nine Worlds. We shall make war, we shall gather tribute, we will take land, and the way things were, once, shall return. Gods be damned. Hel was right. But let it be us, and not them, whom the worlds shall bow down to. Come, Morag of Ymir. Finish your business. You shall be back, one day, to steal Midgard for us.*

I looked at the troops gathered there.

Thrum nodded and marched his thousand through the gate. They shimmered and disappeared. I nodded at Heimdr, who marched his twelve remaining jotuns over Medusa.

I watched them go and turned to Urac, shrinking in size. I wondered at the gauntlet, part of me, and all the secrets it harbored. I noticed he was kneeling before me, and I shook my head to clear it.

Champion of Ymir.

I took a flask. I kneeled next to Medusa and opened a wound on her side. I squeezed out her blood, several drops of it, twenty and more.

Then, I showed it to Urac.

"Tell Nima," I said. "that I am sorry I gave her war and left her facing draugr and civil war. It is best for me to see those who will one day oppose us, fight each other. Tell her she can bow before me and surrender her lands, and I shall one day aid her, perhaps. Tell the others what you will." I gave him the scroll filled with names. "Tell her, that her father conspired to topple her new throne. Tell her she should kill all these men, to stay safe. For some reason, I think she can, and will."

He took the scroll.

"I will, King Morag, tell her all this, and the others? I shall them what I will. Will you not raise your family?" he asked.

I shook my head. "They failed. And I shall not be challenged."

He smiled. "Of course. No challenges." He looked tricky.

I smiled. "Oh, you think there might be a challenge, after all? If you bring back Dana and Shannon, and that Anja," I told him, "tell them only death waits them beyond this point. The Horn is ours now. Jotuntreasure, Urac, and not theirs."

"How will we defeat the draugr?" he asked.

I shrugged. "Use swords and bravery. Bring back the mighty kings and clever queens to fight the dead. Find a ruler, if you can. I doubt you can. As I said, it is best for us that our foes fight amongst themselves."

He looked down. "And if I bring back Baduhanna and Medusa?"

I smiled. "I will kill Baduhanna again. Medusa's corpse comes with me."

I watched a heap of bodies, and the one I had brought with me. Urac pointed at one covered corpse at the edge of the room.

I walked to it and kneeled next to Sand. I smiled and poured a drop of Medusa's blood into his mouth. He began glowing softly, the terrible wounds slowly regenerating into healthy skin. I shook my head. "Not even jotun-gods can do that. A true miracle. My queen?" Asra stepped out and looking with simmering hate the corpse I had brought with me from the depths, grasped Sand, and carried him through.

Urac was frowning. "Why *her*?"

I sat next to Rhean. "Because I love her. I cannot help it. I will love Aras in one way, and her with my heart. I hope she enjoys Nifleheim, our trek to Bolthorn, and her position as a queen of jotun-kin. Do not worry. There will be many queens." I winked. "I think she will dislike me now, and she'll be so unhappy, that I might fall out of love with her."

I poured a drop to her mouth as well, lifted her over my shoulder, and grasped Medusa by her snakes. I handed the blood to Urac, and he took it with a bow. "They will," he said, "come after you. Jotun-treasure. I know the word. It means a contested treasure."

I laughed as I went for the gate, dragging Medusa behind. The bolts embedded in her flesh were snapping as I walked. "Let them come, then. The era of the jotuns is back. The Horn is ours. The Nine will be as well. I am happy to leave Midgard. I love nothing here."

Urac laughed. "Lok the trickster bless you, lord. I wish you the best of luck, Morag of Ymir. If Nima is pregnant, you will one day, perhaps, love something in Midgard."

He walked for the stairs that led down to Mara's Brow.

I cursed Nima, I cursed Rhean, and then, I stepped through the gate. There, after a moment, a breath away, really, I faced my army and a landscape of timeless ice. Far, far in the north, waited Bolthorn, who would rule the Nine with his sisters and brothers, and I, one of them, their Champion.

I put down Rhean, and noticed she was breathing. So was Sand, looking roguish and a perfect fool again.

Then, I put down Medusa, pulled a drop of blood from her side and placed it on her lips. They were bringing fetters for her, and before that, I searched her bag and belt.

I dug out Famine. It was evil, and terrible, and had been waiting for a new carrier, someone with promise. It had, perhaps, waited for Euryale.

It suddenly disappeared in my hands. It was with Hel.

Euryale had died. The dagger was no longer in Midgard. Hel gave up.

Then I remembered Euryale had bitten Medusa in the side. The right side.

I frowned, and looked at the gate, and wondered how contested the Horn would be.

The final book, *Helheim*, shall finish both the Ten Tears Chronicles, and the Thief of Midgard series by December 2018.

If you enjoyed the story, do check out the savage tale of an assassin, the Horn King and his series, and also the Ten Tears Chronicles, which is a sister series to the one you just read. They are very much related, and will have characters that are common, and a plotline that merges later.
If you like the type of story you just read, look at the Roman Era Hraban Chronicles, the Goth Chronicles, and Adalwulf of the Germani Tales. Also check out our Medieval, and Napoleonic Era adventures as well. You can find them in various retail author pages, and our own home- and Facebook pages
Some are free. Don't miss out.

REVIEWS

Thank you for getting this story. If you enjoyed it, I would be grateful if you could leave a review. You need not write an elaborate one, just one line and a rating is enough. Readers who do not enjoy the story, will write such reviews, and a bad rating will make it hard for any author to sell the story, and to write new ones. Your help is truly needed, and well appreciated. This author reads them all, and is very grateful for your help.

NEWSLETTER

Do sign up for our newsletter at: www.alariclongward.com. You will find our blog, latest news, competitions, and lists of our stories in these pages.

FREE BOOKS

We are often offering free e-books for our readers. These are not short stories, but full, often gigantic tales. In many cases, you might get Book 2 free, by signing up to our newsletter. Please check out our author pages in the various retailers, or in our homepage to find out what is available.

OUR OTHER STORIES

If you enjoyed this story, be sure to check our other historical and fantasy tales. We have many related series that often tie together, and are related. We have Medieval stories, several Roman Era tales, story set in the Napoleonic Era, historical mysteries, and many Norse Mythology related fantasy series. None of them are suitable for children, and will serve people who enjoy a surprising plot, fierce battles, and practical heroes and heroines. You can find list of these in our various retail author pages, and our home- or Facebook pages.

ABOUT THE AUTHOR

Alaric Longward was born 1970, which makes him as old as computer floppy disks. Do not worry if you don't know what they are.

Throughout his childhood, he found himself curiously attracted to books. This strange hobby did not take anything away from the computer gaming and occasional sports, but the books stayed and the wonderful stories that could be found in his father's vast library would inspire him throughout his life to appreciate the power of story telling. He loved history, fantasy, and sci-fi.

As time moved on, he graduated from the university with a degree of Master of Political Science, dreamed of a career in diplomacy and ended up making computer games in Nokia N-Gage. He stayed on after the demise of the first serious swing at mobile gaming, and worked as a senior manager and product manager in ICT sector for over a decade, specialising in internet services, innovation solutions, and crowdsourcing.

One day he decided to drive his family nuts, and quit his job to become an author. Now, as a bestselling author of eight books, he hopes to provide you with exciting adventure stories. He is a dad, a husband, and a full time author.

Printed in Great Britain
by Amazon